HIS HEART

CLAIRE KINGSLEY

Always Have LLC

ISBN: 9798590243266

Edited by Elayne Morgan of Serenity Editing

Cover by Lori Jackson

Cover photography by Regina Wamba

www.clairekingsleybooks.com

❀ Created with Vellum

For my dear friend Stephanie, and side-dude, who gave you a new chance at life.

And for the family of the young man who gave you that gift. My heart breaks for your loss. I pray you find love and healing.

ABOUT THIS BOOK

Her greatest tragedy is his second chance at life.

For Sebastian McKinney, wrestling is life. He's focused and determined. Strong and capable. Nothing, not even his biggest rival, will stand in his way.

Except a silent illness that almost kills him.

Brooke Summerlin is no stranger to adversity. Raised by an abusive mother, she's learned to cope as best she can. When Liam sweeps into her life, she believes she's found the impossible—a happily ever after.

Until her happy ending is ripped away. And Brooke's greatest tragedy becomes Sebastian's second chance at life.

Four years later, two souls linked by loss find each other. Although their connection is undeniable, Brooke sinks in grief that threatens to drown her. Sebastian is desperate to help—desperate to save her—even though he has his own uncertainties to face.

But sometimes love transcends the boundaries between life and death—between what is known and what cannot be explained. The heart that loved Brooke still beats for her.

And the one thing that might save them both is love.

Author's note: An intense stand-alone contemporary romance that explores the transcendent, healing power of love. You'll need a few tissues (and maybe some chocolate), but trust me, their beautiful happily ever after is worth it.

PART I

Hope is a dream

the young cling to

the old yearn for

but only the broken understand

~B

1

BROOKE

January. Age sixteen.

IT WAS ALL I could do to simply survive.

High school, to be specific. Phoenix wasn't any different than the other places I'd lived. No matter how many times my mom moved us around, no matter how many schools I went to, they were all the same. Ruled by a hierarchical social structure as stratified as the caste system. Everyone knew their place, and the only safe place was at the top.

Which was the opposite of where I existed.

But the day was over, the last class finished. Some kids hurried outside to catch the bus, or simply to put as much distance as possible between themselves and this prison of a building. Others lingered in the hallway, gossiping with friends, making plans.

Most kids had somewhere else to go that was better than school. Home. Sports practice. A club meeting. A job. I didn't. I took my time, walking alone toward my locker, my eyes on the ground. I wasn't athletic by any definition of the word, and bouncing around from school to school made it hard to get involved in any activities. I was too quiet to make friends easily.

I was the weird girl. Funky clothes. Blue and pink streaks in my dark brown hair. Always sitting in the back of the class, scribbling in a notebook. I wasn't shy, necessarily. I'd just given up trying. It was hard to work your way into an established group of friends. And anyway, by the time I did, my mom would always move us again. So I tried to ignore the social goings-on of high school life. It was January, and I was a junior. That meant eighteen months until graduation. Eighteen months until I would be free. I could make it.

A group of girls stood on the other side of the hallway, across from my locker. The Mean Girls. They wore the label with pride. They even had matching MG stickers on the backs of their phone cases. Since moving here, I'd kept under their radar. I was beneath most people's notice.

But for some reason, the Mean Girls had started to pay attention to me. They stood close together, leaning in to speak in low voices, their eyes on me. I quickly put in my locker combination so I could get out of their line of sight.

"I don't know what's up with her shoes," Karina Bowen said, making no effort to keep me from hearing.

I stopped myself from looking down at my shoes— worn-out blue Converse. I didn't want to acknowledge that I'd heard her comment.

"I can't even with those jeans," Harmony Linwood said. Karina's right-hand bitch. Those two were never far apart. The others huffed and made noises of agreement and disgust. Tapped manicured fingernails. Rolled eyes caked in makeup.

I kept my gaze on my locker and shoved a few books into my bag. *Ignore them, Brooke. Just ignore them.*

"Hey, Brooke," Karina said. "You know, there's a thrift store that's walking distance from here. Might improve your look. Just a tip, sweetie."

Giggles. As if that was such a clever thing to say.

Still, my cheeks flushed hot and I bit the inside of my lip. Anger that my red face was going to betray me when I turned around mixed with the shame they were so good at dishing out.

More whispers and giggles.

"Oh, of course she's a fucking lesbian," Karina said. "Anyone can see that. And it's probably a good thing. What guy would date her?"

I could feel eyes on my back, burning into me like red-hot brands. I balled my hands into fists.

"Hey, Brooke."

The male voice startled me and I glanced up to find Liam Harper leaning casually against the locker next to mine. Blue eyes, careless dark blond hair, and a smile that would have made me feel fluttery and weak even if I *was* a lesbian. Which I wasn't. Especially when Liam Harper was around.

But why was he talking to *me*?

"Um, hi."

The Mean Girls had gone silent and I saw Liam's eyes flick toward them once, then back to me. He opened his mouth to say something, but Karina had crossed the hallway and stepped close.

"Hey, Liam," she said, a phony sweetness to her tone. "Did you see they announced the theme for the Valentine's dance? *Hollywood Nights.*"

His forehead creased a little. "Uh, yeah. Sounds a lot like the theme from last year."

She somehow managed to shoot a micro-glare at me while almost simultaneously batting her eyelashes at Liam. I wanted to take the opportunity to make a break for it, but curiosity had me rooted to the spot. Why had Liam talked to me?

"Well, I think it's going to be amazing," Karina said. "Do you have a date yet?"

I couldn't stop my eyes from rolling. Obvious, much?

"Yeah," he said.

Her face registered surprise, her mouth popping open. That wasn't the answer she'd expected. "You do? Who?"

"Brooke," he said.

Karina huffed, her mouth dropping open. "Brooke Summerlin? You mean, her?"

Liam met my eyes and treated me to a little grin. "Yep. Right, Brooke?"

My mind spun as I stared at him. What was he doing? Was this some sort of pity thing? Or was he waiting for me to agree so he could pull the rug out and laugh in my face? My cheeks flushed hotter and I swallowed hard.

The possibility of being able to look Karina Bowen in the eye and tell her I was going to the dance with Liam Harper was too much temptation. If this was a prank, I'd risk the humiliation.

"Yeah," I said, glancing at Karina. "I'm going with Liam."

Liam's smile widened. Karina's look of disgust was about two steps past ridiculous. You'd have thought someone just told her she stepped in a big pile of dog shit.

"Oh," she said. With another scathing look at me, she flipped her hair and walked back to her minions.

The Mean Girls backed their leader with more glares at

me, but I barely noticed. I stared at Liam, knowing he wasn't *actually* taking me to the dance. There was no way he'd ask *me*. But standing up for me like that had been such a nice— and completely unexpected—thing to do.

"Wow, that was... pretty amusing, actually," I said, watching the Mean Girls flounce down the hallway.

"Amusing?" he asked. "Why?"

"Well, you know, the look on Karina's face," I said.

He glanced over his shoulder, as if he'd already forgotten about them. "Oh, yeah."

I shifted on my feet, feeling a little awkward. My locker still hung open, so I pulled out my bag and slung it over my shoulder, then closed the locker door. "I guess I should get going."

"You live next door to me, don't you?" he asked.

I shrugged, trying to maintain a casual air. But inside I reeled from the knowledge that Liam Harper knew I lived next door to him. Of course, I knew where *he* lived. I'd noticed him within days of moving in. But the fact that he'd made the connection that I was his neighbor left me a little breathless.

"Um, yeah, I do," I said.

"But I don't see you around much," he said.

"I guess not."

"So what are you up to all the time? You know, when I'm not seeing you around?"

"I don't know. I just do my thing. School, other stuff, you know."

"What other stuff?" he asked, still leaning against the locker.

"Um," I said, fumbling. Was he really still talking to me? "I read and listen to music a lot. Try to avoid my mom."

"Yeah," he said with a chuckle. "Cool. So I should get your number."

"What?"

He raised his eyebrows. "Your number. You know, digits? So I can call or text you. I guess I can just come over if I need to talk to you, but it might be nice to have another means of communication since I'm taking you to the dance."

I blinked in surprise. He could *not* be serious. "You're what?"

"Taking you to the dance," he said. "You did just agree to go with me, didn't you?"

"Yeah, but... I didn't think you were serious."

"Well, yeah," he said. "I wouldn't have said it otherwise."

"Oh. Okay, yeah." My heart raced. I gave him my phone number and he typed it into his phone, then gave me his. I was amazed my fingers didn't shake as I entered him into my contacts.

It hit me as I stared at his name on my phone screen that I had nothing to wear to a formal dance, and certainly no money to buy a dress. My mom wouldn't cough up the cash for something like that. Money for weed, or the pills and blow she thought I didn't know about, sure. But for me? Not a chance.

God, it was so disappointing. But better to do this now than have to cancel on him later. "You know, I actually don't know if I can go. I mean, I want to. But the dance is in a couple weeks, and it might be hard for me to find a dress on such short notice."

"Oh," he said, his face dropping. "That sucks." He raised his eyebrows and started typing on his phone again. "You know what? My sister Olivia has a few dresses. She's about your size, and it's not like she's going to wear them again. I'm sure she'll let you borrow one."

I found myself almost speechless again. "I... are you sure?"

"Yeah, I'm texting her right now," he said, still typing. "Since you live next door, you can just come over sometime and pick one. Shouldn't be a big deal."

"Wow, that's really nice. Thank you."

"Sure. Hey, I have to get to practice." He smiled again, complete with a little nibble of his bottom lip. "See you later."

I watched him walk away, his athletic shoulders pulling against his shirt, his cute butt filling out his jeans so well. I felt like I was living someone's teenage dream in a YA novel. Did the weird quiet girl just get asked out by one of the hottest guys at school? The one Queen Mean herself had set her sights on?

It seemed it had actually happened.

Resisting the urge to clutch a book to my chest, lean back against the lockers, and gaze dreamily up at the ceiling, I adjusted my bag again. With a deep breath, I headed toward the exit, my head spinning.

But for the first time in months, I was smiling.

2

SEBASTIAN

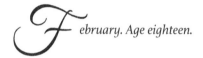 *ebruary. Age eighteen.*

THE NOISE of the crowd beat at me, even through the music playing in my headphones. I liked hearing the crowd as if it were far away—separate from me. Not thousands of people surrounding me in the huge arena.

I paced relentlessly back and forth off to the side of the center mat. There was only one mat now. At the start of the tournament, there had been four, with four matches going on simultaneously throughout the day. Weeding people out. Now it was down to the finals. The last rounds to determine who would be state champions.

In my weight class, it would be me.

Granted, my competition, Charlie Hall, was a fucking good wrestler. Defending state champ, in fact. Now, as a senior, he was determined to defend his title. Probably had a lot of scholarship money on the line.

We both did.

I hadn't wrestled Charlie since last year. He'd beaten me then. Pinned me in the last round, knocking me out of the finals. I took third in state. Not bad for a junior. But nothing less than state champion would be acceptable today.

There are few things as demoralizing as being pinned on your back, immobilized by another guy, completely at his mercy. Wrestlers look muscular and strong, as if the key to winning is in our bodies. But it isn't. It's in our minds. Mental strength, toughness, fortitude—that's what it takes to win. I'd beaten guys bigger and stronger than I was. Guys who were older and had more experience. All because I had it in me to go the distance. To last longer. Endure more.

To never, ever give up.

I could see Charlie, prepping for our match, but I ignored him. He had his rituals, I had mine. What he was doing over on the other side of the arena didn't matter. I was prepared. Months of training, hours in the gym. Strict diet to cut weight and keep up my strength.

Like an animal in a cage, I stalked up and down, my muscles straining against my dark blue singlet. The heavy metal music I always played to pump me up blared in my ears. The crowd noise rose in a crescendo. A match must have ended. From the corner of my eye, I saw Blake, one of my teammates, his arm held up in the air by the ref. Win.

It was almost my turn.

Coach caught my eye and gave me a nod. We had a system. He knew the drill. He'd been coaching me since I was a freshman with a chip on my shoulder and a lot to prove. I'd been wrestling since I was five and thought I was hot shit. Coach had needed to knock me down a few pegs, but it had done me good. Made me better. Under his training, I'd excelled beyond anyone's expectations. I'd gone from a strong wrestler to a fucking beast with an almost perfect high school record.

One loss. To Charlie Hall.

It was going to stay that way. Just one.

I took out my headphones and put them in my bag. Unzipped my hoodie and let it drop. Shook out my arms. Bounced up and down onto my toes a few times. My head was clear, my body relaxed but ready.

The announcer introduced Charlie first. He walked out, his eyes on the ground. Focused. He wasn't letting the roar of the crowd rattle him; he was on his game today.

I walked out and allowed myself one glance at my family. My mom and dad sat a few rows up, right in the center. They'd gotten here when the doors opened so they could get a good spot. Been here for hours to watch me wrestle nine minutes—if it went full rounds.

Cami sat with them, her back straight, her hands clutched in her lap. We'd been dating since fall of Junior year. This was the second wrestling season she'd been through with me, and she still got nervous.

Just as quickly, I put them all out of my mind. The announcer said my name and school—Sebastian McKinney, Waverly Shell-Rock High School—and the crowd erupted with cheers. It washed over me like a breeze, barely registering. This wasn't about them. It was about me, and what I was going to do to Charlie Hall.

Most guys wrestling in the higher weight classes were big and strong, but with a thick layer of flab. Not me and Charlie. The two of us were tall, and our thickness was all muscle. Ripped arms, wide chests, powerful legs. It was part of what made us so evenly matched. Neither of us had a pound wasted on mass that hadn't been developed for our sport.

I fastened the green strap around my ankle. Charlie had black, and the ref wore a matching strap on each wrist. We stepped onto the mat and faced each other, the ref between us. Shook hands.

The adrenaline racing through me made my heart pound. Limbs tingle. Anticipation thrummed through my whole body. It was no longer nervousness. It was excitement. The fuel I would use to power through this match, lending strength to my body and mind.

The whistle blew.

We stalked each other in a slow circle for a few seconds. Charlie was an offensive wrestler, so I wanted to beat him to the first take-down attempt—put him on the defensive. Lowering my center of gravity, I charged in and wrapped my arms around his torso, keeping my head against his ribs. He sprawled his legs backward, but I drove in and spun, trying to get around him. He resisted, but I was a hair faster. I got a hand on his leg and pushed the advantage.

Three seconds later, he was on his back. Take-down, green.

He flipped to his stomach but I clung to him like glue. My breathing quickened and my heart raced, muscles straining. He was strong, his counter moves effective. I got his leg again and moved forward, trying to keep him from getting to his feet. He stretched his arm across my face, pushing me away. The strain pulled my neck, but I simply drove harder.

His stomach hit the mat as I got his leg out from under him. Moving fast, I hooked one arm and leg and pushed, trying to roll him to his back. One heartbeat later, he shifted his weight and spun, getting behind me.

Reversal, black.

Long arms, all muscle, strove to control me. Move me. Turn me over. I fought back with everything I had. He tried for a half-nelson, but I got free. Twisted, spun.

The whistle blew, ending the first round.

We stopped and got up, and I walked a few steps, shaking out my arms. Ground my teeth into my mouth guard. The crowd cheered again, but I kept my mind focused on the battle. On Charlie. On winning.

Round two had me in bottom position—on my hands and knees. Charlie's ear to my back, hand on my wrist, his other arm around my torso. The whistle blew and I exploded to my feet. Charlie got his arms around my waist. He was strong enough to pull me to the side, making it hard to keep my balance. I pushed against his hands to break his grip, keeping my center of gravity low. My height made me look scary, but it could be a disadvantage if I didn't shift my weight in time.

I broke his grip and spun, then took him to the mat. Take down, green. He answered with a reversal, getting behind me and taking control.

This was going to be too close on points. I needed to pin him to win.

We struggled against each other, sweat dripping, making our limbs slick. My chest burned with effort. I could hear Coach's voice yelling instructions—sprawl, spin, turn, drive, drive, drive.

Neither of us could maintain a pinning move for more than a second. He tried for a cradle, but I overpowered him before his grip locked. I almost had him in a half-nelson, but he countered and broke free. We were both the best, at the top of our game. So evenly matched no one watching us could predict who would win.

I knew. It was going to be me.

The whistle blew and we shook out our limbs before the third round. This would be where mental toughness came into play. We were both getting tired. Three minutes doesn't sound like a long time, until you spend every second of it fighting against someone hell-bent on making you submit.

My turn for top position. I knelt behind Charlie, putting my ear to his back. Hand on his wrist. Other arm around his torso. I could see the sequence of moves in my mind. Feel the power in my body.

The whistle blew again. Charlie wasn't going down without a fight. He tried to stand, but I got hold of his ankle and hauled his leg back while driving my body forward. For a second, I had him where I wanted him, but he twisted, his strength matching mine.

The blood rushing in my ears drowned out the noise of the crowd. My body strained, my lungs burning for more air. The two of us fought like gladiators, as if our lives were on the line, not just a title.

He was strong, but I knew his tactics, remembered how he'd beaten me last year. He always went for a cradle. I kept him from getting a grip on me, always countering. I lost track of the points we scored on each other, but I knew it was still too close. I needed to pin him.

I broke his grip yet again and got to my feet. I was getting to him, getting in his head. Frustration showed plain on his face. The round was halfway over, and he was slowing. Fatigue setting in.

I could have wrestled ten more rounds. Energy poured through me, despite my fast breathing and pounding heart. A sense of elation filled me. Almost euphoria. I had this. I could do it.

He went for the takedown and I let him have it. Spun

around and got behind him for a reversal. I wasn't just going to pin him. I was going to *own* him.

Before he could counter, I got control of his arms. Flipped him over into a double arm bar. Few moves are as painful and demoralizing. I kept the pressure on his shoulders, pressing his back into the mat, his arms stretched out. He grunted, trying to break free. But there was no way—not without dislocating both arms.

The ref dropped to the mat, lying on his stomach, swishing his hand back and forth, palm down. Not quite a pin. I pushed harder, drawing on every last bit of strength I had left. Sweat rolled down my face; my muscles burned. My chest was on fire, my heart crashing against my ribs.

Smack. The ref's hand hit the mat. Pin.

I let go and moved so Charlie could get up. He unwound himself and shook out his arms. Blood pounded in my ears, throbbing in my temples. I sat on the mat for a few seconds, catching my breath, letting it sink in.

I'd won.

Charlie reached out a hand to help me up. I took it, meeting his eyes in thanks. Respect. We shook hands and the ref came to take my wrist. Raised my arm above my head.

My heart wasn't slowing, my breath coming faster. Why did my chest hurt so much? Spots of black floated across my vision, followed by sparks of light. I blinked hard, only half hearing the announcer say my name. I tried to find my parents in the crowd, but everything was blurry.

Sudden agony hit me, like I'd just been stabbed. Sharp pains radiated across my chest, down my arm. I cried out, cradling my arm to my body. The ref stepped in. A hand touched my back. Voices, asking me if I was okay.

The pain was unbearable. My legs gave out and I crumpled to the ground. I couldn't think. It was like my entire chest was caving in, my heart bursting apart.

Darkness came for me and I rushed to meet it. Anything to stop the unrelenting pain.

3

BROOKE

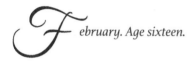 *ebruary. Age sixteen.*

MY PHONE BUZZED WITH A TEXT. I bit my lip, my tummy swirling with nerves. It was Liam.

Liam: Hey, Bee.

He kept calling me Bee. Not just the letter B, but typing it out like that. Bee. No one had ever nicknamed me before. It did funny things to my insides.

I glanced over at our picture from the Valentine's Day dance. I was wearing a dress borrowed from his sister Olivia —fitted shimmery silver bodice with a floor-length pale pink skirt. Liam in a rented tux. We were standing in front of a garish photo backdrop featuring a fake Hollywood sign and a lot of silver and gold stars. It was still a little hard to believe that night had actually happened. That he'd taken me to a dance, in that dress.

Nice things didn't happen to me very often, and that night was one I knew I'd cherish forever.

Me: Hey. What's up?

Since the dance, Liam and I had hung out a little bit—and texted a lot. He texted me in the morning before school, often going to his window to wave at me from next door. We texted in the evenings, sometimes just a message or two back and forth. Other times for hours on end, keeping us both awake late into the night.

We saw each other at school, and he didn't hesitate to talk to me. Apparently my bleak social standing didn't mean anything to him. But school was busy, and there were always other people around. He was nice to me, and he certainly made going to school a hundred times more bearable. But I lived for his text messages.

A crash rang out downstairs, followed by the muffled sound of yelling. I didn't want to know what my mom and her boyfriend, Paul, were doing down there. It could be as simple as one of them accidentally dropping something. Normal people dropped things, right? Or they might be drunk off their asses, stumbling around the house like idiots.

My phone buzzed with Liam's next text, but I went to the door and laid down on my stomach so I could sniff beneath the crack. A hint of cigarette smoke, like always. But no cloying weed odor mixed in. Damn.

If they were stoned on weed, they'd be relaxed—maybe even happy. Drunk meant sloppy and probably angry. They always fought when they drank. Of course, it was just as likely to be a mix of cheap beer and whatever else they could get their hands on. They made half-hearted attempts to hide their drugs from me, but I wasn't stupid. And when they were mixing things, it was the worst. I never knew what I'd get. Angry but half-passed out? Happy but manic? Last week my mom had gone on a drug-induced spree—I didn't know what she'd taken—and painted all the walls downstairs peach.

It was hideous, but she'd thought it was the best idea she'd ever had.

I got up and brushed off my jeans, then grabbed my phone.

Liam: Can you hang out?

Biting my lip, I stared at my phone. Could I? Sometimes sneaking out was easy. If Mom and Paul were high enough, they wouldn't even notice me. But Mom could also get mad, and if she got mad, she got mean. It was always a risk.

But worth it if Liam was asking.

Me: I'll try. Meet you out front.

I never let Liam come up to my door—always found excuses to meet him outside. Even the night of the dance. Olivia had invited me to come get ready with her, and I'd jumped at the chance. I didn't want Liam to see how I lived —didn't want him to know where I really came from.

I grabbed a coat and crept down the stairs. The stench of stale cigarette smoke and mildew permeated the air. We lived in a nice neighborhood, with pretty houses. This one had been pretty too, when we'd first moved in. It wasn't anymore—at least not on the inside.

The stairs descended directly into the living room, and there wasn't much ground to cover to reach the front door. If only I could get to it without them noticing.

No sign of them in the living room, just the usual piles of clutter. Ashtrays. Empty beer and soda cans. Food wrappers. Once in a while I cleaned up, but I hadn't bothered lately.

The sound of voices drifted from the kitchen at the back of the house. From where I was standing at the bottom of the stairs, I couldn't see back there. But there was a clear line of sight from the kitchen to the front door.

I took a deep breath. I'd just have to chance it.

Careful not to step on anything that might make noise, I tip-toed to the door. You'd think as out of it as my mom usually was, she'd be oblivious to the random crinkle of a candy wrapper. But she had an uncanny knack for hearing me move around the house.

"No!" My mom's voice made my back clench painfully.

"Come on, babe," Paul said. His words slurred together. "Upstairs."

Giggles. Groans.

Oh god. Either I'd make a break for the front door, or haul ass back upstairs and put on headphones. Listening to my mom and her boyfriend have drunken sex was one of the most horrifying parts of my life. And it happened way more often than I wanted to admit.

Front door it had to be. I hurried forward and started to open it.

"Brooke!"

Mom's voice again. I froze, my hand still on the doorknob.

"Where the fuck you think you're going?" she asked.

"Outside."

"Like hell," she said. "Did you do your homework?"

"Yes."

"You can't just leave." She stumbled toward me. "I'm your mother, Brooke."

I'd never understood why she felt the need to remind me of who she was as often as she did. I'd been hearing that my whole life—*I'm your mother*. She threw it around like a title, as if *mother* was the same thing as *queen*. When she was sober enough to notice I was around, at least.

"I know, Mom," I said, trying to keep my voice meek. She was on the edge, teetering between blowing me off and deciding I needed punishment for opening the front door without her permission.

Paul stood in the background, his eyes half-lidded, his arms crossed over his chest. I guess I was lucky in that he left me alone—Mom's boyfriends always did. Whether she made sure of it, or she somehow chose guys who had no interest in her underage daughter, I didn't know. She dated some dirtbags. It could have been a lot worse.

But none of them ever tried to stop her when she got violent with me, either.

"Where you going?" she asked again.

"Just outside, Mom," I said. "Maybe for a little walk."

"What? It's getting dark. Who you going with?"

Fuck. I didn't want to tell her it was Liam. If she thought anything was happening between us, she'd forbid me to see him. It wouldn't matter how many times I told her we were just friends. He'd taken me to a dance, and ever since then, she'd been watching me with a wary look in her eyes, like she expected me to announce I was pregnant any second.

She was obsessed with making sure I didn't get knocked up, as if me reaching adulthood without procreating was the primary benchmark of her parenting success. Since my eleventh birthday, she'd been warning me about the dangers of boys. Strange, coming from a woman who was almost never without a live-in boyfriend. She would break up with one and, within days, she'd be madly in love again, shacking up with some new douchebag.

She'd gotten pregnant with me at sixteen, and had told me many times how it had ruined her life. I suppose her strictness when it came to boys might have been a sign that she cared about me. Although, growing up hearing I was a mistake hadn't done much for my self-esteem.

But if I lied to her, and she caught me with Liam, it could

be worse. I turned to face her so I could see her eyes. They were glassy and bloodshot, but too clear for her to be wasted. Desiree Summerlin was never really sober—there had been brief times in the past when she hadn't been using, but they had never lasted. When you were raised by a drug addict, you learned to see the degrees of intoxication. If she was on the brink of oblivion, I could have said anything, knowing she wouldn't remember it later. But there was too much understanding in her eyes, and in this state, she'd know I was lying.

"Liam," I said. "But Mom, we're only friends. We're not doing anything wrong."

Her hand hit my face before I realized it was coming. The slap stung a little, but she was too wobbly to hit me very hard. I moved with the blow, hunching to the side and covering my head with my arms in case she wasn't finished.

"Don't you back talk at me," she said. "I'm doing this for your own good, don't you know that? I'm your mother. I won't let you be some slut who spreads her legs for any boy that smiles at her."

"I'm not, Mom," I said, keeping my arms over my head. "I'm still a virgin."

"Liar," she said, spitting out the word.

"I swear, Mom," I said. "I swear it."

Footsteps went up the stairs. I guess Paul was getting bored watching his girlfriend smack her daughter around.

"Wait, where *you* going?" Mom asked.

"Upstairs," Paul said. "Come on, Desiree."

"Watch yourself," Mom said to me. "You fuck up your life now, and I won't help you. You'll be out on your ass, you hear me?"

I wanted to say, *Promise?* But I kept silent.

She went upstairs, stumbling up the first couple of steps.

I waited until she was out of sight, then slipped out the door as quietly as I could manage.

Fresh air. The breeze against my face. The evening air felt so cleansing, like it washed away some of the filth I lived in. My cheek stung, heat blooming across my skin, but I didn't think it would leave a mark. And at least I was out for a while.

I went quickly up the driveway and rounded the corner. Liam leaned against the fence post a few feet away.

"There you are, Bee," he said. "I thought maybe you changed your mind."

"No, just... had to deal with my mom."

He gave me a crooked grin. "No big deal. I have an idea. Let's go."

He took my hand and the feel of his fingers twining with mine made my heart jump. We went toward his house and up his driveway, stopping at his pickup truck. My eyes darted to the lights in the upstairs windows of my house as he opened the passenger door for me. I'd get in trouble if I got caught leaving with him.

Screw it. I'd just have to hope I didn't get caught.

We drove through town, stopping at a burger place to get cheeseburgers and fries to go. Then Liam drove us down a long two-lane road, winding through the desert hills.

"Where are you taking me?" I asked. "I feel like we're either going out to some secret party spot, or you're going to murder me and hide the body."

He laughed. "Neither. There's just a cool place out here I want to show you. No parties or murders involved."

Liam turned off the road, his truck kicking up dust. The land went up in a sharp incline before leveling off at the top. He stopped, parking in an open area.

"Come on." He got out and grabbed the bag of food.

I followed him to the back of the truck. We both climbed in and sat with our backs against the wheel wells. He dug into the bag and handed me a cheeseburger.

"Thanks."

"Sure," he said. "Did you look up yet?"

Raising my face to the sky, I gasped. Outside the city and absent the glow of lights, the sky was an enormous swath of black peppered with stars. I'd never seen so many stars in my life.

"Wow," I said. "It's beautiful."

"Yeah," he said. "This is probably dumb, but I like to come out here at night. It's so quiet and you can't beat the view."

"This is amazing." I unwrapped my burger. "So, is this where you bring all your girlfriends?"

"Nah," he said. "I've never brought anyone up here before."

I met his eyes. "Really?"

"Really," he said. "Look, I know everyone lumps me in with all the jocks because I do sports. And some of those guys, yeah, they're all about banging whoever they can. But, I don't know, that's just not my thing."

"I didn't think so," I said. "You don't seem like you're anything like those guys."

"Not really," he said. "A lot of them are my friends, and they're cool. But I'm just interested in different things."

"Like what?"

He shrugged. "Books. I like to read and they think that's weird. And I want to travel. There are all these amazing places in the world and I'm supposed to be content with shooting hoops and eating pizza?"

"Yeah," I said with a laugh. "Can I ask you a question?"

"Sure." He took a bite of his burger.

"Why did you ask me to the dance?"

He finished chewing before he answered. "I noticed you when you moved in, and I saw you at school. You were intriguing. I'd wanted to talk to you for a while, I just hadn't gotten up the courage yet."

I laughed. "Why would you need courage to talk to me?"

"Well, you're not very approachable. You're so quiet and you don't seem to talk to anyone."

"I don't mean to be that way," I said.

"Yeah, I know that now," he said. "I should have asked you out a long time ago."

My cheeks warmed and I was glad for the cover of darkness. "So why the dance?"

"I didn't plan that or anything. I saw Karina being a bitch to you and it pissed me off. I kept seeing you in the mornings, coming out of your house, or randomly in the halls at school, and there was something about you. I was curious. And I figured that was my chance. If it got Karina off your back, even better."

"Thanks again for that," I said.

"Sure. Besides, those girls like Karina, they're all the same," he said. "I dated Christy Robertson for a while last year. She was supposed to be like, *the* girl, you know? The guys were all impressed that I got her. But she was boring. We had absolutely nothing in common—nothing to talk about. I didn't want to date someone like that again, but it seemed like the girls at our school were all the same. Until you came along."

"I'm always the different one."

"That's a good thing," he said.

"I guess. It makes things hard, though. I'm such a cliché —the weird, quiet girl who doesn't talk to anyone, just scribbles in a notebook all the time."

"You do it well," he said, a hint of humor in his voice. "Really, you have the whole thing down. Pink and blue streaks in your hair. Ripped jeans. Maybe you should add some black lipstick. Complete the look."

I laughed. "I don't think so. Not really my color."

"What are you always scribbling in those notebooks?" he asked.

"Lots of things, I guess," I said. "Sometimes just thoughts. Or poems. Things I wish I could say out loud but can't."

"Will you read some of it to me?" he asked.

"Oh, I..." I bit my lip. "I don't know."

"Come on," he said. "I showed you my secret spot. I even admitted I come out here to look at the stars. Do you know how badly I'd get my ass kicked if that got out?"

I laughed again, amazed at how easy it was to laugh and smile with him. I'd never been so comfortable with another person. "Okay, fine."

I jumped down and got my bag out of the cab. My tummy fluttered with nerves as I got back into the bed of the truck.

"I've never really read any of this stuff to another person." I pulled out my journal—just a cheap spiral notebook, small enough to fit in my bag—and flipped through the pages, trying to find something that wouldn't be mortifying to read out loud.

"Be honest, you have pages and pages of my name with little hearts," he said.

"You wish," I said.

He grinned back at me.

"All right. This is just... not really a poem, but kind of. Maybe it could be, I don't know." Deep breath. "The air burns my eyes, leaving them dry and gritty. Hurts as it slips past my tongue and into my throat. Don't they realize? But no. They're too numb. Dead to the world, their skin slack and lifeless. Their eyes hollow. They feel nothing, while I am left to feel everything. I drown in a sea of emotions I cannot control, but no one else can see. On the outside, I am glass. Smooth. Serene. Inside, I am a storm."

Hesitating a moment, I kept my eyes on the page, afraid of what I would see when I looked at him. He shifted, moving closer, and put his hand on my knee.

I lifted my chin and he surged in, his lips meeting mine. My eyes fluttered closed as his mouth moved slowly, softly. He cupped my face with his hands and his tongue brushed against my lips. With my heart hammering in my ribs, I shyly met the tip of his tongue with my own. Sparks raced through my body and he pulled me closer. I opened for him and our tongues slid against each other, our mouths warm. I'd never felt anything like it.

Slowly, our lips parted and we paused, our faces close.

"I've really been wanting to kiss you," Liam said, his hands still against my cheeks.

"That was my first kiss," I said, before I could stop myself. *Oh no, why did I say that?*

The corners of his mouth turned up in a smile. "Are you serious?"

"Yeah. I know, it's lame."

"No, that's not lame," he said. "That's one of the best things I've ever heard. I love that I'm your first kiss."

Before I could respond, he kissed me again. Deep and slow. He was intoxicating, the feel of his mouth tangled with mine pushing everything else away. All the stresses, fears, and worries I carried with me melted into nothing in that moment.

Nothing existed but us, kissing beneath the stars.

4

SEBASTIAN

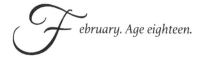ebruary. Age eighteen.

STAYING in the hospital was going to make me lose my mind.

It had been a week since I'd collapsed at the state tournament. The doctors still didn't know what had happened to me—at least, not why. I'd had a ventricular fibrillation, which was a fancy way of saying my heart had quit working right. Something about the electrical impulses getting jammed, so instead of the chambers of my heart squeezing to pump blood through, they'd fluttered—completely useless. By the time I'd hit the mat, I wasn't breathing and my heart had stopped.

They told me Coach had jumped in and started CPR. The arena had an automated external defibrillator, and fortunately for me, someone had found it. Right there, on the mat where I'd just won the biggest match of my life, in front of fifteen thousand wrestling fans, my parents, and my girlfriend, they'd shocked my heart into working again.

At least enough that I hadn't died.

After that, I'd been airlifted to the University of Iowa hospital, where I spent the night in ICU. I had no memory of any of it. All I could remember was winning, then pain, then waking up in a hospital bed with no idea what the hell had happened.

They'd run what seemed like an endless string of tests. Blood work. Chest X-rays. EKGs. Ultrasounds. Still, no one could tell me why my heart had suddenly quit working.

I was eighteen years old, in peak physical condition. The best wrestler in Iowa, a state where wrestling was everything. Clean diet. I'd never done drugs, or drank much. I hadn't even been dehydrated. I'd had plenty of fluids after weigh-in. But for some reason, my heart had freaked the fuck out, and I'd almost died.

My parents had been here every day. Our home in Waverly was almost two hours away, so they'd been staying at a hotel nearby. The first few days, I'd been grateful to have them here. Waking up in a hospital and finding out my heart had stopped had been terrifying.

But as the days had gone by—and we still didn't have definitive answers—my parents' presence had become stressful more than comforting. I knew they meant well, and I couldn't blame them for being concerned. I was their son. But the worry lines etched in my mom's forehead seemed to get deeper every day, and my dad paced all the time. They were keeping me on edge.

Every twinge or pinch in my chest made me nervous, but I tried to keep it to myself so they didn't worry more. But I didn't know if my heart was going to stop again. Until the doctors could tell us why it had happened, I was half-convinced I'd go to sleep one night and never wake up.

I was scheduled for one more test that day—a procedure

the doctors had said should give us the final answers we needed. Knowing I'd had a ventricular fibrillation wasn't good enough. We needed to know *why*.

And apparently that meant they were going to carve off a piece of my heart muscle.

They called it a myocardial biopsy. They were going to slice a tiny hole in my neck and thread a catheter through a blood vessel until it reached my heart. It sounded fucking awful, but if that's what they had to do to find out what was wrong with me, I'd deal with it.

"How you doing there, Seb?" Dad asked. His arms were crossed and he stood near the door.

"Okay." I glanced at Mom. She sat in a chair near the head of my bed. I hated seeing her so upset. But she'd watched her son collapse. His heart fail. That wasn't the kind of thing a mom could brush off.

"I'm fine," I said. "Mom, look at me. I'll get this over with, and pretty soon they'll tell us nothing is wrong and we can quit worrying."

She met my eyes and I could tell she wanted to believe me. But she didn't.

"Are you sure you're not in any pain?" she asked.

"Nope," I said. "Not at all."

Dr. Senter, one of the cardiologists, came in and explained the procedure again. I nodded along as she spoke, but I already knew what to expect. My parents asked a few questions and next thing I knew, I was rolling down the hallway to a procedure room.

Bright lights blazed above me, and there was a lot of equipment—something that looked like a camera and a bunch of monitors.

"Hi, Sebastian," one of the doctors said with a calm smile. She lowered the bed so I was lying flat. "I'm going to give you a mild sedative to help you relax, but it won't put you to sleep."

"Not too much of it," I said. "I don't like the way that stuff makes me feel."

She raised her eyebrows at me. "You're a big guy. And we need you to stay still. This might burn a little."

The sedative flowed into the IV and a mild burning sensation spread through my hand. I focused on a spot on the ceiling, taking deep breaths to stay calm. In seconds, the sedative took effect. My limbs felt too heavy to move and my head swam. I blinked slowly at the ceiling, still staring at the same spot.

Activity swirled around me. I was half-aware of the doctor speaking, equipment being moved and adjusted. The needle stung my neck when they injected the local anesthetic, but I was too sleepy to worry about it.

"Okay, Sebastian, we're going to get started now," someone said. "Lie as still as you can."

Even with my neck numb from the local, it hurt. A lot. I breathed in and out, willing my mind to focus on something else. I would not think about the incision in my neck, or the catheter being snaked through my blood vessel. I would not think about the little device that was about to harvest a sample of tissue from my heart.

I stared at the ceiling, detaching myself from the moment. Focused. Just breathing, in and out. My eyes locked on one spot.

There was nothing quick about it. I was used to being tested mentally—wrestling did that to you. But this tested me in ways I hadn't expected. They worked, moving things, talking, watching the monitors, adjusting, trying again. It took almost an hour before they finally finished and a nurse held a compress to my neck to stop the bleeding.

Even with the sedative, my entire body was tense, my muscles rigid. My mind was fuzzy, making it difficult to use my usual tricks to stay calm.

They brought me back to my room and my parents stood, looking at me as if they'd been afraid I wouldn't come back.

"He'll be tired for a while," someone said. "You should let him rest."

Vaguely, I was aware of my parents telling me goodbye. My mom bending down to kiss my forehead. My dad saying something I knew I wouldn't remember. Then I drifted off to sleep.

I WOKE up to an empty room and a very sore neck. I swore I could feel the entire route the catheter had taken, from the incision to my chest cavity. Groaning, I shifted, trying to get comfortable. But it wasn't much use.

A nurse came in to check on me and just as she was leaving, a familiar face peeked around the curtain.

"Charlie?" I asked.

"Hey, McKinney," he said.

Charlie Hall walked in, his thick body looking nondescript in street clothes—Iowa City West High School letterman's jacket over a t-shirt and faded jeans. He kept his dirty blond hair cut short, although I'd seen him off-season, and he let it grow out a little then.

"What are you doing here?" I asked.

He shrugged. "I wanted to see how you were doing."

"Thanks," I said. "Not really sure yet, actually. Still waiting on some test results. Want to sit or anything?"

"Sure," he said, lowering himself into one of the chairs

next to the bed. "They sent out an email to all the families who were at state. It didn't say much, other than you'd had some kind of heart problem, and you were here for treatment or something."

"Not much treatment yet." I lifted my hand with the IV. "Bunch of drugs. But they won't know what to do until they figure out what caused it."

"It's brutal, man," he said. "Look, you wrestled a great match. You deserved that win. I'm sorry about all this."

"Thanks."

"How much longer are you here?" he asked.

"I don't know," I said. "I guess it depends on what they find out."

"Do you mind giving me your number?" He pulled out his phone. "Just, you know, so we can keep in touch. You can let me know what's going on."

"Sure, man." I gave Charlie my number.

I was so surprised to see him here. Charlie and I didn't know each other well, not outside of wrestling. We went to different schools, in cities far enough apart that our social circles didn't cross. Yet, here he was. Cami had been here twice, and I'd been getting some texts from people at school, but none of my teammates or other friends had visited. Granted, Charlie lived here, in Iowa City. I guess that made it easier.

"You decide on a college yet?" he asked.

"U of I," I said.

He grinned. "Me too. I guess next year we'll be teammates. Assuming, you know..."

I glanced down at myself—at the hospital gown, the IV in the back of my hand. Since we didn't know what had gone wrong, we didn't know my prognosis. But there was one thing I knew for sure. I was going to be healthy enough to wrestle next year.

"Hell yeah, we will," I said. "You're going to have to cut some weight, though. I'm taking the top spot."

"Oh, you think so?" he said. "We'll see about that."

It hurt when I laughed, but I didn't care. Felt like I hadn't laughed—or even smiled—since before state. I was glad Charlie had brought up wrestling. It was good to talk about something normal for a change. Not doctors and heart medications and test results.

Charlie hung out for a while longer and we shot the shit. Talked about school, and graduation, and what college was going to be like. He'd wanted to find an out-of-state school, but U of I had offered him a scholarship he couldn't refuse. I was in the same boat.

He asked about Cami, and whether I thought we'd stay together. We were going to the same school, so I figured we would. He'd broken up with his girlfriend before wrestling season had started—said it was too hard to keep her happy when he was focused on his sport. Now she was dating someone else, but he was over it. Ready to meet some college girls in the fall.

When he got up to leave, I thanked him for coming. But I didn't think I'd done a good job of expressing how grateful I was. Having a normal conversation—with someone who assumed I'd get better and things would go back to normal —did a lot to ease the stress I'd been under since I'd woken up in the hospital.

I was a state champion wrestler. Say what you will, no other sport required as much focus. As much mental toughness. It was just you out there; no one else had your back. To win, you had to learn to dig deep, leave it all on the mat. And I was the best.

Charlie was right. I'd be his teammate next year. I had to be. I didn't know what I'd do without wrestling.

THE DOCTOR CAME in earlier than we expected the next morning. My parents had arrived by nine, looking pale and haggard. Neither of them looked like they'd been sleeping much. Dad was tough. He'd been a wrestler too—state champ in his weight class. He held himself like the athlete he'd been, taking each bit of news as it came, staying focused on what was in front of him.

Mom, on the other hand, was softer. Dad often said she was *made of feelings*. It was hard to see her so concerned. But no matter how often I told her I was doing okay, the fear never left her eyes.

Dr. Senter had a folder of paperwork in her hands. She flipped through a few times after she'd said hello to me and my parents.

"Well, I have mostly good news," Dr. Senter said. "The biopsy gave us the answers we need."

I let out a breath. Finally.

"You have what's called myocarditis. That basically means you have inflammation in your heart muscle. The inflamed tissue caused the electrical impulses that regulate your heartbeat to become erratic. The signals were too uncoordinated, so your heart stopped pumping."

"What caused the inflammation?" Dad asked.

"It usually follows an infection of some kind," Dr. Senter said. "It could be viral, although bacterial infections have been known to cause cases of myocarditis as well. But Sebastian's health history doesn't indicate he's been sick."

"No," Mom said. "He never gets sick. Other kids got ear

infections and coughs and stuffy noses, but never Sebastian. He's always been so healthy."

"No strange symptoms in the last six months or so?" Dr. Senter asked, looking at me. "Fatigue, stomach problems, fever?"

"No," I said. My mom was right. I almost never got sick.

"Well, in some cases, the cause can't be determined," she said. "Sometimes we just don't know why it happened."

"What do we do now?" Dad asked. "What sort of treatment does it require?"

Just like my dad—ready to talk solutions.

"Our first concern is preventing another fibrillation episode," Dr. Senter said, her eyes on me again. "I have several prescriptions you'll need to take. These will help ease the load on your heart and make another ventricular fibrillation less likely."

"But what about the inflammation?" Dad asked. "How do we fix that?"

"We just need to let it heal," Dr. Senter said. "The medications will help. We'll need to keep a close eye on his heart function over the next six to twelve months. For now, you'll need to limit your activity. You're a wrestler, is that right?"

"Yeah," I said. "But the season's over."

Dr. Senter nodded. "That's good. Definitely no wrestling. Or running. Keep it mild so your heart can get better."

I nodded, but I hated the idea of not working out. I took a little time off after wrestling season each year, but I kept in shape year-round. I had to be ready for next season. College was going to be even more competitive. I had to up my game, not take time off.

But I couldn't wrestle at all if my heart quit working again.

I glanced at my dad. "It's just like any other injury. I'll rehab it, and next thing you know, I'll be back at a hundred percent."

He smiled—a look of resolve—and nodded. "That's right."

Dr. Senter had more to say, but it was all worst-case scenario stuff. What would happen if my heart didn't heal—if the inflammation spread. I needed to know what to look out for—how to tell if something was wrong—but I didn't worry about the rest. I'd take my pills, follow my rehab plan, and be back to my old self in time for wrestling at U of I.

That was what was going to happen. Like winning state against Charlie. There was no other option.

5

BROOKE

January. Age seventeen.

MY KEY RATTLED in the front door lock. It always stuck a little, but I managed to get it open. A big black garbage bag, full of who knows what, stood in the way. I had to push it aside to get the door open enough to come in.

I'd spent the afternoon doing homework with Liam and Olivia next door. It had been a little less than a year since the first time Liam had kissed me. After that night, I'd officially become his girlfriend. He'd been my first kiss, and he was the first guy I'd ever dated. I was crazy about him.

The air tickled the back of my throat. My house perpetually smelled of cigarettes and weed, the stale pungent scent permeating everything. It was stuffy—warmer inside than out. Phoenix had great weather in January, but our house was always uncomfortably hot.

The worn-out gray couch—which provided the only

sense that the living room was, in fact, a living room—was piled with flattened cardboard boxes. More bulbous garbage bags sat on the floor, their contents warping their shapes. What was going on?

"Mom?" I called, pitching my voice to be heard in the kitchen at the back of the house. "Are you home?"

Something crashed in the kitchen, a sharp metallic sound, like pots and pans hitting the floor.

"Fuck!"

"Mom?"

I hurried down the short hallway to the kitchen to find my mom in a black t-shirt and jeans, standing over a pile of pots and pans. Her hair was limp and wet, like she'd recently showered. She put her hands on her hips and for a second, I stared at her bony arms. She was so skinny. Not attractive thin, like she was in good shape. She was sickly, with bones protruding from her pallid skin. Her t-shirt was too big, the neck slanting crooked, almost off one shoulder, and her elbows were sharp and pointy.

"Fuck," she muttered again.

"Mom, what's going on?" I asked.

"We're moving," she said without looking at me.

I blinked at her, my breath freezing in my lungs. Moving? Again? In my seventeen years on this planet, my mother had moved me no less than twenty-three times. That I knew of. The number might have been higher, since I didn't know all the places we'd lived before I was three. But by my best guess, this house was number twenty-three.

"What?" I asked. "Moving where?"

"Tucson." She crouched down, revealing her tramp stamp—a set of wings tattooed on her lower back. I'd never been sure if they were supposed to be angelic, or some kind of bird.

"Why?"

She looked at me for the first time then. Her eyes were always bloodshot, so the red veins standing out against the whites of her eyes were nothing new. Today she had dark circles beneath her eyes and a scab on the corner of her lip. Whether that was a cold sore or a place she'd been hit was anyone's guess. Paul didn't usually smack her around, but it happened once in a while if they got really drunk. And she would sometimes leave the house and disappear for a few hours—or days—and return with a bruise or two. I'd never asked what they were from.

"Because we are," she said, her voice sharp. She went back to stacking the pots. "Because Paul is a fucking prick."

I took slow steps backward, my stomach tied in a knot. My mouth hung open, but the words I wanted to say died in my throat. I knew it wouldn't matter how much I protested. Arguing would only get me in trouble. I didn't want to risk getting slapped, or worse.

I decided to try a different tactic. I kept my voice light and conversational. "Wow, Mom. This is unexpected. When did you decide this?"

"Don't argue with me," she said.

"But I was just asking—"

"Goddammit, Brooke," she said, whirling on me. She was smaller than me, all sinew and bone, but I knew how strong she was. "Don't fucking start with me. I'm your mother. We're leaving tonight."

"Tonight?" I asked, my voice strangled, barely escaping my throat.

"You need to listen," she said. "You know I hate repeating myself."

"I know, Mom, but this is really sudden," I said.

"Yeah, well, life's a bitch. Paul took off and I got fired. I'm already behind on the rent on this place. We can crash at my friend Leslie's for a while until I get us back on our feet." She went over to the counter and grabbed a pack of cigarettes, then smacked the pack against her hand a few times before pulling one out and sticking it between her lips. "Where's my fucking lighter?"

With trembling hands, I quickly grabbed a lighter off the counter and handed it to her. She lit her cigarette and took a long drag, then took it out of her mouth between two fingers. She held in the smoke before blowing it out in a cloud.

"Go pack your shit," she said. "Just what we can fit in the car. We'll have to come back for the rest. Or just get new shit, I don't know."

My lungs felt tight, like I couldn't get enough air. Without another word, I turned and went upstairs to my room.

I didn't start packing like she'd told me to. I stood in the center of my bedroom, looking around. I was going to graduate in five months. The last five months of my sentence. Possibly four. In four months, I'd turn eighteen. Even though I'd still have a month until graduation, I'd be a legal adult. Maybe I'd find a way to move out.

I just needed four more months.

But this move shouldn't have surprised me. Mom had been with Paul for a record eighteen months, and we'd lived here for well over a year. We'd been downright settled in this place. It had been stupid to hope we'd live here long enough for me to graduate. I should have known better than to make friends. Get close to Liam.

I glanced out my window at Liam's house. His bedroom was dark, but it was six o'clock. Dinner time. He was probably sitting at the dining table with his family, sharing a meal. Something that required pots and pans like the ones my mom was pointlessly packing downstairs.

Tucson was three hours away. Would Liam's parents let him come visit me? Would he ever have time? He'd have school, and practice, and games.

More importantly, would my mom let me see him if he came?

I'd kept my relationship with Liam quiet, hiding behind my friendship with his sister. It was easier to tell my mom I was going next door to hang out with Olivia than be honest and say Liam was my boyfriend. I was terrified of lying to her, but I was more afraid of what she'd do if she knew the truth. It wasn't that we were sleeping together, like she feared so much. But she'd never believe me if I told her we weren't having sex. To her, that's what a relationship was.

And I *was* friends with Olivia. I didn't hang out with her as much as I did Liam, but I liked her a lot. She was only about six months younger than me, and a junior. She was the first friend I'd had since I was little.

I'd been spending a lot of time with the Harpers. Liam's parents were amazing, Olivia was sweet, and Liam... He was everything. Some people would say I was too young to be in love, but I knew better. I was completely in love with Liam Harper.

How could I leave them?

Anger bubbled up inside me. Why did she have to do this to me? Over and over again? I tried to be a good daughter. I cleaned up after her. Followed her rules, whether they made sense or not. Ignored her drugs. I never ratted her out or called the cops, not even when she hit me.

I'd spent my entire life trying to make her happy. Trying to be good so she'd stay sober for a little while. Because sometimes she did. Sometimes she seemed to get herself together, and things would be okay.

Then I'd come home to her passed out on the couch, or packing up the house to move in with yet another dirtbag she'd picked up who knows where.

And now she was going to move me yet again, right in the middle of my senior year. When I only had four months left before I'd be free.

I couldn't do it. I couldn't pack up and start over again. Not this time.

Instead of pulling out my things and packing for Tucson, I grabbed some of the least-shitty clothes I owned and stuffed them into my backpack. My journals. Hairbrush. Makeup bag. The picture of me and Liam at the dance.

There wasn't anything else I wanted.

With my phone in the back pocket of my ripped jeans, and my backpack slung over my shoulders, I crept downstairs. I desperately hoped I could get out of the house without her hearing. She'd seemed pretty sober, so I didn't have the advantage of her being stoned. If I was really doing this, I had to do it fast.

There was so much crap strewn around the living room, I had to pick up my feet and tip-toe around. Mom was still in the kitchen. I could hear her muttering and the ripping sound of packing tape. What was she doing back there? She only had a sedan—how much kitchen stuff that never got used did she plan on stuffing into the back seat of her car?

"Brooke!"

I froze, my heart pounding. Did she think I was still upstairs? Should I answer? I was too far away from the door. Could I outrun her if she chased me? I'd never tried. I'd always been too scared of what she'd do when she caught me to run away from her.

But I wasn't coming back this time. Not ever. So fuck it.

I sprinted for the front door. Threw it open.

"Brooke, where the hell do you think you're going?"

My backpack bounced as I bolted down the three steps leading to the driveway. One of my journals dug painfully into my back, but she'd do worse if she caught me. I almost made it to the street—although I had no idea where I was going—when I tripped and flew forward, landing hard on the black asphalt.

Pain bloomed across my palms, scraped raw, and my knees burned. I'd tripped over something, but I wasn't sure what. It didn't matter. I just had to get up.

"Brooke, what the fuck is going on?" Mom asked. Her footsteps were getting closer, but she wasn't running.

I glanced over my shoulder. She was only a few feet away. Another step, and she'd be close enough to reach out and grab me. I had to get away.

Pushing myself up with my palms stinging, I struggled to my feet. Blood soaked my jeans at the knees and more ran down my arms. My chin burned; I must have scraped it when I hit the ground.

"You dumbass," Mom said. She had a new cigarette between her fingers and she flicked the ashes into the street. "What are you running outside for? You all packed? I don't have time for your bullshit."

"No," I said.

She put a hand on her bony hip and cocked her head to the side. "Excuse me?"

"I'm not going," I said.

I expected her to erupt with anger, but she simply looked amused.

"Is that so?"

I nodded. "I'm not moving with you."

She took a long drag of her cigarette, never taking her eyes off me. "Yes, you are."

"No."

Anger reached her eyes then. They narrowed and a vein pulsed in her neck. "I'm your mother, Brooke. You're coming with me."

I shook my head. I felt like my scrapes should hurt more, but maybe it was all the adrenaline coursing through my system. That, or all the fear.

The slap came so fast, I didn't have time to flinch away. My cheek erupted with pain and I covered my face, turning away from her.

She hit me again, her fist closed this time. "You little bitch. You can't run away from me. I'm your mother."

"Mom, stop."

Another slap, her palm open. I warded off the worst of it with my right arm, but her fingernail scratched my forehead as it went by.

"This is the thanks I get?" she asked, her voice getting louder. *Smack.* "This is what I get for raising you?" *Smack.* "Putting up with your shit all these years?" *Smack.* "Do you have any fucking idea what it's been like?" *Smack.* She slapped me again, and again, her blows hard and erratic.

"Mom, please." Tears rolled down my cheeks. I staggered backward, my arms up, trying to stop her from hitting me. "Please stop."

"I'm your mother," she shouted. Another hard slap connected with the side of my head, just above my ear.

"Mom—"

"Hey!" Liam's voice.

Oh god, no. No, no, no. Don't let him see this.

"What the hell are you doing?" Liam asked.

I didn't turn to look, but I could hear his footsteps as he

ran toward the street. Mom's hair was disheveled, her face twisted in an angry grimace. Somehow her lit cigarette was still pinched between two fingers, a tendril of acrid smoke rising into the air.

"Mind your own fucking business," she said.

"Did you hit her?" Liam asked.

"I'm her mother," she said.

"Bee, are you—" He stopped, his eyes going wide. "Oh my god."

My entire body shook. I didn't want him to see this. I'd lied about my mom for years, assuring teachers and school counselors that everything was fine. I didn't want anyone to know that this was where I came from. This was my life. I didn't want anyone to see.

Especially not Liam.

Pity and anger stormed in his eyes as he looked me up and down. I'd never felt so ashamed. So dirty. He was seeing the truth of me in all its ugliness. My mother, her baggy clothes hanging off her emaciated frame, the last vestiges of a cigarette in her hand. The door to my disgusting house, wide open, the mess in plain sight.

And me, bleeding, my skin burning, my eyes filled with tears. I'd been so careful not to let him see this. Always met him at the street so he wouldn't come up to my door. Aired out my clothes in the window every night so they wouldn't smell like smoke. Tip-toed around my mom, lying to her, so I wouldn't give her a reason to be mad—a reason to leave a mark on me.

"Listen, you little shit," Mom said to Liam, breaking me from my stupor. "Get your ass back in your house. This has nothing to do with you."

Liam moved in front of me, placing himself between me and my mother. "Don't you dare touch her."

Mom snorted. "Excuse me?"

"You heard me," he said. "Don't touch her. You're never laying a hand on her again."

"And what are you going to do about it?" she asked. "Hit me back? Go ahead, hit a woman. That'll go over well."

He took slow steps toward her, his body tense. Mom's eyes widened and the color drained from her face.

"I won't hit you," he said, his voice dangerously low. "I don't have to because you're going to walk back into that house right now. And Brooke is coming home with me."

"Like hell," Mom said, but there was a lot less conviction in her voice.

Liam shifted toward her and she flinched. "Yes, she is."

"I'm her mother," Mom said weakly.

"Not anymore." Liam turned away from her, as if she no longer existed. "Come on, Bee. Let's get you cleaned up."

I trembled as he led me into his house, too shocked to process what was happening. Liam spoke softly to me, words of encouragement that I couldn't understand. My breath came in shaky gasps, and I clutched my scraped hands against my body.

"Liam, what's going on out there?" his mom, Mary, called from the other room.

"Brooke needs help," he said.

Mary met us in the kitchen. Her jaw dropped and her eyes widened. "Brooke, what happened?"

"Her mom," Liam said, his voice thick with anger.

"What?" Mary asked.

"I went outside and her mom was hitting her in the street."

"Oh sweetheart, you're bleeding." Mary dug through a few drawers and came at me with damp paper towels and bandages.

Someone lifted my backpack off my shoulders. Olivia. She gave me a sympathetic smile and set my bag down.

"I fell," I said while Mary attended to the worst of my scrapes.

"Bee, your mom was hitting you," Liam said. "I saw it happen."

I met his eyes, biting my lip to keep from sobbing. What did he think of me now? He was going to see what everyone at school always did—the real reason they ostracized me. They could tell. I was a nobody with no father and a drug addict mother who slapped me around when she got mad. Who wanted that girl around? No one.

But I didn't see disgust in Liam's face. It wasn't even pity that shone back at me in those bright blue eyes. Anger, yes. He was mad. But there was something else behind the spark of rage. Sadness.

"I know things are awful for you at home," Liam said, his voice soft. "You don't talk about it, and I didn't want to make you. But we know. We've heard things." He glanced at his mom. "Mom suspected there are drugs involved. I wanted to ask you, but I didn't want to make you feel bad. And I wasn't sure if there was anything I could do."

Liam's dad, Brian, had come into the kitchen while Liam spoke. I could see him from the corner of my eye, wearing an expression just like Mary and Olivia. Just like Liam. Sadness.

I gaped at Liam. He knew. They all knew. And they didn't hate me. They didn't think I was awful just like her.

Fresh tears fell from the corners of my eyes. "I can't go back. She's moving to Tucson and I can't go with her. I can't do it anymore."

Liam wrapped his arms around me and pressed me

close. "No way, Bee. You're not going anywhere with her. Never."

Mary rested her hand on my back. "You'll stay here, with us."

"Mom, are you serious?" Olivia asked.

"Yes," Mary said, gently rubbing my back. "Can you share your room with her?"

"Yeah," Olivia said, "of course I can."

"It's settled then," Mary said.

Liam held me close and I rested my stinging cheek against his chest, listening to his heartbeat. "There, Bee. You're safe now."

Somehow, I knew he was right. I knew my mom wouldn't come bang on the Harpers' door and demand I move to Tucson with her. She'd just go, leaving me behind. She was probably throwing stuff in her car right now, relieved she didn't have to deal with me anymore.

The enormity of it left me dizzy, and I was grateful for Liam's strong embrace. His family had always been good to me, but this took my breath away. They were going to let me stay. Live here, with them. A real family. No more smoke and drugs, dirty houses, and creepy men. No more walking on eggshells, wondering which woman I'd find when I got up in the morning or came home from school. No more stinging cheeks and punishments for things I hadn't done.

I wrapped my arms around Liam and held him tight. He kissed the top of my head. The relief that washed through me was so strong it warmed me from the inside, burning away my fear and shame. With Liam, I was safe.

With Liam, I was home.

6

SEBASTIAN

January. Age nineteen.

LETTING my backpack drop to the floor, I slumped down onto the edge of the bed. I was missing my English class, but I didn't have it in me. I was too damn tired.

The medications I took made me feel like I was slogging through mud. Mornings weren't bad. I usually woke up feeling fine. I could walk to class, and even carrying a shit-load of books in my backpack didn't bother me. But by early afternoon, my body was just done.

By the time I got back to my room every afternoon, it felt like I'd been wearing lead shoes all day. My entire body ached, the fatigue settling deep in my bones. I felt like I was ninety, not nineteen.

I lay back on my bed and let my eyes close. When I'd first been diagnosed almost a year ago, I'd figured it would take a few weeks, maybe a month, for my heart to get better.

I'd hated the way the medications had made me feel—getting through an entire school day had been exhausting—but I'd known I could live with it for a while. I'd held on, doing what I had to do. After all, it was only temporary.

A second heart biopsy, eight weeks after the first, had brought bad news. The inflammation wasn't getting better. In fact, it was worse.

They'd changed my dosages, added new medications. I'd slogged through the last couple months of high school as best I could. I probably wouldn't have graduated without Cami's help. She'd been at my house after school almost every day to help me with my homework. The meds made me so tired, I had a hard time staying focused. But I'd passed all my classes, and coasted through graduation.

My friends had all gone out that night after the ceremony. Bonfires. Beer. Couples making out in the backs of pickup trucks. Everyone celebrating the end of childhood, and the beginning of a new chapter.

I'd gone home with my parents and put myself to bed by nine.

Summer had come and gone, and my parents had tried to get me to change my plans for fall. They'd wanted me to live at home, maybe take a few community college classes, or find something online. Something less taxing. But I'd stuck with my resolve to start at U of I.

I needed to do this. I needed to be on my own. Letting my heart condition win wasn't an option.

I hadn't had another ventricular fibrillation, but I'd been having a lot of smaller fibrillation episodes. I could feel them—times when my heart fluttered or beat erratically.

Every time it happened, I was hit with a wave of fear. Was my heart going to stop again? Was there anyone nearby who could help if it did? I wore a medical alert bracelet with instructions, but someone would have to see it, and have the presence of mind to do something if I collapsed.

So far, I'd been okay. But I lived with the worry every day that my heart was going to quit while I was sitting in class, and everyone would just stop and stare at the big guy on the floor.

But even that hadn't deterred me from starting school— or staying once I'd gotten here. I'd made it to January. I was doing okay.

I looked up at the clock. Charlie had a meet tonight, so he was probably already down there, getting warmed up. Charlie and I had decided to room together, and he made a pretty good roommate. I'd assumed I'd be joining him on the wrestling team, but my heart hadn't recovered enough yet. Coach Harris would welcome me to the team as soon as I was well enough to compete. Unfortunately, it wasn't going to be this year.

After a nap I hadn't exactly meant to take—I'd basically passed out on my bed for an hour—I felt a little better. Which was good because I didn't want to miss the meet. Injured wrestlers still supported their teammates. That's all this was. An injury. Athletes got them all the time. Mine was just taking longer to rehab than most.

Before I left, I texted Cami. I wasn't sure what she had going on tonight, but she knew there was a meet, so we didn't have plans. Despite being on the same campus, we only saw each other about once a week. Classes kept us both busy, and Cami was a joiner. She'd pledged to Delta Gamma, and her sorority had a full calendar. I figured it was good for her. I didn't have the energy to do a lot of extra stuff, so her friends kept her busy.

I gave myself extra time to get over to Carver-Hawkeye Arena. Fortunately, I could take Cambus—the free university bus system—to get around, so I didn't have to do too much walking. Coach Harris had given me a wrestling season pass to get me into all the meets, since I couldn't technically be on the team. When I got to the arena, I flashed it and walked inside.

The entire place buzzed with energy. Every college meet was like the high school state finals—packed with cheering spectators. Audience chants. Shouts and cheers for campus favorites. I'd never cared a lot about the attention from the crowd. I'd always been focused on the match ahead, on my competition. But now, the roar of the crowd uncurled a thread of jealousy in my gut.

I should have been doing my pre-match routine right now. Pacing. Listening to loud music. Prepping my mind for the battle to come. Instead, I felt out of shape and weak. I wouldn't last ten seconds against any of these guys. I'd lost weight, and the fatigue I battled every day left me feeling frail. I hated it.

The announcer's voice boomed over the loudspeaker. I made my way through the crowd to the main arena. Coach let me sit down with the team, so I didn't have to be up in the stands. Everyone was focused, so I didn't say anything when I got to their spot. Just took a seat in an empty folding chair on the sidelines.

Charlie was on the floor nearby, stretching. He met my eyes for a second and gave me a brief nod. I nodded back, but kept it at that. I didn't want to break his concentration.

I watched each match. Cheered for my teammates. There were two other guys from Waverly on the team—one who was a year older than me, and another guy from my class. It was weird seeing them here, dressed in singlets and headgear, while I sat on the sidelines in street clothes. They both won. I clapped. They nodded to me in acknowledgment. But that was it. No good-natured bullshitting. No post-win taunts or friendly insults tossed in my direction.

It was like they didn't know what to say to me anymore.

My heart fluttered, the beat suddenly irregular. I took slow breaths to stay calm, my eyes locked on the floor. People moved around me, but I had to stay focused. Will my heart to keep working. My chest tightened and it felt as if my lungs had suddenly shrunk to half their size.

Resisting the urge to put a hand on my chest—I didn't want to scare anyone—I gripped my thighs and tried to breathe. This was the worst episode I'd had in a while. My head swam with dizziness and the pressure in my chest grew. At least I was already sitting down.

"You okay?" someone asked.

I nodded and my voice came out strained. "Yeah, just need a second."

My heart resumed its normal rhythm and the pressure gradually eased. My phone buzzed in my pocket—it was probably Cami—but I needed to breathe through this first. I kept my focus, eyes on the floor. Air in, air out.

I looked up to find Charlie standing in front of me, his hands on his hips. "You good, man?"

"Yeah," I said. Damn it, I didn't want to mess with his routine. "Nothing serious. Just uncomfortable."

"You sure?"

I met his eyes. "Yeah."

He glanced around, then stepped closer and lowered his voice. "No tough guy shit with this, okay?"

"Yeah, man, I know," I said. "Now get out of here and go make that North Dakota asshole cry."

Charlie grinned. "Oh yeah, he's fucked."

I laughed a little, but Charlie's confidence was well-earned. Even at the collegiate level, he was a tough competitor. I watched him wrestle, noting a minor mistake. If Coach didn't point it out, I'd make sure to tell him. I tried not to focus on the fact that the guy I'd beaten last year was kicking ass this season. I was pumped for Charlie to win. But it was still shitty to be stuck on the sidelines.

After the last match, I followed the guys into the locker room. Another wrestler, a junior named Randy, was out for the season too. He'd torn his rotator cuff in practice last week and he'd need surgery soon. He slapped guys on the back, congratulated them on their wins. There were hand-shakes and bro fists.

I realized, as I sat on a bench off to the side, that no one was treating me like an injured team member. Maybe it was because I hadn't started the season with them. A lot of these wrestlers were guys I didn't know well. Older than me, or freshmen who'd come from different high schools. We hadn't bonded like teammates yet.

But even the guys I did know—guys I'd wrestled with for years—looked at me differently.

Everyone knew who I was. Sebastian McKinney, Iowa state champion. But that's not what they saw when they looked at me now. They saw the wrestler who'd collapsed at state. The guy who was still too sick to wrestle. Who'd lost twenty pounds since last season and couldn't work out to put the muscle back on. The guy who had some weird heart condition most people mispronounced.

I'd been trying to deny how much my illness had changed me. Trying to hold on to the guy I'd been before the state finals. Tough. Focused. The best at what I did. My entire identity had hinged on being an athlete. It was all I knew.

But I wasn't him anymore. I could no more win a

wrestling match than run a mile. Hell, I could barely walk a mile.

I pulled my phone out of my pocket, remembering I'd gotten a text.

Cami: Busy tonight, babe. Not sure about this weekend. The girls want to go to a thing. If you're up for it, you can come.

A *thing* probably meant a frat party. Just the thought of a crowded house full of dumbasses drinking beer out of plastic cups was exhausting. She knew I didn't have the energy for something like that. I could tell she was getting bored of our usual stay-in-and-watch-a-movie routine, but what the fuck did she expect me to do? Maybe I should have texted her back, but I didn't.

I heard some of the guys making plans to go out—probably to grab some food. I got up and slipped out of the locker room. I didn't want their pity invite. And the truth was, I'd have said *no* anyway. My limbs were heavy and the pressure in my chest was wearing me down. I was so fucking tired.

I took the bus back to my dorm and tossed my wrestling season pass in the garbage. What was the point of sitting on the sidelines? The rest of the team didn't give a shit if I was there. I made them uncomfortable. Even my old friends didn't know what to say to me anymore. These guys lived and breathed wrestling. I couldn't practice, couldn't work out. I could barely make it to my classes.

Whoever—whatever—I was now, it wasn't a state champion wrestler. I was just a kid with a sick heart. A guy who spent more time in doctor's offices than college parties.

A guy who didn't know who he was anymore.

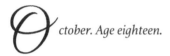

7

BROOKE

October. Age eighteen.

LIAM WASN'T HOME when I got back from class. I dropped my backpack near the door and slipped off my shoes. I'd aced my history test that morning, and my English Lit professor had given me an A on my essay. That was a great way to end the week.

I'd been in college for almost two months, and already I felt like I'd finally found a place I belonged. It was so much better than high school. Granted, the last part of my senior year, living with the Harpers, hadn't been all that bad. I'd had a stable, clean, safe place to live. The Harpers had treated me like part of the family. Dating Liam had made me untouchable to the Mean Girls, so no one at school had bothered me. For the first time in my life, I'd actually been happy.

It had been nine months since I'd seen my mom. She'd left that night, after Liam had brought me to his house. Her car had been gone in the morning, and none of us had seen her since. A week or so later, we'd seen the owner of the house hauling stuff out to a big pickup truck—probably getting the place cleaned up so he could rent it out again. But as far as I knew, Mom had never come back.

She hadn't called either. I was torn between feeling relieved and rejected. She'd been a terrible parent for most of my life, but she was still my mother. Liam insisted that her leaving me was the biggest act of love she'd ever shown —that she'd known I'd be better off without her, and that was why she'd stayed away. I wasn't sure if he was right, but I liked his version better than mine. It was nice to think that she'd left because she loved me, not because I hadn't been good enough to make her stay.

After graduation, Liam and I had decided on a college— Arizona State—and made plans to move. He had a college fund his parents had started when he was little. Between financial aid and scholarships, I'd managed to scrounge enough to make college possible for me.

We'd found an apartment just off campus. There was so much freedom in having our own place. Freedom, and privacy. I was endlessly grateful to the Harpers for bringing me into their home, but they'd been strict with me and Liam. They'd made it very clear that I was to sleep in Olivia's room, and they wouldn't tolerate me and Liam sneaking around.

We had, of course, although not at first. I'd been too afraid of breaking their rules and getting kicked out. But it hadn't taken long before the temptation had become too much to resist. What had started as snuggling and making out under the covers had quickly escalated.

No one had been surprised when we'd announced we were planning to get an apartment together after graduation. Neither of us could imagine living apart. We knew we were young, but that didn't matter. Liam and I were great together. Comfortable. He made me feel secure.

Our apartment was tiny, but adorable. It had a bedroom, a little kitchen, and enough living space for a couch, TV, and a table that we mostly used as a desk. A big window at the front had the ugliest curtains we'd ever seen—olive green with a floral pattern—but they were so hideous, we loved them. I'd strung up twinkle lights and we'd bought some cheap but cute artwork to hang. It was all very college-student-chic, but it was ours.

On the biggest wall, right above the couch, we'd hung a huge world map. We'd decided that after college, we were going to travel. We brought home travel magazines and pored over websites, talking about where we wanted to go. Then we'd put pins on the map to mark the locations. The map was looking pretty full already.

I wondered if we'd ever make it to all those places. Despite having moved around a lot, I'd never really been outside the southwest. Even places like New York seemed exotic and exciting. I couldn't imagine what it was going to be like to hike in a tropical rain forest or wander through a city in Europe.

I opened the fridge and laughed. Liam had obviously been to the store; the top shelf was fully stocked with peach iced tea. He had the weirdest obsession with it. He'd also bought more Coke, which was what I preferred. I grabbed one and brought it to the couch.

He was usually home before me on Fridays, but he'd picked up an extra shift at work. He'd been working so hard since we'd started school. Full load of classes, and he was planning to major in engineering, so it wasn't like they were easy. Plus his job. I worked too, in a little café on campus.

Work and school kept us both busy, but it was shaping up to be a great year.

I decided to shower before he got home. I hadn't washed my hair that morning, and dry shampoo only goes so far, especially since it had been warm out.

After my shower, I toweled off and slipped on a clean bra and panties. I was looking for my favorite ASU t-shirt in the basket of clean laundry when I heard Liam's key in the door.

Dressed only in my underwear, I hurried to the door, struck a pose, and pulled it open.

My eyes widened and whatever seductive line I'd been going to say died a swift death in my throat. It wasn't Liam. Instead, I stood face to face with his sister, Olivia.

Her expression registered surprise and for a few seconds, we stood frozen, staring at each other in shock. Next thing I knew, we were both laughing our asses off.

"Oh my god, get in here," I said between laughs. I grabbed her wrist and pulled. "I need to close the door before one of the neighbors sees me."

Olivia ducked inside, still giggling, and I closed the door behind her.

"Wow, Brooke," she said, looking me up and down. "That's hot, but you didn't need to strip for me."

Maybe I should have been embarrassed, but Olivia had seen me in my underwear—or less—plenty of times. We'd shared a bedroom. And it wasn't like she didn't know I was sleeping with her brother.

I put my hands on my hips and batted my eyelashes. "I just wanted you to feel appreciated."

She laughed again. "I love your guts. But put some clothes on, girl. I'm getting jealous of your boobs."

I laughed again and grabbed my boobs, winking at her. She rolled her eyes and set her backpack down while I went into the bedroom. I found my t-shirt and slipped it on, along with a pair of shorts.

"I take it Liam didn't tell you I was coming," she said when I came out. "Sorry, I should have texted you."

I sat down on the couch next to her. "He didn't; he's such a guy. But it's fine. I'm happy to see you."

"Me too," she said. "I texted him yesterday to see if you guys were free this weekend. He said he was working later than usual today, so I figured I'd come early and keep you company."

"Thanks, O," I said. "Are you staying the whole weekend?"

"If you don't mind," she said.

"Of course not. This will be fun," I said. "How's school?"

She rolled her eyes. "Stupid. I can't wait until I'm out of there."

Olivia was a senior in high school and a little jealous that Liam and I had graduated and gone off to college.

"I bet the year flies by," I said. "Graduation will be here before you know it."

"I hope so," she said. "I'm so over it."

"Well, I guess I don't know when Liam is getting home," I said. "Should we watch a movie or something?"

"Sure. Oh," she said, grabbing my arm, "we should watch that ghost one we didn't get to before you guys moved."

"Done."

I turned on the TV and found the movie while she got up and closed the curtains. Olivia and I were both horror movie junkies. They scared the shit out of us, but we loved it. We settled in on the couch and turned on the movie.

It started out innocent enough, but it wasn't long before the characters were wandering through dark hallways and creepy things were jumping out and scaring them—and us. The eerie music set the tone and I looked over my shoulder a few times, half-expecting to see a ghostly apparition hovering behind me.

I snuggled closer to Olivia and tucked my arm through hers. The movie was so much scarier than I'd thought it would be. My heart raced and I couldn't take my eyes off the screen.

"Boo!"

Olivia shrieked and threw the remote. I clutched the blanket and backed into the corner of the couch. But of course it wasn't a ghost in our apartment. Liam had crept up behind us. He stood next to the couch with a hand over his nose.

"Ow," Liam said. "Damn it, O, you hit me in the face."

"Don't scare us like that," Olivia said, clutching her chest. "You almost gave me a heart attack."

I pushed the blanket off and got up. "Are you okay?"

Liam touched beneath his nose and looked at his fingers. "Crap, I'm bleeding."

"Oh, poor baby."

"Serves you right," Olivia said.

I led Liam into the bathroom and helped him clean up. He wasn't bleeding much. When it stopped, I wiped his face with a wet washcloth. His eyes never left mine.

"What?" I asked.

"I was just thinking about how lucky I am," he said.

"Lucky that your sister hit you in the nose with a remote?" I asked. "I'd say that was pretty *un*lucky. I don't think she even aimed."

He took the washcloth and set it on the counter, then cupped my cheek. "No, I mean lucky because I have you, Bee."

I looked into his eyes and smiled. "I'm pretty sure I'm the lucky one."

"Maybe we both are." He placed a soft kiss on my lips. "I don't know what it is, but I look at you and I just know."

"You know what?"

"That you're my future," he said. "It's weird because none of my friends feel that way, even the guys with serious girlfriends. Everything is temporary to them, like because we're young it doesn't matter."

I nibbled on my bottom lip. Hearing him say that made my heart swell. He thought *he* was lucky? I was the luckiest girl alive. "You're very philosophical tonight."

He tucked my hair behind my ear. "Yeah, I know. I just saw a few of the guys today. They were all bullshitting about stuff, like usual. But it was weird—like I don't know how to relate to them anymore."

Liam had always been different from his friends. He was a deep thinker who liked to ponder big questions and find meaning in simple things. Sometimes I thought I was one of the only people in the world who really saw him for who he was. Most people saw a good-looking, athletic guy. His charisma had always made him popular. But there was so much more beneath the surface. I loved being the one to see it—loved that he shared his thoughts and dreams with me.

I stepped closer and wrapped my arms around his waist. "Maybe that's just part of growing up."

"Maybe." He kissed my forehead.

"Is your nose okay?" I asked.

He scrunched it. "Hurts, but it'll be fine."

"Please tell me you guys aren't getting it on in the bathroom," Olivia called from the other room. "If you need me to leave for ten minutes, just say so."

Liam smiled and banged his hand on the door rhyth-mically.

"Gross!" Olivia said.

I laughed and Liam grinned at me again.

"Should we go finish your movie?" he asked. "I'll hold you if you're scared."

"Sounds perfect to me."

8

SEBASTIAN

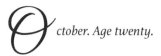 *ctober. Age twenty.*

THE LEAVES CRUNCHED beneath my feet, the crisp fall air refreshing. I'd had to spend a few days in the hospital—again—so it was good to be outside. Students walked past, hoisting heavy backpacks over their shoulders, making their way to classes, or their dorms, or jobs. I just put one foot in front of the other, keeping my pace measured so I didn't tire too quickly.

I'd made it through my freshman year at U of I, and my grades had been decent. Considering I'd missed a lot of school due to a hospital stay in the spring, I was proud of how well I'd done. Proud I'd managed to finish the year at all.

Summer had been spent at home, trying not to go crazy with boredom. My dad owned several car dealerships, and I'd always worked summers there. This year, I'd barely been able to handle part-time hours.

I hadn't seen my friends very often, either. They'd all been busy doing their own thing, and I hadn't hung out with them in months anyway. Cami had been back in Waverly for the summer too, so we'd spent a lot of weekends together— mostly at my parents' place because I still didn't have a lot of energy.

Once again, my parents had tried to talk me out of going back to school in the fall. The doctors had put me on immunosuppressant drugs, hoping that would calm the inflammation in my heart tissue. It made me more suscep-tible to getting sick, and when I did get sick, it was hard to get better, hence a few hospital stays over the last year. It was a bitch, knowing that if I got a cold, I'd probably wind up with pneumonia.

But I'd been determined to go back to school. Cami would be there, and I'd hated the idea of living two hours away from her. It had been hard enough to keep our rela-tionship going since I'd been sick. I hadn't wanted to put any more obstacles in our path.

Plus, if I quit school and moved home, my illness would win. That wasn't going to happen.

Charlie and I lived in a rental house his grandparents owned, not far from campus. I think having Charlie around had helped my parents feel better about me going back to school. My mom thought I didn't know, but she texted Charlie a few times a week to ask how I was doing. I pretended like I didn't notice.

The new semester was kicking my ass, though. My classes were tough. I'd missed a test last week when I'd been hospitalized, and I was scrambling to make up all the work. Thankfully today was Friday, so I'd have the weekend to recuperate and hopefully get caught up.

The walk from the bus stop to my place wasn't long, but

I was winded by the time I got there. I was used to it, now. It had been twenty months since my heart had failed. I'd lost more weight and my energy level was still low—partly because of the medications I took, and partly because my heart was weakening.

I knew that was the truth of it. My parents, Charlie, Cami... they all tried to stay optimistic. They blamed my fatigue on the pills I took, not on the heart that didn't seem to want to heal. But I knew. I wasn't sure what it was going to mean long term, but it was clear to me that I should have been getting better. And the fact that I wasn't was a problem.

For now, I'd keep doing what I'd been doing. Go to class. Study. Eat well. Take my pills, and all the vitamins and supplements I took to help keep myself as healthy as possible. Rely on my mental strength to get me through the bad days, and hope my heart held out long enough for us to figure out a long-term solution.

A solution that didn't involve me dying. I wasn't ready for that.

I got home and put my bag down, glad that I was feeling pretty decent, even after a full day of classes. I was tired, but that was normal. At least I didn't feel like I needed to go to bed at four in the afternoon. I was taking Cami to dinner later and I didn't want to cancel on her. I'd been doing that too much, especially lately. She had her friends, and that was good for her, but I wanted to make sure I could still date her properly. She'd stuck by me through everything. The least I could do was take her out—especially tonight. It was our third anniversary.

"You home, Seb?" Charlie called from his bedroom.

"Yeah."

"You good?" he asked.

Charlie *did* keep tabs on me, but for the most part, he

kept it simple. *You good?* I was mostly honest with him. If I'd had a shitty day or thought something was wrong, I'd tell him—at least if it seemed serious, like last week when I'd had pneumonia again. But he didn't treat me like I was weak or fragile, the way so many other people did. I appreciated it.

"Yep, good day," I said.

I tossed my coat on a chair and went into the kitchen. I wasn't very hungry, but I thought I should probably eat. I didn't have much of an appetite most days, but a lack of food would only make me weaker.

Charlie came out in a Hawkeyes wrestling t-shirt and sweats. He looked me up and down, his brow furrowed. "You look like shit."

"Thanks, asshole."

"We should go get pizza or something," he said. "You need to put some meat back on."

"I don't think pizza is going to help."

"Won't hurt," he said.

I rubbed my stomach. My once rock-hard abs were softer now. I exercised a little, but my body couldn't tolerate much. For a guy who'd been doing sports since he was three, being this out of shape was tremendously shitty. I was already used to following a strict diet for wrestling, and I'd kept up with it so I wouldn't get both fat *and* out of shape. But that only went so far.

"You can't eat that shit, anyway." I made a show of looking him up and down, as if I'd find a flaw. "You're looking a little soft around the middle this year, Chuck."

"Fuck off," he said. "I have two more weeks before I have to start cutting weight. I want a fucking pizza. With everything on it."

I laughed. Charlie was a big guy and when he wanted to,

he could out-eat anyone. "Can't tonight. I'm taking Cami out."

"You sure that's a good idea?" he asked.

"Yeah, we haven't done anything in a while," I said. "Why?"

"Restaurants, people, germs," he said.

"You just said we should go get pizza," I said.

"I'd go get it and bring it back," he said. "Come on, man, you were just in the hospital."

"I can't sit around here all the time," I said. "I feel pretty good today. And it's our anniversary. I want to take my girl out."

Charlie scowled at me. "You're too fucking stubborn sometimes, you know that, right?"

"I'll be fine," I said. "I wash my hands so often people think I have OCD. I'll bring the stupid hand sanitizer."

"Is Cami healthy?" he asked. "Because you know if she even has a cold, you can't be swapping body fluids."

"For fuck's sake," I said.

"I'm just making sure you're not being stupid."

I rolled my eyes. "Look, she's fine. I'm fine. I had a good fucking day and I don't need you playing nurse all of a sudden."

He put his hands up, palms out. "Okay, okay. I'm just looking out for you, man."

"Yeah, I know," I said, but I was still irritated. "I'm gonna go lie down for an hour before I meet Cami."

"All right."

I went to my room and shut the door behind me. He had a point about going out in public. It was always a risk. But I went to classes every day, and I wasn't about to give that up. I stayed home more than any guy I knew. It wouldn't kill me to take my girlfriend out to dinner.

Okay, technically it *could* if I was exposed to something my body couldn't fight off. But quarantining myself was no way to live. I was young. Maybe not as healthy as I could be, but I still wanted to live my life.

I lay down and texted Cami.

Me: Hey babe. I'll meet you at 7. Does that still work?

Cami: Can we do earlier? 6?

Me: Sure. What sounds good?

Cami: Whatever is fine.

I rolled my eyes. Cami not having an opinion about where we went to dinner was about as likely as me being healthy enough to wrestle this year.

Me: You sure? We can go anywhere.

Cami: You pick.

Me: K, how about that pizza place?

Cami: You know I hate that place.

Me: You said anywhere.

Cami: Fine, whatever.

Me: Don't get mad. I'm just joking. How about Short's?

Cami: OK

I wondered what was up with her today. I hadn't seen her since the hospital last week. She'd come to visit me twice, both times sitting with me for an hour or so. I'd talked to her when I'd been discharged, but she'd had a big bio test this week, so I'd told her to stay home and study.

She was probably just stressed about school. Or maybe one of her sorority sisters was going through a crisis again. That seemed to happen at least once a week.

Although I thought I knew what was really bothering her. Based on things she'd said recently, she was hoping for more certainty about the future. I didn't think she was worried I was going to die; she never seemed to entertain that as a possibility. But I got the impression she was hoping for more certainty about *us*.

I didn't think she was itching to get married right this second. We were still pretty young. But I had a feeling she'd love to come home from dinner one of these nights with a ring on her finger. Even if that meant a long engagement while we finished school. A girl in her sorority had gotten engaged a few weeks ago, and Cami had talked about it for days on end. I knew a hint when I heard one.

I wasn't sure if I was ready for that. But we'd been together for three years. Survived the transition between high school and college. Stayed together even though my illness had made a lot of things difficult. We loved each other, and that's what you did when you loved someone. Stuck by them. Stayed loyal.

Cami had been loyal to me. Maybe I owed this to her.

By the time I left to meet her, I'd decided. I'd find her a nice engagement ring and make this official. Show her I appreciated that she'd stayed with me through everything.

We lived on opposite sides of campus, so it was easier to meet her at the restaurant. She was there, waiting for me in the lobby when I arrived. She looked pretty in a light green sweater, her long blond hair down and wavy.

"Hey, babe," I said. I put a hand on her waist and kissed her forehead. "Have you been here long?"

"No," she said. "Just a few minutes."

It was hard not to tell her, but I figured she'd want the whole romantic proposal thing, and I didn't want to spoil it. But as we took a seat in a booth, I felt better than I had in months. Being engaged to Cami would give us something to look forward to—something to focus on that wasn't related to my illness. And it would be an outward display that we both believed I was going to get better.

My chest tightened and my breath felt suddenly labored. I tried to keep my face from showing discomfort. It was just a flutter—nothing too bad. Cami's eyebrows drew together and she watched me while I breathed through it.

"I'm fine," I said when I was sure I could sound normal.

"You're not fine," she said. "You're pale. And those things are happening more than they used to."

"They're not serious," I said.

She tilted her head. "Yes they are, Sebastian."

We weren't starting this date on the right note. I didn't want to fight with her. "I know, sweetie. I'm doing everything the doctors tell me."

"And you're still sick," she said.

"Are you saying I'm doing something to make myself sick?" I asked. "Because, believe me, at this point I'd do anything if it meant I'd get better."

"No, that's not what I'm saying." She brushed her hair back from her face. "It's just been a long time."

"You're telling me."

"I keep waiting for the old Sebastian to come back," she said. "You used to be so... so different."

I wasn't sure what to say to her. Of course I was different. I'd been through hell. What did she expect? "I'm not sure what you're getting at."

She took a deep breath. "Sebastian, I don't think this is working."

"What?"

"I think we need to break up."

I stared at her, my mouth partially open. "You wanted to have dinner with me on our anniversary so you could break up with me?"

"Oh my god, it's our anniversary?" she asked.

What the fuck? "Yeah, I kissed you for the first time three years ago today. We didn't really celebrate it last year because everything was so crazy. But you didn't know that?"

"How can you expect me to keep track of something like that with everything else I've been through?" she asked. "It's been horrible, Sebastian. I was there, remember? I saw you collapse. And every day since, I've been worried that it's going to happen again."

"So your solution is to break up?" I asked.

"I can't handle it anymore." Tears welled up in her eyes. "It's too much. I can only see you if I put in all the effort. You barely have enough energy to go to your classes, let alone spend any time with me. I mean, god, when was the last time we had sex? I don't even know."

"What?" I asked. "Jesus, Cami, I'm doing my best."

"I know you are," she said. "But I fell for the old Sebastian. The guy who was big and strong. Who manhandled his opponents on the mat. He was kind of cocky, and so sure of himself. And we could actually do things. I've tried, Sebastian. Ever since state, I've tried to hold it together. But it's too hard. Being with someone who's sick all the time is too stressful. I'm not cut out for it."

I blinked at her, trying to process what she was saying. She was breaking up with me. Our relationship, over. She wasn't going to stick this out with me.

"Are you serious?" I asked.

"Yes," she said. "I'm sorry. Maybe if things were different…"

"Yeah, if things were different. If I had a heart that fucking worked."

"Sebastian, it's not your fault," she said. "But this is how things turned out."

"Believe me, I know it's not my fault." I stood. My chest felt tight, but not because of a fibrillation. "It's fine, Cami.

Go find yourself a guy who can make you happy. Because I sure as fuck can't."

I walked away without waiting to hear her reply. I didn't want to look at her anymore. How could I have been such an idiot? It was so obvious. She hadn't been hoping I'd propose. She'd been trying to figure out how to break up with me.

Wishing I had the energy to walk all the way home, I hopped on a bus. My mind was restless. Walking across campus would have done me a lot of good, but I knew I'd only exhaust myself. My heart couldn't work that hard.

The ache in my chest spread and my gut churned with emotion. Disappointment. Rejection. Sadness. My friends had mostly drifted away, but I'd thought Cami would be the one who'd stick by me. I'd thought she loved me enough. Obviously I'd been wrong.

Or maybe I just wasn't worth loving through something like this.

9

BROOKE

March. Age eighteen.

I LOVED the beginning of spring. The weather was warm, but not too hot, and everything began to bloom. Citrus trees spilled their fragrances into the air and the mountainsides were covered in wildflowers. Liam and I sat at an outdoor table on campus, enjoying the weather. He was intent on studying for his physics test, and I was working on revisions to an essay on the women's suffrage movement I had to write for my history class.

We only had about two months left before the school year would be over. Finals week was at the beginning of May. But we'd decided to stay in our apartment through the summer and both take a couple of classes. Liam wanted to get more prerequisites out of the way so he could apply to the school of engineering. And I figured if Liam was going to be in school anyway, I might as well take some classes too.

I eyed the paper I was writing. I'd been over it a dozen

times. I probably needed to call it finished and stop tinkering. At this point, I was just wasting time, and I had a math test to think about.

My phone rang and I pulled it out of my backpack. Liam's eyes lifted. I looked at the screen, but didn't recognize the number.

I shrugged at Liam as I answered. "Hello?"

"Brooke?"

I sat bolt upright in my chair, my back stiffening. I recognized that voice. It was coded into my very DNA. My mother.

"Mom?" I asked.

Liam's eyes widened and he closed his book, his face intent on me.

"Yeah, baby," she said. "You still have the same number."

Her words were garbled—hard to make out. She was wasted. On what, I couldn't tell. But hearing her like that was a punch in the stomach. I hadn't talked to her since she'd moved—well over a year ago. Deep down, I'd hoped losing me might finally make her get herself together. That maybe something would change.

"Yeah, I have the same number," I said. "Where are you?"

I heard something muffled, and a man's voice in the background before she answered. "Louisiana, baby. It's beautiful here."

"That's great," I said. "I'm sure it is."

"You should come," she said. "I've got it all figured out. Marcus has a big house and plenty of money. I don't even have to work. I've got a bedroom all ready for you. It will be good this time, Brooke. I swear."

I stared at the table, tears stinging my eyes. What was she talking about? Louisiana? Who the hell was Marcus?

My stomach churned and I felt a little bit like I might vomit.

"Um, I can't come to Louisiana," I said. "I have school."

"School?" She laughed. "You didn't flunk out or something, did you? Aren't you done?"

"No, Mom, I didn't flunk out," I said. Liam's expression hardened. "I graduated from high school last year. I'm in college now."

"I see," she said. "A big college girl, too good for us uned... uned... uneducated tramps, huh?"

"That's not what I said."

She snorted. "Where the fuck did you come from? Are you sure you're my daughter?"

Her words made my throat close up and I couldn't choke out a reply.

Liam grabbed the phone from me. "Desiree, don't call Brooke again."

She said something to him that I couldn't hear.

"You've done enough damage. Just leave her alone." He hung up and put the phone down. "Come here, Bee."

I got up and slipped into his lap, putting my head on his shoulder. He rubbed slow circles across my back. A few tears fell, leaving spots of moisture on his shirt.

"I'm going to take care of you, Bee," he said. "You don't have to worry about her, okay?"

I nodded and sat up, wiping beneath my eyes. "I just wish she was different. She's my mom. Why didn't she love me enough to be a good mother?"

Liam touched my cheek. "Bee, it's not because of you. It's her. She's messed up. And she doesn't deserve you."

"I don't know about that."

"I do," he said. "Come on, let's go get something to eat. Maybe tacos will cheer you up."

I couldn't help but smile. "Tacos *are* good."

"See? That's my girl." He grinned. "Besides, I have something special planned for us tonight."

"Oh yeah? What?"

He tapped my nose. "It's a surprise. But it's something to look forward to. Don't think about her. She doesn't matter anymore. It's you and me, now."

I wrapped my arms around his neck and kissed him. He always knew how to make everything better.

THE SUN WAS SETTING as we drove out into the desert. Liam still had the pickup truck his parents had helped him buy back in high school. We had a to-go bag of cheeseburgers and fries in between us, the smell filling the cab. My stomach rumbled and I hoped we'd get to wherever we were going soon.

I was still a little rattled after the phone call from my mom. No matter how often Liam tried to assure me that I didn't need her, it didn't change the fact that she was my mother. Hearing her voice had reassured me that my worst fear for her—that she had died—hadn't happened. But knowing she was repeating the same mistakes, just in a different place, was so disappointing. I didn't know why I'd expected anything else. She'd been doing the same thing her entire adult life.

But I couldn't help nurturing the hope that maybe someday, she'd get better.

Liam turned to me with a mischievous grin, and I tried to put thoughts of my mom out of my mind.

"So, are you going to tell me what we're doing?" I asked.

"Or are we just going out to eat cheeseburgers in the middle of the desert?"

He didn't answer, just smiled. His blue eyes sparkled.

About ten minutes later, he pulled off the road and stopped. Without saying a word, he grabbed our dinner and got out. I followed and we both climbed into the bed of his truck.

Immediately, I looked up. The sun had set and the stars twinkled against the backdrop of the night sky.

"It's beautiful," I said.

"So beautiful."

I glanced at him, but he wasn't looking up. He was looking at me.

We ate our dinner and chatted. We talked about our summer plans, and the coming year. Olivia had decided to go to ASU with us in the fall. Her parents were already planning a graduation party. It sounded like it was going to be fun.

Then we talked about the future. About a book we'd both read and what we thought it meant. About the places we wanted to visit, and whether we thought we'd be dog people or cat people, or something else entirely.

When we finished, Liam took the wrappers and stuffed them back in the bag.

"Do you remember the first time we did this?" he asked.

"How could I not?"

He smiled. "My life changed that night. From the first time I kissed you, nothing has been the same."

"Yeah, for me too," I said. He thought *his* life had changed? Liam had swept into my life and rescued me. He'd saved me from the hell my mom still lived in.

"I have something for you." He reached into his pocket and pulled out a small box.

A wave of excitement poured through me, making my skin tingle and my heart race. Oh my god. Could that be...? It was so unexpected.

"I know we're young," he said. "So this isn't meant to be something we rush into. If you say yes, we can finish school first and all that. But I also want you to know that you're it for me, Bee. I don't want anyone else, ever. You're my life, and I want you to be with me for the rest of it."

He opened the box and my breath caught in my throat. The ring was a simple gold band with a shimmery light blue opal. It was the most beautiful thing I'd ever seen.

"Brooke Summerlin, my sweet Bee, will you marry me?"

I met his eyes and smiled, my eyes filling with tears. "Yes."

He took the ring and slid it on my finger, then leaned in and pressed his lips against mine. My eyes fluttered closed. We *were* young, but I knew it too. Liam and I were going to be together for the rest of our lives.

10

SEBASTIAN

March. Age twenty.

I HATED HOSPITALS.

Twenty-four days ago, I'd woken up here. The thing I'd feared for the past two years—that I'd have another ventricular fibrillation and my heart would stop—had happened. Fortunately for me, it had been at home and Charlie had been there. He'd reacted fast, calling 911, and the paramedics had arrived quickly enough to revive me.

I wasn't even twenty-one years old, and I'd needed to have my heart shocked into beating again—twice.

This time, there weren't any more drugs to give me. Over the past two years, they'd tried everything there was to try. I was on the maximum dosages, and the side effects had only gotten worse.

My only option had been open-heart surgery to implant what they called a VAD—a device that would shock my heart into working when I had fibrillations. Despite a lot of advances in medical technology, this thing seemed archaic. When they'd first told me I'd need it, I'd assumed it would be something small and entirely internal.

The reality was, I did have a device inside my chest, attached to my left ventricle. But I also had a port where a cable exited my body just below my ribs, and I would have to wear a battery pack and control unit all the time. While I recovered from the surgery, they sat next to me, but as soon as I went home, I'd have them strapped to me like a small backpack.

The worst part was, I'd had my chest cut wide open, and it wasn't going to fix me. They'd only implanted the device because I needed something to keep me alive.

It was only March, but I'd already withdrawn from school. That pissed me off as much as anything. I was so close to finishing my sophomore year. Just a few more months, and I would have been able to go home for the summer, another semester complete. Now I'd had to drop my classes and I'd need to retake them when I got better.

If I got better.

I couldn't keep saying *when* I got better. It was a big *if*. My heart had continued to weaken, and the doctors now considered me in a state of heart failure. Hearing that had nearly made my mom faint, and even my dad had turned white with shock.

The only option I had left for long term survival was a transplant. Three weeks ago, just before the surgery to implant the VAD, they'd officially put me on the list. Shit had gotten real.

I'd listened to the transplant coordinator with a strange sense of detachment. I'd heard things about blood and tissue types, numbers of candidates, chances of finding a match, conditions for acceptance. But all I'd been able to think was *How can this be happening to me?* How had I gotten so sick that I needed a new heart in order to live?

My incisions hurt and my chest felt heavy and sore. I could have more pain relievers if I wanted, but I didn't. They left me feeling drugged and stupid. I hated it.

I hated a lot of things these days. Hated that I had to quit school and move home. Hated that my ex-girlfriend was dating one of the top wrestlers at U of I. Hated that I was on a first-name basis with most of the cardiology staff at the hospital. Hated that I'd have a huge scar running down the center of my chest from a procedure that was only meant to keep me going until they could cut me open again.

Mostly, I hated that I was dying.

Charlie came in, his coat wet from rain. "Hey, man. Ready to go?"

"Yeah." I slowly sat forward, pulling myself up on the sides of the hospital bed so I didn't put too much strain on my chest. It fucking hurt, but I didn't do more than grunt. "Let's get out of here."

I'd been home—or at least, Charlie's home; I wasn't going to be able to live there anymore—three times for increasing durations. It was part of the recovery process. I had to learn how to live with the VAD. So I'd needed to complete practice runs away from the hospital before I'd been fully released.

Now I was ready to get the fuck out. I strapped on my battery pack and control unit and adjusted the straps so they were secure. Charlie helped me into my coat—an old one that was big on me now, but the size made getting in and out of it easier.

My parents had planned to pick me up from the hospital, especially since I was going to their house in Waverly for the time being. But they were getting a new hospital-style

bed for me to use—because apparently that was my life now
—so Charlie had offered to drive me home.

A nurse wheeled me out to Charlie's car—it wasn't his
old pickup truck that he loved so much. He'd borrowed his
parents' sedan. I was glad; his truck was bumpy as hell and I
was in enough pain as it was.

Everything looked different on the drive from Iowa City
to Waverly. I'd been on this highway countless times, but I
saw things through new eyes. Even my hometown seemed
different now. The gray sky dimmed the light of the sun and
washed out the landscape. Faded and dull, just like me.

I thought about my old friends, going on with their lives.
They were training for their sports, studying for tests,
fucking their girlfriends or hooking up with random girls
they met at parties. Living the college life. I thought about
Cami, who had moved on so quickly, she'd been dating
someone new within days of breaking up with me.

She hadn't loved me enough to watch me die.

I didn't want to be bitter. I didn't want to spend the rest
of my life—whether it would be measured in days, months,
or years—being angry. But it was hard not to be.

My life was being cut short. I was still alive—for now—
but I couldn't actually live. I couldn't go to school or work.
Couldn't hang out with friends. I was barely on the edge of
adulthood and I was going to miss it. Miss falling in love—
maybe for real this time. Miss having a family of my own.

I was starting to wonder why I was hanging on so tight.
Letting go would be so much easier than fighting for every
breath, every beat of my failing heart.

We pulled up to my parents' house and Charlie went
around to help me out of the car. I wasn't too proud to
accept the arm he offered me so I could stand—I needed it.

Inside, I slowly made my way up the stairs to my room.

My parents were there, but I didn't have the energy to talk to them. It was all I could do to keep putting one foot in front of the other. My chest was on fire, the pain radiating through my whole body.

Charlie followed me into my room and helped me get settled. I couldn't lie flat, so he adjusted the bed so I was at an incline.

"So, I guess now we wait?" he asked.

"Now we wait," I said.

And maybe that was the hardest part—knowing the outcome of my life was no longer within my control. It wouldn't matter if I stayed mentally strong. My will wasn't enough. This illness was taking me down and there was nothing left for me to do but wait.

Wait, and hope for a miracle.

11

BROOKE

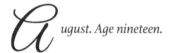*ugust. Age nineteen.*

WE PULLED out of the gas station and Liam got back on the freeway. It was August, and our last weekend before the fall semester began. We'd decided to take a short road trip up to Sedona. Just a quick getaway before we had to buckle down for another term.

Headlights flashed as cars passed us. Liam had worked until eight, so we'd gotten a late start. It would be even later when we made it to Sedona, but neither of us minded. It felt like an adventure.

I twisted my engagement ring around my finger as I watched the dark scenery pass. Liam's parents had expressed some concern about our announcement. Mostly they were worried we were too young, and we were rushing into it. I understood. We *were* young. But we'd reassured them that we weren't planning to get married until after we both finished college. This was simply a promise that marriage was in our future, when we were both ready.

That had made them feel better, and they'd made it clear they'd love to have me as a daughter-in-law. Olivia had been thrilled from the beginning. She'd told her parents it didn't matter how old we were if we were in love and meant to be together.

I wasn't in a hurry for a wedding. I loved that I had his ring and the assurance of a future where Liam would always take care of me. That was more than enough.

Liam took a sip of his peach iced tea and put it back in the cup holder. "So what should we do tomor—"

The world went crazy. A flash of light. Crunching metal. Screeching tires. I was hurtled sideways, my seatbelt digging into my neck. An explosion of pain in my head left me dizzy. I tried to scream, but nothing came out. I couldn't get any air. Everything spun, my limbs flailing. So much noise. Grinding, scraping sounds echoed in my ears. Glass shattered. I tasted the sharp tang of blood and everything turned over again.

We jerked to a stop. For a moment, quiet. Only the faint hum of traffic whirring past. Everything looked wrong. I blinked and tried to focus.

I was hanging upside down.

Craning my neck, I looked down at what should have been up. The ceiling was bent and dented, the windows broken. Granules of glass glittered everywhere.

So quiet. Why was it so quiet?

"Liam?" My voice croaked, the sound scraping through my throat.

No answer.

He hung upside down, his seat belt holding him in

place. His arms were limp, his head bent at an odd angle against the partially caved-in cab.

Oh god. Oh god, no. Please, no.

"Liam? Liam, wake up."

"Are you okay?" A voice from outside. Urgent. "Is anyone in there?"

"Liam," I said, louder now. "Wake up."

"I hear someone," the voice said. A man's face peered through the broken window. "Miss, help is coming, okay? Someone's calling 911."

"Liam."

Liam didn't answer. Didn't move. So quiet. So still.

"Liam, please," I said, my voice cracking. "Please wake up."

"Hang in there, miss," the man said. "An ambulance is coming."

My body hurt in too many places to separate. Bile burned the back of my throat and my stomach turned over. My ears felt plugged, like all the noises around me were deadened. All I could hear was a steady *drip, drip, drip.*

It was Liam. He was bleeding, the relentless patter of his blood dripping onto the warped ceiling.

Bracing myself with one hand, I fumbled for the seat belt latch. I had to get him out of here. It released, and I crumpled against the ceiling. Crawled closer. Touched his face.

"Liam?"

His eyes were closed, his neck bent. Blood flowed freely from a gash on the front of his head. Covered his forehead, stuck in his hair.

Fear made my hands shake. This couldn't be happening. I put a trembling hand in front of his nose and mouth and felt a whisper of breath. Relief poured through me. He was breathing. He was alive.

The man was still talking, but I didn't know what he'd said.

"Hurry," I said, my voice filled with the panic that threatened to overtake me. "Hurry, he needs help."

"They're coming, miss," the man said. "Help is coming."

MACHINES BEEPED and a huff of air poured into Liam's lungs. He looked so fragile. So frail. His head was covered in heavy bandages and a breathing tube went down his throat. There were tubes and wires everywhere. I didn't know what half of them did.

I squeezed his hand, but he didn't squeeze mine back. It had been days, and he hadn't woken up. Hadn't responded. He just lay there, machines doing the work to keep his blood pumping, his lungs inflating.

My injuries hadn't been life-threatening. I was bruised and battered, but nothing was broken. I'd been released from the ER after a few hours, and joined Liam's family in the waiting room.

Sometime the next day, we'd been led to another waiting room. Doctors had talked to his parents and I'd listened in numb silence. Severe head injury. Lack of brain activity. Not much hope. They'd do more tests. Check again.

For the past several days, we'd waited, hoping for a change. Hoping for some sign of life.

Police had come and asked me questions about the crash. I couldn't remember much. They told me we'd been hit by a larger truck. Forced off the road. We'd flipped and rolled over several times. All I knew was that it had happened so fast. Just one second, and the solid ground beneath us had disappeared and the world had gone crazy.

It hadn't really stopped spinning. At least not for me.

The nurse came in and led me back to the waiting room. We weren't allowed to stay with him for very long. I didn't want to leave him, but I knew I didn't have a choice. I'd argued the first time, begging them to let me stay, but they'd threatened to make me leave the hospital. So I'd gone quiet and obeyed.

A doctor was in the waiting room, talking to the Harpers. Brian's face was impossible to read—expressionless—but I could see the strain of him holding something inside. Mary was pale, and tears streamed down Olivia's cheeks.

I stopped in my tracks. Mary met my eyes, her pain reaching out to mingle with mine. In that moment, I knew what they were going to say. I knew why the doctor was there, and it wasn't because he had good news.

"Oh, Brooke," Mary said when I approached. She clutched my hands and I sank into the chair beside her. "Honey, I'm so sorry."

I looked up at the doctor. The compassion in his eyes squeezed my chest. "He's gone, isn't he?"

"Yes," he said. "As I was explaining to the rest of your family, Liam isn't in a coma. There's no sign of any brain activity. That means he's medically deceased."

"His heart is beating," I whispered.

"Only because he's on life support," he said. "I know this can be hard to understand, but Liam isn't alive anymore. He's gone."

I didn't hear the rest. Something about organ donation and giving us time to say goodbye. None of it mattered to me. Nothing mattered anymore.

I SAT WITH LIAM, holding his hand for the last time. His fingers were limp and cold. The machines still did their job, moving blood through his veins, putting oxygen in his lungs. But it was all a sham. He was dead. Whatever made a person who they are, whatever spark had been inside of him that had made him alive, was gone. Extinguished.

Tears slipped down my cheeks, silent and terrible. The heaviness of my grief weighed me down, threatening to crush me. I didn't know if I could live through this. Didn't know how. I'd tried to put my thoughts down on paper, but words had escaped me. There weren't any that could give a voice to this pain.

I stroked his arm, memorizing the feel of his skin. We had only moments left. A few heartbeats. I shuddered and a sob bubbled up my throat.

"I don't want to do this," I whispered, knowing he wasn't there to hear me. "You're my life. You're everything. You can't leave me behind."

I closed my eyes. Heard the swish of the curtain. Footsteps behind me. I felt Mary touch my shoulder. Olivia took my hand.

"Brooke, sweetheart," Mary said, her voice so soft. Full of the pain we all shared. "It's time."

12

SEBASTIAN

 *ugust. Age twenty.*

MY CHEST ACHED with every breath. I would need to lie down soon. Ten minutes of being on my feet was all I could handle. Forget the stairs. I glanced up them. I couldn't remember the last time I'd been upstairs. My parents had cleared out the den and brought the hospital bed down so I could stay on the ground floor. Mom had said she worried about me too much when she was gone—she didn't want me to overexert myself.

I didn't want to tell her that getting up to go to the fucking bathroom was an overexertion.

Mom had been doing her best to put on a brave face, but I'd heard her crying when she thought I wouldn't know. Dad had remained stoic as ever, at least in front of me. But I could see it in his eyes. He knew. We both knew my time was running out.

Picking up my feet was hard work, but I did it anyway. I

just needed to get to the kitchen to refill my water. I could do this.

Just outside the kitchen, I paused in front of a large wall covered in framed photos and memorabilia. Medals, plaques, framed newspaper articles. Photos of me winning. Always winning, the ref holding my arm up in the air. Looking strong, healthy. I shook my head. The wall looked like a shrine. That was appropriate, I supposed. Shrines were for dead people.

I would be, soon.

I glanced down at myself. My t-shirt hung off my thin frame, my body a fraction of its former size. All that muscle, so hard-earned from countless hours of training, melted away. My heart too weak to supply the blood my body needed.

I could feel every beat now. Labored. Heavy. A ticking clock, counting down the beats until my death.

It would have been easier if I'd just died that day at state. At least it would have been over quickly. I wouldn't have had to endure this slow, agonizing deterioration. Two and a half years, countless pills, an open-heart surgery with a brutal recovery. And I was still dying.

I made it to the kitchen and refilled my water. Then came the slow, deliberate walk back to what was now my bedroom.

It was a strange thing, to look in that room and know I'd probably die there. Either there, or in a hospital, but I'd already told them to keep me home if they could. I wasn't going back to a hospital ever again if I could help it. I'd had enough of them, and what did I have to show for it? Scars. Pain. And a heart that was still dying inside my chest.

"Sebastian," Mom said from behind me. I'd almost made it to my room.

"Hi, Mom."

"Honey, why are you up?" she asked. "Here, let me get that for you."

She pointlessly took the water from my hand and walked past me to set it on the bedside table. "Come on, honey, let's get you back in bed."

"I'm good, Mom. I've got it."

She clicked her tongue and took my arm. "I know you do. Come on."

I let her help me into bed, my body aching from the strain of the walk to the kitchen. God, why did everything have to fucking hurt so much? Wasn't it enough that I was wasting away?

She moved the wire from the battery pack and control unit that I was wearing. The VAD had done its job to keep my heart rhythm regular, but it hadn't made my heart any stronger. It hadn't helped me heal.

"I'm taking myself off the transplant list," I said. I didn't know what prompted me to blurt it out right then, but it was something I'd decided a while ago. I just hadn't mustered the strength to tell my parents.

The color drained from my mom's face. "What?"

"I'm taking myself off," I said. "I don't want a donor heart."

"Sebastian, honey," she said, "what are you talking about?"

I closed my eyes—so tired. "I've been thinking about this for a while and I've made my decision."

"No," Mom breathed. "You're just tired. This has been so hard. But it isn't going to last forever. You just have to hang on a little longer."

"I'm sick of hanging on," I said, my eyes still closed.

The bed moved as my mom sat down on the edge. Her trembling hand closed over mine. "Sebastian. No."

The pain in her voice sent a renewed pang of agony through my chest. I forced my eyes open. "I don't want to hurt you. But I'm exhausted. Even if by some miracle I do get a new heart, I'll never be the same person. I don't know what I would do. Who I would be."

"When you're healthy again, you'll come back to your life," she said. "You'll be strong again, Sebastian. I know it."

"Mom, we don't know if I'll ever fully recover," I said. "The chances of getting a new heart are already slim. If I get one, my body could reject it. I don't want to go through another surgery if I'm just going to die anyway."

"But Sebastian—"

"Everything hurts," I said, my eyes closing again. "I can barely get up to go to the bathroom. Every day I wake up worse than I was the day before. I'm dying, Mom."

"Don't you dare say that," she said, heat in her voice.

"Not saying it won't make it not true," I said. "I'm going to die. You have to let me go."

I kept my eyes closed, as much from exhaustion as to spare myself the sight of her tears. I knew they were there, rolling down her cheeks. But what else could I say? It was too late. I could feel it. I didn't want to die, but holding onto false hope had become more painful than facing the truth.

"I'm not giving up on you," she said, her voice barely above a whisper. "You aren't giving up either."

She squeezed my hand. In the two and a half years since my heart had first given out, she'd never once stopped believing. She'd been by my side through everything. Every painful moment.

Tears burned my eyes. I had no idea what it would be like to watch your child die. But I felt the depth of her pain.

And I hated it. I hated what this had done to me, but even more than that, I hated what it had done to her. She was hanging on by an even thinner thread than I was.

I couldn't spare her the pain of losing her son. That was inevitable. But if I gave up, she'd think she'd failed me. I realized, as I tried to squeeze her small hand, that I had to keep fighting. Maybe not fighting to live. But fighting to die in such a way that would allow my mom to find peace when I was gone. I could do that for her. I owed her that much.

"Okay, Mom," I said, squeezing her hand again. My grip was weak, but she squeezed back. "I won't give up."

She smiled through her tears and placed her palm against my cheek. "No, you won't."

MY MOM'S voice woke me. I'd drifted off to sleep after she'd left the room. I took a deep breath, but my chest felt so heavy, like a concrete block rested on top of me. My heart beat slowly—halting, agonizing compressions of the dying muscle. In moments like this, it was hard not to panic. My lungs burned, like I wasn't getting enough oxygen. Because I wasn't. My heart was barely pumping enough to keep me alive.

"He's... no, he's asleep," Mom said. I didn't hear another voice. She must have been on the phone. "Yes. Yes, that's right... What? Yes... Yes, I understand."

The urgency in her voice grew. Instead of sliding back into the relief of slumber, I focused on her words. What had her so riled up?

"We can do that," she said. "Yes, I know how to get there. Yes. Okay, thank you. Thank you so much. Oh my god. Robert! Sebastian!"

I swallowed in an attempt to moisten my dry throat, but my voice was still a weak croak. "Yeah?"

Quick footsteps down the stairs heralded my dad. My mom spoke to him, but I couldn't make out what she said.

"Are you serious?" Dad said. "Oh thank god. Sebastian!"

They both appeared in my doorway, their eyes wide and bright.

"There's a heart for you," Mom said, her voice clear.

Her words settled over me like cold mist. A heart. The transplant I'd been waiting for, without even a shred of hope. When they'd put me on the transplant list, I'd honestly believed it was only for show. There would never actually be a heart for me. What were the chances? People died waiting for organ transplants every day.

"There's... what?" I couldn't fathom that she was serious. That this was real.

"A heart is being flown here right now," she said. "We have to get to the hospital. There are still more tests to do. This isn't a guarantee. But if the tests show it's really a match, and your body can tolerate the surgery, it's yours."

A shock of numbness. That's all I felt. No relief. No joy. I stared at my parents, their faces shining with hope, and I didn't know what to think.

My dad walked in and sat beside me on the edge of the bed. He put his hand on my chest where he could feel the tenuous beats of my dying heart. "Son, it's time."

PART II

FOUR YEARS LATER

Voices of the past echo with sorrow

carry through time

and space

separated by heartbeats

and the pain of living

without you

~B

13

SEBASTIAN

*T*he gym was mostly empty this early in the morning. Just a handful of dedicated—or crazy—people who'd gotten up before the sun.

"Are you serious?" Charlie asked. His hands hovered beneath the bench press bar as I lifted, spotting me in case I needed help.

"Yeah," I grunted, pushing the heavy weight off my chest. God, that felt good. "One more."

Charlie helped me with my last rep and the bar clicked against the rack when we set it down. I blew out a breath and sat up.

"Yeah, I'm serious," I said. "I told you I sent them a letter, right?"

"You did, but a letter isn't *meeting the donor's family*," he said.

"It was actually their idea," I said. "They got my letter and we started emailing. Mrs. Harper asked if I'd consider meeting them in person. I said yes."

"That's some deep shit, dude," Charlie said. "Wasn't he, like, our age?"

I nodded. "A year younger."

"Fuck."

"I know." I rubbed my bearded chin. Charlie gave me shit about it, but I'd let my facial hair grow out after my transplant surgery. I'd always had to shave as a wrestler. But I liked keeping it; it marked the difference in who I was now. "Believe me, I know. They lost their son and I'm alive because of it. But I think it might help give them some closure, you know?"

"Sure," he said. "Get your ass up, though. I need to do my set."

I laughed and stood to help Charlie load more weight on the bar. He was still stronger than I was, although not by much anymore. Since I'd started working out again, I'd regained a surprising amount of my former strength—and size.

My new heart worked like a champion. I still had to take a pharmacy's worth of pills every day, and would for the rest of my life. I had to be careful about getting sick; the anti-rejection meds I took suppressed my immune system. But because I was healthier overall, I didn't get sick nearly as often as I had before the transplant. I'd only had one close call, about a year ago, when I'd gotten a cold that had turned into a sinus infection. Pre-transplant, that would have landed me in the hospital. This time I'd been able to fight it off, although it had knocked me on my ass for a solid week.

I'd never be a competitive athlete again, and things like hang gliding and scuba diving were off limits. But other than that, after I'd recovered from the surgery, I'd been able to lead a normal life. I'd moved back to Iowa City with Charlie. Last year, I started back at U of I. I was beginning to feel like my old self again.

But really, I wasn't him. I wasn't the guy who'd been

laser-focused on winning state. On wrestling for U of I. That guy had died the day my old heart had stopped working.

I wasn't sure who I was now. I had a second chance at life, but I had no idea what I was supposed to do with it. Who I was supposed to be. People seemed to expect me to pick up where I'd left off. Finish college. Go work for my dad at one of his car dealerships in Waverly. But it wasn't that simple.

Charlie told me to chill about it and just let life happen. But I'd always had a plan. A goal to focus on. Not having that made me feel like I was drifting. That fire I'd had inside me—that drive to achieve—had almost burned out. I wasn't sure how to get it going again.

It had been four years since the transplant, and I was still trying to figure it all out.

Charlie finished his set and got up from the bench. "You tell your parents yet?"

"No," I said. "I need to, but you know how they are. Especially my mom. She'll freak out about me being so far away from home."

"Yeah," Charlie said. "So, driving or flying?"

"Driving," I said.

"Cool. When do we leave?"

"We?" I asked.

"Road trip, bro," he said. "It's summer. I'm off until I coach at camp next month."

Charlie was a teacher and an assistant wrestling coach at his old high school. He loved his job and he was amazing at it. He'd thought about pursuing a coaching job at the college level, but he liked working with the high school kids.

"You really want to come?" I asked.

"Yeah," he said. "If you'd rather go alone, it's cool. I mean, you'd be an asshole, but whatever."

"No, it'd be great to have company," I said. "And someone else to drive. But we're taking my car."

"Dude, you have no love for the Beast."

I shook my head. Charlie drove the same old pickup truck—the one he'd inherited from his dad when he was sixteen. It ate through gas like a motherfucker and drove like a tank. But he loved that piece of shit.

"You want to take the Beast, you pay for all the gas," I said.

"Touché," he said. "We take your car."

"We leave tomorrow."

After our workout, Charlie headed home and I went for a run. Because I could. Four years later, and I still hadn't gotten over the way it felt to make my body move and feel it respond. Feel the air going in and out of my lungs. The muscles in my legs working. No dizziness or chest pain. Nothing but the lactic acid building up as I ran, the rush of air in and out of my chest. Deep breaths, filled with oxygen. My new heart thumping a steady rhythm.

It felt really fucking good to be strong again.

Recovery from the transplant surgery had been brutal. But considering they'd cut open my chest, taken out a vital organ, and replaced it with a new one, it wasn't surprising. It blew my mind that it was even possible.

It had taken a year before I'd felt like the surgery no longer impacted my daily life. But I'd been on the brink of death before that, so every day post-surgery had been an improvement. Even those first pain-soaked weeks when I'd felt like I lived with a stack of bricks on my chest had been better than the months leading up to the transplant. At least the new heart gave me some hope.

I'd indulged in that hope with a high degree of caution, especially at first. There were numerous things that could go wrong after a transplant. I'd needed regular tests, including multiple—painful—biopsies to determine how the heart was functioning. Every time, I'd braced myself for bad news. For the doctors to tell me something was wrong. That this heart was failing too, or my body was rejecting it.

It hadn't.

With the help of a cocktail of drugs, my body had accepted the new organ. I hadn't had a single fibrillation episode in four years. I'd been spared any other complications. My new heart worked just as it should.

Now, it was all on me. I had to take care of the heart Liam Harper had given me, and I took that responsibility very seriously. I didn't fuck around with shitty food—at least not very often. Didn't drink or let anyone smoke around me. As soon as I'd been cleared to work out again, I'd hit the gym with a vengeance. I'd been as weak as a kitten when Charlie and I had first started, but as time had passed, my strength had grown.

I fully intended to do everything in my power to keep my body—and my new heart—as healthy as possible. I didn't ever want to be sick like that again.

When I was about half a mile from home, I slowed to a walk to cool down, and pulled out my phone. I'd thought about waiting until I was on the road to tell my parents I'd gone out of town. Or maybe call them from Phoenix. But that could upset my mom even more. I took a deep breath, and called her number.

She picked up on the first ring. "Hi, honey."

"Hi, Mom," I said.

"How are you feeling? Are you okay?"

I tried to ignore the hint of urgency in her voice. It was like she was still expecting me to drop dead. "I'm great, Mom. Just went for a run."

"Honey, you need to be careful," she said. "You don't want to overdo it. And it's so early. Did you get enough sleep?"

"Yeah, Mom, I'm good," I said. "I've been running for the last two years. I'm fine."

"All right, I know," she said. "You should come see us this weekend. Do you have plans? You could come to dinner. Bring Charlie if you want."

"Actually, that's why I called," I said. "I'm going out of town for a few days."

"You're... you're what?"

"I'm going to Phoenix to meet the donor's family."

She went silent.

"Mom?"

"I'm sorry," she said. "I don't know what to say."

"They invited me to come," I said.

"Oh. Well... that's very nice of them," she said. "But Phoenix?"

"Well, yeah, it's where they live."

"Why couldn't they have come here?" she asked.

I stopped on the side of the road, not far from the house Charlie and I shared. I knew my mom would be weird about this. "I offered. It's not a big deal. It's Phoenix, not Mars."

"But what if something happens?" she asked. "What if you need medical attention?"

"Mom, I haven't needed medical attention since... I don't even know when, that's how long it's been. You don't have to worry so much."

"I'm your mom. Worry comes with the territory," she said.

"Charlie's going too," I said. "Does that help?"

"A little," she said. "At least you won't be alone."

"Okay, Mom, I have to go," I said. "We're leaving tomorrow. I'll text you from the road."

"All right, honey," she said. "But don't forget to let us know how you're doing. I don't like you being so far away."

"I know, Mom," I said. "Love you."

"Love you too."

I let out a sigh when I hung up the phone. That had actually gone better than I'd thought it would. It was hard to blame my mom for being concerned about me. But I wished she'd relax. I wasn't sure how to assure her that I was really doing fine. It was like she was afraid to believe me.

Charlie was gone when I got home. His text said he was out getting snacks for the road trip. Dude cracked me up. I was glad he was going with me. As casual as I made everything sound, I was nervous to meet the Harpers. They'd been nice when I'd spoken to them—said they were excited for us to meet. But there was a thick veil of sadness that covered everything. Sure, I'd lived. I'd been given a second chance. But they'd lost their son—a young man in his prime. He'd been in college, recently engaged to his girlfriend.

As grateful as I was for the gift I'd been given, it was bittersweet. I hated that someone else had to die for me to live. My only consolation was that Liam Harper would have died whether or not he'd donated his organs. It wasn't like he'd died *because of* me. But the joy I knew my parents felt at having their son back was mirrored by the grief of the Harpers losing theirs.

14

BROOKE

*T*he noise in the bar throbbed in my ears. Voices and music created a thick layer of sound that filled the space. Pressed against me. The dim light and constant noise wrapped around me, cradling me with their familiarity.

I sat on a stool, running a finger along the rim of my glass of... something. Whiskey, maybe? I'd already forgotten what I'd ordered. Didn't matter. My head was pleasantly fuzzy, the buzz keeping my thoughts aimless. That was all I needed tonight—the haze of booze. The ebb and flow of people moving around me. Distraction. Anything to keep my mind off the hollow space in my chest.

Not that it worked very well. Nothing did. Even the oblivion of sleep never provided real relief. It was always there. The ache. Whether it was hovering in the background of my consciousness, or stabbing my awareness like a knife, the ache was a part of me, now.

It stole through my chest, radiating from the place where my heart had once lived. Nothing was left in that space. Just an empty hole. Sure, I still had an organ to pump blood through my veins. But my heart? It had been torn from my chest. Held outside my body, beating in time with the machines that had kept Liam's organs functioning. It had stopped when Liam's had. Died with him.

In the beginning, the pain had been debilitating. I'd awoken every morning and the ache had ripped through me, burning me from the inside. It would steal my breath, take the oxygen from the air, leave me gasping. It had been shocking to realize that the pain wouldn't kill me. That my body would continue to function in such a state of desperate agony.

But it had. I'd gone on, day after day, still breathing. Still existing.

I took a drink. Felt the burn as it slipped down my throat. A hint of nausea turned my stomach over and my cheeks felt flushed.

"Hey Rick, can I get some water?"

Rick, the bartender tonight, nodded. He got me a glass of ice water and slid it across the bar. "Have you had anything to eat tonight, kiddo?"

I cracked a little smile. "Aw, are you worried about me? Or just worried I'll puke on the bar?"

He wiped a few drops of moisture off the bar top. "You just look a little pale. Maybe you should call it a night. Go get some food and sleep it off."

"You're a sweetheart, Rick." I flashed him another smile I didn't feel. I always gave people a pretty smile. Real or not, it was what they wanted to see. "But I'm fine."

He raised his eyebrows, like he didn't believe me. Which was fine. I didn't believe me either.

I wasn't all that drunk. I knew where I was and what I was doing. But my level of intoxication had nothing to do with whether or not I was *fine*. Another girl could be smashed out of her mind, falling all over the place, puking her brains out, and she'd be more *fine* than I was.

Shifting on the stool, I glanced at the band. They called themselves the *Death Pixies*, which was pretty fucking stupid if you asked me. I thought it made them sound like an all-girl punk band, but they were a bunch of rocker guys in ripped denim and leather.

Jared met my eyes, a slow smile crossing his face while he sang into the mic. It made my stomach turn again. I took a sip of water, hoping it would help. His hair was slicked back, his jaw rough with a week's growth of stubble. Full sleeve tattoos on both arms. Half the girls in here were ready to spread their legs for him, and he acted like he only had eyes for me.

He wasn't my boyfriend. He liked to put on a show in front of other people, claiming some alpha-male style ownership over me. Give a shout out to *his girl in the crowd*, fling an arm around my shoulders, grab my ass when he knew people were watching. Make his groupies jealous. He loved that shit. Ate up the attention like it was booze-filled candy.

But he was just as likely to fuck some random tonight as he was me. He didn't love me, and I didn't love him. Sometimes I wasn't sure if I even liked him. He was an asshole with an ego so big I was surprised he fit in the bar.

It raised the question: What the hell was I doing here, sitting in a crowded bar, drinking too much while Jared and his band played mediocre music?

Mostly, I didn't have anywhere else to be.

I'd lost yet another job, and this time, my apartment with it. I'd known Jared and the other guys in the band for a while. We traveled in the same social circle, if that's what you called a bunch of people who partied together and generally knew each other's names. They all lived in an old house not far from here, and they'd offered to let me come crash with them.

Hooking up with Jared offered me the protection I needed, living with a group of five guys who were drunk or high more often than not. Jared had claimed me, so the other guys left me alone. And he wasn't all bad. We did have fun together. He had a crazy streak—liked to flirt with danger. Chase the adrenaline rush. So did I. He often said he liked me because I was the only one who could keep up with him.

Our non-relationship worked for me. I wasn't capable of loving someone, and that wasn't what he wanted. He liked the appearance, having someone to call his *muse,* without the hassle of having a real girlfriend. And if I slept with him sometimes, there was no harm in it. He was a distraction. Something to fill the empty space inside of me, even if only for a little while.

I wasn't my mother, with a desperate need to be with a man. To not be alone. I hadn't moved from guy to guy since losing Liam. Sure, I lived with Jared now, but it was temporary. I'd get back on my feet and move on.

That's what I'd been telling myself, at least. But as I took another swallow of whiskey—or whatever this was; it didn't taste like anything to me—I knew the truth. Every day I inched closer to being just like her. My only hope was that I retained a degree of self-awareness that she'd lacked. And maybe that would count for something.

My mother had always blamed everyone else for the way her life had turned out. She'd gotten pregnant with me when she was too young. My dad had skipped out on her. The guys she'd dated had screwed her over. Everything had always been someone else's fault.

I *knew* how badly I'd fucked myself over. I didn't claim to be a victim of circumstance. I'd lost my job because I'd stopped showing up. Lost my apartment because I hadn't paid the rent. My life was a disaster, but it was all on me. I could blame Liam for dying, but other people had loved him too. They weren't sitting half-drunk in a dive bar, listening to their non-boyfriend's band, picking up a few shifts at a crappy diner as their only means of feeding themselves.

The problem was, it was hard to give a shit.

I felt as if I'd died when Liam had. It wasn't that I was suicidal. Even in the darkest days after the accident, I hadn't wanted to end my life. But I didn't really care if I lived, either.

I was a ghost, cursed with the torture of half-existence. Moving through the world as if I were alive. But all the important parts of me were dead. All that was left was a shell.

Sometimes I wondered if people could see through me. Did I look as washed out as I felt? Translucent, like a pale gossamer curtain blowing in the wind? Would I eventually fade into nothingness?

After I lost Liam, I'd tried. Tried so hard to keep myself together. I'd gone back to school when the new semester had started. Went to work. Did my homework. Paid my bills. For a while, anyway.

But little by little, I'd stopped doing those things. And of course, there had been consequences. Fail enough classes, and your admission is revoked. Miss enough work, and you get fired. Don't pay your bills, and things get shut off.

Did any of it matter, if I wasn't really alive?

The band finished their set and Jared worked his way over to me. Took his time, stopping to talk to some girl in a black halter top, her boobs spilling out. She looked like most of the girls in this place—rocker girls with lots of makeup, bright red lips, dressed in black. I stood out like a nun in a whorehouse in this place, with my breezy white peasant blouse, cut-off jeans, and collection of beaded bracelets on my wrists. But I didn't care. I wasn't going to change how I dressed for some guy.

Jared met my eyes again and sauntered through the crowd, like the fucking peacock he was. His shirt halfway unbuttoned, ripped jeans slung low on his hips.

"Hey, baby doll," he said. His eyes flicked to Rick behind the bar. "Shot of Jack. And another one for my girl."

I finished off the last of my current drink. If Jared was buying more, I wasn't saying no.

"How'd we sound tonight?" He pulled out a pack of cigarettes and stuck one between his lips, then offered one to me.

I only smoked when I was drunk, but I was close enough. I took it between two fingers. "You sounded good."

"Just good?" he asked, taking the cigarette out of his mouth. Rick slid his drink across the bar and Jared downed it in one swallow.

"Is your ego really that sensitive?" I asked. "If you need someone to flatter you, try Miss Huge Tits in the halter top over there."

"God, I love it when you get jealous," he said.

I laughed and took the shot of whiskey, but didn't bother to correct him. If he wanted to think I was jealous, that was fine. I didn't feel much of anything, so what did it matter?

"Come on, baby doll," he said. "I need a smoke."

He wrapped a possessive arm around me as we walked through the bar, heading for the door. Outside, the heat was still thick. It was unseasonably warm for spring, even in Phoenix.

"Fucking heat," Jared muttered as he lit his cigarette. "Shouldn't be so goddamn hot this time of year. Sometimes I think we should get the fuck out of this place."

He lit mine and I took a drag. Blew out the smoke. Jared talked about leaving Phoenix all the time—usually to move to L.A. "Yeah, the heat sucks."

His phone dinged and he pulled it out of his pocket. Typed something. I wandered up the sidewalk, my cigarette dangling from my fingers. I didn't really want it, so I just let it burn. The smoke curled upward as the ash on the tip grew. I paused and stared at it, seeing her. Standing over me in the street, a cigarette pinched between her fingers. Still burning while she hit me. Liam's voice behind me. *What the hell are you doing?*

I don't know, Liam. I don't know what I'm doing.

"Hey. Got a light?"

I hadn't noticed the guy come up beside me. Too lost in my own head. He was dressed in a black t-shirt and jeans, a battered baseball cap on his head. He held up a cigarette and raised his eyebrows.

"Sorry, I don't."

He shrugged and tucked the cigarette behind his ear. "No big deal."

"You can have mine," I said, offering my half-burned cigarette. "I'm kind of just holding it. It's going to waste."

One corner of his mouth tugged upward as he took it from me. Placed his lips around the tip and inhaled. Turned and blew out the smoke. "That would have been better if you'd have left some lipstick on the tip."

I stepped backward. "That wasn't an invitation to hit on me. Sorry."

The guy opened his mouth to say something, but Jared pushed his way between us.

"Move on, asshole," Jared said.

"Hey, I was just—"

"You were just getting the fuck out of here," Jared said.

The guy seemed to decide it wasn't worth the confrontation. With a half-glare, half-smile that seemed to say *she's not worth the trouble*, he turned and walked away.

Jared grabbed my wrist and pulled me closer. "What the hell was that?"

His grip was tight, digging into my skin. "Nothing. He asked if I had a lighter."

"You know that guy?"

"No. God, Jared, let go. That hurts."

Twisting my arm painfully, he squeezed harder. "Don't fucking do that again. I don't like it." He let go and I clutched my wrist to my body. "I want to get out of here. I'll go get the bike."

Without waiting for my reply, he turned and left, heading up the street to where he'd parked his motorcycle.

I rubbed my wrist. He'd left red marks in the shape of his fingers. It burned, like a demon singed by holy water. I almost expected to see hissing smoke rising from the redness.

In another life, I would have written that down. Now, I didn't have anything with me to write on.

My phone rang, the noise making me jump. I pulled it out of my pocket and my breath froze in my lungs as I stared at the name on the screen.

Mary Harper.

It had been months since Liam's mom had last tried to call. I hadn't answered that time. I'd texted her a few days later, apologizing for missing her call and promising to call back. I hadn't.

In fact, it had been almost two years since I'd seen any of Liam's family. I'd pushed them away so hard, they'd eventually stopped trying. Plus, the last time I'd seen Olivia, she'd made it clear how she felt about me. That had been more than enough to keep me away.

"Hello?" I heard my own voice as if it were outside of me —someone else speaking. Had I answered her call? What the fuck was I thinking? Maybe I was drunker than I thought.

"Brooke?" Mary's voice. So familiar. So kind. It pushed at the ache in my chest, stirring it up so the pain felt almost fresh. "Brooke, is that you?"

"Yeah," I said, hoping I sounded clear. I didn't want her to know I'd been drinking.

"I'm so glad I reached you," she said. "How are you?"

God, that question. But I was good at lying about it. "I'm good. Fine. Just kind of tired. It's late."

"I know, I'm sorry for calling so late," she said. "I need to talk to you about something. It's important. Do you have a minute?"

"Sure."

"We've been in touch with someone," she said. "One of the organ recipients."

Her words didn't register at first. Organ recipients? She couldn't mean...

"What?"

"Four years ago, a young man in Iowa needed a heart transplant," she said. "He received Liam's heart."

His heart? It felt like I couldn't breathe—like my lungs were caught in a vise. "Really?"

"Yes," she said. "He wrote to us. And, well, we've invited

him to meet, here in Phoenix. That's why I'm calling. We were hoping you would come."

I swallowed hard, trying to hold myself together. "When?"

"Tomorrow afternoon," she said. "We're meeting for lunch at Nora's Kitchen, do you remember that restaurant? I'm not sure where you're living now, but if you need a ride, I'm sure we could come pick you up."

Pick me up? Wait, no. This was moving too fast. "No, you wouldn't need to do that. I know where that is."

"I know this is difficult," she said. "But I think it will be a positive experience for all of us. Show us the good that came from Liam's death."

I bit my bottom lip to keep from shouting at her. Nothing good had come from Liam's death. Not a single fucking thing. I didn't care about some asshole in Iowa who'd needed a heart. Why was his life so special? Liam had been taken from me—from all of us—and nothing was ever going to make that okay.

But I didn't want to make Mary feel bad. I'd done enough of that already. "I'm just not sure if I can make it tomorrow."

"I'm sorry, I should have given you more notice. And if you just... well, if you just can't, I certainly understand. I know how hard this is."

Goddammit, why did she have to be so *good*? I knew they were disappointed in me, but Mary was always understanding. Sometimes I wished she'd just yell at me. Get angry. Call me names and lay the blame for everything at my feet. At least I'd deserve it.

But I desperately wanted to make her happy. She'd been a better mother to me than mine ever had, and I knew I'd hurt her by pushing her away after Liam died.

It wasn't just the pain of seeing his family. That *was* hard. But I didn't want her to know—didn't want any of them to know—what a mess I'd become. How far I'd fallen. I was ashamed of myself for falling apart and not being strong enough to put the pieces back together.

Still, I found myself answering. "Yeah, okay. I might be able to come."

"Yes?" She seemed to cover the phone or turn to speak to someone else. Probably Brian. "Yes, she said she might come." Clearer, now. "We would all love it so much if you did. We've missed you."

Not all of you.

"So, I guess I'll just meet you there?"

"Yes, meet us there at noon," she said. "Thank you, honey. We're all looking forward to seeing you."

Jared pulled up beside me, the roar of his motorcycle making it impossible to hear.

"Um, I have to go," I said, half-shouting into the phone. I couldn't hear if she replied.

My hands shook as I ended the call. What had I done? I'd just agreed to see the Harpers. Tomorrow. To meet the man who'd received Liam's heart, of all things.

I'd been in some messed up situations in the last few years, but this took the cake, hands down.

I put my phone in my pocket and climbed on the back of the bike, slipping my arms around Jared's waist. Out of nowhere, I swore I could hear Mary's voice, asking me why I wasn't wearing a helmet.

Because it doesn't matter, that's why.

"Ready, baby doll?" Jared asked, raising his voice to be heard over the rumbling engine.

"Let's get out of here."

He pulled out onto the street and hit the gas. My body

thrilled at the sudden burst of speed. The danger. The wind blew my hair back from my face and I leaned over just enough to watch the lights race toward us. Alcohol and speed was a potent combination, one of the few things that worked anymore. One of the few things that made me feel as if I were still alive.

15

SEBASTIAN

a wave of nervousness hit me as I stood outside the restaurant. This was it. I was about to meet the family of the man whose heart had saved my life.

The trip down here had only taken a couple of days. Charlie and I had taken turns driving and stopped at a cheap motel in the middle of nowhere for a night. We'd arrived in Phoenix last night, tired and cramped from so many hours on the road.

A bead of sweat trailed down my back as I opened the door. Cool air-conditioned air wrapped around me when I stepped inside. I hesitated near the front, wondering if the Harpers were here yet. I was a few minutes early. Charlie had stayed behind at the hotel.

I recognized Mrs. Harper the second I saw her. Shoulder-length blond hair. Blue eyes. I'd seen her picture— looked her up on Facebook. She met my eyes and even from across the restaurant, I could see her gasp in a small breath.

A man who looked to be about fifty or so sat across from her. He was lean, in a button-down shirt, his hair mostly gray. He reached across the table and rested his hand on hers.

The other person at the table was a young woman, maybe about my age. She was either Liam's sister, or his girl-friend. Had to be sister. She looked like their mom—pretty, with blond hair, blue eyes, and a similar mouth.

They all stood as I approached their table. I was several inches taller than Mr. Harper, and a lot thicker, but I was used to being the big guy. I didn't crowd their space, but stepped close enough to reach out and shake his hand.

"Sebastian McKinney," I said. Mr. Harper took my hand and shook, introducing himself. I shook Mrs. Harper's hand, and she introduced me to Olivia. Definitely the sister.

Olivia shook my hand and stared at me, wide-eyed. "Wow, you're huge. Does my brother's heart really work in your body, or do you need two of them?"

Mrs. Harper gaped at her daughter. "Olivia."

"It's a fair question," Olivia said. "Look at him."

"Maybe we should all just have a seat," Mr. Harper said.

"It's okay," I said. "I'm used to it."

I sat at the end of the table, with Mr. Harper on my right, Mrs. Harper and Olivia on my left.

"We're so grateful you were willing to come all this way," Mrs. Harper said.

"I'm happy to," I said. "It's the least I can do."

A moment of awkward quiet settled over the table. Just as I was about to say something, the waitress came. We gave her our lunch orders—Olivia raised her eyebrows at me when I ordered a salad with grilled chicken—and she left ice waters for each of us.

"So, what was wrong with you?" Olivia asked. "Why did you need a heart?"

It looked like Mrs. Harper was going to apologize for

Olivia, but I held up a hand. "It's fine, really. You can ask me anything. And I figured you'd want to know what happened to me."

They watched intently as I told my story. I didn't want to make it sound melodramatic, but I was honest. I left a few things out—particularly Cami. They didn't need to know about her. Mr. Harper had a lot of questions about my illness, and I did my best to answer. And they all wanted to know how I was doing now. Partway through, the waitress brought our lunches, and I continued talking while we ate.

It made me feel good to be able to tell them I was healthy now. Their son's heart hadn't gone to waste.

"What an amazing journey you've had," Mrs. Harper said.

"I don't really know how to say this and have it come out right," I said. "I struggle with knowing that my second chance at life brought someone else a lot of pain. But I want you to know how grateful I am."

Mrs. Harper reached across the table and put her hand over mine. "We're grateful too. We miss Liam terribly. Nothing will ever take his place. But it helps so much to know that something good came out of that tragedy."

I nodded, feeling a little choked up. Damn, this was tough. I'd only just met these people, and I felt like I'd known them my whole life. Like they were somehow my family, too.

Tears rolled down Olivia's cheeks and she wiped them away. "Oh my god. This is the craziest thing. I'm so pissed Brooke isn't here. She really needs to meet you."

"Maybe she's just running late," Mrs. Harper said.

"Doubt it," Olivia said, rolling her eyes.

"I'm sorry," Mrs. Harper said. "Brooke was Liam's

fiancée. We invited her to join us, and she said she'd be here. We actually haven't seen her for quite some time."

"I don't blame her," I said. "If I were in her shoes, I don't think I'd want to meet me either."

Mr. and Mrs. Harper exchanged a sad look.

"I wish I'd have done more for her," Mrs. Harper said.

"Grief can make it hard to do the right thing for the living," Mr. Harper said. "We did our best at the time."

"Yeah, Mom, you need to stop beating yourself up about her," Olivia said. "It's not your fault."

"You're right, I know," Mrs. Harper said. "We'll give her more time. Maybe she'll still come."

They asked me more questions and the conversation lightened. They wanted to know about Iowa, and my family. Turned out Mr. Harper was a sports fan, and he chimed in with more questions. I told them about losing to Charlie junior year. How we'd become friends after I'd gotten sick, and how he'd come to Phoenix with me.

Then we talked about Liam. I wanted to know all I could about the man, but I hadn't been sure if they'd want to talk about him. But rather than being sad or somber, their reminiscing was filled with fondness. They brought out some pictures. Told me what he'd been like as a kid. The sports he'd played as he got older. About meeting in Brooke in high school, and how she'd eventually come to live with them.

We ate and talked and even laughed. I loved hearing about Liam, and the more we talked about him, the more the sadness seemed to lift.

When our meal was finished, and the server had cleared our plates, Mrs. Harper reached out and touched my hand again. "Thank you, Sebastian. This meant so much to us."

"Me too, Mrs. Harper," I said. "I'm really glad I got to meet all of you."

As we said our goodbyes, the Harpers all glanced toward the front door several times. Probably hoping Brooke would show at the last minute.

I couldn't explain why, but I hoped so too. Every time they'd mentioned her name, I'd felt a tightness in my chest. A tingling in my limbs. Like a foreboding, a sense that something was about to happen. But she hadn't come, and I was filled with an inexplicable sense of disappointment. I had no idea why. I didn't know her. I had no reason to be so concerned.

But I was. I was filled with unease. Why hadn't she come? Was it simply that she'd decided it would be too difficult to meet me? That was understandable. But I couldn't get rid of the sense that something deeper was wrong. Not as we finished up our conversation, talking about meeting again, maybe in Iowa this time. Not as we stood and exchanged long hugs, the embraces bringing both Mrs. Harper and Olivia to tears again.

Mr. and Mrs. Harper opened the door, but Olivia hesitated.

"I'll be right there," she said to her parents, then turned to me. "Look, I know this doesn't really matter, since you'll probably never meet Brooke. But I don't want to give you the wrong idea about her. I knew she wouldn't come, but it's not because of you. It's because of me."

"What do you mean?"

She sighed and glanced down at her feet. "The last time I saw her was... it was bad. I was so angry after my brother died. I said things to her that I really regret. Well, we both said things, but there's no excuse for how I treated her. And I haven't seen her since."

"So, you didn't just lose your brother," I said.

"Exactly," she said. "I was hoping she'd be here. I owe her an apology, and I thought maybe today would be the day I'd have the chance. Anyway, I don't know why I'm telling you all this. It's not your problem. I just didn't want you to leave thinking she was a flake."

"Thanks," I said. "I hope you get the chance to talk to her."

"Yeah, me too," she said. "Thanks again for coming. I'm glad I got to meet you."

We hugged again and said one last goodbye.

I stopped in the restroom, then left the restaurant. I was still thinking about Brooke. Wondering what had become of her—of the woman Liam Harper had loved. Wondering if she was okay.

I was still thinking about her when I turned up the sidewalk, heading to where I'd parked. Still thinking about her when I saw a woman across the street, sitting at a little café table, looking at her phone. She was dressed in a tank top and shorts, long dark hair spilling down over her shoulders. I paused and watched her glance up, looking in my direction.

And I knew, with every ounce of my being, that she was Brooke.

16

BROOKE

*T*he Sunrise Diner had seen better days. Tucked away on a side street and housed in a rundown building, the diner could have been one of those hole-in-the-wall places known for great food. If it'd had great food. Which it didn't. The booths were worn out, the kitchen outdated, and the neon sign outside blinked *PEN*, the *O* having long since burned out. They never had many customers, but somehow the place stayed open. I had no idea how.

I opened the door, the jingling bell announcing my arrival. Betty Jean looked up from her newspaper. "Hey there, sweetie." Her bright pink lipstick cracked when she smiled and her hair was a shade of strawberry blond that didn't exist in nature. "You working today?"

"No," I said. "Just killing time."

I slipped into a booth. Betty Jean owned the place and she let me work sometimes. I knew they didn't really need me. But Betty Jean seemed to have realized I was in a bad spot. I tried not to think of it as a pity thing. She swore up and down I gave her a break, since she couldn't afford to hire someone full-time. If I worked some shifts, she could get other things done. It was a win for both of us.

It helped keep me afloat, even if it wasn't enough money for me to get my own place. But at least it was something.

"Are you all right?" Betty Jean asked. She stood by the table, a full coffee carafe in her hand.

"Yeah, I'm okay." I turned over the white coffee mug. "Just tired, I guess." *And fucking hungover.*

She poured. "It's almost lunch time, but I bet you haven't eaten anything. How about some breakfast?"

I shrugged. I knew I should eat, but I never had much of an appetite. "Sure."

"I'll get you the usual," she said. She always made me eat something. Only charged me for it about half the time, too.

She left to give the cook my order and I pinched the bridge of my nose. My head felt like it was going to split open. I dug out bottle of Tylenol from my bag and took a few. Hopefully they'd take the edge off. I glanced at another bottle in my bag. Vicodin. That would definitely get rid of the headache. But I didn't want to be out of it when I met the Harpers later.

God, what had I been thinking? How could I face them? And how could I face the man who had Liam's heart?

I sat in the booth and sipped my coffee. Picked at my food after Betty Jean brought it. Checked the time. Watched it get closer to noon.

And I didn't get up.

Noon passed. They were at the restaurant, now. Sitting with him. I wondered what they were talking about. What this guy looked like. Who he was and why he'd come here. Did he want to know about Liam? Why did the Harpers want to meet him? Hadn't they been through enough already?

Another hour. I had a text from Mary, asking me if I was still coming, and if I needed a ride.

I didn't answer.

Betty Jean glanced at me now and then, in between helping the few other customers who came in. But she didn't ask me what I was doing. In some ways, I wished she would. Maybe if I told her what I was avoiding, she'd agree with me. Tell me I was right to stay away, and I could stop feeling bad.

Or maybe she'd tell me to go.

Maybe I shouldn't have been waiting for someone else to tell me what to do. The restaurant was walking distance from here. If I got up now, I might still catch them.

Before I could talk myself out of it, I grabbed my bag and stood. "Betty Jean, I have to go. Can I pay for this later?"

"It's on me, sweetie," she said.

"Thanks."

Outside, the temperature had risen. It was warm for spring. I hurried down the street, adjusting my backpack on my shoulder. It was heavy, but I was used to it. I carried a lot of my stuff around with me since I'd moved in with Jared and his band.

Thoughts warred in my mind. I should go. It would make the Harpers happy, even though I was late. I could do this for them. They were probably getting ready to leave, so I wouldn't have to stay long. I could say hello, talk to them for a few minutes, and be done with it.

But god, I was such a mess. On the outside, I looked fine. My long hair down, brushed nicely. Bracelets on my wrists. My clothes—a loose white tank top that laced up the front, cut-off jean shorts, and brown sandals with turquoise beading—were the same boho style I'd worn since college. And I knew how to put on a pretty smile. But the Harpers knew me better than anyone. They'd see right through me.

I turned and saw the restaurant up ahead, across the street. Stopped in my tracks.

Mary and Brian were there, standing on the sidewalk. Olivia came out of the restaurant. They each hugged her, then Brian put his arm around Mary's shoulders. Olivia wiped her eyes. I didn't see anyone else. A few people walked up and down the sidewalk, but the guy from Iowa must have left already.

My chest tightened and my back was tense. The ache inside threatened to overwhelm me. I stepped backward, still watching. They turned the other way and walked down the sidewalk—probably heading for their car.

I let them go.

I hated myself in that moment—more than ever before. Hated that I was too weak to face them. Hated that I'd let myself sink this low. I knew I couldn't answer their questions. *Where are you living now?* With a bunch of guys in a band. Once in a while I let the singer fuck me so the others will leave me alone. *What about a job?* I get paid under the table to work at a shitty diner because the owner feels bad for me. *Are you thinking about going back to school?* I can't, I flunked out and lost all my scholarship money.

The café next to me had a few outdoor tables. I slumped down in one of the chairs, leaving my bag at my feet, and took out my phone. I should at least text Mary. I didn't want to make her worry any more than I already had. I'd just tell her I'd been called into work or something. It's not like she'd know I was lying.

"Excuse me?"

The deep male voice startled me and I fumbled my phone, almost dropping it.

"I'm so sorry," he said. "I didn't mean to scare you."

The man standing in front of me was enormous. At five-foot-seven, I wasn't short, but if I'd been standing, he would have towered over me. And he wasn't just tall. The guy was built like a tank. Wide shoulders, broad chest, huge arms. He had dark hair and his square jaw was covered in a thick beard. And his eyes. Deep green in the center, fading to almost brown at the edges of his irises. They were so striking. *He* was striking.

I stared at him, but it was hard to look away. He looked familiar, like someone I should know but couldn't place. But there was no way I'd met him before. I'd never forget a man like this.

"That's okay," I said. "Do you need something?"

"This is going to sound weird, but are you Brooke?" he asked.

I blinked at him. "Um, yes. How do you know my name?"

"I'm actually not sure," he said. "I'm Sebastian McKinney. Maybe Mrs. Harper told you about me? I just had lunch with them."

Holy shit. This was *him*? "Yeah, she did, but I, um... I couldn't make it earlier."

He nodded. "Yeah, it's no problem. I just saw you over here and..."

"How did you know it was me?" I asked.

"I honestly don't know," he said. "A feeling, I guess."

I had no idea what to think about that. We stared at each other for a moment and I felt something stir deep inside.

Maybe it was just curiosity. I'd thought I didn't want to see this guy. But now that I was face to face with him, I wondered who he was. What he was like. Why he'd needed Liam's heart.

And those eyes. They reached into me and took hold. A tiny spark lit inside of me, making my tummy tingle with what almost felt like nerves. It was so faint, it would have been easy to dismiss it as nothing. The stress of the day—or of my life.

But it was there. A glimmer.

"That's weird," I said.

He smiled. It softened his eyes and took the intimidating edge off his demeanor. "It *is* weird. Sorry, I'm not a psycho or anything."

"Are you sure? Because that seems like something a psycho would say to convince people they're not."

"That's a good point. But last I checked I'm pretty safe." He glanced around the street. "Listen, can I buy you a cup of coffee or something? Or lunch, if you're hungry. If you can't, or don't want to, it's fine. I'll go and leave you alone."

I swallowed hard. I didn't want him to go, and I couldn't explain why. "Sure, coffee, I guess."

He smiled again and gestured to the café. "In here? Or do you want to go somewhere else?"

"Here is fine," I said.

I got up and he held the door for me. We went inside and I picked a table near the front. I felt like I needed a clear path to the exit in case this got weird. A waitress came and took our orders—coffee for me and an unsweetened iced tea for him—and left.

He blew out a breath. "I don't know about you, but this weather is freaking me out. I'm not used to it being this hot in April."

"I guess I'm used to it," I said. "And I don't think your beard helps."

He rubbed his bearded jaw. "Yeah, you're probably right. It's perfect for winter in the Midwest, though. So, did you grow up here?"

"Sort of," I said. "We moved a lot. Texas, New Mexico, Oklahoma. California for a while. And here."

"Wow," he said. "My parents still live in the same house they bought before I was born. Small town Iowa."

"It must be nice to have a home to go back to," I said.

"Yeah," he said, but there was a hint of sadness in his voice. "A lot of memories there."

"I guess that's not always good," I said.

He shrugged. "Most of the memories are good ones. Enough of them, at least. Kind of thought I was going to die in that house, though. Seems different now."

I realized my eyes had settled on his chest. The top of a scar was barely visible right at the neckline of his shirt. I tore my eyes away, hoping he hadn't noticed.

"I'm sorry you had to go through that," I said.

"Thanks, but *I'm* sorry," he said. "For your loss."

I didn't want to talk about Liam. Not with this guy. But I did want to know about him. "Can I ask what happened to you? Were you born with a bad heart or something?"

"No," he said. "I was always healthy before I got sick."

The waitress brought my coffee, but it sat untouched as he told his story. It sounded awful. The shock of almost dying at such a young age. All the tests, the worry. Getting worse no matter what the doctors tried. The ache in my chest throbbed when he talked about what it had been like just before he'd learned there was a heart for him. How he'd wanted to give up.

I knew what that felt like.

I thought about where I must have been when he first got sick. He'd been a senior when I was a junior, and he'd said it had been in February. His heart had given out around the time Liam had asked me to the Valentine's Day dance.

That silly, sad teenage girl with her journals and streaks in her hair. She seemed like a different person. Her life had been messy, but what would that girl think of me now?

She'd be horrified.

"Sorry, that was probably more than you wanted to hear," Sebastian said.

"No, it's fine," I said. "I'm glad your life is better now."

I knew my words sounded hollow, but there were too many thoughts pinging through my brain. Too many feelings beating against the door where I kept them locked away.

"What about your life?" he asked.

"My life is fine," I said.

He narrowed his eyes and I knew he could tell I was lying. But he didn't press the issue.

"Oh, I had a question," he said. "It's about Liam, if that's okay. I meant to ask the Harpers, but I forgot."

"What?"

"Did he like peach iced tea?"

I gaped at him. How could he know that? "Yeah, it was his favorite."

He shook his head. "That's so weird."

"Why?"

"Well, they say it's a myth that when someone receives a transplant they take on some of the likes or dislikes of the donor. I asked the doctors about it, and they said there's no real evidence that it happens. But I swear to you, before four years ago, I wouldn't have touched peach iced tea. Now I get the weirdest cravings for it."

I didn't know why it was talking about peach iced tea that did it, but I couldn't take any more. This man's presence was too much. He was too big, too overwhelming. The ache in my chest was going to rip me open, letting my emotions spill out onto the floor. I couldn't let that happen.

"I should probably go," I said.

"Yeah, okay," he said. "But wait one second? Please?"

He flagged down the waitress and asked for a pen and paper while I watched him, confused. The waitress fished a pen out of her apron and tore a piece of paper from her notepad. After writing something on the paper and folding it in half, he passed it to me.

"It's my number," he said. "Just in case."

"Just in case, what?"

"I don't know," he said. "But if you ever need anything, call me. I know, I live fifteen hundred miles away, and I'm a total stranger. I just feel like I need to do this. Take it. Please."

His voice was so stern, so serious, I didn't think I could refuse. Narrowing my eyes at him, I picked up the folded piece of paper and slipped it into my pocket. "Okay."

"Thanks," he said. "It was really nice meeting you, Brooke."

He held my gaze and I found myself trapped by his mesmerizing eyes. Were they more green now? It was like their color had shifted. That tingle in my stomach was back and I had an almost overwhelming urge to reach out and press my palm against his chest.

I tore my eyes away and grabbed my bag. "Nice to meet you too."

Shouldering my backpack, I hurried out the door. I had to get away from him. Away from those eyes. Away from the feelings that threatened to claw their way to the surface when I looked at him.

I couldn't deal with all this emotion. I needed to be numb. Numbing myself against it all was the only way I could survive.

17

SEBASTIAN

a waitress took our order and Charlie went back to being glued to his phone. Between meeting the Harpers, and sitting with Brooke afterward, it felt like I'd been in restaurants for half the day. And here I was at another one. But Charlie and I had spent the rest of the afternoon in the hotel pool, and we were starving.

"What's going on, man?" I asked.

"Nothing." He typed for a few more seconds, then put his phone away. "Kimmie's being weird."

Kimmie was Charlie's on-again, off-again girlfriend. Apparently they were *on* at the moment. I wasn't Kimmie's biggest fan. But it was Charlie's business, not mine.

"She mad about something?" I asked.

"Just bitching about me leaving town," he said. "I told her I was going with you, but she's still pissed. I don't know what her problem is."

I wanted to say her problem was that she's a whiny drama queen, but I didn't. I just shrugged. "Who knows. Women, right?"

"I don't understand them." He took a sip of his water. "Speaking of, are you and Tracy still a thing?"

"No," I said. "We weren't much of a thing anyway. But I called it off."

"Shitty," he said.

"I guess."

Tracy and I had dated for a while, but nothing come of it. Just like Jessica. And Brianna before her. I hadn't had a serious, long-term girlfriend since Cami. They had all been nice girls. Pretty. And come on, I liked sex as much as the next guy. But there hadn't been anything there. We just went out, talked a little. Maybe fucked afterward, if we'd gotten that far. I wasn't sure what I was looking for, exactly, but it wasn't that. I wanted a woman who did something to me. Set me on fire. Made me feel alive.

That made me think of Brooke, and I wasn't sure what to do with that.

"How did it go today?" Charlie asked. "You haven't really said anything."

"It was intense," I said. "They were such nice people. It sucks that their son died. They wanted to know about me and my illness and everything. And they told me a lot about Liam. It was good, though. I think they felt good about meeting me."

He nodded. "Sounds like it was worth the trip."

"Definitely," I said. "A weird thing happened afterward, though."

"Yeah?"

"Liam's fiancée, Brooke, was supposed to be at lunch, but she didn't show. It was obvious the Harpers were really worried about her. And their daughter, Olivia, was kinda pissed."

"She was pissed at this Brooke chick for not being there?" he asked.

"Yeah, but more frustrated because she was concerned about her, I think. Anyway, when I left, I saw Brooke across the street."

"How did you know it was her?" he asked. "Did they show you pictures?"

"No, I'd never seen her," I said. "But I took one look at her, and I knew."

Charlie furrowed his brow. "How the hell did you know?"

"I said it was weird. I have no idea. But I saw her and there was no doubt in my mind it was her. So, I talked to her."

"You what?"

"I went across the street and talked to her," I said.

He chuckled. "What did you do, just walk up and ask who she was?"

"Basically, yeah."

"Only you, man," he said. "What was she like?"

"Beautiful," I said before I could stop myself.

Charlie raised his eyebrows. "Um, okay. What's that about?"

"Never mind," I said. God, where had that come from? But she hadn't just been beautiful. She'd been haunting. I hadn't been able to stop thinking about her since we'd met. "That doesn't matter. She wasn't sure about me, but I wound up buying her a cup of coffee and talking to her for a while."

"Wow," he said. "How did that go?"

"Okay, I think. She didn't stay long. But I gave her my number before she left."

"Dude," Charlie said. "You can't hit on her. That's just... really wrong."

"Fuck off, I wasn't hitting on her," I said.

Charlie raised his eyebrows at me in disbelief. The waitress brought our dinners and we paused while she set our plates in front of us.

"Then why did you give her your number?" he asked when the waitress had left. "That sounds like hitting on her to me."

"It just seemed like the right thing to do," I said. "In case she ever needs anything, I guess."

He picked up his fork and shook his head. "Sure. It had nothing to do with the fact that she's cute."

"No, it didn't," I said. "And I never said anything about her being cute."

"Right, you said *beautiful*. That's completely different."

I cut into my chicken and took a bite. "That's not why. It was the look in her eyes—her expression."

"What do you mean?" he asked. "What did she look like?"

"Like she's broken," I said. "I know that look. It's how I looked before the transplant, when I'd given up."

Charlie paused and nodded. He understood. He was one of the few people who'd seen me in those last days before the surgery. I *had* given up. I'd been waiting for a death that wouldn't come fast enough. Brooke had looked as if she were waiting for the same thing.

I'd hated seeing her that way. It was strange, because I didn't know her. I didn't remember her smile, or what she'd sounded like when she'd been happy. But the deadness in her eyes had been gut-wrenching.

My phone rang and I pulled it out of my pocket to glance at the screen. I didn't recognize the number. "That's weird."

Charlie just shrugged and took another bite.

I swiped to answer. "Hey, this is Seb."

A woman's voice. "Um..."

I waited a second, but she didn't say anything else. "Hello?"

More silence. I figured it was a wrong number and was about to hang up when she spoke again, her voice halting.

"Seb... Sebastian?"

"Yeah," I said.

"Oh god, I'm sorry."

"Brooke?" I asked. Charlie's eyebrows lifted. The other end of the line went quiet again, but noise in the background told me the call was still connected. "Brooke, is that you?"

"Yes."

I sat up straight, my food forgotten, all my instincts on high alert. Something was very wrong. "Brooke, what's going on? Are you okay?"

"No."

I shook my head at Charlie. *She's not okay.*

"What's wrong?" I asked.

"I shouldn't have called you," she said.

"Yes, you should have," I said, worried she was going to hang up. "It's cool. What happened? Are you hurt?"

Her voice was so small. "Yes."

I nodded at Charlie. He pulled out his wallet and tossed some money on the table as we both got up.

"Where are you?" I asked. We were already out the door, on the way to my car. "Don't hang up, Brooke. Stay with me. Just tell me where you are."

We got in the car. Fastened seat belts. Started the engine.

"I'm... um..."

God, Brooke, don't hang up.

"It's a restaurant," she said. "Sunrise Diner."

I repeated it and Charlie punched it into his phone.

"Got it," he said.

I put Brooke on speaker and pulled out onto the street. "Brooke, hang in there, okay? Don't move. I'm on my way."

"Okay."

The relief in her voice hit me square in the chest. This girl was scared. Not just scared—terrified. It made me wonder what we were about to walk into. But there was no way I could leave this alone. Not when it was her.

I followed the navigation across town, my back tense. "You still with me?"

"Yes," she said.

It took ten minutes to get there. I kept talking to Brooke, making sure she stayed on the line, and hoped we were going to the right place.

Charlie pointed to a rundown building with a broken neon sign. "That it?"

"Yeah." I found a parking spot out front. "Brooke, we're here."

She hung up, so I pocketed my phone. The bell on the door jingled when we walked in. A woman with orange-red hair and bright pink lipstick stood next to a booth toward the back, her arms crossed. Her name tag said Betty Jean. She eyed us with open suspicion as we walked toward her.

Of course, Charlie and I were big guys. We probably looked pretty intimidating.

Brooke was curled up in the booth, in the corner by the wall. Her hair hung over her face.

"Hey," I said, crouching down and resting my hands on the end of the table. "What happened?"

She looked up and my heart squeezed. Charlie muttered, "Holy shit," behind me. She had the beginnings of a black eye and one side of her mouth was swollen. Anger flooded through me. Someone had hit her. I'd fucking kill them.

Her eyes darted from me to Betty Jean. "I'm sorry. He broke my phone. I had your number in my pocket."

"Yeah, good," I said. "I'm glad you called me."

She sniffed. "I wasn't sure what to do."

"She didn't want to call the cops yet," Betty Jean said. "You guys are friends of hers?"

I stood and glanced back at Charlie. "Yeah, we're Brooke's friends. We'll take it from here."

Brooke clutched her bag but Betty Jean made no move to get out of her way so she could get up.

"You hurt this girl, and I'll find you," Betty Jean said. "I'll find you and I'll cut your balls off. I don't care how big you are. Got it?"

"Yes, ma'am," I said with a nod. I had no doubt she meant it.

She seemed satisfied, and stepped out of the way. Brooke got up and put her bag over her shoulder.

"Let's go," I said, keeping my voice gentle. I looked at Betty Jean. "Thanks for helping her."

She just nodded.

I led Brooke outside to my car. She got in the passenger's side and Charlie got in the back, behind me, like he was giving her space.

"Who did this to you?" I asked.

She didn't look at me. "Guy I'm staying with."

"We should call the police," I said.

"No," she said, fear and desperation in her voice. "Please don't."

Tears glistened in her eyes. I wanted to wrap my arms around her—hold her and tell her everything was going to be okay. Which was crazy. I barely knew this girl. But god, the urge was so strong.

"Okay, no cops for now," I said.

She nodded and gingerly touched her lip.

Charlie hadn't said anything, but I knew he was going to think I was nuts. Or stupid. But I didn't care. I punched the address to our hotel into my phone.

"Brooke, this is Charlie," I said, nodding toward him. "He came out from Iowa with me. We're staying at a hotel not far from here. I'm going to take you there for now, okay?"

She nodded again.

We drove to the hotel in silence. I wanted to know what had happened—who had hurt her. Whoever he was, I wanted to break his face. Make him look ten times worse than Brooke. Fucking coward.

Brooke kept her arms wrapped around herself, her face turned away from me. She had her bag on her lap; she'd had it with her earlier too. We pulled up in front of the hotel and I found a parking spot.

The three of us went to the room. Charlie and I waited while Brooke disappeared into the bathroom.

"What are we going to do?" Charlie asked, his voice low.

"I don't know." I sat down on the edge of one of the beds.

"Bro, you don't know anything about this girl," he said. "And she looks like a fucking mess. You have no idea what you're getting involved in."

"I know."

"Okay, so why are we not calling the police and letting them handle it?" he asked.

"Look, I just wanted to get her somewhere safe," I said. "When she comes out, we'll figure out what to do."

"Yeah, okay," he said.

The bathroom door opened and we looked up. Brooke

came out looking marginally better. She was still wearing the cut-off shorts I'd seen her in earlier, but now she had a shirt with long, wide sleeves and tiny flowers embroidered down the front. She'd cleaned the dried blood off her lip, but her bruises stood out, purpling red against her skin.

"She should put some ice on that," Charlie said. He got up, grabbed the ice bucket, and left.

"I'm sorry to do this to you," Brooke said. "You don't even know me."

"I told you, it's okay," I said. "I wouldn't have given you my number if I hadn't meant it. I'm glad you had someone to call."

She nodded.

"Are you hurt anywhere else?" I asked.

She pushed up the sleeves of her shirt, revealing dark red splotches on her wrists and forearms. "Here, too. But that's all."

"Who did this?" I asked. "Your boyfriend?"

"He's not really my boyfriend," she said. "I guess he thinks so."

"Will you tell me what happened?"

She pulled her sleeves down and sank onto the bed beside me. "I've been crashing at his place for a while. After I saw you earlier, I went home. When he came back a couple of hours later, he kind of freaked out on me."

"Why?"

"I told him no."

Rage swirled in my gut, but I kept a lid on it. This wasn't her fault, and I didn't want to scare her by getting angry. "We should call the police."

"No," she said. "I don't want to deal with the cops."

"Why not?" I asked. "He assaulted you."

She stood. "Back off."

"Hey, I'm just trying to help."

"Jesus," she said, rolling her eyes, her demeanor suddenly defensive. "I took some stuff earlier that's not exactly legal and I'd rather not get arrested for it, okay?"

"What did you take?" I knew she'd probably been drinking. She smelled faintly of alcohol. But I needed to know what else I was getting into here.

"Just some Xanax," she said. "It's not a big deal. But I didn't get them from a pharmacy, you know? And after the last few weeks I've had, it would be just my luck and I'd get busted."

"You do that often?" I asked.

"No," she said. "Just once in a while."

"But you drink a lot?"

"Why are you asking me about this? It's none of your business."

"Maybe it's time someone made it their business," I said.

"I have to go." She grabbed her bag and made for the door. "I shouldn't have called you."

I stood. "Brooke."

She stopped in front of the door.

"Do you have a place to go?" I asked, knowing she probably didn't. There was a reason she'd called a perfect stranger, and it wasn't because she had a lot of options. "I'll take you if you do."

She didn't answer.

"What about the Harpers? Should I call them?"

"No," she said, whirling around. "Please don't. I can't let them see me like this."

The pain and desperation in her eyes cut through me. The desire to hold her was almost more than I could resist. "Only if you stay. If you leave, I'll call them. And the police."

Charlie came back in with the ice and handed me the bucket. "If you've got this, I could use a shower.

"Yeah, thanks, man." I grabbed a towel and wrapped some ice in it.

He nodded, and after a quick glance at Brooke, he went into the bathroom.

Brooke put her bag down and sat on the edge of the bed. Carefully, I held the ice up to her face. She put her hand over it and took a shuddering breath.

"I'm sorry, Sebastian," she said. "I'm really screwed up. I should go and get out of your way. You don't want my mess in your life."

"Don't worry about that right now," I said. "When was the last time you ate?"

"What?" she asked, glancing at me. "I don't know."

"Here's what we'll do," I said. "I'll go get some food. You eat something, drink some water, and flush that shit out of your system. You can stay here tonight—sleep everything off. Charlie and I won't mess with you. You'll be safe here."

"I can't ask you to do that."

"You didn't. I offered," I said. "We'll figure out what to do next in the morning, okay?"

She nodded. "Okay."

I got up, satisfied that we had a plan. "I'll be right back. Don't take off."

"I won't," she said, her voice quiet. "I don't have anywhere else to go."

God, it hurt to hear her say that. What had happened to this girl?

"I'll see you in a few." I opened the door.

"Sebastian?"

I looked at her over my shoulder. Even with bruises and tangled hair, she was so fucking beautiful. Her eyes did something to me. Her voice spoke to a place deep in my soul. I couldn't explain it. But it made me think I should find a place to drop her off as soon as possible and get my ass back to Iowa. This girl was dangerous.

"Yeah?"

"Thank you."

I just nodded and left to get her some dinner.

18

BROOKE

*A*fter bringing us all dinner, Sebastian sat with me and ate. Made sure I drank a huge bottle of water. I was going to have to pee at least half a dozen times tonight after so much liquid. But he was probably right—I needed it. I already felt a little better.

Charlie cast wary glances my way, but he didn't say much. After we finished eating, the guys cleaned up. They gave me one of the two beds, and shared the other one. I tried to tell them I'd sleep on the floor, but they both looked at me like I was nuts for even suggesting it.

My face throbbed where Jared had hit me, but the ice had helped. A little, at least. I scooted back on the bed and laid down, resting my head on the pillow.

Meeting Sebastian earlier had left me reeling. I'd gone back to the house and downed some Xanax that I'd bought off a guy recently. I hadn't lied to Sebastian about the drugs. I didn't take shit like that very often. I didn't want to turn out like my mother.

But Sebastian had ripped me open, leaving my grief raw

and exposed. I'd needed to be numb again. I couldn't cope with all those emotions.

I'd expected Jared to be gone all night, so I'd chased the pills with a few shots of cheap whiskey. All I'd cared about was dulling the pain that threatened to break me. But their drummer and bassist had both come down with food poisoning, so they'd canceled their gig and come home.

While two of the guys took turns puking in the bathroom, Jared had wanted to spend his evening fucking me.

I'd slept with him before. Why had today been any different? I'd been pretty wasted, so it shouldn't have been a big deal. But I hadn't been able to do it. I'd taken one look at him and realized I'd never sleep with him again.

All I'd been able to think about was Sebastian.

Why, I had no idea. Sebastian wasn't anyone to me. He'd seemed like a nice enough guy, but I had no responsibility to him. Meeting him shouldn't have changed anything.

But it had. Meeting him had changed everything.

Jared had been pissed when I'd said no. He'd accused me of cheating. I'd pointed out we weren't exclusive, considering he slept with other girls whenever he wanted. That had only made him more angry, and he'd hit me.

I'd been hit before. But being smacked by my mom was nothing compared to being punched by a grown man. He'd hit me so hard, I'd spun with the impact and wound up on the floor. The pain had been shocking, making me gasp for breath.

The next few minutes were a haze. We'd struggled. Hands had gripped my arms. At some point he'd hit me again. Smashed my phone. Snarled at me, his breath thick with the stench of cheap booze.

He'd been trying to wrestle me to the floor when I'd managed to knee him in the groin. I'd grabbed what I could of my things and left while he lay on the ground, clutching his nuts. Snarling, saying he was going to kill me.

I believed him.

My only thought had been to get away—and make sure Jared didn't follow. So I'd taken a bus across town, all the while trying to keep my head down so no one would notice my face. The bus driver might have, but he hadn't said anything. I'd gone to the only place I could think to go. Sunrise Diner.

A few customers had been leaving when I'd walked in, but they hadn't really looked at me. Betty Jean had freaked. She'd tried to get me to call the cops, but in the end, I'd convinced her to just let me use her phone. Told her I had someone to call who would help.

Maybe I should have called the police. What were the chances they'd do a drug test on a woman who'd just been assaulted? And even if they had, it was just some Xanax. But I hadn't exactly been in a rational frame of mind. I'd been terrified, and still fuzzy from the pills and whiskey. And the last thing I needed was to find out that rock bottom included drug charges.

I'd still had Sebastian's number on that folded piece of paper in my pocket. So I'd called.

It was crazy. I'd met him once, for maybe twenty minutes, and he was who I turned to in a crisis?

Granted, without my phone—and half wasted—I didn't know anyone else's number. Not even Mary's. It had been an act of desperation.

I lay there in the hotel room, staring at the ceiling. Sebastian and Charlie watched TV for a while, but eventually turned it off and went to sleep. I listened to them breathing. Sebastian was on the side next to my bed, sleeping on his back with one arm above his head.

I didn't mean to stare, but all I could think about was how I'd felt when I'd heard his voice on the phone. What it had been like to watch him walk into the diner.

He was so big, his presence had filled the restaurant. I'd been relieved to see him—calmer as soon as he'd walked in the door. This guy barely knew me, and he'd dropped whatever he'd been doing to come pick up some random girl. I wasn't sure what to think about that.

But now, I was so damn tired. Despite the way my face hurt, I could feel myself falling asleep. The bed was comfortable. I pulled up the covers and let my eyes close. With a full stomach and an odd sense of peace, I let unconsciousness take me.

WHEN I WOKE up in the morning, my head was clear. My face hurt, but that was to be expected.

Sebastian and Charlie were still asleep in the bed next to me. I sat up and had to stifle a laugh. Two big, muscular men crammed together on the same bed. They were kind of adorable.

I got up quietly so I wouldn't wake them and went into the bathroom. I was afraid to look in the mirror, but it wasn't as bad as I'd feared. Granted, I looked awful. My lip was swollen and I had purple bruising beneath my eye. But it could have been worse.

I took a shower and got dressed. Thankfully I had a change of clothes in my bag. I set it down next to me on the bed and carefully unzipped one of the pockets. Peeked inside. It was where I kept the photo of me and Liam at the Valentine's Day dance, and the box with my engagement ring. I couldn't look for very long, but I had to know they were still there. Had to know they were safe.

By the time I came out, Sebastian and Charlie were up. Charlie was as big as Sebastian. His hair was lighter and his eyes blue, rather than that mesmerizing mix of green and brown. But they were both so tall, and thickly muscled. Sebastian had said he'd been a wrestler. Charlie must have been, too.

Sebastian smiled at me. "Morning. Feeling any better?"

"Yeah," I said, trying not to let his smile get under my skin. But it prickled my insides. "The bed was comfortable."

Charlie snorted. "At least someone was comfortable last night."

"I slept fine," Sebastian said.

"That's because you're a fucking blanket hog," Charlie said.

Sebastian just chuckled. He stepped close and touched my chin with gentle fingers. He tipped my face to one side, then the other, his eyes intense and scrutinizing.

I held my breath, torn between wanting to pull away from his touch, and melting at the warmth of his fingers on my skin.

"God, this pisses me off." He let go. "Sorry, Brooke. I really want to kill the fucker who did this to you."

"Yeah me too," I said.

Sebastian glanced at Charlie, then back at me. "I think you need to go to the police this morning. He shouldn't get away with this."

I stepped backward. Going to the police opened such a can of worms. What if it made the news, and the Harpers found out? Or I reported it, but Jared went free? He'd already said he'd kill me. This would only make things worse.

And where was I going to live now?

"I don't know," I said.

Sebastian put a hand on my arm. "I'll go with you, okay? You don't have to do it alone. But this isn't right. Have you looked at your face? Let's just go talk to them and see what they say."

I still wasn't sure if this was a good idea, but I agreed.

Sebastian drove me to the nearest police station. He came in with me, but when the woman at the front asked what we needed, I hesitated, looking to him.

"Go ahead," he said. "You've got this."

"I need to report an assault," I said, surprised that my voice came out so clear.

The officer was businesslike, but compassionate. Sebastian sat quietly next to me while I explained to her what had happened. She asked questions, took some pictures, and got Jared's name and address. When she asked for my contact information, I wasn't sure what to say. My phone was broken, and at this point, I was basically homeless.

"Can I give you my number for now?" Sebastian asked.

"And you are?" the officer asked.

"Sebastian McKinney," he said. "I'm Brooke's friend."

"All right," she said, and took down Sebastian's number. "We'll be in touch soon."

"Thanks for your time," I said.

Sebastian touched me gently on the back as we walked out of the police station. It was comforting. I'd wanted him to answer all the questions, even though he hadn't been there. But he'd been quiet until the end, only nodding encouragement when I'd looked at him. His silent presence had helped, as did his light touch on my back, guiding me to his car. I was shaky, and part of me wanted to fall apart. To cry, and drink too much, and go to bed. Get numb and sleep it all away.

But I took a deep breath as I got into his car, and held the pieces of myself together. For now, anyway.

"Breakfast?" he asked when he got in next to me.

Was it simply hunger that rumbled in my stomach? I so rarely had an appetite. But I felt cleaner than I had in a long time—more normal. Maybe I did want a good breakfast.

"That sounds good," I said.

"Great. Let's go get Charlie. Even if he had breakfast already, he can always eat."

We picked up Charlie and they checked out of their hotel. There was a restaurant that served breakfast nearby, so we went in. Sebastian and Charlie proceeded to order more food than I could eat in a week. Eggs, hash browns, pancakes, bacon, French toast, sausage. It was like they were trying to one-up each other. I opted for scrambled eggs and toast. I still felt a little wobbly, and I wasn't sure what my stomach would be able to handle.

"So, when are we heading out?" Charlie asked in between bites of food.

They both sat across from me, like they were trying to give me space, the two of them crammed into one side of the booth. Sebastian stopped eating and his eyes rested on me.

I tried not to squirm beneath his scrutiny, but it was difficult. His eyes were so intense. Was he trying to figure out what to do with me? Where to take me? I didn't know the answer to that, so how could he? I had nowhere to go.

"Seb?" Charlie asked. "Simple question, man. Just wondering what the plan is."

"Come with us," Sebastian said to me.

"What?" I asked, trying not to fidget beneath the heat of his gaze. But it was as if he could see straight through me.

"Come to Iowa," he said, his eyes never leaving mine.

"Um, Seb, can I talk to you outside for a minute?" Charlie asked.

"No," Sebastian said. He still didn't look away from me. "I know what you'll say. You'll tell me this is crazy and it's a terrible idea. And you'll ask me if I've thought this through. But I agree with you. It *is* crazy, and maybe it's a terrible idea. I don't know, I haven't thought it through."

"That's not very convincing," Charlie said.

"Brooke, think about it," Sebastian said, apparently ignoring his friend. "We both know you can't go back to the guy who hurt you."

"No, but..." I trailed off, unsure of what to say.

Charlie looked between me and Sebastian, his eyebrows raised. "This is messed up, Seb. No offense, Brooke."

"You could have a fresh start in Iowa," Sebastian said. "Charlie and I would be there to help you get settled. Give it a shot, and if you hate it, I'll drive you back to Phoenix myself."

I couldn't actually be considering this. I couldn't just take off with two guys I'd met yesterday, and move halfway across the country. They were practically strangers. How did I know I could trust them?

But I did. And as much as it terrified me to admit it, I didn't want Sebastian to go. The thought of him leaving hurt in ways it shouldn't. And that right there should have been reason enough to say no. To say goodbye.

Sebastian was dangerous. Not like Jared. Sebastian wasn't going to hurt me physically. But his very existence threatened to rip down my walls and strip me bare. It would only be a matter of time. And I wasn't sure that was something I could survive.

"Okay," I heard myself say. It was almost as if someone

else was speaking. "I'll go."

Sebastian's smile lit up his face and made my stomach tingle. "Awesome. This is great. What about all your stuff?"

"Oh, I don't have much of anything," I said. "I sold my furniture when I had to move. I have some stuff at Jared's, but honestly I'd rather leave it. It's mostly just clothes, and I don't want to go back there." I had everything that meant something to me in my bag.

"That makes it easy," Sebastian said. "Although I'd love to pay a visit to that piece of shit."

"I actually agree with you there," Charlie said. "But are we sure about this?"

"Yeah," Sebastian said. "It's not like I'm kidnapping her. She wants to come."

"That's not what I mean," he said. "Can we talk outside, or are you really going to make me do this in front of her?"

Sebastian didn't answer, just raised his eyebrows at Charlie.

"Fucking balls," Charlie muttered. "Fine. Brooke, I swear I'm not hating on you right now, but Seb, are you nuts? She's... well, obviously she has some issues. And you just met her. And she's... you know." His eyes moved meaningfully to Sebastian's chest.

"Yeah, I know," Sebastian said. He looked at me again. "If you want to do this, I'm in."

I had a feeling that when Sebastian went in on something, he went all in. There was no reluctance or hesitation in him. Just a burning intensity that called to me—drew me in and made me want to get closer.

I took a deep breath, like I was about to jump into cold water. "Yes. I want to do this."

He smiled again and I melted a little. "Okay. Let's get going. We have a long drive ahead of us."

19

SEBASTIAN

The drive back to Iowa took two days. Charlie and I traded off driving, and Brooke even took a couple of turns. It went by fast with the three of us. We stopped at a motel for a night and got on the road early the next morning.

We'd been driving for several hours when I got a call from the Phoenix police department. They'd picked up Jared. Turned out he had outstanding warrants in four different counties, plus two prior DUIs. The county prosecutor wouldn't even have to work very hard to put that guy away.

Brooke spoke with the officer and said she was in the process of moving. He said it wouldn't be a problem. It was unlikely they'd need her to testify. The other charges Jared was facing were more than enough to get him locked up for a long time, and they had the evidence they needed from her assault. But they'd get in touch if anything changed.

I was just glad to be getting her away from that bastard, whether he went to jail or not. Every mile of pavement that passed beneath the tires made me feel better.

Brooke spent a lot of time staring out the window. I wondered what she was thinking. Was she nervous? Questioning whether she'd made the right decision? Or maybe she was just watching all the wheat and corn fields. She said she'd never seen so much corn before. But that was the Midwest for you.

We rolled into Iowa City late Monday night. Charlie was snoring in the backseat when I pulled into our driveway.

Brooke glanced over her shoulder, then looked at me. The corners of her mouth turned up.

Holy shit. She smiled.

I grinned at her. "He's a loud sleeper. I feel sorry for his future wife."

We got out of the car and Charlie stumbled out behind us. I grabbed my bag—Brooke had hers—and led her inside.

Charlie and I lived in an old house his grandparents owned not far from the university. It was two stories with a covered porch and wood floors that creaked, especially when the weather was changing. A huge maple tree in the front yard dumped leaves all over everything in the fall.

Brooke hesitated in the front room, holding her bag on her shoulder.

"We have an extra bedroom upstairs," I said. "There's not much in there, but it has a bed. No one's used it in a while."

"Thank you," she said. "I can sleep wherever, so that's great."

Charlie hoisted his bag over his shoulder and headed for the stairs. "I'm going to bed." He paused and glanced at Brooke. "Don't murder us in our sleep or anything, okay?"

"Wasn't planning on it," she said.

Charlie trudged up the stairs and we followed. I showed Brooke to the extra room and made sure she had everything she needed. She assured me she was fine, so I left her to it and went to my room.

Although it was late, I sent a text to my mom, letting her know I was home. I wasn't sure how I was going to explain Brooke. How do you tell your parents you had brought home the girl who'd been engaged to your organ donor? That was going to be an interesting conversation.

I was well aware of how crazy this was. I could have called Mrs. Harper. Even though Brooke hadn't wanted me to, they would have helped her. I could have left her with people who clearly cared about her, and gone home.

There were so many reasons I should have done just that, not the least of which was the fact that she'd been engaged to Liam Harper. Plus, she clearly had problems. I didn't know if she was a drug addict or alcoholic. Whether the guy who'd beat her up was some psycho who'd come looking for her if he got out of jail. She'd said she'd been staying with him temporarily, but why? And she'd left town on almost a moment's notice. She'd borrowed my phone to make a couple of calls before we'd left—one had been to the lady from the diner—but that was it. What kind of person could just take off? What did that say about her?

I'd thought about all those things before I'd asked her to come with me. I'd thought about them again, over and over, on the long drive. And even though they were all true, I still didn't regret bringing her here.

That part, I couldn't explain. Just like I couldn't explain how I'd known it was her when I saw her for the first time. Or why I'd insisted on giving her my number.

What I did know was how I felt when I looked at her. I wanted her here. I couldn't walk away.

Which was, of course, fucking insane. But I guess I'd

decided to embrace the insanity. I'd told her I was in, and that was the truth.

It was good to be home and back in my own bed, so I put aside my worries for the night and went to sleep.

The next morning, I came downstairs to find Brooke in the kitchen, cooking. Her hair was up, looking a little messy and careless, and she was dressed in a sleeveless crocheted sweater over a white tank top. Her shorts showed off her legs, and her feet were bare.

I really needed to stop looking at her legs.

"Hi," she said. "I hope you don't mind me using your kitchen, but I thought you might want breakfast. You guys have a waffle iron, and I make pretty good waffles."

"Thanks," I said. "You definitely know the way to Charlie's heart."

She gave me a small smile and brought two plates of waffles to the table. I got out a bottle of syrup and forks.

"Do I smell food?" Charlie came into the kitchen, rubbing his eyes. His hair stuck up at a weird angle.

"See?" I said.

"Um, yeah, I made waffles." Brooke put two more on a plate, then handed it to Charlie.

"Thanks," he said.

We all sat at the kitchen table to eat. Brooke was right, she did make good waffles.

"I didn't poison them," Brooke said, looking at Charlie.

He hadn't taken a bite yet. "That's not what I was thinking."

Brooke just smiled. Her bruises still showed, although the ones on her arms were getting lighter. Her black eye had faded to a dull purple. It would probably be gone in a few more days.

We ate in silence for a while. Charlie inhaled his food,

then helped himself to two more from the stack Brooke had left on the counter.

Her plate was only half empty, but she put her fork down. "I haven't done a very good job of thanking you guys for what you've done for me. Waffles don't mean very much, but I want you to know I'm really grateful that you came when I called you."

"Actually, these waffles are really fucking good, Brooke," Charlie said.

"Thanks," she said.

"I'm glad we could help," I said.

"Well, if I'm really doing this, I need to get my act together," she said. "I'll get a job and find a place to live. I don't want to be in your way any longer than necessary."

"It's really no big deal," I said. "But you can use my laptop to look for jobs, and we'll help you get around if you need a ride."

"I can probably help with the place to live part," Charlie said. "My grandparents own this house, and they own a few more. They rent them out. I don't think my gramps will rent to someone who's unemployed, so you'll need a job first. But they have a rental that's not far from here. You know the one, Seb, the little red house. It's been empty for a couple of weeks while they're doing some maintenance on it. If I put in a good word, I'm sure they'll rent it to you."

"Wow, that would be amazing," Brooke said. "Thank you so much."

I met Charlie's eyes and nodded. He shrugged and went back to his waffles.

"I have so much to do, I feel like I need to make a list or something," Brooke said. "This whole *starting over* thing is a little overwhelming."

"Here, let me get you something." I got up and rooted

around a couple of drawers until I found what I was looking for. I took the small spiral notebook to the table and handed it to Brooke. "I usually keep these around, for school and stuff. I don't think this one's been used."

She stared at it, flipping through the pages of the little green notebook. The paper swished through her fingers. "Thank you."

"Pretty neat invention," Charlie said. "You know, paper held together in a little book. You can even write on it."

"Shut up, smartass," I said.

Brooke shook her head at Charlie. "No, it's just... never mind."

Someone knocked on the door and I looked at Charlie. "Is Kimmie coming over?"

"I don't think so," he said.

"I'll get it, then."

I got up and opened the door to find my mom standing on the other side.

"Oh, Mom, hi," I said. What was she doing here? "I didn't know you were coming. And so early."

"Hi, honey," she said, stepping inside. She hugged me and I patted her on the back. "I thought for sure I replied to your text and said I'd be stopping by. I had to be in Iowa City this morning for an appointment."

"Um, I don't think so," I said. But that wasn't surprising. My mom was notoriously terrible at texting. Half the time she didn't read them until days later, and when she did, she often forgot to reply.

"Hmm. Well, I wanted to come over and see how you're doing. I figured I'd get here first thing so I didn't miss you. How was your trip?" She headed for the kitchen, clearly expecting me to follow.

Oh, boy. This was going to be interesting.

"My trip was good."

"Good morning, Charlie. Oh—" She stopped in the doorway to the kitchen. Charlie and Brooke looked up from their breakfast. Brooke's eyebrows rose and she shifted in her chair. An amused smile crossed Charlie's face and he folded his arms. I glared at him. *Dick.*

My mom was kind of old-fashioned, so finding a girl having breakfast with us—implying she'd slept here— would bother her even if she knew the girl. And here she was, faced with Brooke—a woman she didn't know, with a black eye and visible bruises—sitting at our kitchen table.

"Mom, this is Brooke," I said. "Brooke, my mom, Lorraine McKinney."

Mom's eyes darted around between the three of us a few times. I think she was trying to figure out if Brooke was here with me, or Charlie.

"Nice to meet you," Mom said.

"Hi, Mrs. McKinney," Brooke said. "It's nice to meet you too."

Points to Brooke for calling my mom *Mrs. McKinney.* My parents were both big on formality.

Charlie's grin widened. "Morning, Mrs. McKinney. Brooke, here, is from Phoenix."

I glared harder at Charlie. *Fucker.*

"From Phoenix?" Mom asked. "Are you here for a visit, Brooke?"

Brooke started to answer, but I cut in. "Not exactly, Mom. Can I speak to you out here for a minute?"

I led my mom out to the covered porch and shut the door behind us.

"Sebastian, what on God's green earth is going on?" she asked.

"I met Brooke in Phoenix," I said.

"Yes, we've established that," she said. "What is she doing in your house?"

"I'm just giving her a place to stay until she gets settled," I said. "She needed a fresh start, so I offered to bring her out here. That's all. She slept in our extra bedroom last night."

"Sebastian, don't be vulgar," she said, as if the mere mention of where she slept was somehow a sexual reference. "You were only out of town for a few days. How did you meet her?"

"She..." I trailed off, because I knew this was going to freak her out. "She was Liam Harper's fiancée before he died."

"You mean... the man who..."

"Yes, Mom," I said. "The organ donor who saved my life."

"You brought his fiancée back with you?" she asked, her voice rising. "What were you thinking?"

"Look, it's a long story," I said. "She needed some help, and this felt like the right thing to do."

"I'll say she needs help," Mom said. "She has a black eye, Sebastian."

"Yes, I know."

Mom's brow furrowed, her worry lines creasing. "Honey, this is reckless. You can't just bring some strange girl home with you. Especially *that* girl."

The way she was talking about Brooke made my hackles rise. I didn't like it. But I was also raised to never be rude to my mother, and I didn't want her to worry. I'd already given her enough worry for a lifetime.

"I know. I get it. This is a weird situation. But you always taught me to be willing to help other people if I could. Brooke has been through a lot. She just needs a chance."

She took a deep breath. "Be careful. I don't want anything bad happening to you."

"I know, Mom. I'll be careful. I always am."

"I suppose I should go," she said, although I could hear the reluctance in her voice. "I have my appointment to get to. But come home for dinner soon and tell us about your trip. The rest of it, I mean."

"Yeah, I will."

Mom and I said our goodbyes, and I went back into the kitchen.

"That was awesome," Charlie said with a laugh.

"Thanks for that, asshole," I said.

"Come on, man," Charlie said. "You can't expect me not to make things awkward. It's what I do."

"You're a dick."

"I'm sorry," Brooke said. "Is your mom upset that I'm here?"

"No, she's fine," I said. "You just took her by surprise. And she worries a lot."

"And there's also the fact that this whole thing is insane," Charlie said. "Even if Brooke does make good waffles."

"You're right," Brooke said with a shrug. "Coming here with you guys was nuts."

"At least you admit it," Charlie said. He pointed to me. "And you. *Come to Iowa with us?* Who does that?"

"Yeah, well, maybe it is crazy, but we're here now." I turned to Brooke. "I'll grab you my laptop and then I'm going to hit the shower. I'm free all day, so let me know what you need and we'll make it happen."

"Thank you," Brooke said.

"I should get moving too," Charlie said. "I guess I need to go see Kimmie."

"Have fun with that," I said.

Charlie grunted as he got up from the table, then went upstairs.

"You good for now?" I asked.

Brooke met my eyes. God, she was beautiful. I needed to be careful with her. I was going to get myself into trouble.

"Yeah," she said. "I'm good now."

20

BROOKE

*I*n the beginning, Iowa was good for me.

Moving here had been impulsive. Maybe even reckless. But I hadn't had anything to lose. Starting over, and putting some distance between me and Phoenix, seemed to wake me up. A little bit, at least. I'd been in Iowa for two months and felt better than I had in a while.

I glanced out the window of the bookstore as I finished the new display. The blue sky was deceptive. It was beautiful outside, but not nearly as warm as it appeared. I tugged the sleeves of my sweater over my hands and hugged my arms around myself. Joe, my boss, was baffled at how I could be so cold all the time, even on a sunny day. But I'd grown up in the Southwest where the weather was warm—if not stifling hot—most of the year. As far as I was concerned, the seventy-degree June weather was barely warm.

I'd found my job at Booklover's Corner my first week in town. Joe had hired me without so much as an interview. Just took my application, asked me a few questions about my availability, and gave me the job on the spot. Maybe it was serendipitous. It had avoided the need for me to answer awkward questions about my employment history. But mostly Joe was distracted and a little scatterbrained. And I think he was tired of hiring college students and having to work around their schedules. He was about sixty, with a thick white mustache and wire-rimmed glasses that constantly slipped down his nose. He tended to be distant, but he was a decent boss. He was easygoing, and he'd given me a break when I'd come in late a few times.

I was trying—hard—to hold it together and not screw this up. But some days, just getting out of bed still felt impossible. The ache in my chest left me feeling hollow, and that same sense of apathy would overtake me. I knew if I didn't get up, I'd probably lose my job. But would it matter? Did I care?

On days like that, I'd force myself out of bed. Make myself go through the motions of living. And most of the time, I'd be glad that I had.

Charlie had made good on his offer to help me find a place to live. His grandparents' rental house was a short walk from where he lived with Sebastian. It was small, but I didn't need much space, and the whole interior had been freshly painted. I'd been slowly adding things as I could afford them. A bed. A couch. Kitchen stuff. Charlie's grandma had given me an old table and chairs. Sebastian had helped me repaint them, and now they looked great.

Sebastian. It was disconcerting how often he was on my mind. I saw him, and Charlie, frequently. The three of us had become good friends. Charlie still joked about me being a crazy person who was plotting their murders, but jokes and insults were how Charlie showed affection. He did it to Seb all the time, and those two had the cutest bromance I'd ever seen.

But whereas my friendship with Charlie was laid-back

and fun, my relationship with Sebastian was something else entirely.

Sebastian was unlike anyone I'd ever met. He was so serious. Not that he didn't smile or laugh—he did. But he had an intensity that smoldered beneath the surface. I could feel it radiating from him whenever he was near. His presence did strange things to me—stirred up emotions I barely recognized.

I didn't know what to do with all those feelings.

We didn't have any customers, so I wandered into the back and sat down at a little table surrounded by half-empty boxes. I opened my spiral notebook—the same one Sebastian had given me on my first morning in Iowa. The first page still had the list I'd made—things I needed to do to start over. I'd checked them off, one by one. And for a while, I hadn't written anything else. The rest of the pages had remained blank.

There had been a time when I'd never been without a notebook. I'd gone through dozens of them. In high school, it had been a way to pass the time. Something to focus on so people wouldn't notice me. A place to put all the thoughts I'd been afraid to share.

When I'd been with Liam, I hadn't felt stifled by my life anymore. But I'd still filled notebooks with words. Poems. Lyrics. It had been such a part of who I was, even when the words were happy ones, they'd still found a home on those lined pages.

Not after he died.

I'd stopped writing things down. It had felt like I no longer had anything to say. The once-constant stream of words had dried up. Gone silent.

There were words in this notebook. Halting phrases. Half-finished thoughts. Eraser marks and parts crossed out or scribbled over. Some pages had more doodles than words. But they were there.

Too many of my words were about Sebastian.

I never wrote his name. But I'd be lying to myself if I said what I wrote wasn't about him. I felt like I should be writing about Liam. Remembering him, or processing my grief. But my mind always went back to Sebastian. To the way he filled up the space wherever he was. To the color of his eyes. To the way my heart beat a little harder every time he was near.

So I let the words come as they would, feeling guilty all the while.

The bell above the front door tinkled, a soft sound that could barely be heard in the back room. Joe had gone home, leaving me to close up. I shut my notebook and went to see if the customer needed help.

Sebastian stood near the front, looking at a shelf of mysteries. He tilted his head to one side, like he was reading the titles on the spines. I paused and watched him, a little flutter tickling inside my chest. The sleeves on his University of Iowa t-shirt looked like they might burst open beneath the muscles of his arms. He rubbed his chin, his fingers sliding through his thick beard. I'd never been into facial hair on men, but on him? God.

He was gorgeous. There was no way around it. He was one of the most beautiful men I'd ever seen, with his thick dark hair, sexy beard, and captivating eyes. His body that exuded so much strength and power. There was a tension inside of him, like he was constantly holding something back. Like there was a fire within that he kept carefully controlled.

His fire made the spark inside of me want to jump to life. To burn. But I was afraid it would turn me to ash and I'd blow away in the wind.

As if they were compelled by some outside force, my eyes drifted to his chest. I swallowed back the rise of emotion I always felt when I thought about who he really was. About the heart that lived inside of him.

"Hey," I said. The air was warm, but I hugged my sweater around myself. "What are you doing here?"

"I had to meet with one of my professors," he said. "Since I was nearby, I thought I'd see if you were getting off soon. Maybe walk home with you."

I got around fine without a car, so I hadn't bothered with the expense of buying one. Sebastian drove, but I'd noticed he walked places a lot, even when he didn't need to.

"Yeah, we close in about ten minutes," I said.

"I can wait."

I finished up the last few things I needed to do while Sebastian wandered through the store. Being alone with him like this left me feeling off-balance. Conflicted. Even when he was hidden behind tall shelves, I could sense him there. It was frightening to admit how much I liked it. How the sight of him picking up books and flipping through their pages—waiting for me—made my breath quicken and my skin prickle.

"Finished," I said.

He shelved the book he'd been looking at and smiled.

I looked away quickly so he wouldn't see the warmth creeping across my cheeks. "I'll just grab my stuff."

I went into the back and slid my notebook into my handbag. Grabbed my coat. I walked out front and Sebastian held my coat while I slipped my arms into the sleeves. He was close enough that I caught a hint of his scent. He always smelled fresh, like clean cotton, with a spicy undertone that wasn't the product of any cologne. It was just him. My body responded to that smell in ways that made me enormously uncomfortable.

But god, he smelled good.

After I turned off the lights, we went outside and I locked the door behind us. I tucked my hands in my coat pockets against the chill in the air. The sun had set, leaving the streets to fade in the dimness of twilight. We walked in silence for a while. Slow. Taking our time, as if we both wanted to draw this out for as long as possible.

Finally, Sebastian broke the silence. "How's work going?"

"It was quiet today, but weekends are busy," I said. "It's a good job."

"Any problems with the house?" he asked.

"No, the house is great," I said.

"Seems like Iowa's treating you pretty well," he said.

"Yeah, I like it here."

He paused for a moment and our pace slowed even more. "Do you?"

I wondered what he was getting at. "Yeah, I do. Why?"

"Just making sure."

"Are you afraid I'll skip town and disappear on you?" I nudged his arm with my elbow.

"Kind of," he said. I'd meant it as a joke, but his tone was serious. "Yeah, I guess I do worry about that."

"I wouldn't do that to you," I said, my voice quiet.

"Have you told the Harpers you left Phoenix?" he asked.

A flash of anger hit me. They weren't any of his business. "Why are you asking me about them?"

"I want to know," he said. "Did you tell them?"

"I don't know why you care."

He stopped and turned to face me. "Because they care

about you. And I want to know if you just walked out on them."

"I've been here for months, and *now* you're worried about this?" I asked.

"Stop avoiding the question," he said.

"Yes, I did. Jesus. I told them I moved, right after I got hired at the bookstore. I texted Mary with my new number."

He held my eyes. I wanted to look away, but when he looked at me like that, I was powerless to resist.

"Okay. Good."

There was relief in his voice. I didn't understand where it was coming from—why he'd brought it up. We'd never really talked about the Harpers before.

I *had* told them. Sebastian had put Mary's number in my phone—a wordless hint that I should contact them. I'd texted her and simply said I'd moved away and was doing fine. She'd replied to ask where, but I hadn't responded. I wasn't sure why I didn't want them to know where I was. Maybe I was waiting to make sure I didn't fail. When I did reply—when I told them where I was and what I'd been doing—I wanted to have something to be proud of. As it was, there were still too many broken pieces of me lying around. Pieces that didn't fit together.

Sebastian didn't say anything else the rest of the walk home. It was so tempting to touch him. I wanted to brush my hand against his or lean closer so our arms touched. But he never touched me. Not even by accident. He had, once or twice, when we'd first met in Phoenix. But now, he always kept a little distance between us. It made me feel like I shouldn't violate it—like he didn't want me to.

He followed me up to my front door and stood next to me while I got out my keys.

"Thanks for walking me home," I said.

"Sure," he said. "Look, I'm not trying to give you a hard time. You just... you keep things to yourself. Sometimes I wonder what's going on in that head of yours."

I lifted my eyes to his. Felt his gravity pulling at me, urging me closer. A wave of heat poured through me. But it wasn't the fire of ruin. It was the tantalizing warmth of hope. Of life. Of creation, and power, and passion. Of all that had once lived inside me that I'd lost.

"Nothing, really," I said, stepping back and tearing my eyes from his. "I'm just doing my thing, you know? I'm fine."

"Okay," he said. What was I hearing in his voice? Skepticism? Disappointment? I couldn't tell. "I'll see you later, then. Goodnight, Brooke."

"Goodnight."

I watched him walk away, feeling suddenly cold and alone. Missing him before he was really gone.

21

SEBASTIAN

The stupidest thing I'd ever done was fall in love with Brooke Summerlin.

There was no point in denying it. In a way, I'd loved her since the first moment I saw her, sitting at that table outside a restaurant in Phoenix. It didn't matter whether it was possible. Whether love at first sight was crazy, or unrealistic. It had happened, and I was trying to figure out how to live with it.

I'd never really loved anyone before. Not even Cami. At the time, I'd thought I was in love with her. But that hadn't been love. It had been comfort and familiarity. Cami was the proverbial girl next door. Our relationship had been what was expected. I'd liked her, and it had hurt when she'd left me. But there hadn't been any heat. No fire, or passion. Things hadn't worked out between us, but someone like her was still the safe choice.

There was nothing safe about Brooke.

She was unpredictable. She might show up randomly at my house with armfuls of groceries and cook an enormous dinner. Insist we go for a drive to get out of the city, and race down the highway at a hundred miles an hour, shouting at the top of her lungs. We might stay up all night so we could sit outside and watch the sky turn pink with the sunrise, even though we both had places to be the next day. She'd sit with me for hours, talking. Telling me stories about her childhood. Listening to mine.

Or she might go dark for days on end. Not answer her phone. Miss work. Twice I'd been worried enough to go check on her. I'd found her at home, looking pale and tired. Both times, she'd chased me off, claiming to be sick. I hadn't believed her.

She was a walking contradiction—so beautifully damaged. Fearless, without a care for her physical safety, yet weighted down by sadness and grief. Spontaneous and impulsive, but still guarded and reserved. I could see fire in her eyes, fierceness in her spirit. But more often than not, it was masked by a pain she'd never talk about with me.

From the first time we'd met, she'd lodged herself deep inside of me. One look in her eyes and I'd seen her truth. She was broken. Ready to give up. That had been me, once. And I'd known, in that moment, that I had to teach her how to live again.

But I didn't love her because of her sadness—or in spite of it. I just loved her. She made me happy. Made me feel alive. Looking at her felt like home.

Loving Brooke was a mistake, but it wasn't because she was unpredictable. It wasn't because I half-expected her to disappear someday. It was because I was in love with a woman who couldn't love me back.

I was the embodiment of everything she'd lost. The heart of her pain lived in me. Literally.

So I held back. We were friends, and I wasn't willing to lose that, even though there were times when it killed me to be near her. I texted her. Spent time with her. Walked her home some nights after work. Checked on her when she seemed to be slipping away. But I kept distance between us so she wouldn't know. So she wouldn't see what she did to me. How much I wanted her.

God, I wanted her.

Charlie saw right through me, but he didn't comment. If he ever did, I'd just remind him of his train-wreck of a relationship with Kimmie. Those two seemed to fight more than they got along. When it came to the wrong woman, both of us were doing a damn good job of fucking ourselves over, just for different reasons.

I grabbed my keys and headed to my car. Charlie was taking Kimmie to the county fair, and he'd roped me into meeting them there. Because apparently I was a glutton for punishment, I'd invited Brooke. I did *not* want to be the third wheel to Charlie and Kimmie. But in reality, I hadn't needed an excuse to ask Brooke to come along. It was blindingly stupid, but I'd take any chance to be with her.

I was really fucked.

When I got to her house to pick her up, she came out looking adorable in a loose gray sweater that hung off one shoulder, the sleeves covering the bracelets she always wore. Her jean shorts were so high they showed off most of her thighs. Gray socks went over her knees and she wore a pair of tall brown boots. She was killing me with that short shorts and tall socks combination. It was sexy as fuck.

"Hey," I said. "Ready for a good old-fashioned country fair?"

"Just tell me they have funnel cake," she said.

"I'm pretty sure they do," I said. "What's with the sweater, though? It's hot out."

"It's like seventy-five," she said. "That's *not* hot. Talk to me when it's a hundred and ten. That's hot."

"Whatever, chilly." *She* was hot, but I wasn't going to say that out loud.

We got in my car and drove out to the fairgrounds. The parking lot wasn't full, so I found a spot not far from the entrance. I texted Charlie to see if he and Kimmie were here. He texted back, saying they were right inside, just past the admission gate.

Kimmie was pretty in a former-Johnson-County-beauty-queen way. Long hair she kept dyed platinum blond. Stylish clothes. Never seen in public without makeup. She reminded me of Cami. Kimmie had been a sorority girl too. Charlie had met her at a party in college. She'd been a wrestling groupie, and they'd hooked up a few times. After Charlie had graduated, he'd run into her again and asked her out. Since then, they'd dated on and off—and fought a lot.

Now was no exception. Brooke and I found the two of them facing off. He stood straight with his arms folded across his big chest. She had her hands on her hips, and by her expression, she was clearly unhappy.

"Again?" Brooke asked.

"Guess so," I said. "Should we wait for them to battle it out, or just walk by?"

"Let's keep going," Brooke said. "They can catch up. Or, you know, not, if Kimmie keeps being a bitch."

I laughed. "Tell me how you really feel."

"Sorry," she said, but she didn't sound sorry. "Charlie is so awesome. I wish he was with someone who actually deserved him."

I felt stupid for the little pang of jealousy that hit me at hearing her call him *awesome*. Brooke and Charlie got along fine, but she'd never acted interested in him.

"Yeah, me too."

We wandered around the fair for a while. It was crowded, but people tended to move out of the way for a big guy like me. I bought Brooke a funnel cake and she shared a few bites with me. It tasted amazing. I so rarely ate food like that. I was always too concerned with keeping my heart healthy. But the worst part wasn't the tempting food. It was watching Brooke lick powdered sugar off her fingers. That gave me a hard-on that was downright uncomfortable.

I needed a distraction, so I led her through the booths to play a few games. She laughed when I lost at a ring toss, then laughed harder when she lost too. The sound of her laughter rang in my ears, carrying above the din of the crowd around us. I loved making her laugh. It was like winning the lottery every single time.

"I know this is ridiculous, but I need some cotton candy," she said when we'd gotten bored of playing carnival games.

"You know that's pure sugar, right?"

"That's the point," she said. "But it's a nostalgia thing. My mom took me to a big fair once. I don't even remember where. Oklahoma, maybe? Anyway, she bought me cotton candy. We had a good time that day."

She almost never talked about her mother, but I'd been able to put the pieces together. She hadn't gone to live with the Harpers as a teenager because she'd had a great home life. And she'd told me a few things. But I always felt like she was skirting around the edges of her story, afraid to tell me the whole truth.

"I can get on board with that," I said, leading her to a booth that sold cotton candy. She offered to pay, but I just looked at her like she was nuts. The lady handed her the bag—it was bright pink—and Brooke smiled.

"Thanks." She pulled off a piece and stuck it in her

mouth. "Oh my god, it tastes exactly like I remember. Want some?"

"I'll pass," I said.

The sun was sinking lower and the carnival lights were coming on. We walked slowly while Brooke picked at her cotton candy. I checked my phone and had a text from Charlie.

Charlie: Sorry to bail. I'm over it with her. Took her home. I'm done. For real this time.

"I think Charlie broke up with Kimmie again." I tucked my phone back in my pocket.

"Really?" Brooke asked. "Do you think it'll stick? Or will he go running back next time she texts for a booty call?"

"I hope it's finally over," I said. "I don't know why he's let it go on this long."

"I don't know either," Brooke said. "Maybe the familiar is easier than the unknown."

"Yeah, very true," I said, but I wasn't going to worry about Charlie too much. He'd figure it out.

I wondered if Brooke would talk more about her mom if I asked. I wanted her to let me in—to know she could trust me.

"So, was the last time you went to a fair like this with your mom?"

"I think so. I must have been eight or nine. It was during one of those rare times when she was single." She paused and put another bit of cotton candy in her mouth. "I, um, I don't know who my dad is, and my mom was almost always with some guy."

She glanced over at me, her eyebrows drawn together, like she was worried. I just smiled.

"Anyway, she... god, I can't even tell this story without getting into all my mom's bullshit." She took a deep breath.

"Okay, I've told you my mom was an addict. She was wasted, like, a lot. But once in a while, she'd go through a short sober period. I don't remember why this one happened. Sometimes it was like she really wanted to try, so maybe that's all it was."

We walked out toward a group of picnic tables and sat.

"Things were always so much better when she was sober," Brooke continued. "She'd take care of me like a normal mom. I didn't have to worry about making her mad all the time. And she'd actually do things with me, like the fair. We went and I just remember walking around and hearing all the noises and seeing all the lights. She must have spent a fortune playing games, trying to win me this pink teddy bear. She did, and I kept that thing for years."

"What happened to it?" I asked.

"I don't know," she said with a shrug. "I guess I outgrew it, and I'm not sure what happened to it after that. Probably lost one of the times we moved." She pulled out another wispy puff of pink and set it on her tongue. "She never bought me treats, but that day I guess she wanted to go all out. Maybe she was spoiling me to make up for all the shitty stuff she did when she was drunk or high. I wanted cotton candy, so she bought me some. She let me have the whole thing all to myself. It felt like such a big deal."

"When was the last time you saw her?" I asked.

"I was seventeen," she said. "She moved and I didn't go with her. She called me a year or so later. Said something about being in Louisiana and I should come live with her again. I said no, and I haven't heard from her since."

I wanted to touch her—hold her hand or caress her cheek—but I didn't. "I'm sorry. That's really shitty."

"It's for the best," she said. "She's my mom, and I'll always love her. But I couldn't save her. I wanted to. For a long time, I wished I could be enough to make her want to get better. I don't know where she is now, but I hope someday she gets the help she needs."

I reached over and pinched a bit of cotton candy between my fingers. It was soft, but gritty. A little bit like Brooke.

"Me too," I said.

She stuck out her pink-stained tongue. "I don't think I can finish this. Do you want the rest?"

"No, I'm good," I said.

"We should go on some rides." Her eyes lit up but her smile faded quickly. "Wait, can you go on rides? Because of... you know."

"Yeah, I can go on rides," I said. "There's actually not much I can't do."

"Really?" she asked. "You can do pretty much anything?"

It felt weird to talk about my heart. We didn't very often. And the way she said *pretty much anything* made me wonder what she really meant. Although I was kidding myself if I thought she meant sex. Obviously she wasn't thinking about that. Even if I was.

"Yeah, I don't have many restrictions," I said. "Mostly things with big pressure changes, like scuba diving. I can't fly in a small plane because of the unpressurized cabin, or go hang gliding. But that's about it."

"Wow," she said. "It seemed like there was more."

"Why?"

"I don't know, you're just always very careful," she said. "That's good, don't get me wrong. I figured it was because the doctors had given you a long list of things that were off limits."

"No, I'm in good health, so I'm free to live how I want for the most part," I said.

"That's good." She gazed at me for a few seconds. What was she thinking? Then she blinked and her smile was back. She looked past me, her eyes focusing on something. "Oh my god. What about that one?"

I looked where she was pointing. It was a huge contraption that looked like a human slingshot. A two-person seat was strung on thick cables between a set of four poles. I watched while a couple got strapped in. The seat bounced and swayed a little as the cables went taut. Then an air horn blew and the seat launched straight up, shooting past the height of the poles. The seat rocked and turned over as it fell. The tension in the cables kept it bouncing up and down, until finally the seat was lowered and the couple stumbled off, laughing and high-fiving each other.

"You want to go on that?" I asked.

"Did you see how fast they flew up?" Brooke asked, her voice filled with awe and excitement. "Have you ever been on it before?"

"I've never even seen it," I said. "It must be new."

"Let's do it," she said.

"I don't know if I should."

"You just said you can do pretty much anything," she said. "It's not like it goes as high as an airplane. Come on, Seb. Live a little."

It was probably stupid for a twenty-four-year-old man to worry about what his mother would think, but that was the first thing that came to my mind. My mom would faint if she found out. But Brooke was right. I was far enough out from my surgery that I had very few restrictions. I *could* go on it.

"Please?" Brooke asked. She bit her lower lip and scrunched her shoulders.

Like I could tell her *no* when she looked at me like that. "Fuck. Okay. Let's do it."

"Yes!"

She grabbed my hand and half-dragged me to the ticket booth. I was having second—and third and fourth—thoughts as we waited our turn. Watching the thing launch again, closer this time, made me wonder what the hell I was doing. How could I knowingly put myself in danger like that?

Before I knew it, I was in the seat, strapping myself in. The over-the-shoulder harness almost didn't fit. It pressed against my chest when it locked into place, but the compression made me feel a little better. I glanced over at Brooke and she grinned.

"Ready?" she asked.

Before I could answer, the horn blared and we shot into the sky. The air whooshed by so hard it made me feel out of breath. Adrenaline coursed through my veins and my heart beat fast. My stomach dropped as we fell and bounced upward again.

But it felt fucking amazing.

For a brief moment, I felt free. Brooke screamed and laughed, and I let the exhilaration wash over me. Embraced the fear. Turned it into excitement.

We soared up and down for a while before they lowered us back onto the platform and the ride attendants helped us out. My legs felt wobbly and Brooke had to lean against me for a few seconds before we walked down the short set of stairs.

Brooke's hair was windswept, her cheeks flushed. I loved it when I got to see this side of her—when the light in her eyes drove out the sadness. I knew it was temporary, so I'd enjoy it while I could.

"Wow, that was intense," she said.

"No shit." I put my hand on my chest and took a deep

breath. I felt fine. Better than fine, actually. I couldn't remember the last time I felt so... alive.

"Are you okay?" she asked.

"Yeah," I said. "That was awesome. I'm great."

She laughed again and we walked up the midway. Shivering, she pulled her sleeves over her hands, clutching the edges with her fingers.

"God, it's getting cold. Are you really not cold?"

I shrugged. "Nope."

She rubbed my arm and squeezed my bicep. "I guess you have all that muscle to keep you warm."

Her touch sent a lightning bolt of electricity straight to my groin. I struggled not to let it show on my face as I stopped and turned toward her. "I guess we should go, if you're getting cold."

"Yeah," she said, her eyes lingering on mine.

People walked past, but the crowd had thinned. Music played from loudspeakers and the rides whirred in the background. The lights reflected in her eyes, making them sparkle like fireworks.

It was the perfect moment for a kiss. We stood there, watching each other, like we both knew it. I wanted to kiss her so badly, I could almost taste the cotton candy on her lips. My heart beat hard and my skin prickled with anticipation.

Her eyes flicked down to my chest.

And there it was, the reminder of who I was to her. Of her pain that lived inside me.

I stepped back and shoved my hands in my pockets. "Okay, chilly. Let's get you home."

22

BROOKE

*S*unlight peeked through the gap in the curtains, creating a slice of brightness across my sheets—right in my eye. I groaned and turned over. My head hurt and the stupid sun was pissing me off.

The last few days had been gray and cloudy—matching my mood. Fall weather. It was September, and I'd been living in Iowa for over five months.

I grabbed my phone to check the time. Eleven. I was going to be late for work if I didn't get up. My entire body felt heavy, like I couldn't lift my limbs. Even rolling over had been hard. I wanted to sink into the softness of my bed, close my eyes, and pretend the world didn't exist.

I'd already missed the last two days of work. Joe would be pissed if I called in sick again, even if he didn't find out I was lying. I wasn't sick. I didn't know what was wrong with me. But I couldn't muster the energy to get up and do anything.

I hadn't felt this lethargic since before I'd moved to Iowa. Even my bad days here hadn't been anything like this. The deadness was eating its way through me again. Seeping into the cracks in my psyche, worming its way through my veins. A parasite, devouring my spirit.

It had started with a crying spell a few days ago. I'd come home and the tears had burst out of nowhere. Shaking with sobs, I'd curled up on the couch and cried until my back was sore and my throat raw. Afterward, I'd dug out a bottle of Vicodin I still had from somewhere. I hadn't taken any pills —hadn't even had a drink—since moving here. But I'd dumped a few into my trembling hand and swallowed them, desperate for anything to make me sleep. To turn off the deluge of pain that had suddenly gripped me.

The next morning, I hadn't felt any better. If anything, I'd been worse. I hadn't cried again. Hadn't even wanted to. But it had taken me four hours just to get out of bed for the first time.

Nothing had happened. I didn't know what had changed to send me spiraling into this decaying orbit. It wasn't an anniversary, or Liam's birthday. I hadn't gotten any surprising or upsetting news. Things had been fine at work. I'd seen Sebastian a few days before. We'd watched a movie with Charlie. Nothing unusual.

But I was back to feeling like a ghost. It had hit me so hard, it was as if all my color and substance had been ripped away, like the siding on a house in a tornado. I was formless. Transparent. Fading into nothing.

I texted Joe to tell him I was still under the weather, and went back to sleep.

It was dark when I woke up. My bladder screamed at me, so I dragged myself out of bed and went to the bathroom. The clock said nine. God, I'd slept all day. I hadn't even taken anything. That was crazy. I probably should have been alarmed, but that required too much energy. I didn't have it in me to care.

I had a text from Joe, saying he hoped I got better soon. But if I was going to be out for a while to let him know so he could hire someone else in the meantime. I wanted to feel bad about that, but I felt nothing. So I'd lose another job. I'd lost a lot of jobs in the last several years. Did it matter?

Another text was from Sebastian, asking if I was busy tonight. He always seemed to know when I was having a tough day and he'd invent reasons to get together. Usually it worked. Tonight, I didn't bother to answer.

I glanced into my open closet—to the bag I'd carried around with me in Phoenix. I'd taken most of my stuff out. The only things left were my treasures. My mementos of Liam.

My rational mind knew that now was not the time to get them out. I wasn't in any state to handle it. But I did it anyway. I pulled out the dance photo and the box with my ring, and brought them over to the bed.

Seated cross-legged among my tangled covers, I stared at the photo. Traced my finger across it. Liam with his cocky teenage smile—the look of a young guy without a care in the world. I had stars in my eyes bigger than the ones in the Hollywood Nights backdrop. That evening had been pure magic.

A few tears slid down my cheeks. They were more painful than the deluge from the other night—hot and dreadful, rolling silently down my cheeks.

How you doing, Bee?

"I'm dead, Liam," I said aloud. I knew he wasn't talking to me, but the memory of his voice still echoed in my mind. "I died too, but I'm stuck here."

There was no answer.

The strange thing was, I wasn't pining for Liam anymore. I missed him, and I probably always would. My love for him had been real, and I'd carry it with me for the rest of my life. But the grief that plagued me now wasn't for him. I didn't understand it. If I could gaze at his picture and know my sorrow for him was no longer drowning me, why was I still so broken?

Suddenly the walls felt too close, the air stifling. I had to get the hell out of this house.

A voice in my head told me to call Sebastian. Tell him I wanted to get together. That would be the smart thing—the safe thing—to do.

Fuck safe.

I needed a rush. Speed. Intoxication. I needed to bury my pain, blur it out. I rooted through my things and found the bottle of Xanax. I took the few that were left, swallowing them without water. I didn't have any booze in the house, so I threw on some clean clothes—a loose floral blouse with wide sleeves and a pair of tight jeans—put my hair up, and left.

Standing outside, I ordered an Uber. The Xanax kicked in while I waited. It had been so long since I'd taken anything, and it hit me hard. My eyes grew heavy, but I embraced the numbness that stole through me. It felt so good. The edges of my mind went smooth and fluid, my thoughts dancing across the surface of my consciousness. Nothing mattered tonight but finding a distraction. Having fun. Making myself feel alive, somehow.

My ride arrived and I got in.

The driver was a young guy wearing a U of I shirt. Skinny, with sandy blond hair. "Where do you need to go?"

"I guess I need to figure that out." I blinked sleepily at him. "I want to go out and have a good time. What do you suggest?"

He shrugged. "Have you been to Deadwood?"

"I don't know," I said. "Is it a good place to party?"

"Yeah," he said as he pulled away from the curb. "It's basically *the* place to party around here."

"Sounds perfect."

I swam in blissful numbness while he drove me to Deadwood. He dropped me off, telling me to have a good time. I waved at him and went inside.

It was the perfect sort of dive bar, with low light, dark red carpet, and a bar top that looked worn and weathered. The place was packed. It looked like a mix of college students and older twenty-somethings. I didn't much care who was in there, as long as I could down some drinks and keep this buzz going all night.

I found an empty stool and ordered a shot of Jack Daniels. To my right, a guy in a John Deere t-shirt and camo pants put the moves on a blonde in a mini-skirt. To my left, a group of about half a dozen guys all took a shot together, then slammed their glasses back on the bar. They were all dressed in plaid flannel, unbuttoned over t-shirts. Most wore worn out baseball caps. Bunch of corn-fed Iowa college boys.

The bartender brought my drink and I downed it in one swallow, then ordered another.

"That was impressive."

It took me a second to realize the guy was talking to me. One of the college boys. He leaned against the bar and grinned.

"What was impressive?" I asked.

"The way you took that shot," he said.

The bartender came back with my second drink. I tossed it back.

"Damn," the guy said. "You're fucking awesome."

"Dude, Joel, stop being a cheese dick," one of the other guys said.

Joel rolled his eyes. "I'm just talking to... what's your name?"

"Brooke."

"I'm just talking to Brooke." He turned back to me. "So what's up tonight? You must be meeting someone."

"Nope."

"You're here alone?" he asked.

"I just came to drink."

"Fuck yes," he said. "Guys, this is Brooke. She's hanging with us tonight."

"No, I'm not—"

My reply was cut off by a round of cheers. These guys were already pretty hammered. But one of them ordered another round of shots, including one for me.

It looked like I had six new best friends for the night.

A few hours later, I was so wasted I barely knew where I was. We were still at Deadwood, all of us packed into a booth. At least, I thought that's where we were. I didn't remember leaving, and I didn't really care. My brain was soaked in Fireball and I'd been telling the best stories. Joel and his buddies had been laughing so hard, they were doubled over, slapping their knees. One guy—I had no idea what his name was—had run off to the bathroom, probably to puke. The rest were holding their liquor.

Joel had his arm slung around my shoulders. There was something about that I didn't like. But it was hard to remember why it mattered. The room spun, and whenever I blinked it took me a little too long to open my eyes again. Voices carried around me, but I wasn't following the conversation anymore.

"You coming, sugar?" Joel said, close to my ear.

"Where we going?"

"For a ride," he said. "Come on."

I got up and left the bar, Joel's arm still around me. My sense of unease grew, but it was taking all my concentration to walk straight. Leaning against him helped, so what was the harm in him holding me up? I'd probably fall if he wasn't there. It was fine.

We walked up the street and I found myself being hoisted into the back of a big pickup truck. My phone rang and I pulled it out, squinting at the name on the screen. Sebastian?

"Hey, Sebby," I said. "What's up, baby?"

"Brooke?" Sebastian said. "Are you okay?"

"I'm so good," I said. "So good."

One of Joel's friends smacked his arm. "Dude, that's probably her boyfriend."

Joel shrugged him off. "Who the fuck cares?"

It seemed like there were more people in the truck than there should be and I realized I wasn't the only girl. When had these other girls showed up? God, I was fucked up.

"I didn't even see them," I said. "They're all so pretty. Why are you so pretty?"

"What?" Sebastian asked. "Didn't see who? Brooke, where are you?"

The truck rolled down the street and the wind blew through my hair. I leaned my head back and laughed.

"Dunno," I said. "Driving."

"What the fuck is going on?" Sebastian asked. "Who are you with?"

I turned to Joel. "Who are you?"

He grinned. "That guy bothering you, sugar?"

I laughed, like he'd just told the most hilarious joke.

"Brooke, for fuck's sake, where are you?" Sebastian asked.

I looked around at the scenery whizzing by. Lights flashing. I blinked hard and tried to focus, but everything was blurry. "On a road. I don't know. I'm free tonight, Seb. I have to let it all go."

"I need to know where you are," Sebastian said.

The sharp note of alarm in his voice cut through my intoxication and I turned to Joel. "Where are we going?"

"Just for a drive," Joel said. "You're okay. I've got you."

I giggled. The truck pulled onto the highway and picked up speed. I turned around and held onto the edge of the bed, facing forward so the air blew my hair back.

I didn't remember hanging up on Sebastian, but at some point, I was no longer talking to him. Joel's arms were around my waist, holding me like he was trying to keep me in the bed of the truck. I held up my arms and leaned into the wind, laughing.

"Careful, Brooke."

"Goddammit, she's fucking crazy."

"What is she doing?"

"Holy shit, hold onto her."

Maybe I *was* crazy. I didn't care.

Someone was helping me out of the truck, but I didn't remember stopping. I had no idea where we were. I stumbled as I got down. Arms held onto me. Didn't make sense. What time was it? When had we stopped driving? Where was Sebastian?

I tried to ask, but my words came out in an incoherent jumble.

"Dude, she is fucked up," someone said. "What are you going to do with her?"

Something wasn't right again. The arm around me felt wrong. I pushed against him. Tried to move away. "Let go."

"It's okay," he said. Was it Joel? He spoke softly into my ear. "It's not what you think. You're all right. Just hang in there, sugar."

He led me up a set of stairs and into a house. I could barely stand. The floor felt like it lurched beneath my feet. Footsteps moved around me, but hands held me in place.

Next thing I knew, I was on a couch. How long had I been there? I looked around, but I didn't recognize anything.

"Hey," Joel said. "There you are. I think you passed out."

I smiled, mostly because it seemed like there were three faces in front of me, their edges blurring together.

"Who do you want me to call?" he asked.

"What? What's going on?"

"Look, you're really fucked up," he said. "And I don't do that shit, okay? A lot of guys do, though, so you're lucky you wound up with me tonight. That Sasha chick is drunker than you are, and my fucking roommate still took her to his room."

"I don't know what you're talking about." At least, that's what I meant to say. It came out slurred.

"Brooke, focus for just a second," Joel said. "Should I call Sebastian? You have a bunch of missed calls from him. But if he's like your ex or something, I don't want to mess around with that."

"Seb's not my ex," I said. That made me laugh again.

"Okay, I'm calling him."

I was half-aware of voices. Then I was waking up again —someone's hands on my shoulders, shaking me gently.

"Brooke?"

I forced my eyes open and saw Sebastian. "Seb?"

"Goddammit."

Why did he sound so mad?

"You need a drink," I said. "Let's go get another one. My buzz is going to wear off."

"Not likely," Sebastian said. My eyes closed again but I could still hear him talking. "Thanks for calling."

"Sure," Joel said. "Look man, if she's your girlfriend, she never said anything. She just seemed like a cool chick and she wanted to party."

"She's not my girlfriend."

Sebastian's voice was so hard. So cold. The way he said that sliced through me.

"Let's go," Sebastian said.

I tried to stand, but my legs were jelly. Sebastian's thick arms wrapped around me and he lifted me up, cradling me like I weighed nothing.

He smelled so good. So familiar. Even so wasted I could barely keep my eyes open, I realized this was the closest I'd ever been to him. Cradled in his arms, my head resting against the top of his chest. His beard tickled my forehead. I wanted to nuzzle my face into his neck, but he stuck me in the passenger's seat of his car.

I shivered, suddenly cold. His body hadn't just been warm. It had been smoldering hot.

He got in the car. "I'm taking you to my house. I want to make sure you don't fucking die in your sleep."

"I'm not gonna die," I said, my voice dreamy. "I can't die now. I already did."

23

SEBASTIAN

I'd never been so relieved to see someone, yet so angry I could fucking kill them at the same time.

Brooke sat in my passenger's seat, muttering drunk nonsense. I didn't bother trying to figure out what she was saying. She was so out of it, there wasn't any point in talking to her. So I stayed silent, my eyes on the road. Seething.

She'd seemed weird the last few days. I'd stopped by the bookstore yesterday, but Joe had told me she'd called in sick. She'd said the same thing when I'd called her—that she wasn't feeling well. I knew it was bullshit. She wasn't sick this time, any more than she'd been sick the last time she'd done this.

When I didn't hear back from her earlier today, I'd gotten worried. I went to her house, expecting her to open the door a crack and make a show of not wanting me to get her germs. But she hadn't been home.

She hadn't answered her phone, either. Not until a couple of hours later when she'd finally picked up, sounding drunk as fuck. I'd heard voices in the background

—a guy's voice specifically. And what had sounded like an engine, and maybe road noise. Then she'd hung up on me.

I'd blown up her phone after that, but nothing. I'd gone out looking for her, still trying to get through. After looking everywhere I could think of, I'd been about ten seconds away from calling the police. Then her number had lit up my phone.

Some guy had been on the other end. I'd almost come unglued, but he'd been calling in the hopes that I was someone who could come get her.

I was pretty sure I'd scared the piss out of him when I'd shown up at his door. I hadn't meant to be a dick; I was grateful he'd been a decent human being and hadn't taken advantage of her. But I'd also been angry as hell, and I'd stormed in there like I was ready to rip anyone and everyone to pieces.

If he had hurt her, I would have.

She was passed out again by the time we got to my house. I picked her up, cradling her like a baby, and took her inside. Charlie looked up from the couch. He'd stayed home in case she showed up here while I was out looking.

"Holy shit," he said. "Is she okay?"

"Just piss fucking drunk," I said.

"Need any help?" he asked.

"No, I've got her."

I took her upstairs, and before I realized what I was doing, I put her in my bed. I could have dumped her in the extra room, but I didn't move her.

She didn't seem like she was going to wake up, so I took off her shoes and pulled the covers up around her. I was exhausted, so I stripped down to my boxers and a t-shirt. I stood next to the bed, hands on my hips, looking at her for a moment. Debating what to do. Should I leave her here and go sleep in the extra room? Sleep in here on the floor? In the end, I decided to say *fuck it all* to good decisions and got in bed with her.

BROOKE WAS STILL SOUND ASLEEP—OR passed out—when my alarm woke me in the morning. I hadn't slept well. My body ached from sleeping in an awkward position, trying to give her room. As much as I'd wanted to wrap my arms around her and hold her while she slept, I'd resisted the urge. Being pissed had made that easier. But none of it had made for a restful night.

Thankfully, she hadn't puked in my bed. I held a hand close to her face to make sure she was still breathing—she was—and got up. I was glad I'd woken up first. I didn't want to deal with the awkwardness of waking up in bed with her when she probably wouldn't remember most of last night.

I went downstairs to take my pills. It was important for me to take them at the same time every day, hence the alarm. After swallowing them all, I put on a pot of coffee and sat down at the table. They always made me a little shaky after taking them, so I waited for the feeling to pass.

Soft footsteps came from the stairs. They weren't Charlie's heavy footfalls. He wasn't up yet. I wasn't expecting to see Brooke this early, but she crept into the kitchen, her face a mix of confusion and worry. Her hair was a tangled mess, her shirt disheveled, and her shoes dangled from one hand.

I leveled her with a hard stare. I wasn't going to let her get away with this shit.

"You don't know how you got here, do you?" I asked.

She had the decency to look guilty, and shook her head. "No."

"How about I tell you what I know, and you can fill me in on the rest," I said.

"Okay."

"You were apparently too sick to work yesterday, but not too sick to go out," I said. "You got wasted out of your goddamn mind and took off with a bunch of fucking frat boys."

She stared at the ground.

"Do you know how lucky you are?" I asked, my voice rising. "That guy you almost hooked up with could have done anything to you last night. You were passed out on his fucking couch. He could have violated you in a hundred different ways."

"I wasn't going to hook up with him," she said, her eyes still on the floor.

"No?" I asked. "He sure seemed to think so. At least you picked a guy with a conscience."

"That wasn't what I was doing," she said.

"Bullshit," I said, spitting the word at her. "I don't know what happened at the bar, but you left with a pack of fucking party boys and got in the back of a pickup truck. You tried to jump out while they were joyriding down the goddamn highway."

"What?" she asked.

"They had to hold you down," I said. "You could have fucking killed yourself. And then they took you back to their house. You only ended up with me because you were so out of it, the guy decided he didn't want to fuck some girl's unconscious body. He called me to come get you."

Brooke stared at me, stricken. Her face was pale, her eyes bloodshot. "I'm sorry. I didn't mean to."

"What were you thinking?" I asked.

"I don't know."

"That's it?" I asked. "You don't know. You could have been raped, or killed. I was going out of my fucking mind trying to find you, and you *don't know*."

"I didn't mean to get so out of control," she said. "I just wanted..."

"What?"

"Nothing," she said.

I waited to see if she would say anything else. If she'd try to explain what she'd been doing last night. Nothing.

"Fine." I stood up. "I'll take you home."

She stared at me for a second, looking like I'd just slapped her. I tore my eyes away from her pain and grabbed my keys.

"Let's go," I said. "I have shit to do today."

"Don't bother. I'll walk," she said, her voice trembling.

She walked away. I stood in the kitchen and listened to her footsteps, then the door open and close.

"Fuck." I pushed the chair across the wood floor and it slammed against the wall. Probably left a dent I'd have to fix later.

Charlie poked his head in. "Is it safe?"

"Were you listening?"

"I caught the end," he said. "Sorry, I came down and you guys were talking. Or, you were mostly."

"Whatever. I don't care."

He grabbed the chair and pulled it back to the table.

"I don't get it," I said. "I know she's been through some shit, but why is she so goddamn self-destructive? Just when it seems like she's better—she's not so sad and fucked up all the time—she pulls this crap. She could have died last night."

"She needs help, Seb," Charlie said. "Not the kind of help you can give her."

"I know she does," I said. "I've told her that, but she blows me off."

"Maybe last night will be a wake-up call," he said. "Like hitting rock bottom."

"Will it, though?" I asked. "On her last day in Phoenix, she was a step away from being homeless. Living with a guy who beat the shit out of her. You know why she didn't want to call the cops that night? She had drugs in her system. She was afraid of getting arrested. Shouldn't *that* have been rock bottom?"

"Holy fuck, Seb," Charlie said. "Why didn't you tell me that?"

"Because I'm an idiot?" I said, shaking my head. "Because I wanted to help her, and I wanted to believe her when she said she didn't get high all the time."

"Do you think that's what she's doing now?" he asked. "If she's using hard drugs, that's serious, man."

"She might be," I said. "Yesterday I would have said not a chance. But after last night? I don't know."

"What are you going to do?" he asked.

"I don't know that either," I said.

He patted me on the shoulder. "Let me know."

"Yeah, I will," I said. "Thanks, man."

I went upstairs and lay down on my bed. Turning into the pillow she'd used, I took a deep breath. It smelled like her. Not the scent of alcohol coming off her pores. Just her. That warm, soft scent that made my eyes roll back and tension build in my groin.

God, I was stupid. I should walk away. Let her run her life into the ground. But I knew I couldn't. I was pissed at her, but I wasn't ready to give up on her yet.

I sat up and grabbed my phone. I should have done this months ago, regardless of what Brooke had said. What she wanted and what she needed were two different things, and I was done letting her dictate either of them. At least when it came to this.

"Hello?" Mrs. Harper said when she answered.

"Hi, it's Sebastian," I said. "Sebastian McKinney."

"Sebastian, hello," she said, obviously surprised to hear from me.

I took a deep breath. "Okay, here's the thing…"

24

BROOKE

*T*wo days went by, and I didn't hear a word from Sebastian. I'd left his house with a horrendous hangover, but that hadn't held a candle to how bad I felt for what I'd done.

For what it had felt like when he'd written me off.

He was done with me. I'd gone too far, and I knew there was no going back. I had no excuse. I'd let myself get completely out of control, and I'd done it on purpose. I hadn't intended to put myself in danger, but I hadn't cared if I did, either.

And for the first time, it mattered.

Letting random guys buy me drinks in bars, hopping on the back of Jared's motorcycle when neither of us were sober, blowing off appointments or work—before I'd met Sebastian, none of those things had seemed to matter. I hadn't really cared whether I lived or died, so why not take a risk? Chase the high? Disappear? The consequences hadn't held any weight.

But seeing the hurt in Sebastian's eyes, suddenly there was a consequence I cared about. Deeply.

He'd been trying to find me that night—afraid for me. And when he had, not only had I been completely shit-faced, I'd been with some other guy.

Hooking up hadn't been on my agenda. I hadn't gone looking for a one-night stand. If I'd been anywhere close to my right frame of mind, I wouldn't have given those guys the time of day. Technically, I was single—no man had any claim on me. If something had happened with the guy from the bar, I wouldn't have been cheating—I didn't have anyone to cheat *on*.

Except it still felt wrong. And I knew what I'd done had hurt Sebastian just as it would have if he and I had been something more than what we were. Something more than friends.

That was the betrayal I'd seen in his face when he'd looked at me the next morning. I hadn't had an answer to it. I'd wanted to apologize—I still did—but I didn't know how. How could I look him in the eyes and ask for his forgiveness when I didn't deserve it? Not from him. Not after hurting him like that.

I walked home from work, alone in the growing darkness. Thankfully Joe hadn't fired me. I'd resolved to be stronger and not let myself get buried in apathy again. I didn't want to lose my job and wind up like I'd been in Phoenix. But I didn't have much confidence in my ability to hold to it. What would I do if—or when—the deadness overtook me? Would I be able to force myself to keep going? Was it possible to cope without completely self-destructing? I didn't know.

Inside my house, the quiet was deafening. I'd thought about calling Sebastian so many times, but I hadn't done it. I still didn't know what to say. And his silence spoke a clear message. He didn't want to hear from me, anyway.

Joe had brought us some takeout late in the afternoon, so I wasn't hungry. I flipped on the TV—anything to cut the silence—and went into the kitchen to make tea. Maybe some chamomile would help me sleep.

There was a knock at my front door and my heart jumped. Oh my god, was it him?

I opened the door and my mouth hung open. It wasn't Sebastian, but I couldn't believe what I was seeing. Olivia?

She was dressed in a thin white cardigan over a floral sundress, and sandals that showed her ruby red toenails. Her blond hair was down and she had a rolling suitcase sitting next to her.

"Hi," she said.

I swallowed hard. Was I really looking at Olivia Harper, standing on my doorstep in Iowa City? "Hi."

"Can I come in?" she asked, her voice hesitant. "Maybe?"

"Yeah, sure. You can come in." I stepped aside and she rolled her suitcase inside. I closed the door behind her with a click and twisted the deadbolt.

"Thank you," she said. "I'm sorry to show up unannounced like this, especially after, you know... everything."

The tea kettle whistled. I was so shocked at the sight of Olivia, I wasn't sure what to say. "Um, I'm making tea. Do you want to come in and have some?"

"Yeah," she said with a small smile. "I'd love that."

I turned off the TV, and she followed me into the kitchen. I bustled around, getting our tea ready, trying to figure out what the hell she was doing here. How she'd known where to find me. But I didn't ask yet.

We took our mugs to the couch and sat down.

"Look, I'm basically incapable of bullshit, so I'm not going to dance around everything," Olivia said. "The last time we saw each other, I was angry, and I took it out on you. I'm so sorry for what I said. I didn't mean it."

I closed my eyes for a moment against the sting of tears. The last time Olivia and I had seen each other, we'd gotten into an argument. I'd said some things I regretted too. But she'd told me I wasn't really part of their family, so I should just take my mess and move on.

"I'm sorry too." I swiped away a tear that broke free from the corner of my eye. "I'm sorry I pushed you and your family away like I did."

"It's okay," she said. "I pushed you away too. You didn't deserve that."

I reached over and squeezed her hand. "Thank you."

She squeezed back. "Oh my god, I've missed you so much."

"I've missed you too," I said. "But how did you find me here?"

"A certain big muscular bearded guy," she said.

"Sebastian?"

"Yep. He called my mom a couple of days ago. She was going to fly out here, but I insisted I would come."

"Why did he call your mom?" I asked. Now I was completely confused.

"Because he's worried about you," she said. "But you need to let me ask the questions for a minute. I love you, but you have a lot to answer for, you crazy bitch. Why didn't you tell anyone you moved out here?"

"Because it was nuts," I said.

"Shit yeah, it was nuts. Although I've met Sebastian, so..." She paused, her eyes on me. "Are you on drugs?"

Her question caught me off guard, like a shove from behind I wasn't expecting. "What? No. Why would you ask me that?"

"Because Sebastian is worried that you're using," she said.

"I'm not using drugs," I said, my voice sharp.

"Be straight with me, Brooke," Olivia said. "With your history... I need to know if I'm here for an intervention or what."

"My history?" I asked. "You mean my mom."

"Well, yeah, growing up with an addict makes you more susceptible. But mostly I'm asking you because Sebastian told me what you did the other night."

I hesitated, staring into my tea. I felt like I was at a cross-roads with Olivia. I believed her when she said she was sorry. Both of us had been angry that day, our anger fueled by grief. And if I pushed her away again now, I'd never get another chance. She'd been like a sister to me once, and I still loved her like one. I always had.

I met her eyes. "Last week I took some Vicodin. And Saturday night I got wasted out of my mind on Xanax and alcohol. But before that, I hadn't touched a thing since I moved here. Not even a single drink. I swear."

"Where'd you get the pills?" she asked.

"In Phoenix before I left."

"Do you have more?"

It took me a second to answer, a lie sitting unspoken on my tongue. It bothered me that my first instinct was to protect my stash. That wasn't a good sign. "Yes."

"Where?"

"There's more Vicodin in my sock drawer. I have a bottle in my purse that says Advil, but that's not what's in it. I'm not even sure what those are; there's a few different things. And I took the last of the Xanax. I promise, that's it."

She raised her eyebrows and got up. I waited on the couch while she dug through my purse and pulled out the bottle. She went to my room and I heard her go through my things. I let her do it.

The toilet flushed and she came out, brushing her hands together. "Gone. We cool?"

"Yeah."

"Do you have any booze?" she asked.

"No."

"Damn," she said, and one corner of her mouth lifted. "I could really use a drink."

I laughed. She sat down again and picked up her mug.

"You look really good," she said, her voice softer than before. "I was kind of worried I'd find you looking like a strung-out crack whore. But you don't at all. You look beautiful."

"Thanks," I said. "You look great too. How have you been?"

She shrugged. "Okay, I guess. Let's see, since I last saw you... I transferred to NAU. After graduation I moved back in with my parents, though. That sucks, and I'm going to get my own place as soon as I can. I got what I thought was a great job, but they laid me off a few weeks ago. Me and like six other people. So that sucks too. I don't know, that sounds really depressing, but it's not so bad. I'll find another job. It's all just kind of... anti-climactic. Adulthood, you know? I'm itching for something more."

"What about relationships?" I asked. "Are you with someone?"

"No," she said. "I was dating this guy I met at school for a while. A couple of years, actually. But we had kind of a dramatic breakup."

"What happened?"

She rolled her eyes and sighed. "I wanted to get serious, so I brought up moving in together. I thought we could at least *talk* about it. He responded by getting drunk at his company Christmas party that night, and fucking one of his coworkers in a bathroom."

"Oh my god," I said. "That's horrible."

"Yeah, it was," she said. "I was really upset at first. But then I realized if I'd have stayed with him, I would have totally been settling. It was still a bullshit thing for him to do to me, but it was for the best that we broke up."

"I'm sorry," I said. "What an awful thing to go through."

"Thanks," she said. "Okay, so I talked to Sebastian after my mom did. I know you two met the day we had lunch with him. Then you left town with him and came here. He didn't tell me why exactly, but I'm going to guess it wasn't because your life was all sunshine and roses."

"No," I said. "Truth?"

"Truth."

I took a deep breath. "I lost my job, and my apartment. Then the guy I was living with gave me a black eye and a split lip."

"Holy shit," she said. "Why didn't you call my mom?"

A lump rose in my throat and my voice trembled. "He broke my phone. But mostly I didn't want her to know."

"Give her some credit," she said. "What do you think she would have done? Tossed you out on your ass? You know my family better than that. We would have helped you."

"I know," I said. "But I kept doing stupid things. And I knew it, I just didn't care enough to do anything differently. Everything felt so fucking hard after Liam died."

"Well, yeah, you never got any help," she said. "That wasn't something you should have gone through on your own. My parents and I went to therapy. Have you seen a counselor? Or even just talked to someone about it?"

"No."

"Maybe it's time," she said. "I mean, Jesus, you were there. You lived through it. I know it was so hard on you."

I looked down at my tea, still clutched in my hands. "I don't have the words."

She put her hand on my knee and squeezed. "So, what's going on now? Sebastian made it sound like he thought you were pretty happy here until you imploded the other night. What was that about?"

"I don't know," I said. "I spent a few days feeling really down. It happens sometimes, but this was the worst in a while. I wanted to get rid of that feeling. So I took some pills and went to a bar to drink."

"And that's how you ended up hanging out of the back of a pickup truck with a bunch of drunk frat boys?" she asked.

"Basically, yeah."

"Fuck, Brooke, you're a dumbass," she said. "I love you, but really?"

"I know," I said. "And the worst part is..."

"What?" she asked. "Tell me."

"The worst part is what I did to Sebastian," I said. "I really hurt him."

"So, you and Sebastian are like..." She raised her eyebrows. "Right?"

"What, together?" I asked. "No. We're just friends."

"Hmm," she said, narrowing her eyes at me. "You sure about that?"

I took a sip of tea to give myself a second before I answered. "Of course I'm sure. I think I'd know."

"Nothing has happened between you," she said. "No ill-conceived make-out session you never spoke of again, or a sweaty drunken night together that you're trying to pretend didn't happen?"

"I told you, I haven't been drinking," I said. "And he never does."

"Not even a tender moment of longing where something almost happened, but didn't?"

"No, I..." But I trailed off before I finished protesting. There had been a moment like that. Actually, there had been many moments like that. At least, moments that could have been. I wasn't sure.

I knew Sebastian was more to me than just a casual friend. He'd gradually worked his way into the hollow space where my heart had lived, filling it with his warmth.

What did he see when he looked at me? A girl who was a walking disaster, no doubt. But what did he feel? Friendship? Something more?

"I don't know, but it doesn't matter," I said. "I ruined it."

"Making a mistake doesn't mean you ruined a friendship forever," she said. "Right?"

"Yeah, but Sebastian isn't going to put up with me anymore."

"You realize how much he cares about you, right?" she asked. "If he didn't care, he'd just bail and let you run around with all the frat boys you want. But he didn't. He reached out to my mom, hoping she could help you. He picked me up at the airport and drove me here. I saw the way he looked when he was talking about you. Maybe he's mad, but he's not walking away."

I stared at her as what she was telling me sank in. He hadn't written me off. I still had a chance. Maybe I hadn't lost him.

"Oh my god, I need to go talk to him." I put my mostly-full tea down on the side table and got up, my entire body filled with urgency. "Do you know if he's home?"

"Calm your tits, crazy," she said. "Yeah, I think he's

home. I'm supposed to call him after I talk to you and tell him how you're doing."

"Okay, call him, then. Talk to him."

"Maybe we should just go over there," she said. "And you talk to him. It's close, right?"

I nodded. "Yeah, we can walk."

"Let me go use the bathroom first."

My heart raced while I waited for her to come out. I paced around the living room, too agitated to sit. It all made so much sense now. I'd been trying to deny it—trying to push my feelings away. Afraid of what they would mean.

But I knew the truth. I was in love with Sebastian, and nothing would ever be the same.

PART III

The whispers of my heart grow

until they are

more than a breath of air

sound

fury

passion

things I did not know

until I found you

_~B_

25

BROOKE

*O*livia knocked on the door while I tried to hide behind her. Charlie answered, dressed in a t-shirt and jeans.

His eyebrows lifted and his lips turned up in a smile. "Hi. I guess you're looking for Seb?"

"Oh my god, you're huge too," Olivia said, her voice awed.

"Uh, yeah. I guess so?" He held out a hand. "I'm Charlie."

"Sorry." Olivia took his hand. "I'm Olivia. You have really beautiful eyes. And I obviously have no filter right now."

Charlie grinned. "That's okay. It's nice to meet you."

They kept shaking hands, their eyes locked, for a lot longer than necessary. I had a feeling neither of them remembered I was there.

Sebastian came down the hallway and I peered at him from behind Olivia. He wore a pair of gray sweats and his sleeveless shirt displayed his muscular arms in all their glory. His hair was carelessly unkempt, his beard a little thicker than usual. My heart felt like it was going to beat right out of my chest and my tummy swirled. Tingles of emotion bubbled up from deep inside, feelings long buried trying to make their way to the surface.

"Oh, hi," Olivia said, taking her hand back from Charlie.

"Did you talk to her?" Sebastian asked.

"Yeah," she said. "She's okay, but I think maybe you should just talk to her."

She stepped aside and I found myself under the intense gaze of those gorgeous green and brown eyes. Sebastian stared at me, his face unreadable.

Charlie glanced behind him, then at me. "So, Olivia, you must be hungry after your flight. Want to grab some dinner with me?"

"I'd love to," Olivia said. "I'll be back in a little bit, okay, Brooke?"

I nodded, my eyes never leaving Sebastian.

Charlie grabbed his keys, then walked Olivia out to the driveway. I stepped inside and closed the door as Charlie's truck roared to life.

I decided to take a page from Olivia's book, and get straight to the point.

"Sebastian, I'm so sorry. I know telling you that I'm a mess is a stupid excuse. There's no excuse for what I did. But I *am* a mess, and I'm sorry for that. I'm sorry I put myself in danger, and that you had to rescue me. But more than anything, I'm so sorry I hurt you."

He just looked at me for a moment and I tried not to let my knees shake.

"I need to know why you did it," he said.

"Because I felt hollow." I swallowed hard, tears suddenly threatening, coming out of nowhere. "Because I spent days feeling like I couldn't get out bed. Like I was fading away. And I wanted to *feel* something."

"You wanted to feel something with him?" Sebastian asked.

"No, that wasn't it, I swear. I got so out of control, I had no idea what I was doing. I just wanted to feel free—to drown out all my thoughts. Numb my feelings."

"Why?" he asked.

"I don't know how to explain it."

"Tell me," he said, moving closer.

"I said I don't know how."

He surged forward and got right in front of me, caging me against the door with his arms. He was so close, I could feel his body heat, smell his seductive scent.

"Tell me."

"Because sometimes I feel like I died," I whispered. "And I don't know why I'm here. I feel like my heart stopped beating when Liam's did."

His eyes held mine. I couldn't look away. He took my hand and brought it to his chest. My fingers trembled as I opened them, brushing lightly against his shirt. Then he covered my hand with his and pressed my palm against him.

"His heart is still beating," he said, his voice low and quiet. "It didn't stop."

A tear trailed down my cheek as I felt the rhythmic *thump, thump, thump* of his heart. I closed my eyes. His hand over mine was warm, his chest firm and strong. The beats of his heart pulsed against my palm.

His other hand settled gently on my chest, and his voice was so soft. "Neither did yours."

I covered his hand with my own and he leaned down so our foreheads touched. The rhythm of his heart thrummed through me. It was sensation and desire. Fear, and hope. It was life.

"I'm sorry," I whispered.

"Brooke, this heart beat for you when it lived inside him," Sebastian said. "It still beats for you now that it lives inside me."

He dropped my hands and ran his fingers through my hair, his face close to mine. His fingertips pressed gently into my scalp. Heat poured through me at his touch, and I held onto his thick arms as if I might crumple to the ground.

"Tell me no." His nose brushed against mine. "Tell me you can't do this, and I walk away."

My body screamed the *yes* my lips struggled to produce. I wanted him in every way—wanted him more than I'd ever wanted anyone.

"Yes."

Without a second of hesitation, he took my mouth in a hard kiss. His beard grazed my skin and his lips pressed against mine, demanding I give in. Demanding I give him everything.

I surrendered.

His kiss was fierce, and I answered his passion with my own. Our mouths opened. Tongues caressed. Tastes mingled. I wound my arms around his neck, and his hands moved down my back, our bodies pressing together. He was so big. So overwhelming. His strong arms enveloped me, his thick muscles tense.

He pulled away suddenly, leaving me breathless. I didn't want him to stop. He placed his hand alongside my face and looked into my eyes.

"I've wanted you for so long," he said. "I want to make your heart beat. Hard, like mine does when I'm with you. I want to make you gasp for breath. I want to make you *feel*, Brooke. If I can make you feel half of what I do right now, you'll know you're alive."

I nodded, too enthralled to speak. He kissed me again,

his mouth hungry and aggressive. My body came to life, nerve endings lighting up. Pieces of me I'd kept buried exploding to the surface.

He picked me up and pushed me against the door. I wrapped my legs around his waist and his hands gripped tight to my ass. His solid erection pressed between my legs. Even through our clothes, the feel of him sent sparks of pleasure racing through me.

It had been years since I'd had a real orgasm. It was as if that part of me had shut off. The pressure of Sebastian's cock grinding against me brought it back in a rush. Tension built and I moved my hips, aching for more. Desperate.

As if he already knew the intricacies of my body, he moved in a steady rhythm, rubbing against me in just the right spot. I held tight to his back as every muscle in my core contracted. He didn't stop, his movements relentless, his breath hot on my neck. My eyes rolled back and I moaned, the sensation overtaking me. Holy shit, he was going to make me come like this. Right here against his front door.

I clutched at his back. The heat between my legs built, wetness soaking my panties. Tingling waves of pleasure rolled through me as Sebastian's stiff erection pressed against me. His hips drove forward, his cock grinding against my clit. This was insane.

My climax peaked. I let it happen, coming apart in his arms. I gasped with every pulse of my orgasm, the heat of it coursing through me.

"Oh my god." I was breathing hard, the final tremors pinging through my body like little jolts of electricity. He held me up and I clung to him, my arms wrapped tight around his neck.

He waited for me to relax, then gently lowered me to the

ground. He touched my face and kissed me, soft this time. My lips. Cheek. Neck.

"What do you feel now?" he asked, low into my ear. Kissed my neck again.

"Alive," I whispered. I ran my hand down his chest, over his abs. His body was so solid, so thick with muscle. Past the waistband of his sweats. Wrapped my hand around his cock. "But I want more."

"You don't have to," he said, but I heard the desire in his voice.

"I want to."

Without saying a word, he took my hand and led me upstairs to his room. He shut the door behind us, shrouding the room in darkness. We tore off our clothes and our mouths crashed together. The feel of his skin against mine lit me on fire. He pushed me down onto the bed and climbed on top of me.

Before I had to ask, he reached for his bedside table and pulled out a condom. It only took him a few seconds to rip it open and roll it down. I stared at his thick erection. I'd felt it through our clothes, but seeing it was another thing entirely. Sebastian was big, and his cock was no exception.

The intensity in his eyes pierced through me, even in the dim light. He settled between my legs, the tip of his cock spreading me open. He took his time, kissing my lips, sliding in more.

With a swift thrust, he pushed himself deep inside me. Held there, his thickness filling me. He groaned into my neck and tension rippled through his body.

"God, you feel good," he said.

My eyes fluttered closed as he started to move, driving his hips, plunging in and out. "So do you."

But he felt so much more than *good*. He felt amazing.

Skin sliding against skin. Mouths tangled together. Our bodies joined, moving as one. It was unlike anything I'd ever experienced before.

The inevitability of this moment washed over me. Since the day we'd met, everything had been leading us here. Every walk home. Every late-night conversation. Every breath. Every heartbeat.

I ran my fingers through his hair. His beard grazed across my skin, pleasantly rough. He drove faster—harder. I moved my hands across his back, feeling the hard planes of muscle contracting above me. So strong and powerful. Down to his glutes, flexing with each thrust. I splayed my hands against his ass and pushed him in deeper, wanting more.

Hot tension grew inside me. He was relentless, the pressure of his cock exquisite. His rhythm perfect. The energy between us built into a frenzy until I was gasping for breath. Clutching his back. Crying out, my inhibitions long gone.

His erection hardened, thickening inside me. It slid through my wet pussy, the friction intense. Stimulating every nerve. He grunted and growled, his voice low in my ear, reverberating through my chest.

Oh my god, he was going to make me come again.

"Fuck," he breathed. He lifted up, the muscles in his arms bulging. Met my eyes. "I want to keep fucking you, but I don't think I can stop." Hard thrust. "Fuck, you feel so good."

"Don't stop," I said. "Come, Sebastian. Come inside me."

His brow furrowed and he groaned, driving into me, over and over.

"Yes, yes, oh fuck yes," I said as the ground beneath me opened and I tumbled into space. Soared through the air. The second orgasm was even more intense than the first. My pussy clenched hard around his pulsing cock and he groaned louder. I called out, hot waves of pleasure rolling through me. The intensity leaving me breathless.

When it was over, he kissed me, deep and slow. There was still so much passion in his kiss. It was luxurious and unhurried, but powerful. Full of feelings we hadn't yet spoken aloud.

After a final soft kiss on my lips, he looked deep into my eyes. I'd never felt so vulnerable, yet so secure.

"I love you," he said.

A potent mixture of joy and relief filled me at hearing his words. I hadn't realized how badly I wanted to hear them until he spoke them aloud.

"I love you, too," I said, touching his face.

With a hint of a smile on his lips, he nodded and kissed me again. He got up to dispose of the condom, then came back to bed. Drew me close, into his arms. Kissed my forehead.

I rested with my head on his chest, listening to the beats of his heart.

26

SEBASTIAN

*B*rooke's breathing was slow and even, her body warm against mine. I caressed her silky skin and took a deep breath, smelling her hair. Her scent was warm and feminine. Intoxicating.

The darkness and quiet sheltered us, as if nothing existed beyond the feel of her in my arms. I was relaxed— sated in a way I'd never been before. It was more than the physical release of an orgasm. More than the glow of amazing sex—and it had been amazing. I'd felt something deeper as I made love to her. Something primal—maybe even spiritual. As if our souls had mingled while our bodies connected.

I wasn't sure if she knew it, but I'd given her a piece of myself. And I didn't ever want it back.

I pressed my lips against her forehead and she stirred.

"Hi," she said, lifting her head to look at me. Her voice was sleepy.

"Sorry," I said. "Did I wake you?"

"I wasn't sleeping," she said. "Just relaxed."

I touched her face and kissed her mouth, slow and soft.

A gentle caress of my lips against hers.

"Thank you," she said.

"For what?"

"For everything," she said. "For keeping me safe the other night. For forgiving me. For not giving up on me."

"You're worth it," I said. "But no more of that, okay?"

"No," she said. "I'm not using, Seb. I promise. Not like that. I took some stuff the other night, but that was the first time since I met you. And Olivia flushed the rest of what I had down the toilet."

"Good," I said. "I guess you're not angry with me for calling Mrs. Harper?"

"No, I'm not angry," she said. "But why did you?"

"I had to do something," I said. "I couldn't sit back and watch you self-destruct."

"So you brought in the big guns," she said with a little laugh.

"Can you blame me?" I asked. "I knew they cared about you, and they'd find a way to help. I wasn't exactly expecting to pick up Olivia at the airport today, but she called this morning."

"I still can't believe she came. I didn't think she ever wanted to see me again. And then, there she was, knocking on my door. Here, in Iowa." She paused, her fingers absently caressing my chest. "I didn't think you wanted to see me again, either."

"Of course I did." I rolled her onto her back and leaned over her. "I'm in love with you, Brooke. I don't say that lightly. If I'm going to do something, I give it my all. I learned that when I was a wrestler. So if we do this, I'm going all in. I'm too familiar with my own mortality for casual flings or that friends-with-benefits bullshit. I want to be with you. But I need you to want to be with me too."

She looked into my eyes and I could see her taking it in. Processing what I said, and what it meant. I was glad she didn't answer right away. This was important. I'd held back, trying to hide my feelings from her, because I hadn't known if she was capable of returning them. If she wasn't, I had to stop this before it went any further, regardless of how much I wanted her. How much I loved her. Because me loving her would never be enough if she couldn't love me back.

But I knew it was there, inside her. I'd felt it in her body. In the way she'd responded to me. In the way she'd surrendered. Heard it in the very breaths she took. She'd said it, let the words escape her lips, and I'd heard the truth of them. *I* knew she loved me. But she had to know it too.

Her eyes moved to my chest. To the scar that ran down the center, right between my pecs. She trailed her fingers across the raised skin, caressing me with a light touch, then met my eyes.

"I'm in love with you, too. I want to be with you. More than anything."

I leaned down and kissed her. She tasted so good. So sweet. There were so many things I wanted to show her. Do with her. It was as if a whole new world had opened—a world in which maybe Brooke Summerlin could really be mine.

She giggled and I pulled away. "Is my beard tickling your face?"

"A little." She stroked my jaw. "But I love it."

"How do you feel now?" I asked.

The corners of her mouth turned up and her eyes sparkled. "Happy."

I leaned in and kissed the delicate skin below her ear. Ran my hand up her body, from her hip to her breast. Her nipple hardened against my palm and she moaned softly.

"Again? You can't be—"

I pressed my hard erection against her. "Yes, I can."

"Oh my god," she said, her voice breathy. "But what about Olivia?"

I squeezed her round breast, enjoying the firmness in my hand. Kissed her neck again. "What about her?"

"She'll probably be back soon."

"Don't worry, Charlie will keep her entertained." I kissed my way down her neck to her collarbone. "You're mine now. I'm not sharing you tonight."

She lifted her arms above her head while my mouth made its way to her tits. They were so perfect. I kissed around her nipple, then slid my tongue along the hard peak. She sighed, her body twitching. I took it in my mouth, pinching her other nipple gently between my thumb and forefinger while I sucked. Licked. Kissed. Sucked again. I loved the taste of her skin. The feel of her tits in my mouth.

"Oh my god, Sebastian," she said. "How do you do this to me?"

I groaned, kissing my way down her stomach. Past the swell of her hips. Pressed my lips into the crease of her thigh. I pushed her legs open and started with slow swipes of my tongue. Exploring. Tasting. Her soft sighs were music to my ears. I loved making her feel good.

She writhed and whimpered as I sucked on her clit. Massaged her with my tongue. Her pussy tasted so fucking good. Holding her body captive like this was such a rush. The way she moved and moaned. Breathy whispers of my name. She slid her fingers through my hair and rolled her hips. I felt her getting close, but I wasn't ready to let her finish.

I stopped and she gasped. She was breathing hard, her body tense. My cock was rock solid, aching to be inside her again. Grabbing her hips, I flipped her over and she got onto her hands and knees. After rolling on another condom, I positioned myself behind her and leaned down.

"I want to fuck you again," I growled into her ear. "Hard this time."

"Yes," she said, and the desperation in her voice drove me insane. "God yes, fuck me hard, Sebastian. Now."

She was so wet, I slid in easily. Her ass pressed against my groin as she arched her back. I gave her a few gentle thrusts, and then I unleashed.

I plowed into her, hard and fast. My hands held tight to her hips, pulling her back as I drove my cock in. Her hair spilled across her back and shoulders, dark against her skin. The lines of her back, narrow waist, and round hips looked amazing—soft feminine curves. She looked back at me over her shoulder, her eyes glassy, her lips parted. So fucking beautiful.

"Harder," she said.

I gave her what she wanted, slamming into her pussy over and over, grunting with every thrust. My heart beat wildly and the tension in my groin built fast. I pounded her again and again, while she called out her ecstasy. We were loud and uninhibited, letting passion sweep us away.

I wanted to give her everything. Take away all her pain. I wanted to fuck the sadness out of her—see nothing but desire in her eyes.

My muscles were taut, flexing hard. I took one of her wrists and pulled her arm back. She lowered her chest to the bed and I grabbed her other arm. She wrapped her hands around my wrists as I held hers, her arms stretched out behind her. With her ass in the air and her body in my control, I fucked her relentlessly.

Her throaty moans spurred me on, the heat of her pussy

driving me crazy. Where our first time had been passionate and tender, this time I released the animal inside me. The drive to possess her. Own her. Love her with my body with all the ferocity of a predator.

"Oh fuck," she said, her voice a whimper. "Fuck, yes... oh god... yes... harder."

The walls of her pussy tightened, the pressure agonizing. My balls drew up tight, almost ready to explode. I thrust again and felt her tumble over the edge. She cried out, her face almost buried in the mattress, as she came hard all over me.

I couldn't hold it in any longer. Like a bomb going off, I detonated inside her. Hard, hot pulses of my cock overwhelmed me. My mind went blank and I kept fucking her, grunting through the biggest fucking orgasm I'd ever had.

I slowed, my chest heaving with ragged breaths. I let go of her wrists and pulled out. She collapsed onto the bed, breathing hard, her hair damp and tangled.

Still trying to catch my breath, I got up to deal with the condom, then fell back in bed with her. She hadn't moved. I gathered her up in my arms and held her close. She laid her cheek against my chest and I slid my fingers through her hair.

The intensity of the moment made my chest feel tight. Even broken as she was, she'd been so vulnerable with me. Trusted me so completely. I wanted to engulf her with my arms, cocoon her with my strength. She held me with the same force and severity. The power of our connection was mind-blowing. I'd known I loved her for months, but this... This was raw and open and beautiful.

"I love you," she whispered.

I squeezed her, kissing her head. "I love you too, Brooke. More than I know how to say."

27

BROOKE

"*H*ey, Joe." I closed the door to the bookstore as quickly as possible to stop the blast of cold air. It was freezing out there. "How's it going?"

Joe leaned against a tall stool behind the front counter, an open book in his hands. "Quiet. Are you early?"

"Yeah," I said. "I had an appointment and it was easier to come straight here, rather than go home. I'll just go sit in the back for a few if you don't mind."

He nodded. "No problem."

I went into the back and sat down at the little table, wondering if Joe would let me put a space heater back here. I huddled down in my thick coat and rubbed my hands together. Sebastian had warned me winter was going to be cold. As far as I was concerned, I was surprised it wasn't snowing. And it was only October.

I was glad I had a little time before I had to be on the clock. My appointment had been with my new therapist, and even though we hadn't delved too deeply into anything serious, it had been emotionally draining.

Although logically I could see the benefits of therapy, I

wasn't convinced it was right for me. Or maybe I just hadn't found the right therapist. But I'd promised Sebastian I would give it a shot, and Olivia had backed him up. I'd complained about them ganging up on me, but they hadn't backed down. So off to therapy I went, once a week on Wednesdays.

My phone dinged with a text. I fished it out of my handbag.

Seb: Hey, love. I have class tonight but can I come over later?

Me: You better. I miss you.

Seb: Miss you too. At work?

Me: Yep. It's cold in here.

Seb: Don't worry, I'll warm you up.

Me: Can't wait. Love you.

Seb: Love you too, chilly girl.

I smiled and touched his name on the screen. It felt so good to smile. I'd been doing a lot more of it since Sebastian and I had gotten together. It had been about a month since that unbelievable day when he'd kissed me... made love to me... then fucked me into oblivion. I was so in love with him, sometimes I didn't know what to do with myself.

But I still carried a hint of fear. What if I wasn't strong enough to love him the way he deserved? He was so big and powerful. So fierce and determined. I hoped my spirit had the strength to match his.

With a little time left to kill, I pulled out my notebook. I wrote down a few lines that had been bouncing around in my head all morning.

The future
Has a face

Where it did not before
Potential, and hope, and possibility
But only
If the darkness
Always looming
Does not prevail

IT WAS SHORT, and simple. But I looked at my words and left them as they were—satisfied. For now, at least. Sometimes I needed pages and pages to express my thoughts. Other times a few lines felt right.

I closed the notebook and put it away. I'd filled the original one Sebastian had given me, and a few more since then. This one had a deep orange and blue paisley cover. It almost matched my sweater.

When it was time for my shift, I reluctantly left my coat on a hook and came out into the shop. Although now that I'd been inside for a little while, I wasn't all that cold.

Joe glanced up from his book. He seemed a bit melancholy. "You can close up early tonight if it's still a ghost town."

"Okay," I said. "Is everything all right?"

He closed his book and set it on the counter. "Yes, fine. Business has been so slow. There are always ups and downs, but I'm getting a little worried."

I wasn't surprised to hear that—it *had* been slow—but I hated seeing Joe look so stressed.

"Well, if you need to cut back my hours or anything, just let me know," I said.

He smiled. "It's not so bad as all that, yet. And things

usually pick up around the holidays. It just seems like it gets slower and slower every year."

Some days we had a lot of customers, but I often wondered how Joe managed to keep the place open. I glanced over at the curtained-off area on the far side of the store. There was a counter there that had once been a little café, serving coffee and tea. "Have you thought about reopening the café counter? It might give people more of a reason to come in if they could get something warm to drink. Especially with the weather getting colder."

"It didn't seem to make much of a difference when I had it open before," he said.

I tilted my head and took a good look at the space. "Was it just like this? The layout, I mean. Did you have places to sit?"

"There were two tables," he said.

I walked toward the curtained-off nook, thinking about the current placement of the bookshelves. There was a lot of wasted space. The building was sizable, and Joe had everything spread out. It did make it feel open and airy, but it wasn't a very efficient use of the square footage.

"What if we had more seating?" I asked. "Not just a couple of tables, put there as an afterthought, but a whole section. There's room if we move things around." I gestured toward the rear of the store. "And we're using that whole area for storage, but couldn't we put that stuff in the back room? It would free up a ton of space."

"Space for what?"

"For people." I paused for a moment, thinking. "What if this wasn't just a bookstore? What if it was like... a gathering place? We need ways to encourage people to come in and shop here, instead of ordering online or going to one of the big chain stores."

"Well, sure," he said. "That's why we have our local authors section, and the staff recommendations. Those are popular with customers."

"Yeah, but is it enough?" I asked. "If you had places for people to sit, you could host some of those local authors. Invite them to do readings. Open it up to book clubs." My mind spun with the possibilities. "You could have open mic nights for poets or even acoustic musicians. This is a college town. College kids love that stuff."

He nodded slowly, his eyes moving around the space. "But I've never had much luck getting the college crowd in here."

"They'd come if you gave them a cool place to hang out," I said. "All we'd have to do is organize a few poetry nights or something, post fliers around campus, and I bet it would be packed."

"I'd have to hire someone to run the café," he said. "I tried before, but I don't know anything about operating that sort of business. Books, I know. Overpriced coffee? Not so much."

"Okay, but let's say you could hire someone," I said. "Or lease the space and let someone bring their own small business in here. What about the rest of it?"

"I'm open to it," he said. "Although with my knee, I can't do any of the rearranging. That's why I've left it like this for so long. The bookshelves are too heavy for me to move around."

I grinned. "Don't worry. I have the muscle covered."

He laughed. "That's right, I've met your boyfriend."

I felt a surge of excitement. "So, we can do this?"

He narrowed his eyes and his white mustache twitched.

"How about this," I said. "I'll see what I can find as far as seating and give you the costs. Rearranging the layout is no problem, Sebastian and our friend Charlie can help with that. And I'll come up with some ideas for events. I'll keep the costs down. And if you need help with getting the café going again, I can do that too."

"It's very hard to say no to all of that," he said.

"I think this could be really great," I said. "I won't pretend like I know what I'm doing, exactly, but I'll do my best."

"All right," he said. "But I need to approve the new layout first."

"Of course," I said.

"Thank you, Brooke. It's good to have someone in here with a little enthusiasm," he said, smiling again. "Well, it's time for me to go home. Like I said, close up early. You don't need to sit around if there aren't any customers."

"I will. Thanks, Joe."

After Joe left, I started sketching layout ideas in my notebook. I had a few customers in the late afternoon, but after that, all was quiet. I closed the shop an hour early and went home.

The porch light was on, but the living room was dark when I got there. I wondered where Olivia was. She'd been here for weeks and I wasn't sure how long she was planning to stay. At first, she'd said she could stay for a week. But a week had come and gone, and she was still here.

She'd asked if I minded, and I told her I didn't. It was nice having her here. I got the feeling that she liked being away from Phoenix—and not living with her parents. Even though they were nice people, I didn't blame Olivia for not wanting to live with them. She'd been on her own while she went to college, so moving home must have taken some adjusting.

Plus, we had fun together. Olivia had always been a spitfire, so we'd had our moments. Just a couple of small arguments, nothing serious. The longer she stayed, the more we fell back into the comfort of our old relationship. We loved each other like sisters, but we sometimes we fought like sisters too.

I shut the door behind me and flicked on the light. I was hungry, but I figured I'd wait for Sebastian. Maybe he'd want to grab dinner. Who was I kidding, Seb always wanted to grab food. His diet was the healthiest of anyone I'd ever known, but he was a big guy. It seemed like he was always hungry.

A bang coming from another room startled me. Maybe Olivia *was* home.

"Olivia?" I called.

She didn't answer, so I got out my phone to text Seb.

I heard another sound and it made me pause, mid-text. Was that a moan? It sounded like a woman's voice. I shook my head and grinned. Maybe Olivia was enjoying some alone time.

More noise, and another voice. Definitely not Olivia's. It sounded like a man. Was she watching porn back there? I shrugged and finished my text. I was going to tease the crap out of her when she came out.

Then the noise kept going—a rhythmic banging. Like two objects hitting each other. Or more like... a bed knocking against a wall.

Oh, shit.

She was either watching porn and getting really into her special-me-time, or she had someone back there with her.

The moaning got louder. Two voices. This was getting a little bit mortifying. I wondered if I should leave. She obviously didn't know I was home. If she did, she'd at least attempt to keep it down. As it was, they both kept getting louder. Who was she with?

The worst part was, it was kind of a turn-on. God, I was never going to tell her that. But listening to people having what was clearly some very amazing sex made my core tingle. Damn it, my panties were getting wet.

Well, at least Sebastian was coming over soon. Although maybe I'd suggest we hang out at his house tonight. There was slightly more privacy over there—at least the bedrooms were upstairs, instead of right next to the living room.

Sebastian hadn't answered yet, so I curled up in the corner of the couch and waited for them to finish. And what a finish. They were either having one intense simultaneous orgasm, or Olivia was hard-core faking.

I poked around on my phone for a little while, looking at furniture ideas for the café. I was so excited to get started. I'd never had a job that I really cared about before, but I really wanted to see Booklover's Corner succeed. It would be heartbreaking if it had to close—and not because I'd need to find a new job. It was a great store with so much potential. It just needed a little boost.

Olivia's bedroom door opened and an imposing figure walked out. Tall. Thickly muscled. For a split second, his silhouette reminded me of Sebastian and a chill ran down my spine. But then he stepped closer to the light.

Oh my god, I should have known. Charlie. *Of course* it was Charlie.

He stopped in his tracks in front of the bathroom and looked at me. Dressed in nothing but boxer briefs, he had his shirt over his wrists like he was about to put it on.

"Oh, hey, Brooke," he said. "You're, um... you're here."

"Yep," I said.

Olivia stumbled out of the bedroom, giggling. She was

dressed in a fitted t-shirt that wasn't long enough to hide her bright pink underwear. She wrapped her arms around Charlie from behind, then seemed to realize he was looking at something. Her eyes moved to me and they widened in surprise.

"Oh god," she said. "You were supposed to be at work."

"Sorry," I said. "I came home early."

"How long have you been here?" she asked.

"Long enough," I said with a wink.

"Well, fuck," she said.

Charlie just laughed and pulled his shirt over his head, then looked at me. "How was work?"

"Um, fine," I said. "But maybe you should put on pants?"

He glanced down at his muscular legs and shrugged.

"Shit, I'm not wearing pants either," Olivia said. "Charlie, get in here."

He grinned, then followed Olivia back into the bedroom.

They came out a few minutes later, both fully dressed. I pretended to be very interested in something on my phone while they said goodbye. Or kissed goodbye, rather. It took a while.

Charlie finally left and Olivia closed the door. She came over to sit on the couch, her cheeks flushed, her eyes dreamy.

"So, Charlie?" I asked. "Did this just happen?"

She bit her lower lip. "Um, not exactly."

"What?" I asked. "When?"

"Well..." She drew out the word, scrunching her nose. "Kind of the first night I was here."

My mouth dropped open. "What? You slept with Charlie the first night you met?"

"Yeah, I know," she said. "It was crazy. We went out to dinner so you and Seb could talk. But then *we* wound up talking for hours. We didn't leave until the restaurant was closing. When we got back to his place, you were still in Sebastian's room. I didn't have a key to your house or anything, so he invited me to stay and hang out. So, we did. And then, well, we did."

"Why didn't you tell me?"

She sighed. "I almost did, but I felt weird. Like you were going to be mad, since I'd just met him and he was your friend. I don't know, maybe that doesn't make sense. And at first, I didn't know if it would amount to anything. But then we started texting, and talking. And we got together again, and well..."

"Wow," I said. "I'm not mad. Just surprised. Either you guys have been hiding it pretty well for the last few weeks, or I haven't been paying attention."

"Mostly the second one," she said. "You've been a little wrapped up in Sebastian."

"Yeah, I guess I have," I said. "So, what is this between you guys? Are you just messing around?"

She shook her head. "No, that's the really crazy part. I don't think we are. At first, I wasn't sure what was going on. That's why I didn't tell you. It was this whirlwind of insanity, like in a movie or something. He's... god, Brooke, he's amazing. I really, really like him. And it's not just the sex. Although oh my god, the sex is incredible."

"Yeah, so I gathered."

"Consider it payback for the times I've had to listen to you and Seb."

I cringed. "Touché."

"It's no big deal," she said. "My roommate in college used to fuck her boyfriend under the covers with me in the same room. You get kind of desensitized after a while."

"Ew," I said. "Is this why you've been procrastinating on going back to Phoenix?"

"Pretty much," she said. "Can I tell you something that's probably going to make you think I'm insane?"

"Yeah..."

She bit her lower lip. "Charlie doesn't want me to go back, and... I think I might stay."

"Why are you worried I'd think you're insane?"

"Well, because I just met him and I'm considering packing up my life and moving halfway across the country," she said.

"Um, you do realize who you're looking at, right?" I asked. "I was on the road with Sebastian after knowing him for less than twenty-four hours."

"Good point," she said. "I knew I liked you for a reason. I'm way less crazy compared to you. I'll definitely use that argument on my mom when I tell her."

I laughed. "I don't think *but Brooke did it* is a very good argument."

"You just said yourself, you did *worse*." She smiled and tucked her legs up on the couch. "What is it about these big Iowa boys that makes us want to pack up and change our lives?"

"I don't know, but they're very persuasive."

"Are you sure you're not mad?" she asked. "Not even that I didn't tell you at first? We were going to. We talked about it today, actually. He hasn't said anything to Sebastian either."

"No, I'm not mad," I said. "You guys are two of my favorite people. This is fantastic."

"Thanks," she said. "I keep using you as an excuse to my parents for why I haven't come home, but I'm going to need to tell them the truth soon. I was hoping to find a job first, though. You know, so I could soften the blow and make it sound less like I'm stupidly moving for a guy I've known for like a month."

I gasped, feeling as if a light bulb had just lit up above my head. "Oh my god, O. You have a degree in business, right?"

"Yeah, business management with a minor in new media. Why?"

"And you worked at a coffee shop?"

She nodded. "All through college."

"Hear me out on this," I said. "The bookstore has space for a café, but it's been closed for a while. It's not much, I think they used to serve coffee and tea, plus maybe a little case with muffins or something. But I'm trying to talk Joe into reopening it, and getting some more seating in there. Doing little events and stuff, like readings and open mic nights. He's interested, but he needs someone to handle the café. What if..."

Her eyes widened as I spoke. "Brooke, I could do that."

I sat up taller. "And you were doing all that social media management stuff at your last job, weren't you? Joe is hopeless at that. He tries to pretend the Internet doesn't exist. You could work with him on that side of things. I know it would help us get the word out about the store and the events and stuff."

"I'm kind of freaking out right now," she said. "Is this a real possibility?"

"I'd have to talk to Joe," I said. "But yeah, I think so."

"Oh, Brooke, this would be amazing," she said. "That bookstore is so cute, but you're right. It needs seating. And maybe some cool art. Oh, and better lighting. You know what would be adorable? I saw these hanging lamps shaped like stars in a store downtown. They had different patterns and colors, and they weren't expensive."

"That's perfect," I said. My phone dinged, so I picked it up. "I'll see Joe tomorrow at work and I'll ask him. I bet he'll be relieved he doesn't have to look for someone."

Sebastian: On my way.

I smiled down at my phone.

"You know, you have the prettiest smile," Olivia said.

"Thanks," I said. "But where did that come from?"

"You just seem really happy lately," she said. "I kind of forgot what happy Brooke looked like."

I lowered my phone. Obviously, Olivia knew what had happened between me and Sebastian. We hadn't been hiding our new relationship from her, or Charlie. But it was difficult to talk about with her, beyond a little comment here and there. Liam had been her brother. I wasn't sure if she'd think I was disloyal for being with someone else.

Although the truth was, *I* was afraid I was being disloyal.

"Does me being with Sebastian bother you?" I asked.

"No. Like I said, it's great to see you happy."

"Yeah, but..." I glanced down again, not sure how to put this into words. "You know, if things had been different—"

"I know," she said. "But things aren't different. We lost him. That doesn't mean you have to be alone forever. It's okay to move on. You should. That's healthy."

I tucked my hair behind my ear and nodded. "I don't know what I believe about what happens to us after we die. But I wonder if he can see me, you know? Sometimes I almost feel him. Like he's here, in a way. Maybe it's just my imagination."

"No, I do too," she said. "Not all the time. But once in a while, he pops into my head out of nowhere. I always wonder if that's his way of saying he's still with us."

A sudden rush of emotion hit me and I blinked back tears. "But, if he can see me, what must he think? It's one thing for me to move on. But O, Sebastian isn't just some guy I met. He has..."

"Liam's heart," she said, her voice soft. "I know. I'm not gonna lie, it's a little weird. And maybe kind of morbid if you think about it too hard. But it's obvious you really care about him."

I nodded. "I did love Liam, you know that. But this is different. I don't know if I can explain it. Liam was comfortable. Like a cozy blanket. But Sebastian is..."

"Like a triple shot, don't hold the whipped cream, melt your panties off orgasm?"

"Yes, exactly," I said. "Everything with him is like life on steroids. I didn't know it could be like this."

She smiled. "Then let go of the guilt. Sebastian is good for you. Let yourself be happy."

As if on cue, he knocked on the door. I got up to answer, my tummy filled with the sudden rush I always got when he was near. Sparks and tingles of excitement mingling with arousal. My body awakening to his presence. I opened the door and his smile warmed me like the sun.

"Hey," I said.

"Hi, beautiful."

He brushed the hair back from my face and kissed me. And there was nothing wrong with any of it.

28

SEBASTIAN

I parked outside my parents' house and glanced at Brooke. She had a coat on over her dark blue off-the-shoulder dress. It had wide sleeves and a brown leather belt, and she'd put on the knee-high boots I loved so much. Her long hair draped around her shoulders and she wore the necklace I'd bought her recently—a silver chain with a little corn cob charm. For Iowa.

She smoothed down her dress. "Are you sure this is okay?"

I smiled, my eyes moving up and down, unabashedly enjoying the sight of her. "You look beautiful."

"Maybe I should have worn the long one," she said. "Are you sure this isn't too short?"

"I like this one," I said, glancing down at her legs. I wanted to fuck her later in those boots. "It's not too short."

"Okay."

I leaned over and kissed her. "You'll be fine. My parents won't bite."

"Get a room," Charlie said from the backseat.

I glanced at him in the rear-view mirror and scowled.

That was rich, coming from the guy who'd spent most of the almost-two-hour drive making out with his girlfriend in the back seat. Those two were like a couple of teenagers.

My parents had asked me to come home for dinner tonight. It had been a while since I'd seen them. Charlie had invited himself along—which was normal. He usually came with me when I visited my parents. My mom was a great cook, and she always made enough food to feed an army. Charlie coming along meant Olivia too—those two were only apart when forced by things like work.

And it was the first time I was bringing Brooke home to meet my parents.

Before we'd started dating, I'd invited her to come to Waverly with me and Charlie a couple of times, but it hadn't worked out. I knew my mom had been leery of Brooke— and, to be fair, her circumstances had been a little questionable—but now I couldn't wait to show her off to my family. My parents knew we were together, but I hadn't officially introduced them. This felt like a big step, but a good one.

I kissed the back of Brooke's hand. "Ready?"

"I think so."

We all got out of the car and I took Brooke's hand in mine.

"Wow, you grew up here?" she asked.

"Yeah," I said. "Why, does it look different than you imagined?"

"Very. You said *small town Iowa.* I was picturing an old-fashioned farmhouse, not a freaking mansion."

I glanced up at my parents' house. It was nice, but it wasn't a *mansion.* It did have a four-car garage—my dad was really into cars—and a covered porch supported by white columns. The exterior was a combination of wood and brick, and lights glowed in most of the windows.

"It's not that big," I said.

Brooke just squeezed my hand.

I opened the front door—didn't bother to knock—and ushered everyone inside. Brooke paused in the entryway and glanced around.

"Hey, Mom," I called out. I could hear noise coming from the kitchen and the scent of food filled the air, making my stomach rumble. "Something smells great."

I helped Brooke out of her coat as my mom came down the hallway. Except when I glanced up, it wasn't my mom.

It was Cami.

Charlie started coughing behind me. I stared at Cami, like a deer in headlights. She looked the same as I remembered—wavy blond hair, light pink cardigan, floral skirt, heels. But what was she doing here?

"Hi, Sebastian," she said, her voice hesitant as her eyes swept over the four of us.

Brooke looked up at me, then at Cami. Instinctively, I wrapped an arm around her and pulled her close.

"Hi." My brow furrowed and I was relieved to see my mom come down the hall. *She better have a good explanation for this.*

"Good, you're here," Mom said, but her smile faded when her eyes landed on Brooke. "Oh. I didn't realize you were bringing... guests."

"I texted you, Mom," I said. "Did you forget to check your texts again?"

"I guess so," she said.

The awkwardness level was off the charts. Cami's cheeks flushed and she seemed to be trying very hard not to look at Brooke. Charlie finally stopped coughing and Olivia patted him on the back, quietly asking him if he was all right. I kept my arm around Brooke, my hand on her bare shoulder.

I'd never felt this way in my parents' house before. Defensive and territorial, my instincts on alert. This place had always been home, but tonight it felt like walking into a trap.

I decided to ignore the fact that my ex-girlfriend was inexplicably here, at least for the moment. "Mom, this is Brooke. You met her once before, but that was quite a while ago. And this is Olivia Harper."

My mom blinked when I said *Harper*, but quickly recovered her manners. "It's lovely to meet both of you. Hi, Charlie."

"Hi, Mrs. McKinney," Charlie said. "Uh, hi, Cami."

Cami gave him a weak smile.

"Well, isn't this lovely?" Mom said. "I'll set some extra places at the table. There's more than enough for everyone."

My mom went back to the kitchen, Cami close on her heels. Charlie met my eyes, giving me a *what the fuck* look. I just shrugged. I didn't know what was going on. I held Brooke back while he and Olivia went into the kitchen.

"I'm so sorry about this," I said, keeping my voice low. "Cami is... well, she's my ex-girlfriend."

"Yeah, I gathered that," she said.

"I have no idea why she's here," I said. "My mom is friends with her mom, but I thought she lived in Chicago or something. I haven't seen her in years."

"She's from... before?" Brooke asked.

I nodded. "High school. Early college. I'll get my mom alone and ask her what the hell is going on when I can. But if you'd rather go..."

Brooke put her hand on my chest. "No, we don't have to leave. It's fine." She glanced toward the kitchen. "I just hope Olivia doesn't make it worse. She's really good at that."

"Yeah, this is going to be interesting." I touched her chin, tilting her face up, and planted a soft kiss on her lips. From the corner of my eye, I thought I saw Cami watching us from the other room, but when I looked up, she wasn't there.

I led Brooke into the kitchen where everyone else was standing around. My dad came out of his den and looked even more surprised to see Brooke and Olivia than my mom had. He gave Mom a sidelong glance—there was a distinct *I told you so* in his expression—and politely greeted both of them.

God, this was going to be the weirdest dinner ever.

Mom asked Cami to help her pour wine, and it didn't escape my notice that Cami seemed to know where everything was. Brooke and I both declined a drink.

"Oh my god, Seb, look at you," Olivia said. She stood in the hall just outside the kitchen in front of all my old wrestling pictures. "You look so different without your beard."

"Yeah." I wished my parents would take all that shit down. "Those pictures might as well be a different guy."

"They're still you," my mom said with a smile. "You're still the same."

Hearing her say that didn't sit well with me, but I wasn't sure why. Brooke slipped her hand into mine and squeezed. I glanced down, and she met my eyes with a comforting smile. It was like she understood what was going on inside me, even when I didn't.

"I barely recognize you with that baby face," Olivia said. She turned to Charlie. "Did you look this young when you were a wrestler?"

Charlie usually kept a few days growth of stubble, rather than a thick beard like mine. But we'd always had to shave when we were wrestling. He rubbed his jaw. "Yeah, except I'm way better looking."

"You wish," I said.

Cami helped my mom get the food on the table. We all sat down and passed things around, dishing up our plates. The tension in the room was so thick I was surprised any of us could breathe.

My mom's expression was calm, but the worry lines in her forehead deepened every time she looked at me. My dad was either oblivious, or choosing to ignore the awkwardness. Charlie met my eyes with an amused grin. He was clearly enjoying my discomfort. I kind of wanted to punch him in the face.

Brooke stayed quiet. I put a reassuring hand on her leg.

"This is really good, Mrs. McKinney," Olivia said. "Thank you."

Mom smiled. "You're very welcome."

My dad cleared his throat. "Sebastian, how's the new semester going?"

"It's good," I said. "I'm taking a full load."

"That must be about it, then," he said. "Almost finished with that business degree?"

"Not quite," I said. I'd been back in school for the last two years. With the credits from my first year and a half at U of I, I should have been almost finished. But I'd thrown in some extra math classes that weren't required for my major. And I wasn't so sure about that business degree anymore. But I hadn't discussed that with anyone yet—especially not my parents.

"Well, hurry it up, son," Dad said. "I need you at the dealerships. As soon as you're finished with school, that assistant manager position is yours."

"Family business," Olivia said. "Nice. Are you and Brooke planning to move out here, Seb?"

The tension heightened, but either Olivia didn't notice,

or she'd said *you and Brooke* on purpose. Charlie choked back a snicker while Olivia looked at me with an innocent smile. Definitely on purpose.

"I'm not sure," I said. "We haven't really talked about it."

"Of course he is," Dad said, apparently ignoring the *and Brooke* part of her comment. "That was always the plan. Waverly is home."

I just shrugged. I didn't want to talk about this.

"Well, Cami, how are you adjusting to life back in town?" Mom asked, giving Cami a pleasant smile.

"I'm really happy to be back," Cami said. "There were things I loved about Chicago, but I realized life in the big city isn't for me."

"No, you're a Waverly girl at heart," Mom said. "You're right where you ought to be."

Cami nodded and her eyes flicked to me. "I think as we grow up, we learn more about what we want in life, and it isn't always what we once thought."

"So very true," Mom said. "It's perfectly normal to experiment a little when you're young. Maybe go off to college, or live somewhere new. Make new friends. But home always brings you back if you let it—back to the people you're meant to be with."

For fuck's sake, this was ridiculous. My mom couldn't have invited Cami in an attempt to get the two of us back together. But the way she kept looking at Cami, then at me —and ignoring Brooke—made it really fucking obvious that was exactly what she was doing.

I squeezed Brooke's thigh under the table, then grabbed the half-empty bread basket and stood. "I think we need more bread. Mom, can you come help me with that?"

She opened her mouth like she was going to say the basket wasn't empty, but I leveled her with a hard stare.

Plastering on another smile, she put her napkin aside and stood.

I stalked into the kitchen and tossed the basket on the counter, then led her into Dad's den. I didn't want everyone at the table to hear this.

"What is going on?" I asked, keeping my voice low. "Why is she here?"

"Cami?" Mom asked. "She moved back to Waverly recently. I thought it would be nice for all of us to reconnect."

"Did you forget what she did?" I asked. "I know you're friends with her mom and you never wanted to say anything bad about her. But she left me when I really needed her. That doesn't bother you?"

"That was a difficult time for everyone," she said. "And people grow up and mature. They change."

"So I'm supposed to overlook the fact that she bailed on me because she couldn't handle it when things got hard?" I asked.

"She was young," Mom said.

"I can't believe you're making excuses for her," I said. "You, of all people. I was dying, Mom. If she was the person I was *meant to be with*, she would have stayed."

Mom took a deep breath. "I know, honey. I was angry at Cami for a long time, too. It put a lot of strain on my friendship with her mother. But she came to me recently and we had a very long talk. She deeply regrets what she did, and she wants the chance to apologize to you."

"I'm not angry at Cami," I said. "And it's nice that she wants to apologize. That's fine, I don't hold a grudge against her. I moved on. But if you think you're going to orchestrate some kind of reunion that's going to lead to me dating her again, you need to get that out of your head right now."

"Well—"

"Mom," I said, cutting her off. "My *girlfriend* is sitting at the table across from her. I didn't bring Brooke to dinner because I wanted a pretty date. Have I brought a single girl home since I got better? No, not one. Because I was never serious about anyone. I'm serious about Brooke. I'm in love with that woman and you better get used to it, because if I have my way, she's going to be around for a very long time."

"Honey," she said in a soothing tone that was really getting on my nerves, "I can understand why you're interested in Brooke. She probably seems very exciting. But she's not the kind of girl you settle down with."

I gaped at her, speechless. I couldn't believe what I was hearing. "Did you really just say that to me?"

"Sebastian, you've been through a lot," she said. "But your illness is behind us now. Things are back to normal. You can finish school and move back here to work with your father. I'm sure Brooke is a very nice girl, but I don't see how she fits in with your plans."

I'd never been so angry at my mother. My back tightened and I balled my hands into fists. I needed to get out of here before I said something I'd regret. "Mom, I love you, but I'm leaving."

"Sebastian..."

She tried to say more, but I was already walking back to the dining room. Everyone looked up from the table, staring at me in alarm. Except Charlie. He still wore that smart-ass smirk of his.

"Let's go."

Charlie's face sobered and he nodded, touching Olivia's elbow as he stood. Brooke bit her lip, her eyebrows drawing together with concern, but she got up and followed me toward the front door.

"Sebastian, where are you going?" Dad called from the table.

I didn't answer. There was no way I was letting them disrespect my woman like that. I should have turned around and walked out the second I saw Cami. That was my mistake, and I'd apologize to Brooke for it when I was calm. For now, I just needed to get us the fuck out of here.

We piled into my car and I pulled out onto the street. I gripped the steering wheel and ground my teeth, anger flowing like liquid silver in my veins.

"Sorry," I said.

Charlie acknowledged me with a silent nod. I didn't have to say anything else. He understood me.

Brooke reached out and touched my leg. I took her hand and brought it to my lips. Placed a hard kiss on the back of it. I twined my fingers with hers and squeezed, trusting that she understood. I wasn't angry with her. I just needed time to calm down.

If my parents thought Brooke was some kind of experiment—a phase I'd outgrow—they had another thing coming.

29

BROOKE

*W*e spent the long drive back from Waverly in silence. Charlie and Olivia spoke to each other in hushed whispers in the back seat, but other than that, it was quiet. Sebastian was tense, his bulging muscles flexed and rigid, the veins in his forearms protruding. Heat emanated from his body, like his blood was actually boiling. Under different circumstances, it would have been sexy as hell.

He held my hand, kissing the back of it now and then, letting me know he wasn't upset with me. He didn't need to say it. I understood.

That had been one of the most uncomfortable situations of my entire life. I'd known without Sebastian telling me that Cami had to be his ex. There was no mistaking the way he'd looked at her. I didn't know much about her, or what had happened between them, except that she'd left him when he'd been sick.

I hated her for it.

It wasn't the general dislike a woman might have for her boyfriend's ex. It didn't bother me that he had a girl in his past, even one he'd been serious about. What made me hate her was knowing she'd abandoned him when he'd been weak.

And now that he was strong again, she wanted him back.

That was perfectly clear. She hadn't been at dinner because she was an old friend who wanted to see how Sebastian was doing. Or to catch up after years apart. I knew a thirsty girl when I saw one.

But the worst part had been Sebastian's mother. An ex-girlfriend who thought she might have another chance was one thing. A mom who had orchestrated the meeting, obviously thinking her son would come alone, was another. She'd invited Cami because she wanted Sebastian to get back together with her. Even knowing he was with me.

Made it obvious what she thought of me—and my relationship with her son.

The first time we'd met, I'd been one step away from homelessness, sporting a black eye and a split lip. I knew what she must think. I was trash—not good enough for her son. It wasn't because I wore beaded bracelets, peasant blouses, and boots. Although maybe if I'd come over in a cardigan buttoned up to my neck and a modest skirt that hung below my knees, like a good little Iowa girl, she would have thought twice about judging me.

But it wasn't just the way I dressed or my lack of a manicure—though I'd seen her notice that too. She didn't need to know the details of my past to see it. She could tell. Some people just could. I didn't know how to explain it, but sometimes I encountered people who could read my past. As if the story of my fucked-up life was tattooed on my skin. Often it was because they shared a similar history—a child of an addict or an abusive parent recognizing a kindred spirit. But others took one look at me and knew I'd grown up poor and neglected—and instantly looked down on me for it.

Mrs. McKinney had done just that. She'd done it the first time we'd met, when her eyes had widened with alarm at the thought that her son was associating with *that* kind of girl. And she was doing it now—even to the point of attempting to sabotage our relationship by getting Sebastian to hook up with his ex.

It made me sick to my stomach. I didn't want to cause a rift between Sebastian and his family. But it was probably too late.

We dropped off Charlie and Olivia at the guys' place, then drove the short distance to my house. We went inside, and as soon as the door closed behind us, he grabbed me with rough hands and kissed me. I melted against him, draping my arms around his thick neck. Raised up on my tip-toes and pressed my body against his.

He held me tight, his kiss hard and aggressive. Filled with the anger coursing through him—turning rage into lust and desire. I could feel the urgency in his thick muscles, in his tight biceps and flexing chest.

"I love you," he growled into my ear, backing me up toward my bedroom. "I love you and I'm sorry."

His mouth on mine cut off my reply. There would be time for talking later.

In my room, we yanked off our clothes, but he stopped me from taking off my boots. He slipped my panties down over them, then turned me around and bent me over the side of the bed.

"Fuck, that's hot," he said.

I looked back at him while he got out a condom and rolled it on. His hard length stood up straight, protruding from his lean hips. He had the perfect amount of hair on his broad chest—enough to make him look manly and powerful—and the sexiest happy trail running down his lower abs. The veins in his arms stood out and his mesmerizing eyes roved over me.

"I've wanted to fuck you in those boots since I watched you put them on," he said.

He slid his hand down the center of my ass until his fingers brushed across my opening. I practically vibrated at the light touch. He put pressure on my clit and rubbed slowly while his other hand gripped my hip, holding me in place. I tried to arch back, to make him give me more, but he held me fast.

"I know, baby," he said. "You want my cock, don't you? You want me inside you."

"Yes."

He rubbed faster and my eyes rolled back. He knew exactly where to touch me to make me insane. Slipping his fingers into my pussy, he groaned.

"That's my girl," he said. "So wet for me. I'm going to fuck you so hard, baby. Are you ready for this?"

"Oh my god, yes," I said.

In one quick movement, he took out his fingers, grabbed hold of my hips with both hands, and thrust his cock in. I called out at the abruptness of it. The fury. He held tight, his fingers digging into my flesh, and plunged into me—hard. Over and over. His hips drove his thick cock in and out, his body slamming against mine.

I clutched the sheets for dear life, arching my back to take all of him in. His power and strength were overwhelming. I wanted him to take it all out on me—all his anger and frustration. I wanted to forget how I'd felt, wilting under his mother's judgmental gaze. The humiliation and shame. The guilt. I wanted him to fuck it all out of me.

He was relentless. Fierce. Slamming me into the mattress, making the bed scrape across the floor. He grunted and growled with every thrust, his voice primal and raw. No one had ever done this to me before—fucked me with so much passion and intensity. I didn't know how much more I could take, but I never wanted it to stop.

The heat in my core built, almost to the breaking point. Tension mounted, like a rubber band being pulled tight. Just when I was about to plunge over the cliff, he slowed. His grip eased and his thrusts relaxed.

He pulled out and turned me over. I backed up onto the bed and he climbed on top of me. His breathing was ragged and he was covered in a sheen of sweat. It glistened off the hard lines of his body, accentuating every angle and curve. His eyes held mine and I watched as they went from glassy and unfocused to piercing, all that intensity trained on me.

His cock slid in again. Gentle, this time. Slow, powerful thrusts had me riding the edge of climax, the mind-numbing pleasure soaking through me. With our eyes locked, we moved together, a slow dance of bodies teeming with heat. With tension and passion. A moment of connection that filled the space in my chest, once left hollow. Filled it to bursting.

I felt his cock thicken inside me and I knew he was close. Desperate for release, I clutched at his back, grinding my hips into him with each thrust. He wouldn't break eye contact, the fierceness in his gaze demanding I do the same. He could see through to my soul, see every bit of me. I was more naked and exposed than I'd ever been, my whole self on display.

His brow furrowed and his back stiffened. He drove harder, and the first pulse of his orgasm sent me careening off the edge. I burst into flame, hot sparks lighting up every inch of my body. My senses ceased to function, my brain only processing the almost violent waves of pleasure.

The magnitude of it left me gasping, clinging to him. He tucked his face against my neck, his breath hot against my skin. We held each other, sweat mingling, bodies pressed together. Soaking in the moment.

He lifted himself up and brushed my tangled hair from my face. His kisses were gentle—reverent. Our eyes met and the fullness in my chest almost brought tears to my eyes.

"I'm sorry for what happened," he said. "It doesn't matter what anyone else thinks. All that matters is us."

I nodded. "It's okay, and it's not your fault anyway."

He kissed me again, then got up and went into the bathroom. I took off my boots and set them beside the bed. A minute later, he climbed back in bed with me and drew the covers up around us. I tucked myself into the nook of his strong arm and rested my head against his chest.

"Can I ask you something?"

"Of course," he said.

"Do you really want to work for your dad?" I asked. "You've never talked about that before. I didn't realize that was what you were planning."

"That's because I don't know if it is anymore," he said. "That was the plan, once. I guess back in high school, it made sense. My dad had been a wrestler, gone to college. He opened his first dealership when he was my age. It seemed natural that I'd follow in his footsteps."

"But that was before," I said, my voice soft.

"That was before," he said. "I don't understand why no one wants me to be any different. It's like I was traveling down a road, and when my heart gave out, I veered hard to the left. And I kept on veering, taking unexpected turns. I wasn't even going forward anymore. Sometimes backwards, sometimes sideways. Then after my surgery, I started to get better. At the time, it seemed like it was never going to end, but eventually I was healthy. It seems like ever since, people in my life keep waiting for me to get back on that original road. But I veered so far away from it, I don't even know where it is anymore. And if I found it, I don't know if it would be the right one."

"That road ended in Waverly," I said. "Working at your dad's dealership." *Married to Cami, or at least someone like her. An Iowa girl with corn silk hair.*

"Exactly." He paused, still caressing my skin. "I almost died. And it was agonizing and slow. I don't know how my parents could watch me go through that and not see how it changed me."

"I guess sometimes people see what they want to see," I said.

"Yeah."

"What do you want?" I asked. "If you don't want that life in Waverly."

He took a deep breath, his chest expanding against me. "Promise you won't laugh?"

"Why would I laugh?" I asked. "Unless you're going to say you want to be a drag queen. Then I make no promises."

"No," he said with a chuckle. "I've been thinking about going into architecture."

I propped my head on my hand so I could look at him. "Really?"

"Yeah. I've always been interested in it. Although back in high school, I was so focused on sports, I didn't think about much else. I figured I had a job waiting for me after college, so why worry about it? But when you can't do sports, and you've lost almost all of your friends, you have a lot of time on your hands. I did a lot of reading when I was sick. I read about a lot of things, but architecture fascinated me. I actually had a subscription to *Architectural Digest* for a while, but I stopped getting it."

"Why did you stop?"

"I don't know," he said. "It seemed stupid. I'm already so close to finishing school. There's nothing wrong with a business degree, even if I don't work for my dad. I can do a lot with that. I'm already behind, you know? I lost years to my illness. If I start over now, with a completely different major, it will take that much longer before I'm finished."

"It doesn't seem like the time should hold you back," I said. "But college is expensive."

"Yeah, but that's not a big issue," he said. "I don't want to sound like an asshole about it, but my parents have plenty of money. They gave me my entire college fund and let's just say it was overkill. I haven't even gone through half of it yet."

"Wow, that makes it easier," I said. "Then what's holding you back?"

"That's a good question," he said. "Maybe I'm still trying to figure out what road I'm supposed to be on."

I settled down against his chest again. The warmth of his body was so relaxing. But I couldn't help but wonder if the road he was meant for was a road also meant for me.

30

BROOKE

*W*ork was crazy. Joe had decided to give Olivia a chance at reopening the café, and she'd attacked the project with gusto. We spent our time searching for deals on furniture and décor to spruce up the place, comparing suppliers and costs, and trying to get Joe to sign off on the new store layout. He had some very particular requirements and didn't want to budge. It was no surprise he hadn't been using the space efficiently. It was hard to get it all organized to his satisfaction.

We'd been hoping to get the first events going before the holidays, but things had taken longer than we'd anticipated. It was mid-December, and there was still work to do. But Joe hadn't minded waiting, and the store was getting more business as people shopped for gifts.

This week the chaos had settled to a dull roar. Olivia was in Phoenix to visit her parents and sell some of the things she didn't want to move. Charlie couldn't go because of work, so he'd been pouting since she'd left. The first night, Sebastian had declared him impossible to live with, so he'd come to my place.

He'd been staying at my house all week. I didn't mind. I loved falling asleep next to him every night, and waking up to him in the morning. I think we were both starting to realize it was something we could get used to.

The house was empty when I got home after work, but Sebastian texted me minutes later.

Sebastian: We still on for our date tonight?

Me: Yes! What are we doing?

Sebastian: Movie? New horror flick is out.

Me: OMG WE ARE THERE

Sebastian: Done. Already checked times. Should we do 9?

Me: Sounds perfect.

Sebastian: I'll be at the library another hour or so. Finals are going to be brutal.

Me: Come straight here when you're done. I'll make us dinner.

Sebastian: Have I told you lately how much I adore you?

Me: Yes, but you can say it again.

Sebastian: I'll tell you with my tongue later.

Me: Promise?

Sebastian: It's either a threat or a promise. You can tell me after you're done begging me to stop.

I laughed and set my phone on the counter. If he kept talking like that, I was going to have to change my panties. I thought about sending him a dirtier text—maybe see what it took to get him to pack it in and come here now—but I decided to try it another time. He'd been studying his ass off for finals. If he needed another hour, I shouldn't mess with him. He'd have time to make good on his tongue threats later.

My phone rang, so I grabbed it. Mary. That was strange. I hoped everything was okay with Olivia.

"Hi, Mary."

"Hi, Brooke," she said. Her voice was serious, putting me immediately on edge. "Do you have a minute?"

"Yeah," I said. "Did Olivia make her flight?"

"She did. She should be landing in about an hour," she said.

"Okay, good," I said. "What's up?"

"Well, there was an accident on one of the freeways, just outside Phoenix," she said. "The driver who caused it was killed."

My heart felt like it was in my throat and my hands trembled. I didn't understand why she was telling me this. Car accidents happened all the time. Why was this one important?

"Um, okay."

"The driver who caused the crash was intoxicated," she said. "I think that's why it made the news. That and the fact that multiple cars were involved with only one fatality. But... honey, the driver who died was your mother."

"What?" A sick feeling turned my stomach. My mother? "How do you know?"

"The news article online gave her name," she said. "I made some phone calls to confirm that it was her. She had a Texas driver's license, plus an old one from Arizona."

I stared at the counter, numb with shock. "She... she caused an accident?"

"Yes," Mary said.

"But she didn't kill anyone?" I asked.

"No."

"Were people hurt?"

"The news said there were minor injuries, but no one was hospitalized," she said.

"Oh god." I pressed my hand to my stomach, wondering

if I was going to throw up. "Do you know anything else? Why was she in Phoenix?"

"I'm afraid I don't know," she said. "I have the name of the funeral home where her body was taken. Do you want me to call for you?"

I took a deep breath. "No, I can call if you give me the number. Can you text it to me?"

"Yes, of course," she said. "If you need to come to Phoenix, you're welcome to stay with us."

The Harpers still lived in the same house. I wasn't sure if I could face that again. "I don't know, Mary, I'll think about it."

"Brooke, I am so very sorry," she said. "If there's anything we can do, let me know. I mean that."

"Thank you," I said. "And thanks for letting me know."

"You're welcome," she said. "At least let me know if you come to town."

"I will."

We said goodbye and a minute later, I got her text. This was so surreal. What had my mother been doing back in Phoenix? Why had she been driving drunk? What had she been doing all these years?

I couldn't help but wonder if she'd gone back to Arizona looking for me.

AN HOUR LATER, Sebastian came back from campus. He found me in my bedroom, packing.

"What's going on?" he asked. "Is everything all right?"

I folded the shirt I was holding and put it in my bag. "I have to go to Phoenix. My mom died."

"Oh my god."

Instantly, his arms were around me. I leaned into his thick chest and breathed him in. Let him hold me. I didn't feel like crying. I wasn't sure how I felt. I was still too shocked to feel much of anything.

"I'll come with you," he said.

I pulled back. "You have three finals this week. You're not missing those."

"Fuck my finals," he said. "I'll get them rescheduled."

"Seb, I'm okay," I said. "I'm going for a few days, that's all. Her current boyfriend already took care of a lot of stuff, so it's not like I'm being saddled with funeral arrangements."

"Is there going to be a service or something?" he asked.

"I think maybe something small, but I'll find out more when I get there."

"I'm absolutely going," he said.

"No." I put my hand on his chest. "I just need to go take care of some things. I know it's my mom, but... god, this makes me sound like a horrible person, but the last time I saw her she tried to beat the crap out of me. And that was years ago. It's not like we were close."

"It doesn't matter," he said. "I'm going."

"I already booked my flight," I said.

"I don't care—"

I gently touched his lips. "Sebastian, listen to me. I'll feel terrible if you miss your finals. There's no way I'm doing that to you. It's bad enough that I have to go. Please don't make this worse for me."

"What about Olivia?" he asked. "Can she stay in Phoenix with you?"

"She's on a plane coming back here right now," I said. "I can't ask her to turn around and go back. She has to work."

He put his hands alongside my face. "Will you stay with the Harpers?"

"They offered, but…"

"Stay with them, and I'll stay here and take my finals. I don't want you to be alone."

I took a deep breath. "Okay, I will."

His brow furrowed and he brushed my hair back. "I still don't like this. I should be there with you."

"I know, but I'll feel so much better knowing you're getting your finals out of the way," I said. "Please. This is what I need you to do for me right now. Ace those tests. I'll be back Friday and we can celebrate."

He kissed my forehead and wrapped me in his arms again. I knew he didn't like it, but the guilt would kill me if he missed his tests because of this.

31

SEBASTIAN

I walked out of the classroom, knowing I'd just crushed my final. Considering how distracted I'd been since Brooke had left, it was something of a miracle. I was good at compartmentalizing—staying focused on just one thing, even in the middle of chaos. But this thing with Brooke's mom was weighing on me, making it hard to focus.

Still, I'd pulled it off, and I'd done it for her. She wanted me to ace my tests, so I was going to ace the shit out of those fuckers.

Still, I kept feeling like I should have gone with her.

I hated that she was down there dealing with something as intense as her mother's death without me. I'd had a bad feeling when she'd left, and now it was worse. She'd been texting me to keep me updated, and this morning she'd said she'd need to stay a few days longer than she'd thought. I'd been ready to go to the airport and get on the first flight I could—or maybe just fucking drive the twenty-four hours to Phoenix—but she'd stopped me. Again. I had another final on Monday, and she wanted me to stay and take it.

She'd insisted this was what she needed from me. I

wanted to give her what she needed, but I didn't have to like it.

I was free for the rest of the day, although I had to spend more time studying. I also needed food, so instead of going to the library, I drove out to Billy's, a diner I liked that served great breakfast. If it wasn't too busy, I could get some studying done there anyway.

The restaurant was quiet, so I got a table by the window and ordered a breakfast burrito. I pulled out a stack of envelopes from my backpack and laid them out in front of me.

Admissions packets. I'd requested them from five different universities with good architecture programs. There was no guarantee that I'd be accepted if I took the leap and applied. But I had a shot. My grades were good, especially since I'd been back at U of I. I'd taken most of the prerequisites.

But I still wasn't sure.

I didn't have to ask to know what Brooke would say. She'd tell me to apply. I knew she'd have my back.

Something was still keeping me from taking the plunge. This would mean leaving U of I—leaving Iowa. All the schools I was interested in were out of state. I liked the idea of moving somewhere new—that wasn't a problem.

But it would also be the point of no return. It would officially set my life on a different path—one that didn't end in Waverly with me running one of my dad's dealerships and coaching wrestling on the side.

Like I'd told Brooke, I hadn't been on that path since the day my heart had stopped. It had been almost seven years and I was still trying to figure it all out. Who I was. Where I was going. I'd gone from believing I was going to die before I was old enough to order a beer, to being healthy again, able to pick up the pieces and go back to my life.

But in trying to pick up the pieces of who I used to be, I'd stalled out. Some of those pieces didn't fit anymore. I wasn't the guy who'd thought wrestling was a metaphor for life—who'd thought winning was everything. Who'd been content to follow the path that everyone expected.

I didn't want to be like those guys I used to hang out with, who never thought beyond the obvious. Who got jobs they didn't care about and married their high school or college girlfriends, simply because that's what you do. Not because it was what they wanted. Not because that life had anything in it that set their soul on fire.

"Hi, Sebastian."

I glanced up, surprised to see Cami standing next to my table. I'd been so lost in my thoughts, I hadn't noticed her.

"Hi." I quickly scooped up the admissions packets and stuffed them in my backpack. "What are you doing here?"

"I met a friend out here for coffee this morning. I drove by and saw your car outside so I stopped. Do you mind if I sit?"

"I guess not." I shifted uncomfortably in my chair. I didn't really want to sit and talk with her. I was still annoyed with my mom for the dinner debacle. But that hadn't really been Cami's fault.

"Thanks." She lowered herself into the chair across from me. "So, how have you been?"

"Great," I said. "How about you?"

"Okay," she said. "It's weird to be back in Waverly. It all looks the same, but it's not, you know?"

"Yeah, things change."

"They do," she said. "People do too."

The waitress brought my breakfast and asked Cami if

she wanted a menu. Cami glanced at me, like she was hoping I'd invite her to stay, but I didn't. She told the waitress she'd stick with water.

"Sebastian, I've really been wanting to apologize," she said. "I was hoping I'd get the chance when your parents had us over for dinner last month, but..."

"Kind of hard when I was there with my girlfriend," I said. Cami flinched, but I didn't feel bad about it. I was with Brooke and it was better that she knew where things stood.

"Yeah," she said. "Well, what I wanted to say was that I'm sorry. I abandoned you when you needed me. It was immature and selfish. I was so caught up in sorority life and parties. I thought I wanted a boyfriend who could spoil me and show me off. But all I got out of that was drama. Guys who didn't care about me. Who cheated on me and treated me like I was disposable. And then I went off to Chicago and I thought I'd be living this glamorous big-city life. But none of it turned out the way I expected."

I felt bad for Cami. Life had obviously knocked her around a bit. I understood what that was like. "I'm not mad at you anymore. It was a long time ago. And I'm sorry if you went through stuff that was shitty."

She met my eyes and smiled. "Thank you. That means a lot to me."

I figured she'd leave, now that she'd said what she wanted to say. But she traced her finger along the outside of her water glass. I just ate my breakfast.

"So, what have you been up to?" she asked. "Are you still at U of I?"

"Yeah," I said. "For now."

"Do you think you'll move back to Waverly after you graduate?"

I paused and put my fork down, meeting her eyes. "No."

"Oh," she said. "Why not?"

I was surprised at the sudden sense of conviction I felt. But hearing Cami—who had been as much a part of that plan for the future as the job at my dad's dealership—ask me that question began to harden my resolve. "Because that isn't the life I want."

"You're going to turn down your dad's job?" she asked. "You know in a few years he'd have you running things. Maybe even make you part owner. You'd make a fortune. You could live like a king in Waverly."

"So?"

"So? He's handing you a career on a silver platter. You could have your life back." She paused and batted her eyelashes a few times. "You could have everything back if you wanted it."

"I don't want it," I said, and a spasm of pain crossed her features. I didn't want to hurt her feelings, but Jesus, why couldn't anyone understand? "I'm sorry, Cami, but this isn't about you. My life is different now. The Sebastian you knew in high school isn't who I am anymore."

"Of course it isn't," she said. "I've changed too. That's what happens when you grow up and start experiencing things. But that doesn't mean you should throw away the chance to have a comfortable life."

"I don't want comfortable," I said. "And you know, I don't think I ever did. Even if my heart had never gotten sick and I'd never gone through any of it, I wouldn't have been satisfied with comfortable. I would have resented it."

"Then what do you want?" she asked.

"I want to take risks," I said. "Go places I've never been. I want to pursue my dreams and fail and try again. I want passion. If I'm going to be here, I want to really live. Otherwise, what's the point?"

"But why can't you have both?" she asked. "And what if some things are just meant to be?"

I pushed my plate away. I was getting tired of this conversation. "Did you come here to try to talk me into something?"

"I don't know," she said.

"Look, I accept your apology," I said. "But if you're fishing for some sign that you and I might have another shot, you're in the wrong place. It's not because I'm mad at you. It's because I've moved on. I have someone in my life who means the world to me. You want to know what I want? Her. The rest, I honestly don't know yet. But Brooke is the one thing I'm sure of."

"What if that's a mistake?" she asked.

I raised my eyebrows. "You're asking me if Brooke is a mistake?"

She paused, pressing her lips together, her eyes on the table. I couldn't tell if she was thinking about what to say, or just being dramatic.

"I know how you met her," she said finally.

"What does that have to do with anything?" I asked.

"Seb, your mom told me she was supposed to marry him —the organ donor. And then he died, and they were so young. That must have been a devastating loss. Hasn't it ever occurred to you that maybe *that*," she said, pointing to my chest, "is why she's with you? That she doesn't really want you? She wants what's left of him?"

"Why are you discussing Brooke with my mom?" I asked.

"Because we're worried about you," she said.

"Cami, you lost your right to worry about me, or who I'm with, when you broke up with me."

She crossed her arms. "We've known each other since kindergarten. Our mothers have been friends for years. Just because we stopped dating doesn't mean I can't worry about you."

"There's nothing to worry about," I said. "And if my mom has an issue with my life, or my girlfriend, she should take it up with me. Not discuss it with my ex."

"It's not like she's gossiping," she said. "She's concerned for her son and she doesn't think you'll listen to her."

"Well, I'm telling you she doesn't have anything to be concerned about. And neither do you. And as for Brooke, and this," I said, touching my chest, "that's not only morbid, it's insulting."

"I'm not trying to insult either of you," she said. "But I don't understand how you can throw away the life you were supposed to have. It was almost taken from you, and now you can have it back. You just have to reach out and grab it. But you won't."

"What if I told you I was moving back to Waverly after I graduated?" I asked. "That I was going to work for my dad, and buy a nice house, and be a volunteer wrestling coach, just like everyone always figured I would—but I was going to do it all with Brooke. Would that make a difference? Is it really my career and financial stability you're worried about?"

Her lips parted and her eyes narrowed, but she smoothed out her features before she replied. "I'm worried about all of you. About your life, and your happiness."

"I've got it covered, Cami," I said. "I *am* happy. Happier than I've ever been."

She tucked her hair behind her ear and gathered up her purse. "Well, that's good, then. I hope you're really as happy as you claim to be."

I didn't say anything else as she walked out the door.

God, my mother. It pissed me off that she'd been talking

about Brooke with Cami. My mom didn't know Brooke. She'd obviously made some ridiculous assumptions. Brooke didn't want me to be some kind of second-choice replacement for Liam Harper. If that had been the case, she would have sought me out. As it was, she hadn't wanted to meet me at all.

And this heart in my chest still sometimes felt like a wall between us. Not the way it once had, but I did wonder if she'd ever be able to truly let go. Truly move on. My heart wasn't the reason she wanted me—it was one of the reasons she'd been afraid to be with me.

Moving back to Waverly, working for my dad, marrying Cami... living in a nice house with our two-point-five kids and a minivan in the driveway... that was safe. That was why my mom wanted it for me. But it wouldn't be living—just existing.

I didn't want safe. I didn't want friends like the guys I'd known in high school. I wanted Charlie, who'd had my back every step of the way, even when he was still basically my rival. I didn't want a girl like Cami, who was more interested in her reputation and finding someone to take care of her. I knew why she wanted me. She saw me as the means to a life of comfort—a fancy house and a new car every year. A life where she was the envy of all the other wives in Waverly.

I pulled out my admissions packets again. Maybe there *was* a piece of myself that I still needed to recapture. The drive and focus I'd once had. That single-minded resolve to do whatever it took to achieve my goals. It was why I'd won state. In a lot of ways, it had gotten me through my illness. I might not have survived long enough to get the transplant if I hadn't been mentally tough. Driven. It had only been at the end that I'd wanted to give up.

But since I'd been better, I hadn't applied that drive to

anything. Not school or my future. I'd always thought of myself as an all-in guy, but the only thing I'd gone all in on was Brooke.

She'd brought that out in me. With her, I felt a flame burning inside. A desire to really *live*, not just exist.

I ripped open the first envelope and spread the letter out on the table. It was time to start living.

32

BROOKE

*T*he first thing I realized when I got to Phoenix was that I wasn't used to the weather anymore. It was mid-December, and it had been cold in Iowa. I'd worn my heaviest coat and a pair of gloves to the airport. When I got to Arizona, it was sunny and in the seventies. Like an Iowa summer. I complained about being cold all the time, but the warm sun in Phoenix felt wrong, especially with Christmas decorations everywhere.

The first two days were difficult, but I handled it. I met with the funeral director and got in touch with my mom's boyfriend. We made arrangements to meet so he could give me some of her things.

I had a tearful reunion with Mary and Brian Harper. It was good to see them again, but staying at their house was almost more than I could take. Every room was full of memories of Liam.

I didn't know how to feel about him anymore. I looked at his pictures on the walls and tried to remember him as he'd been back then. But he was fading from my mind. The sound of his voice didn't come to me so easily now. I couldn't remember what his hands had felt like on my skin, or his mouth on my lips.

Sleeping there was worse. If Liam's spirit existed anywhere in this world, it was in his parents' house. I slept in Olivia's old room—a room that had once been mine too. But Liam's bedroom seemed to call to me from across the hall. They'd emptied it years ago and turned it into a guest room. The door hung open and for a moment, it looked like his room again. The same room I'd crept into in the dead of night. Where we'd nestled under the covers together and discovered what it was like to love.

The house next door—the last place I'd seen my mom— was freshly painted with a brand-new fence and kids' toys strewn around the yard. Nice cars in the driveway. It looked happily lived in—not like when we'd been there. I figured the inside must look nice too. By now someone had to have repainted the walls, covering that hideous peach my mom had chosen. Repaired the dents and scratches, washed away the stench of smoke. Removed the scars of the broken family who had lived there.

The funeral was scheduled for Monday, so I decided to stay. But I didn't think I could sleep at the Harpers' again. I let them think I was flying out Friday, and checked myself into a hotel on the other side of Phoenix.

Sunday afternoon, I drove my rental car to meet my mom's boyfriend at their house outside Mesa. It was on a quiet residential street and from the outside, it looked like it might be a nice place to live. I could imagine a normal family living there, with pots and pans they actually used for cooking. A dining table where they shared meals. A living room that wasn't piled with junk. But I knew outsides could be deceiving.

I knocked and a man with shaggy hair, a scruffy chin,

and skin that was tan and weathered opened the door. He had deep lines in his forehead and around his eyes, but I guessed he was younger than he appeared. He looked like he'd probably spent a lot of his life working outside in the sun. He was dressed in a faded blue t-shirt and a worn pair of jeans.

"You must be Desiree's daughter," he said with a slight Texas drawl, and stepped aside. "I'm Mack. You can come on in."

"Thank you," I said.

I wasn't sure what I'd been expecting when I saw where she'd last lived, but it wasn't this. It was clean, for one thing. Mostly, anyway. There were two full ash trays on a coffee table, but the couch was clear. No beer cans or poorly hidden drug paraphernalia. The odor of cigarettes hung in the air, but no weed. No stench of mildew or the sickly-sweet scent of a bag of garbage that had been in the house too long.

Mack glanced around, then gestured to the couch. "Here, you can have a seat. I'd offer you something to drink, but I don't have anything except water. Guess I should go to the store, but I haven't bothered."

The hurt in his voice caught my attention, and I took a better look at his face. His eyes were bloodshot, and he had the greasy look of someone who needed a shower. But he was stone cold sober. The redness in his eyes and the way he fidgeted weren't because he was drunk or high, trying to act normal. I could spot that a mile away. He was sad. Grieving.

I could spot that a mile away too. I knew it all too well.

"It's okay." I lowered myself onto the edge of the couch where he'd cleared a space. "I don't need anything."

"Always wondered if I was going to meet you someday."

He sat on the other side. "You remind me of her. Although I'm guessing maybe you look a bit like your dad, too."

I shrugged. "Maybe. I don't know."

"Well, you probably have questions," he said.

God, where did I even begin? "Yeah. I suppose you know I haven't seen her in a long time. The last time I heard from her, she was living in Louisiana with... I can't remember what she said his name was. How long have you known her?"

"Three years," he said. "We met in Houston."

"Three years?" I asked. "Were you together all that time?"

He nodded. "Yep. It was rocky sometimes, but I'll tell ya, I loved your mama."

She'd never had a relationship last so long when I'd been with her. And I couldn't remember ever hearing a man say he loved her—not in a way that was believable, at least. "Wow, that's amazing. When did you move here?"

"About a year ago," he said. "She'd been sober a couple of months by then, and decided a change of scenery would do her good. She always said Arizona was her home, no matter where else she'd been. So I brought her back here."

I'd barely heard a word since *sober*. "She was sober? But I thought... the accident..."

"She had almost fourteen months of sobriety," he said. "Obviously she fell off the wagon again."

"So, you were with her when she was using? Since you've been with her three years and she had fourteen months sober." I wanted to ask if he'd been using too, but it felt awkward.

"She was clean when we met," he said. "That time lasted about six months, and I met her toward the beginning of it. When she relapsed, I stuck it out. Thought maybe I loved her enough to get her through it—get us both through it. And after a while, it worked. She did two months in rehab and when she got out, I swear, she was a new woman."

"Um, I'm sorry if this is too personal, but are you an addict too? I only ask because the men she dated when I was a kid always were."

He shook his head. "Naw, never touched the stuff. Well, I smoke, and I reckon that's what'll put me in my grave someday. But I don't even drink much, let alone the other stuff."

"So, she was sober and doing well when you moved here," I said. "How long ago did she relapse?"

"I can't say for sure," he said. "I only found out a few days before the wreck. But I work two jobs, so I'm not here all that much. She had a job too, but I guess a few months back, she'd started missing work. Didn't tell me about it. She got fired a few weeks ago for not showing up. Didn't tell me that either. I was at work when she got in the wreck. If I'd been with her, I wouldn't have let her drive."

The guilt in his voice cut through me. "No, it wasn't your fault. You can't blame yourself for what she did."

He shook his head, his eyes on the floor. "I swear to you, I tried everything. And she'd been doing so good for so long. I thought the worst was over."

"I'm so sorry," I said, my voice quiet. "But thank you for helping her. I always wanted to believe that it was possible for her to get better. That maybe she was happy somewhere. It sounds like she was, for a little while anyway."

"The worst part is, I should have known better," he said. "People are who they are, Brooke. You can't change them. I couldn't change your mama. I think I always knew it was going to end this way. I wanted to believe she could change, but some things are so deeply ingrained, you may as well be trying to shoot the moon out of the sky. Didn't matter how long she went without drinking, or the drugs, or picking fights with me. Eventually, it always came back to that. She always went back to being who she was."

I stared at him, a deep sense of dread filling me. The air felt thick and my eyes were dry and gritty. Suddenly, I had to get out of there. "Okay, well, thanks for meeting me. I hope... I hope you'll be okay. But I'm sorry, I don't think I can stay."

"Oh, hang on a minute. I have something for you."

He got up and disappeared through a door. My back clenched painfully and my stomach roiled with nausea. I almost got up and left—this place was suffocating me—but Mack came out, holding a black plastic file box.

"This is some stuff you might want to keep," he said. "I'm not sure what all's in it, but she always took care to make sure we had it when we moved and whatnot."

I stood and took the box. It wasn't heavy enough to be full of files, but it definitely had weight. "Okay, thank you."

He nodded. "And Brooke, I'm sorry. She talked about you a lot. About how smart you are, and how pretty. I think she wanted to see you again, but she was afraid."

My eyes filled with tears. I took a deep breath so they wouldn't spill. Not yet. "Thanks, Mack. I'm glad to know she had some happy times with you. Even if it ended badly."

"Me too," he said. "Will I see you at the funeral?"

"Yeah," I said, even though it was a lie. "I'll see you then. Take care."

THE MUSIC WAS LOUDER than I remembered. It wasn't live, although it reminded me of Jared's band. I wondered what had happened to those guys. With their front man in jail, they'd probably gone their separate ways. I couldn't even remember most of their names.

"Well, holy shit," Rick said. He walked down the bar to where I sat in the last stool at the far end. "Look at you, kiddo. Long time, no see."

"Hi, Rick," I said.

"The usual?" he asked.

I hesitated for a second, knowing this was all a terrible idea. There was no reason for me to be here. But I'd gone back to my hotel and felt like I was crawling out of my skin. Everything Mack had said raced through my brain, kicking up the dust of faded memories. Bringing up old pain.

"Sure," I said, although I didn't remember what my *usual* had been.

He left for a moment and came back with a glass of what looked like whiskey.

"You look good," he said, sliding the glass across the bar. "What have you been up to?"

"I moved to Iowa."

"No shit?" He grabbed a towel and wiped a few spots on the bar. "What for?"

"I needed a change," I said.

"What brought you back here?" he asked. "Tired of freezing your ass off?"

"No." I took a sip. It wasn't good, but I could drink it. "I just had to take care of some things. I'm not staying."

He nodded. "I'm glad you came by, then. I wondered what had happened to you."

I could tell by his tone that he'd had his theories, and they hadn't been good. I swallowed the rest of my drink. "Yeah, I guess I kind of disappeared. I'm okay, though."

"Good." He took my glass and went to refill it.

I didn't stop him.

33

SEBASTIAN

*H*er smile didn't fool me.

When I picked Brooke up at the airport, my relief at seeing her—god, I'd missed her—was dampened by the look in her eyes. She smiled. Said things had gone well. She'd missed me and it was good to be home. But her eyes told a different story.

The haunted look was back.

I took her home and although she invited me in, something wasn't right. Olivia was with Charlie, so we had the place to ourselves. And we hadn't seen each other in almost a week. But she didn't seem interested in any sort of passionate reunion. She asked about my finals, but I'd already told her how they'd gone. There wasn't much more to say. I wanted to talk about what she'd done in Phoenix— and what she'd learned about her mom—but she only gave me vague answers. I could tell she didn't want to talk about it.

When she said she was exhausted and just wanted to go to bed, I didn't argue. I wasn't tired, but I crawled into bed with her. It was enough to hold her—wrap myself around her and feel her soft body against me. I inhaled her scent, and she smelled good. Like Brooke. But something was different. It was subtle, and I couldn't explain what it was. A hint of something I didn't recognize.

Whatever had happened in Phoenix had left a mark. As I held her beneath the sheets, I wanted to kick myself for letting her talk me into staying here. I'd known it was a bad idea. Every instinct had told me to go with her. I should have let her be mad, and gone anyway. She'd needed me, and I hadn't been there.

Fuck.

I just hoped she'd feel better after she got some rest, and she'd open up about what had happened.

BROOKE DIDN'T OPEN UP.

Not the next day, or the day after. Not when she'd been back for a week. Not after two. Christmas came and went. We celebrated with Olivia and Charlie. I called my parents, but didn't go home to see them. Things were still too tense.

We went out for New Year's Eve to a bar with some friends. Charlie and Olivia were there, and some other people we knew. Brooke had a glass of champagne, and I didn't think anything of it. Even I indulged in a glass. She had another and drank it so fast, I almost didn't realize the third glass was new. By midnight, she was laughing at everything and too drunk to walk straight.

The next morning, she brushed it off. New Year's Eve only comes once a year. It had been a party, and she'd had a little too much fun. She'd nurse her hangover with coffee and a big breakfast, and everything would be fine.

But it wasn't fine.

Over the next couple of weeks, I started checking her house for alcohol or bottles of pills. I felt shitty for doing it, like it meant I didn't trust her. But it wasn't about trust. I could feel her drifting away from me, little by little. I only found something once—an open bottle of wine in her fridge. She told me she bought it for cooking. I chose to believe her. After all, it was out in the open. She wasn't trying to hide it.

But whether or not she was drinking, I could feel the change in her. Could see it in her eyes. We still went out. I took her on dates, and we hung out together at home. We double-dated with Charlie and Olivia. She went to work, and I went to class. I brought up the possibility of transferring to another school, and she enthusiastically told me to go for it.

And I told myself that maybe things were normal. Maybe it was just my imagination. I'd been so concerned about how she would handle her mother's death, I'd assumed the worst. I kept expecting her to crash. But maybe she wouldn't. Maybe I'd done enough to love her through it, and she'd be fine.

By the end of January, she and Olivia were busy getting ready for the bookstore's first event. Olivia had opened the café counter after the first of the year, and things seemed to be going well. Olivia was happy, at least.

She and Charlie were as serious as ever. Their relationship had moved so fast in the beginning, I'd been a little worried. But I'd never seen Charlie this crazy about anyone. They got into it sometimes, but nothing like he and Kimmie had. And Olivia was a spitfire. I figured the occasional outburst—and unfortunately for me, loud makeup sex—was simply part of the deal with her. She wasn't bitchy or malicious—just a little intense. And I could tell she loved Charlie just as much as he loved her. I was happy for them.

I got out of class one Friday afternoon and texted Brooke to see when she was off work. I figured I could head over to the bookstore and pick her up if she wasn't going to be there late.

Brooke: I'm not at work. Don't feel well.

Sebastian: I'm sorry, baby. What can I bring you?

Brooke: No, don't come over. I can't get you sick.

I looked at her message, frustrated. I did have to be careful about exposure to illnesses. But I couldn't shake the feeling that she wasn't really sick. That she was having a bad day, and she'd made up an excuse so she didn't have to go anywhere.

Instead of texting her back, I stopped at a deli to pick up hot chicken soup, and went to her house. She answered the door dressed in a rumpled t-shirt and leggings, with thick socks and a big blanket draped around her shoulders. She hadn't complained about the Iowa winter nearly as much as I'd thought she would, but she did have a growing collection of blankets that she wore like some girls wore jewelry.

She peered at me through the partially open door. "Hey. I told you not to come over. I don't want to get you sick."

Instead of hesitating on her front step, I used my size. I crowded up close and gently pushed until she had no choice but to let me in.

"I'll be fine. If you're really that sick, I'll just wash my hands a lot and keep it G-rated." I kissed her forehead. "I brought soup."

I grabbed a spoon from the kitchen and brought her soup into the living room. She sank down onto the couch and curled up in the far corner.

She took it and smiled. "Thanks."

"You bet," I said. "Gotta take care of my girl."

"You shouldn't stay, though," she said. "I'd feel awful if you got sick because of me. You know you can't mess around with that."

"I know. Do you have a cold or something?" I asked. She didn't sound congested.

"Something like that." She blew on a spoonful of soup and took a sip.

I watched her for a moment. She was a little pale, but still so goddamn beautiful. Even with her dark hair in a messy bun, disheveled clothes, wrapped up in a blanket. But she was fading, the light in her eyes growing dim.

"You know you can talk to me, right?" I said. "About anything."

"Yeah, of course," she said.

"Are you going to tell me what else is going on?" I asked.

She looked up. "What do you mean?"

"You're not just sick," I said. "Do you think I can't tell when something is bothering you?"

"I'm fine," she said. "I'm just feeling a little under the weather. It's that time of year; it happens. I've got people sneezing all over shit in the store. I'm surprised I didn't catch something sooner."

"Okay," I said. "But I still feel like you're not telling me something."

"Do you think I'm lying to you?" she asked. "What are you implying?"

"Nothing," I said. "It's just that ever since you went to Phoenix, you've seemed... off. Like there's a lot going on in your head that you aren't talking about."

"I told you what happened in Phoenix," she said. "My mom died. Her boyfriend told me she'd been sober for a while, but relapsed. It was really sad, and I felt bad for him too. That's about it."

"Did you open the box of stuff he gave you?" I asked.

She hesitated, looking down at her soup. "No. Not yet."

"Are you afraid of what you'll find?" I asked, my voice gentle.

"I think so," she said, and for a second, I thought her protective barrier was coming down. "But, honestly, it's not that big of a deal. It's probably just a bunch of useless crap anyway. She kept weird stuff sometimes."

God, why wouldn't she just talk to me?

"What has your therapist said about all this?" I asked. "Has she been helping?"

"I haven't really been to see her in a while," she said.

"What?" I asked. "I thought you went every week."

"Well, I was going every week, but I had to cancel when I went to Phoenix. And you know, stuff gets in the way. I just haven't rescheduled."

"Brooke, don't you think you should?"

"I will," she said. Her flippant tone was pissing me off. "It's just hard to fit in with work and everything."

"Yeah, but you need to make that a priority," I said. "Especially now."

"What do you mean, *especially now*?"

"I mean, you lost your mom. And then the holidays and everything. Those can be hard for anyone. I can see it in your eyes. There's something there, and you're not talking about it. If you won't talk to me, at least go talk to her."

"I don't have anything to talk about." She moved her blanket off her shoulders and stood. "I'm fine."

She walked into the kitchen and put her soup away in the fridge. When she came back, she settled on the couch next to me. I wrapped an arm around her and she tucked herself against me.

"Don't worry so much about me," she said.

"Brooke, I love you," I said. "Of course I'm going to worry about you."

She took a deep breath. "I love you, too. And I'm sorry."

"For what?"

"I don't know. Everything."

I set my chin on her head and held her close. I hated feeling so helpless. No matter what she said, I knew she wasn't okay. Depression was serious. I'd been doing everything I could to coax her out of it. To love her through it. But she still held back. Kept it to herself. It was like she didn't want to burden me with her problems. But I wanted to help her carry them. And I'd told her that. Tried to show her. I was here for her. I could help.

But if she didn't want help, what else could I do?

I felt her slipping down a slope and if something didn't catch her, she was going to crash. I could see it coming. The last time, I'd called in the *big guns*, as she'd said. Olivia coming to Iowa, and giving her the chance to reconnect with the Harpers, had been good for her. It had helped. For a while, she'd been doing so well.

But who could I turn to this time? What was my plan B if she didn't come around? There wasn't anything more Olivia could do for her. I'd hoped her therapist would make a difference, but if she wasn't going to her appointments, that didn't do any good. Short of driving her there and watching her go in—which I was seriously considering—I couldn't force her to go. And if I made her go to therapy, would it help? Would she open up?

I knew what it was to struggle. To have circumstances

beyond your control threaten to take you down. It was serious shit, and it could be hard as hell to deal with.

The heart that had loved Brooke had saved me. I wanted to return the favor. I wanted to save her. Not just for her, or for me. For Liam Harper, too. For the man who would have loved her through dark times if he had lived, and I had died.

I just didn't know if I could.

34

BROOKE

*E*ven though I was vaguely aware of what was happening, I felt powerless to stop it. I'd called in sick to work again—the second time this week. Told myself I was just tired. Fighting off a cold. But the heaviness in my limbs and the deepening sense of lethargy that plagued me wasn't because I'd caught something at the bookstore.

I hated that I'd started to fall apart in Phoenix so badly. Before I'd come to Iowa, I'd kept myself numb. I'd swung from being too depressed to get out of bed, to staying too drunk to care. I'd found ways to bury my grief. Whether it had been drinking myself senseless, or taking stupid risks for the rush, I'd self-medicated. Kept myself from feeling things too much.

Now I didn't have that protection. I'd opened myself up again, but that meant being vulnerable. I'd gone to Phoenix without any way of defending my emotions from the onslaught of memories. Liam's house. My mother. It had all flooded in, overwhelming me.

There was an inevitability to all of it. A pattern I was locked into repeating. I had read that the human body strives for homeostasis—a state of balance it's always trying to maintain. Perhaps the same could be said for a whole person. I had a norm, a default setting, and I was always going to return to it.

Just like her. Just like my mother.

Was it because of losing Liam? Had his death torn me apart so thoroughly that I was unable to recover? Or was it because of my childhood? I'd spent my life being shuffled from place to place. Hurt and neglected. Exposed to things no child should ever see.

Or was this just the way I was made?

My experiences had shaped me, but at the end of the day, I was my mother's daughter. She'd lived in a loop of chaos. For brief periods—usually measured in weeks or months—things had been good. She'd been happy. Sober. A mother to her daughter, a good friend to the people in her life. But those times had always been temporary. Even with a man in her life who had tried, who had seemed to truly love her, she'd failed. Returned to the person she really was inside. And it had killed her.

I couldn't get Mack's face out of my mind. He'd looked so sad. So devastated. He'd sacrificed for her, thinking he could do enough. Thinking he could save her. And in the end, all he'd been left with was the pain of loving someone who was too broken to love him back. And the grief of losing her, even though he'd tried.

I couldn't escape the feeling—the fear—that I was exactly the same.

Olivia opened the door, letting in a blast of cold air. I pulled my blanket tighter around me.

"Still sick?" she asked.

"Yeah," I said. "How's the shop?"

She didn't answer right away—kept her back to me and

took off her coat. The hairs on the back of my neck stood on end and anxiety tingled my belly. Olivia was pissed.

"The shop?" She turned and put her hands on her hips. "Well, it's fine, I guess. We have an author signing coming up and I don't know what the fuck is happening with it, since you decided you needed to stay home and hold the couch down or something."

"I'm sorry," I said. "I haven't been feeling well."

She rolled her eyes. "Yeah, right."

"What's that supposed to mean?" I asked.

"Don't even get me started." She walked into the kitchen and opened the fridge.

"No, really," I said. "You're obviously mad. I'm sorry I've missed work. I'll be in tomorrow. Or we can go over the event stuff now, if you want."

"I wouldn't want to interrupt your sulking time," she said.

"I'm not sulking," I said. "What the hell?"

"Whatever it is you're doing, I'm getting tired of it." She slammed the fridge closed.

"I'm just not feeling well," I said.

"Will you stop? You might have everyone else fooled with that act, but I don't buy it. I never did."

"I'm not acting," I said.

"No?" She came out of the kitchen and folded her arms. "I call bullshit. You're very good at getting attention when you want it."

"Excuse me?"

"You'll just sink into your little pity hole and wait for everyone to come dig you out. Then bask in their adoration."

"What the fuck, Olivia?"

She shook her head. "Quit pretending you don't know

what you're doing. I've seen you do it before. I even fucking fell for it again. I came all the way out here because I thought, shit, I said some hurtful things and if she's in a bad place, maybe I can help. But it was just the same game again. What is it this time? Has Sebastian been too busy to pay attention to you? You have to invent more fucking drama so people will tell you how sweet you are?"

"Is that what you think of me?" I asked. "That I manufacture drama to get attention?"

"You get everyone to make excuses for you," she said. "My parents did it. Of course Sebastian does it. He's blind when it comes to you. But now Joe, and even Charlie. God, it's like people meet you and they want to fucking fall all over themselves to make you happy."

"What are you talking about?" I asked. "I've never asked anyone to make excuses. I missed a couple of days of work. Why are you being so dramatic about it?"

"Oh, I'm not the one being dramatic," she said. "I don't know why Joe doesn't just fire you."

Anger blazed to life, making my cheeks hot. I stood, clenching my hands into fists. "What have I ever done to you?"

"Where do I begin?" she asked. "You put my parents through hell after Liam died. They bent over backwards to help you, and you just bailed."

"I bailed because you told me you didn't want me around," I said. "You told me I wasn't part of your family."

"Because you were already such a fucking mess," she said. "And all they could talk about was *poor Brooke. That poor girl.*"

"So they shouldn't have given a shit about me?" I asked.

"Maybe they should have given a shit about *me*," she said, stepping closer. "He was my *brother*."

"Is that why you resent me so much?" I asked. "Because of the way your parents treated me after he died?"

"You have no idea what it was like," she said. "And it never really stopped. Everyone jumps to come to your fucking rescue. I lost my brother and everyone was so busy worrying about you, they didn't bother to worry about me."

"And you think that was my fault?" I asked. "You think I asked for that? For any of it? I would have done anything to have him back. To have not gone on that stupid trip."

"But you did," she said. "He wanted to rescue you, too. He couldn't fucking help himself."

The meaning behind her words screamed at me. It made my anger boil, running through my veins like fire. "Because he loved me."

"Yeah, and it killed him," she said. "He fucking died because of you."

My hand flew, my open palm striking her cheek with a loud smack. She stepped back, grabbing the side of her face while I stared at her in horror. Without a word, she grabbed her coat and ran out the door. Slammed it behind her.

I staggered backward, my heart racing. Oh my god. What had I done? I'd hit her. I'd gotten so angry, I'd slapped her across the face.

Just like my mom had done to me.

Her tires squealed as she backed out of the driveway. How could I have done that? To her, of all people. I covered my mouth as I choked out a sob.

God, what was wrong with me? Why was I such a fucking disaster? I stumbled to my room and shut the door behind me. I thought about getting my phone—trying to call or text her. But what different would it make? It was better if she left me—if she stayed away. It would be better if everyone did.

35

BROOKE

When Sebastian opened the door, I couldn't look him in the eyes. I saw the first twitch of his smile, but I glanced away and stepped past him into his house.

"Hey," he said. "What's wrong?"

I took a few more steps, trying to keep distance between us. If he held me—if he so much as touched me—I'd lose my resolve. I wouldn't be strong enough to do what I knew had to be done.

"I need to talk to you," I said.

"Sure," he said. "We've got the place to ourselves. I don't know where Charlie went. Is he with Olivia?"

Oh my god, he didn't know. "I guess so."

"Brooke, you're really freaking me out right now," he said. "What's going on?"

"I hit Olivia."

He didn't say anything. I glanced back over my shoulder, terrified of what I'd see.

His eyes were intense, piercing through me. "What happened?"

"She came home angry at me for missing work," I said. "We got in an argument and I hit her."

"Holy shit," he said. "When?"

"A little while ago," I said. "She left. I assume she's with Charlie now. Hopefully."

"You guys argued about work?" he asked. "How did that turn into..."

"It doesn't matter."

He took a step toward me, tentative like he was afraid of scaring me away. "Actually, it kind of does."

"I got angry, and I slapped her," I said. "That's what happened."

"You can tell me the whole story," he said. "I'm not going to flip out on you."

"I told you, it doesn't matter," I said.

"Okay," he said. "Here's what we'll do. Give her time to calm down. I'm sure Charlie's working on that. She'll sleep here tonight, and we can all get together in the morning. We'll figure this out."

"No, we won't," I said. "There's nothing to figure out."

"So, you're just going to throw away your friendship with her?" he asked. "Over one fight?"

"Not because of one fight," I said. "Because all I've ever done is fuck things up for her. She had this nice family, living in a nice house, and then I showed up. She had to share everything with me, whether she liked it or not. Her room. Her parents. Her brother."

"I don't think it was like that," he said. "You and Olivia were good friends back then, weren't you?"

"Everything fell apart when he died," I said. "And maybe she was right. Maybe it was my fault."

"Whoa," he said, holding up a hand. "Stop right there. Is

that what she said? Did Olivia tell you Liam's death was your fault?"

"It was, in a way," I said. "If he had never met me, he wouldn't have been on the road that day."

"Brooke, you can't think like that," he said.

"I put his family through hell," I said. "I was too weak to handle his death. So I just said fuck it. And then they kept trying to help me, Seb. They kept fucking trying. And for what?"

"For you," he said. "They kept trying because they cared about you."

I shook my head and my breath came in shaky gasps. "They shouldn't have. They should have sent me back home the night my mother left. Or called social services. They never should have let me in their lives."

"Brooke, what the fuck are you talking about?"

"This is what happens with me," I said. "Don't you see it? I'm a mess. That's all I'll ever be. It's going to keep happening, over and over. It doesn't matter if I do okay for a while. I can't sustain it. She couldn't, and I can't either."

"She?" he asked. "Are you talking about your mom? Brooke, you're not your mother."

"No," I said. "I'm not her. But I'm made of the same stuff. For a while I thought maybe I wasn't. I didn't get pregnant when I was a teenager, or get addicted to drugs. But the details don't matter. Just like her, sooner or later, I hurt the people I love. I fuck things up. I get my shit all over their lives. I can't do that anymore."

"So you're going to blow off Olivia?" he asked.

"I'm not talking about Olivia."

His face hardened and he crossed his arms over his wide chest. He stood with his feet shoulder width apart, a huge immovable wall of man, glowering at me. His eyebrows drew down and the veins in his muscular arms stood out.

"I know what you're doing," he said.

"Sebastian, you have to understand." My throat felt thick. "My mother's greatest act of love was to leave me. She did it to give me a chance. It's not her fault it didn't work. She had her own demons to fight, and they killed her. She left someone behind who was gutted and broken, because he couldn't save her. You can't save me, either. And I love you too much to let you torture yourself trying."

He didn't respond. Just stared at me, arms crossed.

"I'm sorry," I said. God, this hurt so much. "You need to go do all those things you want to do. Go finish school. Get your architecture degree. Live your dreams."

"What are you going to do?" he asked.

I blinked at him. "What? I don't know."

"Are you going to go to work?"

"What does that have to do with anything?" I asked. "I'm telling you I can't be with you, and you're worried about my fucking job?"

"I'm wondering how badly you're planning to self-destruct," he said. "I see what you're doing right now, Brooke. If this is what you think you need, then fine. Walk away. But I see through your bullshit."

"This isn't bullshit," I said, my voice rising. "I don't know why you want to be with someone like me anyway. Look at your family, where you grew up. Do you think I fit in that world? You know where I come from, Seb? Houses filled with cigarette smoke. Weed. Fucking piles of beer cans, or little pieces of foil with burn marks lying around. I grew up with a mom who'd hit me for looking at her wrong. Who was so skinny, she looked like she never ate. We were so poor, one year my only Christmas present was a half-used coloring book and a ballpoint pen from our landlord."

"None of that is your fault," he said. "None of that is *you*."

"No?" I asked. "I had a fiancé and a family who loved me. And sure, for a while, I lived like a normal girl. I even went to college. But after a while? I went right back to what I really was. The drunk girl in a fucking bar, hanging on a guy who'd give me a black eye."

He shook his head. "We both know that isn't who you are."

"That's what I'm trying to tell you," I said. "That's exactly who I am. It's where I go back to, every time. Nice, normal people try to help me, and all I do is leave more damage in my wake."

"Brooke—"

"No," I said. "I'm not going to ruin your second chance at life. That heart inside of you deserves better. Liam did, and you do too."

He blocked my path to the door, so I veered around him, keeping my head down. I couldn't look at his face. I didn't want to hurt him, but that was inevitable. At least this way it would be over and he could move on with his life. That was what I wanted for him. To live. To take that second chance he'd been given and run with it. Not spend it pointlessly trying to fix someone like me.

I slammed the door behind me. Sebastian didn't follow.

I walked home in the cold, my breath misting out in a cloud. I tried to imagine what my mom had felt, the night I'd gone to the Harper's for good. What had she been thinking when she'd walked back inside that house? When she'd driven away, leaving me behind? I'd always thought she must have been relieved. I'd been a burden she'd been stuck with. A consequence for not being careful.

Liam had said she'd left me because she'd loved me. I'd never really believed that until now. Until I was faced with the same choice.

But if she'd felt relief that night—even relief that her daughter was in better hands—I didn't feel the same. I'd hoped I would feel lighter, knowing I'd done the right thing. But all I felt was the oppressive weight of loneliness. The ache in my chest spread wide, consuming me. I was so hollow. So empty.

Sebastian had put my heart back inside of me, and for a while, it had beat in time with his. But I'd left it with him. He could keep it. I didn't need it anymore.

36

SEBASTIAN

*I*f Brooke was aware of how often I checked up on her, she didn't let on. Maybe I was stealthier than my size would imply. I didn't let it mess with my life. I went to my classes. Studied. Hung out with Charlie sometimes. But I always found ways to see what she was doing.

It wasn't difficult, considering how rarely she left her house. She didn't go to work. I had no idea if she'd actually quit, if she was pulling her sick routine, or if she'd just stopped going without explanation. I wanted to go talk to her boss, but I decided against it. Even if he listened to me, what good would it do? It wasn't like I could drag her down there and make her show up.

She was self-destructing, and it was fucking painful to watch.

At first, I'd figured I'd let a few days go by, give her space, and wait for her to come back. But a few days turned into a week, and I didn't hear from her. It was hard not to call, or go see her. I knew she was hurting, and every bit of me wanted to make her feel better. But I waited.

Olivia basically moved in. None of us talked about

Brooke. It was this giant fucking elephant in the room that we all pretended to ignore. It was stupid, but the one time I'd almost brought up what was happening, Charlie had tried to murder me with his eyes.

I didn't blame Olivia for being mad. Hearing Brooke had slapped her had been a shock. It wasn't cool, but I knew there was more to it. If Olivia had thrown Liam's death in her face—said it had been Brooke's fault... well, she didn't deserve to get hit. No one did. But it made it easier to understand why Brooke had been mad enough to do it.

But Brooke had pushed everyone away. She was completely alone, and I hated it.

I'd been putting off seeing my parents, so when they asked me to come to dinner, I agreed. I drove out to Waverly —alone this time. Didn't even tell Charlie I was going. I wasn't in the mood for any of it, but at least I'd get my mom's cooking out of the deal.

Although, if Cami was there, I'd turn around and leave.

Thankfully, it was just my mom and dad. I went inside and chatted with them in the kitchen while they finished getting dinner ready. Small talk, mostly. They didn't ask about Brooke, or why I'd come alone.

My mom had made enough food to feed ten people, but that was typical. We sat down at the table together, but the quiet was distracting. I couldn't remember the last time I'd been here without at least Charlie along. But this was how it had been, once. Just us three.

"How are your classes going?" Dad asked.

"Fine." I hadn't told them about applying to other schools, but it was one of the reasons I'd come. "I actually switched a couple of classes last minute, but it's worked out fine."

"Switched?" Dad asked. "Why?"

"So I could get prerequisites out of the way," I said. "I'm applying to architecture programs."

Dad put his fork down. "Architecture? Why would you do that?"

"Because I want to be an architect," I said. If he was going to ask an obvious question, I'd give an obvious answer.

"Since when?" he asked.

I shrugged. "I've thought about it for a while. This is what I want to do."

"But honey," Mom said, "you're almost finished with your degree. You don't want to be in school that much longer, do you?"

"That was a consideration, but I decided it would be worth it."

My parents looked at each other like they were baffled.

Dad's brow furrowed. "I guess this means..."

"It means I'm not going to move back here and work for you," I said. "I'm sorry, Dad. I know that's what you wanted for me. But that just isn't what I want to do with my life."

"Son, this is something I can do for you," Dad said. "Something I can give you. I built up this business from nothing. I wasn't just going to have you work for me. You'd do that until you had some experience, and then I was going to hand it over to you."

"I know," I said. "But I don't need you to give this to me. You've already given me everything. You guys raised me well, gave me a good, solid home." I met my mom's eyes. "And you didn't give up on me when I was ready to throw in the towel."

My mom took a deep breath. "I'm not sure what to say."

"I've been trying to figure out what I'm supposed to do

with my life ever since it sank in that I was going to get to have one," I said. "And I think I'm finally starting to."

Dad nodded slowly. "All right, then. What schools are you thinking about?"

I couldn't help but grin a little. On to practical matters. That was my dad. "I've applied to Virginia Tech, University of Texas, and University of Michigan."

Mom's mouth hung open, her worry lines deepening.

"Mom," I cut in before she could say anything. "I know, they're far away. But they're the best fits."

"You've already applied," Dad said. It was more a statement than a question.

"Once I made the decision, I was all in," I said.

Dad chuckled. "Of course you were. I wouldn't expect anything less."

"Oh, Sebastian," Mom said.

Dad put his hand over hers. "He'll be fine. Look at him. You wanted our son back. I'd say we got him, and then some."

It felt damn good to hear him say that. "Thanks, Dad."

"What about your girlfriend?" Dad asked, and Mom looked down at the table. "She going with you?"

I knew they'd ask about Brooke, and I didn't have a good answer. I hated living without her. It felt wrong down to the very core of my being. And the longer I went without seeing her, the more I started to wonder if she was ever going to come around.

I'd tried to imagine moving away without her. Going to school in another city and leaving her behind. The problem was, without her, all my plans fell apart. All my dreams and aspirations had her in them.

"I'm not sure," I said, and it was the honest truth.

"All right," Dad said. "I can't say I'm not disappointed. I

was looking forward to having you close by. But I'm proud of you."

"Thanks, Dad."

After dinner, I drove home with a full stomach—and half a cheesecake I knew Charlie would devour. I felt good about the way I'd left things with my parents. They'd hugged me at the door, and both of them had told me again that they were proud of me.

But the closer I got to Iowa City, the deeper my sense of unease grew. I'd been making sure Brooke wasn't out doing anything that would get her hurt—or worse—and so far she hadn't done anything crazy. At least, not that I knew of. But her silence was painful. I was starting to look at the future with a new sense of who I was, and who I was going to become. But none of it mattered without her.

I didn't love her because of some weird transplant phenomenon. It wasn't like the random cravings I got for peach iced tea. But there *was* an element I couldn't explain. Liam's heart had recognized hers the day we met.

But the bond we'd forged was ours. It was built on the ashes our former lives—our former selves. We were two people who had been through fire. We'd suffered pain, tragedy, and loss. And yet, in the aftermath, we'd found each other. And as far as I was concerned, a life lived together was the only option.

She had my heart, and she always would. It had belonged to her before it had belonged to me. It belonged to her still. I just hoped she'd realize it before it was too late.

37

BROOKE

*T*he bartender put a glass of whiskey on a napkin in front of me. I nodded my thanks, and he left to see to his other customers.

It wasn't busy. Enough people that a low hum of conversation hovered in the background. Not so many that it was crowded. Music played, but I didn't recognize most of the songs. The lights were low, the bartender never smiled, and the guy sitting two barstools down kept falling asleep, his scruffy chin resting on his chest.

I took a sip of my water, leaving the whiskey to sit on its napkin. I had my notebook open, my pen in hand. I hadn't written a word since I'd left Sebastian. But my thoughts were eating at me from the inside, and I hoped I could get them out on paper. Maybe quiet them down.

It had been my therapist's idea. Almost on a whim, I'd called her this morning. I couldn't remember the last time I'd seen her. She hadn't had time in her schedule for a full appointment, but she'd fit me in for fifteen minutes in the afternoon.

It had taken so much effort to make myself go. In the

time between making the call and going to her office, I'd invented at least a dozen excuses to cancel. But in the end, I'd gone. She'd asked me a few questions, and then suggested I try her writing exercise.

Just write, she'd said. Not with form or intent. I wasn't supposed to worry about sentences or punctuation or even making sense. Just write whatever came to mind—whatever thoughts and feelings were *in* my mind.

I began, and my pen moved across the paper, leaving a trail of blue ink. I kept my eyes moving forward—didn't allow myself to read what I'd written. I just needed an outlet. A place to put all these feelings. I filled the page, so I turned to a new one and kept writing. Glanced up at the whiskey. Still didn't take a drink.

I wrote more. Filled pages and pages. My hand cramped and once in a while I had to pause to stretch my fingers. But still the words tumbled from my mind, through my pen, and onto the paper.

Eventually, I stopped. The swirl of madness in my head wasn't spinning so fast, the whirlpool of thoughts was slowing. Calmness crept over me. My muscles relaxed and the tension in my shoulders eased. I put my pen down and flexed my fingers, opening and closing my hand a few times.

Then, with a tingling sense of trepidation in my stomach, I looked back on what I'd written.

At first, it was random. Single words, some phrases. Things like *hollow*, *tears*, and *I'm lonely*. By the top of the third page, my ramblings took on more form. Lines and sentences. Complete thoughts. Questions.

Is there a door on the other side of the darkness, and if there is, will I be able to find it?

How does the cycle end?

Am I strong enough for this?

And there, among the words I'd written, his name. Sebastian.

He was always on my mind. I missed him desperately. The warmth of his strong body. His big hand holding mine. The way his beard scratched my neck or my cheek... or my thighs. The way he kissed me, so fierce and passionate. Just thinking about him brought tears to my eyes and made the hollow space in my chest ache.

I closed my notebook and tucked it away in my bag. Tossed some money on the bar—more than necessary, even with a tip—and walked out the front door.

I left the whiskey sitting, untouched.

My house was dark and cold. I turned up the heat and flicked on a few lights. Shivering a little, I went to my bedroom and found a thicker pair of socks and a long knit sweater. As I put them on, the half-open closet caught my eye.

I took out my backpack—the one I'd carried around in Phoenix. The box holding Liam's engagement ring was still tucked inside. I opened it and ran my finger over the smooth gold band. Then I put it aside, and pulled out the dance photo.

How you doing, Bee?

"I don't know," I said, touching his face in the photo. "Not so well, I guess."

I gazed at the picture for a minute. But Liam couldn't help me. He wasn't here to save me anymore. With a deep breath, I put it all away.

My mom's box was still in my closet, unopened. I'd been too afraid to look. I had no idea what a woman like her would have kept. Was there anything meaningful in there? Or would it be another disappointment? A box full of junk I'd have to throw away.

I put it on the bed and sat in front of it, cross-legged. My heart fluttered as I lifted the lid and set it aside.

It was full to the top. I found papers, some in envelopes. Most of them looked old—faded and yellowing. A copy of an old lease for an apartment in Albuquerque. Two bus tickets from Fort Worth to Tulsa. An envelope, shaped like it had once held a greeting card, with a handful of pictures— all of people I didn't recognize. None of it meant anything— at least not to me—so I dug deeper to see what else was in there.

My hand touched something soft. It was a strange contrast to the smooth feel of paper around it. I grabbed it and pulled it out of the box.

It was the pink teddy bear my mom had won for me at the fair.

I stared at the tattered stuffed animal. Its fur was unevenly worn, one foot so threadbare the stuffing showed through. It had lost an eye and I'd tried to fix it by drawing one in sharpie, but it was crooked compared to the original. The piece of thread that had been its mouth was loose, and its once-bright pink color had faded considerably.

Of all the toys I'd ever owned—there hadn't been many —this one had been my favorite. It had meant the most. I'd slept with it every night. Set it carefully on my pillow each morning. I'd sat in my room and held it, telling it stories. Whispering prayers and wishes. Cried with it clutched tightly in my arms.

By the time it had gone missing, I'd outgrown it. But I'd still been sad to realize it had gone. I hadn't been sleeping with it anymore, but it had still meant something to me. It had been a memory of a good day with her. A day that had stood out in its goodness because there had been so few.

A tear broke free from the corner of my eye and slid

down my cheek. She'd kept it. I didn't know when she'd taken it and added it to her box, but at some point, she'd decided to save it. Had she done it for herself? Had she remembered that day like I had?

Maybe it had represented the same thing for her that it had for me. A memory of something good between us. A dream of what could have been, if things had been different.

One thing I knew without a shred of doubt. It meant she'd loved me.

I touched its face, biting my lip to keep from crying too hard. Although I wished I'd had the chance to see her again, in some ways this was better. It whispered the words I'd needed to hear so badly, said them directly into my heart: *I love you, Brooke.*

With a trembling breath, I sniffed hard. Instead of putting it back in the box, I put it in my backpack, along with my dance picture and engagement ring. It felt like it belonged there, with the other moments that had shaped me. The good ones. The memories where love had won.

I wiped my cheeks and went into the bathroom to blow my nose. As I was tossing the tissue into the garbage, I heard a knock at my door.

It didn't sound like Sebastian's big fist. His knock was louder. I walked out and opened the door, my tummy full of nerves. It was Olivia.

"Hi," she said.

I was so surprised to see her, I didn't know what to say.

"Look, if you don't want to see me, I get it," she said. "But um, could you let me know one way or the other so I can either come in or get back in my car? It's freezing out here."

"Come in."

"This Iowa winter shit sucks," she said, rubbing her hands together as I shut the door behind her. She wore a thick coat and a knit hat with a little crocheted flower on one side. "So, I came over because I think I was actually the bigger asshole. Can we talk, maybe?"

"Sure," I said.

We sat down at the little table Sebastian and I had repainted. That seemed so long ago.

"Okay, I'll go first," she said. "What happened to Liam wasn't your fault. I didn't mean that, and I never should have said it. I admitted it to Charlie, and he kind of ripped me a new one. He's still pissed at you for slapping me, but he did tell me I was a huge jerk for saying something so awful to you."

I nodded, but the guilt I felt was overwhelming. "It doesn't matter what you said. I never should have hit you. I'm so sorry."

"It's okay," she said. "I deserved it, at least a little bit."

"That's what my mom would have done," I said, my eyes on the table. "She hit me when she was angry."

Olivia put a hand over mine. "I know. Actually, when you did that, it made me realize what that must have been like for you. A little bit, anyway. I hadn't thought about it very much before. I kept thinking about how angry I'd been because my parents were so concerned about you all the time. But, I think it was because you needed it so much more than I did. I had this great childhood with nice parents who were still married. The worst thing that ever happened to me was when some kid pushed me off a swing when I was nine, and I broke my arm. And it wasn't even all that bad. Mostly I remember getting ice cream after they put on the cast."

I breathed out a soft laugh and she squeezed my hand.

"But you... you lived through things I can't even fathom," she said. "And you were always so alone."

"Yeah."

"Charlie made me realize something else," she said. "I was lying in bed with him and it was one of those moments that's so good it takes your breath away. Do you know what I mean?"

I nodded.

"It wasn't sexual," she said. "It was pure contentment. In that moment, I was so happy and so in love, I wanted to cry. And I was thinking about how lucky I am that we met. And how amazing it was that we love each other so much. There's nothing lopsided or off balance. You don't find that every day, and when you do, you don't want to lose it. In fact, you'll do anything to keep it."

She paused and met my eyes. Took a deep breath before she continued.

"That's when it hit me," she said. "If I lost Charlie, I don't know if I'd be able to live through it."

I took a shaky breath and nodded. I wasn't quite ready to speak.

"You did live through that." Tears filled her eyes. "You loved him *like that*, and you had to watch him die. And then you had to try to go on living without him."

I nodded again. It was all I could do.

"God, Brooke," she said. "I get it now. You're not weak. You're strong as fuck to keep breathing after that. I don't know how you do it."

"Not very well," I said. "Obviously. I'm a fucking disaster."

She laughed. "Yeah, you're a goddamn mess. But honestly? You're not as bad as you think you are."

I wished I could believe her.

We both took deep breaths and wiped our eyes.

"Do you think we can survive this?" she asked. "Because I love you and I really don't want to lose you."

"I don't want to lose you either."

We stood and wrapped each other in a tight hug. It made us cry all over again, so we held on, letting the tears come.

"I know I'm an asshole," Olivia said through her tears. "I'm trying to work on that, though. I'm trying not to lose my temper so much that I'm a horrible person to the people I love."

"I love you too," I said, and sniffed hard. "And believe me, I'm an expert on being horrible to the people I love."

She pulled away and brushed the hair out of my face. "What do you think you're going to do now? Go back to work, maybe? Joe wants you to come back."

"Why would he want me back?" I asked. "I'm the worst employee ever."

"Not the worst," she said. "You should go talk to him. I can go with you, if you want."

I sat back down and Olivia followed. "I'm not sure what I should do. Being here is so painful. I keep thinking about going somewhere else. Starting over again. But I don't know where. And nothing about *me* would be different. I'd still be a mess. But I wouldn't have to walk around through memories all the time."

"I hope you don't leave," she said. "God, life is fucking hard."

"It really is," I said. "I don't know. I feel so lost."

"I wish I could help you find what you're looking for," she said.

"I know," I said. "But I don't think anyone can."

38

SEBASTIAN

I went downstairs after waking from an unintentional nap. I hadn't been sleeping well lately, but when I'd lain down, I'd only meant to rest for twenty minutes or so. Three hours later, I'd come to like a coma patient struggling to regain consciousness. Now I was groggy and dehydrated. I felt like shit.

Although that was basically the norm for me lately. I wasn't moping around like a baby. I was handling my business. But on the inside, I was a wreck. It felt a little bit like I was slowly dying again. Like my heart was struggling to keep up, the compressions labored. I guess when your heart breaks, it feels a lot like a case of myocarditis. It fucking sucked.

I grabbed some water out of the fridge and went over to the couch. I'd stopped checking my phone quite so often, hoping Brooke had sent a message. But I still did it, and still felt the let-down that she hadn't. I could have been the one to call, but it didn't feel like the right thing to do. If I muscled my way back into her life, we'd only wind up right back where we started. Something needed to change first.

I went over to the couch and plopped down. Olivia was in the big overstuffed chair by the window.

"Hey," she said.

"Sup, O," I said. "Where's Chuck?"

"Store," she said.

I took a drink. "I hope he's getting me dinner."

She smiled. "Yeah, you know he has your back. Although that means it'll be something healthy. Bo-ring."

I tapped my chest. "Gotta take care of the ticker."

"Yeah," she said. "Speaking of... I saw Brooke yesterday."

That got my attention. "You did? Where?"

"Her house."

"And?"

"Well, I apologized for my role in the assholery that occurred recently," she said. "And she did the same."

"You guys made up?"

She nodded. "Yeah, we're good. I kind of figured some things out that I should have realized a long time ago. You know, life experience and stuff. It makes a difference."

"Sure does. How is she?"

"Not great," she said. "Maybe not as terrible as I thought she'd be. It looks like she's eating and all that. And there was a notebook sitting out with a pen next to it. If that means she's writing, it could be a good sign. I think she works stuff out that way, you know?"

"She does," I said.

"But, I don't know, Seb. I told her she should come back to work, because I know Joe will take her back. He misses her dumb ass. But she said no. She said she's thinking about leaving and starting over somewhere."

Oh, fuck no. "She what?"

"She wasn't packing or anything," she said. "But you

never know with her. She upped and left Phoenix. I'm a little worried she might do the same thing again. And if she decides to disappear, it's pretty hard to find her. Trust me. She didn't even have to leave the area after my brother died and it was impossible to track her down."

I stood, spilling my water. But I didn't give a shit. I grabbed my coat and my keys. This had gone on long enough.

"Good luck," Olivia said.

I was already out the door.

Brooke's house was dark. I banged on the door. No answer. Again. Fuck. She couldn't have left. Olivia said she'd only mentioned it.

God, Brooke, don't do this. Don't disappear on me.

I still had a key, so I let myself in. She could be pissed at me all she wanted for it. I walked through the rooms, but her stuff was all there. Even her backpack was tucked away in the closet. I knew what she kept in there, and I didn't think she'd leave it behind. That made me feel better.

But I was still worried. Where had she gone?

I checked her kitchen for bottles. Looked in the garbage. Nothing. Checked her bathroom and the drawers in her bedroom. I kept thinking about her on the couch in that frat house, so wasted she could barely stand. I hoped she wouldn't do something like that again. But if she was unraveling, I didn't know what she'd resort to in order to escape her pain.

It would be hard to find her if I just drove around. She didn't have a car—she walked places, or used the bus or Uber—so I couldn't find her that way. It was cold as shit outside, so she probably wasn't walking. She could be pretty much anywhere.

I took out my phone and called her, but it went straight to voicemail. She'd either ignored my call, or her phone was off. Maybe she'd forgotten to charge the battery. Or hadn't bothered. Damn it.

I texted her anyway, in case she just didn't want to talk to me. Maybe she'd read it.

I'll leave you alone if you want but please tell me where you are.

I also texted Olivia and Charlie, asking them to call me if they heard from her. Olivia texted back a few minutes later to say she'd called her, but it had gone straight to voicemail.

There were a few places I could check—places I knew she liked or might go. The bookstore was closed. I stopped at a restaurant we'd been to a bunch of times, but she wasn't inside. If there was a horror flick playing, she might have been at the theater. I checked the movie times, but none of them seemed like something she'd go see.

If she wanted to drink, she might be at a bar. But fuck, it was a college town. There were bars everywhere. I drove around town a while longer, but there was no sign of her at any of the places I tried.

My last hunch was a little tavern that was walking distance from our neighborhood. I didn't think she'd have walked in the cold, but I'd checked everywhere else. Might as well stop there, too.

As soon as I stepped inside, I knew she was there. It took me a few seconds to find her. She was on a stool at the far end of the bar. It looked like she was leaning over a notebook and writing something. She had a glass of water near her left hand, and a glass of what was probably whiskey sitting in front of her.

Something came together inside of me at the sight of her. That drive I'd always had. The determination. I felt it again, stronger than ever before. More intense than before any wrestling match—even before I'd faced Charlie at state. It coalesced into a razor-sharp point, and I made a decision. I was going all in. I knew exactly what I needed to do. And there was no turning back.

39

BROOKE

I sensed Sebastian before I saw him. It wasn't the door. I was too far away to hear it, or feel the gust of cold air. But my heart fluttered and I looked up, knowing he was there.

Tall and thick and strong. His presence sucked the air from my lungs and made my heart pound.

He stalked toward me, his face all hard lines etched in stone. His brow was furrowed, his dark eyebrows drawn together. His mouth was set, his shoulders rigid. It wasn't anger in his expression, although it could easily have been mistaken for it by someone who didn't know him.

Eyes followed him as he moved toward me. The bartender, in particular, had him in his sights.

I closed my notebook and turned on the stool. "What are you doing here?"

"Come with me," he said.

The focus in his eyes was startling. Their shifting colors seemed brighter than usual, even in the dim light of the bar.

"Where?"

His voice didn't change. Urgent, but almost monotone. "Just come."

Something about the way he said it made him impossible to refuse. I dug in my little handbag and pulled out some money.

"You okay, miss?" the bartender asked as I tossed the bill on the bar.

"Yes," I said with a nod, meeting his eyes. I knew what this looked like. Big, bearded, hulking man comes barreling into a bar, looking aggressive and scary. And he did. Even I felt a chill at the look on his face. But Sebastian was the last person in the world who would hurt me. "I'm good. I'm safe with him."

"You sure?" The bartender's eyes flicked to Sebastian, then back to me.

"Absolutely," I said. "But thank you for asking."

"All right," he said.

I slid my notebook into my bag and got down off the stool. Before my feet were flat on the floor, Sebastian turned and walked away. He didn't look back until he held the door open for me.

Still without saying a word, he walked to his car. I got in the passenger's seat and fastened my seat belt.

"Where are we going?"

He didn't answer.

We drove outside the city. His body was tense, his hands tight fists on the steering wheel. My nervousness grew as the lights of civilization faded behind us. Where was he taking me? And why?

He turned down a bumpy road. It was dark, so I couldn't see much of the scenery. We followed the street as it wound around and finally came to an end. From there, he turned again and kept driving. Now I really didn't know where we were. Not on a road. A twinge of fear ran through me. I didn't understand what was going on.

The headlights lit the way, but ahead of us all I could see was black. It was as if the ground simply stopped. He kept driving, the black chasm drawing closer. When we'd almost reached it, he stopped the car.

He put it in park and left the engine running. "Get out."

"What?"

He opened his door. "Get out and trade places with me."

Bewildered, I got out and walked around the back. He stalked past me without saying another word, and got in the passenger's side.

Glancing around, I realized where we must be. It looked like a quarry. And we were parked on the edge of a tall cliff.

I got in the driver's side and shut the door.

"Sebastian, what's going on?" I asked. "You're scaring me."

He shifted in his seat and looked at me. It was hard not to flinch under the heat of his gaze. "I'm not trying to scare you."

"Okay," I said. "Then what are we doing out here?"

"Do you remember the first time we met?" he asked.

"Yes."

"Something happened that day. I can't explain how I knew who you were. I'd never seen you before. I had no idea what you looked like. But I knew you." He put his hand on his chest. "This heart knew you. I don't know how that's possible, but it's true. It's why I approached you. Why I insisted you take my phone number. There was a connection between us, from that first moment."

"I know."

"But that's not why I fell in love with you. I fell for you because of who you are, not because of what's in here." He tapped his chest again. "I fell in love with your spirit, even when it was hidden by sadness. I fell in love with your sense of humor and that spark of adventure you let out sometimes. With your body and the way it fit together perfectly with mine. I fell in love with the way you made me feel alive again."

He paused and looked down for a second. "Loving you is both the easiest and the hardest thing I've ever done. At first, I thought the fact that my heart had been his would be too much. That maybe you'd been too hurt to love someone again—especially me. But that wasn't the case, and for a while there, *god* it was fucking good. We were amazing together, Brooke."

I nodded.

"I recognized something in your eyes," he said. "I saw it when we met, and I see it now. It's the same look I had when I was waiting for a new heart. I wasn't really waiting for a transplant. I was waiting to die. And I know you've been through hell. But goddammit, you don't have to keep living in it. Because you're alive. You didn't die."

"I know."

"Do you?" he asked. "Because I'm not sure."

He was right. I wasn't entirely sure either.

"You know what the craziest thing about this whole situation is? You reminded me how to live again. The girl who can't seem to decide if she's going to live or die is the one who showed me what living is. Jesus, Brooke, don't you realize that? I wasn't living before. I was existing. I kept trying to play it safe. But I don't want safe. I want passion. I want to take risks. I want to push boundaries and try shit I've never done and go places I've never been. You brought that out in me."

Tears burned my eyes, but I didn't know what to say.

"I've tried everything," he said. "I tried to help you. I tried to love you. I even tried to live without you, and that's been a fucking nightmare. But through all of it, I realized something. I can't fix you. I can't make you want to live. That has to come from you."

He looked out the windshield and took a deep breath. "I can't do this anymore. I can't keep trying to drag you through your own life, hoping you'll wake up and start living it. I can't save you, Brooke. You have to save yourself."

"What are you saying?"

"I'm saying I can't be your hero," he said. "Because you don't need one. No one has the power to do this for you. I can be here to support you and love you, but ultimately, none of that is enough if you don't choose to live."

I nodded and looked down at my hands. I knew he was right about that, too.

"But here's the thing," he said. "I love you, and I've told you before, I don't take that lightly. But I can't go on like this. It hurts too goddamn much. I also know I can't live without you. It's like there's something inside of me that's intertwined with you. Living without you isn't an option."

He paused and I looked up. I'd never been afraid of him, but I was now. Afraid of the truth—and the unwavering resolve in his eyes.

"You need to decide, right now," he said. "Are you going to live, or are you going to die? And whatever you decide, I'm going with you."

"What?"

"If you don't want to live—if you just can't do it—put the car in drive and stomp on the gas. Get it over with."

I looked in horror out the windshield. We were only feet from the cliff. It wouldn't take more than a few seconds to reach it. We'd drive right over, and—

"But if you do want to live—and I mean really live, Brooke. No more self-destructive, reckless bullshit. No more checking out and pushing everyone away. If you want to live your life, put it in reverse. Pull back. We'll switch seats and I'll drive us home. But you have to make the choice, right now. And whatever you decide is for both of us. If you're going over the cliff, I'm fucking going with you. Because I know, in the deepest place in my soul, that I can't live without you. I love you, and I don't know how to do anything half-assed. It's the way I'm built. I go all in, or I don't go at all. So if you want to live, with me, put the car in reverse. But if you don't, gun this fucker and we'll go out together."

I stared at him, my lips parted. It felt as if my heart had stopped. He wasn't bluffing. He hadn't brought me out here to scare me into making the choice to live. For all he knew, I'd put the car in drive and kill us both. And he was completely willing to risk it.

He sat motionless. Silent. Giving me time.

He was right. I kept wavering back and forth, between living and fading away. In the process, I'd hurt people I loved. Hurt him.

And I did love him. God, I loved him so much he consumed my soul. I'd loved Liam like a child. It had been simple, and pure. But Sebastian. Our love was like fire. Like a lightning storm. Full of energy and chaos and passion.

He'd taken the shattered pieces of me and tried so hard to hold them together. But he didn't have that power. He could fit them back into place, but they'd only fall apart again, unless I decided to glue them back together.

I had to decide.

Was I nothing but a ghost? An echo of a girl who'd once loved a boy? A copy of a woman who'd hurt her own child?

Decide. The word hummed in my mind, repeating over and over in Sebastian's deep voice. It reverberated through my chest—made my fingers twitch.

I grabbed my notebook from my bag. Sebastian didn't say anything. He kept his eyes focused on me while I opened it and thumbed through the pages. *Decide.*

There it was, written in blue ink. I didn't know where it had come from, because the words didn't seem like mine. But I'd written them down while sitting at the bar, a glass of whiskey I never meant to drink nearby. A reminder of who I could be, and the choice I was making to be someone else.

The choice is yours, Brooke. Yours, and no one else's. You get to decide who you are. That's the beauty of it. The houses you lived in or the messes inside them don't define you. Your mother doesn't define you. Loss doesn't define you. What matters are the decisions you make. You can't control what happens to you. And sometimes that means pain and suffering. Grief and loss. But the worst pain wouldn't exist without the love that preceded it. And isn't that love worth something? In fact, isn't that love worth everything? But you can't love if you're not living. So you're going to have to decide.

I took a trembling breath and put the notebook down. Grabbed the steering wheel with both hands. Pressed my foot down on the brake as hard as I could. And put the car in reverse.

Sebastian didn't crumple with relief as I backed us away from the edge. He watched me, his eyes still burning with the same intensity. I stopped and put the car back in park.

"You're sure?" he asked.

I nodded, trying not to cry. Feeling the deluge of emotion as it bubbled up my throat. "Yes. I'm sure."

He grabbed the back of my head and pulled me to him. Our mouths connected and the relief that poured through me was staggering. He kissed me hard, holding my face against his.

I climbed across the center console and into his lap, still kissing him. His lips on mine and his beard against my skin felt like fate. Like coming home. I straddled his large body and he wrapped his thick arms around me.

"I love you," I whispered into his mouth. "I love you and I don't know what I've ever done to deserve you."

He pulled away and looked deep into my eyes, brushing the hair back from my face. "Maybe love doesn't have to work like that. It's not a game. Someone doesn't have to lose for you to win. I love you because you're my heart. You're my life. And if I choose that—if I choose to love you and be the man you need—we both win. Love wins."

I nodded. "Sebastian, I know I have so much work to do. But I'll do it. I swear."

"Don't do it just for me," he said. "Do it for you."

I kissed him again. Stroked his beard. "For me. For you. For us."

He smiled, then, and much like the first time we met, it took the edge off his intensity. Sparks raced through my veins and the emptiness in my chest filled—filled with his love. His light. His life.

Something inside me had known, when I'd met Sebastian, that my life would never be the same. But I'd never have guessed how true that could be. In him, I'd found my future. My home. My life. And I was never letting it go.

I'd make that choice, every day. The choice to love, and to live. For me, for him, for us.

40

SEBASTIAN

*B*rooke came out of the building and her eyes lit up when she saw me. Her loose yellow dress fluttered in the summer breeze and her bracelets sparkled in the sun. She brushed her hair out of her face and adjusted the strap of her handbag as she walked toward where I was parked.

God, that woman was sexy as fuck. Curves and long legs. Soft skin. I couldn't wait to get her home.

Our home. I'd moved out of the house Charlie and I had shared for so long, and into Brooke's place. Olivia and Charlie had wanted to make their living arrangement permanent, so it made sense for me to move out. But even if they hadn't, I would have moved in with Brooke. We were starting a new life together. Going all in.

We'd be in Iowa City for another year, and then off to a new adventure in Virginia. I'd been accepted to two of the three schools I'd applied to. I chose Virginia Tech. It seemed like the best fit for me. And neither of us had ever been there. That made it even more perfect. A new part of the country to explore. New things to experience. It was going to be strange, not living in Iowa. But for me, home wasn't a place. It was a person.

She stopped on the sidewalk to answer her phone. Smiling again, she held up a finger, letting me know she needed a minute. I waved. *Take your time, baby.*

Brooke was going back to school too. She'd been accepted to the University of Colorado's online program to finish her English degree. Since she'd failed some classes at Arizona State after Liam had died, she'd had to jump through extra hoops to get accepted. She'd written the admissions department a long letter—a letter that had turned into something much more—telling her story.

Not only had she been accepted, they'd directed her toward several scholarships and encouraged her to submit her writing to various publications. She hadn't submitted anything yet, but I'd been encouraging her. What she'd written was so poignant. Her words were heartfelt and beautiful, even when they described some of her darkest moments.

She'd been expanding on it, weaving my story in with hers, a chronicle of the journeys we had taken. Highlighting the moments that had brought us to where we were. The tragedies that had brought us together.

My phone rang. Charlie.

"Hey bro," I said. "What's up?"

"Dude, talk me down," he said. "I'm freaking the fuck out right now."

"Why, what's going on?"

He took a deep breath. "I'm doing it. I'm asking her."

"Are you serious?" I asked. "You're proposing tonight?"

"No, not tonight," he said. "Like, now. Or when she comes in."

"If it's now, why the hell are you calling me?" I asked. "You're not having second thoughts, are you?"

"Fuck no," he said. "I'm gonna marry the shit out of that girl. No, I think I screwed it up already."

"How?"

"I wanted this to be a big surprise," he said. "And I've been trying to throw her off so she wouldn't guess. The problem is, I think I did too good of a job, and now she's mad at me. She's sitting in the driveway in her car, talking on the phone. She looks pissed."

I glanced up at Brooke. She was nodding her head slowly, then said something. It looked like *everything will be fine*.

"Yeah, I think she's talking to Brooke," I said. "Listen, calm down. Focus. Stick to the plan. You'll be fine."

"God, I'm so nervous," he said. "I don't think I was this nervous before I had to wrestle you at state."

That was funny to hear. We didn't talk about stuff like that very often. Guy thing—we didn't want to admit to it. But I knew how he felt. I'd been nervous to face him too. Plus, I had a surprise in the works for Brooke that was making *me* nervous. It was hard to keep her from finding out.

"Remember, it's not nerves," I said. "It's excitement."

"Right, excitement. Oh shit, she's coming. I gotta go."

Brooke put her phone in her bag and walked out to my car.

"Hey," she said when she got in the passenger's side. "Sorry. It was Olivia. I missed her call earlier so I wanted to take it."

"No problem. What's up with O?"

She rolled her eyes. "She's just being Olivia. She's freaking out because she thinks Charlie has been acting weird. I told her Charlie is always weird, but that didn't help."

I laughed. "She doesn't have anything to worry about."

"Why? Did you talk to him or something?"

"Yeah. I'm probably not supposed to tell you this, but he's proposing."

"Oh my god." She covered her mouth with her hand and stared at me, wide-eyed. "Really? When?"

"Now," I said. "She was sitting in the driveway talking to you and he was waiting for her inside."

"That is so freaking funny," she said. "Olivia was pissed because Charlie asked her to go run some errands earlier. And she didn't want to, or something, and they got in a fight about it. She didn't understand why he wanted her out of the house so badly."

"That was why, apparently." I'd known Charlie had planned to propose—I'd even gone with him to buy the ring —but he hadn't filled me in on the details of when and how he was doing it.

"She's going to lose her mind," Brooke said. "I'm so excited for them."

I started the car and pulled out of the parking lot. "Yeah, me too. Although does this mean I'll have to wear a suit?"

"Probably." She looked me up and down and licked her lips. "Oh my god, I can't wait. You're going to look delicious in a suit."

I just laughed and handed her a lidded cup. "Here."

"Did you get me a milkshake?" she asked as she took it from me.

I laughed. "Protein shake, baby. But I found a place that makes really good ones. Organic whey protein, low sugar, all the good stuff."

"Mm, healthy," she said with a wink, then took a sip. "Oh, this *is* good. Chocolate peanut butter?"

"Yep."

"Yum."

"I figured you could use some sustenance after your appointment," I said. "How was it?"

She took another drink, then set it in the cup holder. "Hard. Really hard, actually. We decided to stop early, and she gave me some time alone in her office. That's why it took me a little while to come out. I needed to recover a bit."

Her therapist was amazing, but her sessions could be exhausting. She'd been going every week for months now, slowly working through all the trauma she'd experienced. It wasn't always easy, but it was making a huge difference. Starting on the right medications had also helped her. It had taken a couple of months to get the dosages right, but they were another one of the tools she was using to get better.

The bottom line, though? She was doing the work. I had her back every step of the way, but it was her strength shining through. Her joy sparkling in her eyes.

I was just lucky enough to be the guy to enjoy it.

"You can always take your time," I said. "I don't mind waiting if you need some space to process or whatever."

"Thanks," she said. "Half an hour ago, I felt like crawling into bed and crying. But I wrote some things down and just kind of let myself feel it all for a while. I think I have to do that sometimes, instead of hiding from it. Even when it hurts."

I caressed her cheek with the backs of my fingers. "How are you now?"

"Good," she said, and by her tone I could tell that surprised her. "Really good, actually. I feel cleansed. Like I'm fresh and clean on the inside."

We stopped at a red light, so I leaned over and kissed her softly on the mouth. "Good."

"Thanks for picking me up today," she said. "You didn't have to. I could have taken the bus."

"I love it when I can come get you. But I've been thinking maybe it's time to get you a car. You have enough going on, I think it would make things easier for you."

"Yeah, it would be nice," she said.

"And I know a guy who'll give you a great deal." I winked at her.

She laughed. "Your dad has been waiting to get me into one of his cars, hasn't he?"

"Of course." My parents had really come around. Once they'd gotten to know Brooke, they'd fallen in love with her, just like I had. I had failed to mention the part about me driving her to the edge of a cliff and telling her I'd go over it with her. That wasn't something they needed to know.

I hadn't been lying to her that day. Taking her out to that quarry hadn't been a ploy to scare her into changing. I'd been dead fucking serious. We were either going to live, or die, and we were going to do it together. Obviously, I was glad she'd chosen to live—and that she kept making that choice every day—but I would have gone out with her if that's what it took. Did that make me crazy? Maybe. But it was all or nothing for me. I didn't know any other way to be.

"What do you say?" I asked. "Should we go to Waverly this weekend? You can let my dad give you the star treatment. He'll make you test drive at least ten different cars, just to warn you. But the upside is, we can have dinner with them afterward. I bet if I ask nicely, my mom will make chicken Parmesan."

"I will test drive a hundred cars with your dad if I get to eat your mom's chicken Parmesan."

"Cool. I'll let them know."

"Yeah, but don't text her," Brooke said with a smile. "She might not read it until next week."

"I know," I said. "I'll call."

When we got home, I took her inside and gave her a long back rub. She deserved it. Plus, I'd take any excuse to get my hands on her bare skin. Afterward, we snuggled up in bed together and talked for a while. She had some things she needed to get out after her session earlier.

Eventually my slow and gentle kisses, meant for comfort, escalated. Our bodies wanted more. We wanted more. I made love to her in our bed, tangled up in our sheets. I savored every touch, every kiss, every bit of her skin. Loved her in every way I knew how. She was my life.

And soon—very soon—I was going to make sure the rest of our lives were lived together.

41

BROOKE

*T*he bookstore was quiet. The rows of neat shelves arranged in precise order seemed to absorb sound. It was a hushed silence, like a field covered in fresh snow. Inviting, and peaceful. It smelled like books—paper, leather, and ink. A hint of coffee, and a breath of lavender.

After the success of our first several readings and events, Joe had added more seating so we could accommodate larger crowds. A handful of people sat at the tables, books laid out in front of them. Some had coffee or tea. Star-shaped light fixtures dangled above the coffee counter, and framed prints of classic book covers decorated the walls. Strings of white lights hung around the perimeter, adding a touch of sparkle and magic.

A muffled sound came from the back, like cardboard sliding across the floor. Probably Joe.

I found him moving boxes of books from a recent shipment.

"Hey," I said. "Quiet afternoon?"

"It's probably the calm before the storm," he said. "Although it was busy this morning."

That made me smile. Business had picked up considerably. Joe was still distracted—often reading while he was supposed to be doing something else—but the changes we'd made to the store had worked beautifully. People came in for more than books. They came for the ambience. It had become a popular hangout for college students, particularly the more literary-minded. Study groups met here, as did book clubs. There was even a knitting club who came once a month.

People packed in for events. Author readings and book signings were popular. But open mic nights were the big hit. Joe had invested in a small sound system, and people loved taking the stage. And it wasn't just students. The store drew in people from all over the community. Last week, we'd had readings from a college freshman with a blond ponytail, a middle-aged man in a suit and tie, a young guy as big as Sebastian wearing a football t-shirt, and an eighty-nine-year-old African-American man with a raspy voice and a knack for storytelling.

"Do you need any help back here?" I asked. "Or should I go get things set up for tonight?"

"I'm fine," he said, pushing his glasses up his nose. "Just making a little room."

I went out front and took care of a few things. Waited on customers. Olivia came in and waved to me with a broad smile. Her pale pink shirt looked perfect with her blond hair, and I'd have to tell her later that her jeans made her ass look fabulous. She'd been lit up like the sun ever since Charlie had proposed. They were planning a destination wedding in the Caribbean next year. She'd already asked me to be her maid of honor, and I had absolutely no complaints about a tropical vacation to watch two of my best friends get married.

Olivia wasn't working tonight, but she checked in with the barista. She'd done an incredible job with the store. Not just reopening the coffee counter, but helping redecorate, and working with me and Joe on promotions. She'd put together a whole new website and was handling all the store's social media.

Joe treated us both like granddaughters, and Olivia had already told him he had to fly down to her wedding—he didn't have a choice. He acted like he wasn't thrilled—he hated to fly—but we knew he was touched that she wanted him there.

I was going to miss him when Sebastian and I moved next year. But we'd come back to visit. And who knew what the future held. Maybe we'd wind up back in Iowa someday. Right now, I was excited at the prospect of going somewhere new. It felt like an adventure. But I knew that ultimately, I wanted us to settle down. Find a place where we could put down roots and be a part of a community. Create a safe and stable home.

Evening fell and the sun went down. I got the last of the things ready for open mic night as more people wandered in and the tables began to fill. Sebastian and Charlie arrived. They were both so big, they dwarfed everyone around them. It was even more noticeable when they were together. They went over to Olivia's table and I left the front counter to join them.

Sebastian slipped his arm around me and squeezed. We waited for Charlie and Olivia to finish their mildly-inappropriate greeting.

"Hang on," Charlie said. He put his hand on Olivia's arm to stop her from sitting. "We have a surprise for you."

"For both of you," Sebastian said.

Before we could ask any questions, they pointed to the front door.

Brian and Mary Harper walked in, their eyes searching. Olivia squealed, then clapped her hand over her mouth. She ran over to her parents and threw herself at them, awkwardly trying to hug them both at the same time.

Sebastian and I waited by the table while Olivia introduced them to Charlie; I didn't want to intrude on their moment. I teared up a little watching Brian shake Charlie's hand and Mary wrap him in a tender embrace. Olivia held out her hand so they could admire her engagement ring.

The beauty of the moment filled my heart. All of them, so happy. So full of life and love.

Mary met my eyes from across the store. Strands of silver were like sparkles in her blond hair, and her blue eyes—so much like Liam's—crinkled at the corners with her smile.

She came over and took my face in her hands. "I'm so proud of you, my sweet girl," she said, and kissed me on the forehead.

I stepped into her embrace and she held me tight. It was so good to see her again. Brian hugged me too, then shook hands with Sebastian. Mary was having none of this polite hand-shaking. She held her arms open for Sebastian. He leaned down and gave her a gentle hug, his big arms engulfing her.

"Wow." Sebastian cleared his throat as he stepped back. "I think there's something in my eye."

"I can't believe you're here," Olivia said. "How could you keep this from me?"

"We wanted it to be a surprise," Mary said.

Olivia turned to Charlie and smacked him on the arm. "How could *you* keep it from me?"

"Hey, don't blame me," Charlie said. "Seb invited them."

Sebastian's lips quirked in a little smile and he shrugged.

Mary squeezed Sebastian's arm. "And we're glad you did. It's not easy having all our kids so far away."

The way she said that—*all our kids*, looking straight at me and Sebastian—made the tears I'd been trying to hold back win their battle. I touched my lips and took a deep breath as a few slid down my cheeks.

But they weren't tears of sadness or grief. They were tears of joy.

We all took our seats at one of the round tables. The buzz of noise grew as more people arrived, the tables filling. Olivia jumped up to help the barista for a little while when the line got too long, and I had to go check out a few more customers at the front counter.

At eight o'clock, I made my way to the little area we referred to as the stage, and opened the evening. Olivia or I always had to act as host. Joe wouldn't go near the microphone. He stood near the front counter, watching from a distance.

I thanked everyone for coming and turned over the mic to the first performer of the evening. I went back to our table and sat next to Sebastian. He took my hand in his and I leaned my cheek against his shoulder.

We listened to a piece by a man who'd spent the last year in South America. The next guy had a thick accent, but he was so animated, we all seemed to understand at least the spirit of his words. A young woman wearing a U of I sweatshirt looked so terrified, at first I wondered if I should get up and rescue her. But she closed her eyes, took a deep breath, and recited a lovely poem she'd written about her mother. I think we were all touched, not only by her words, but by her bravery.

"You ready?" Sebastian asked quietly into my ear.

I nodded. "As ready as I'll ever be."

With a deep breath, I stood and took my place at the microphone. I'd never done a reading before. The closest I'd ever come was reading a few things aloud to Sebastian. I'd never shared any of my writing publicly. Looking at Mary and Brian, Olivia and Charlie, and Sebastian—and even Joe —in the crowd, I couldn't have imagined a better time than tonight, with my whole family here.

I pulled out my piece, swallowed hard, and began.

"Enshrouded in the darkness of grief, her heart breaks. Emptiness consumes her. Where contentment and joy once lived, the shattered pieces of a life scatter across the floor like broken glass."

I paused, my eyes lifting. Sebastian nodded.

"But life is not linear. It is not a line drawn in sand, only moving in one direction, ceasing to exist where it meets the waves. It is circular. Repetitive. Death leads to life. Despair leads to hope. Destruction leads to rebirth.

"For what is emptiness if not a vessel in which to pour? The hollow space in her chest lies ready, waiting. Abiding in the faith, however small, that it will once again be filled.

"Unspoken thoughts and smoldering coals hide beneath the surface. Green fades to brown, speaking of the truth held within. Touched by death. Saved by tragedy. Life and love exist in the beats of his heart. A heart shared by two. Loved by one.

"And therein lies the beautiful sadness of existence. Joy and sorrow. Happiness and heartache. Light and darkness. But above all, love."

Stepping away from the microphone, I let out a long breath. The crowd applauded and my face flushed. I tucked my hair behind my ear and smiled, feeling a sense of fullness and satisfaction.

Sebastian's proud smile warmed me from the inside out. He clapped along with everyone else, but the love in his eyes held me captive. So unyielding. So determined. He'd never given up on me, not even when I'd given up on myself. He'd known the truth—that together, we could rise from the depths of tragedy. And his faith in that truth was still unwavering.

Liam's death had almost destroyed me. But I'd come to realize that even the worst circumstances could lead to something beautiful. Our lives had all changed forever the day he died. It was impossible to know what life would have been like if it hadn't happened. But that wasn't the point, anymore. It *had* happened. It had been an ending, and a beginning. A tragedy, and a gift.

Liam's spirit lived on. In his sister's laughter. In his parents' generosity and kindness. In the love that had blossomed between Charlie and Olivia.

And of course, in Sebastian. His heart had given Sebastian a second chance at life—a gift of immeasurable value. But it had given me a second chance, too. Sebastian and I had both lost a part of ourselves and been faced with a world—and a future—that had been irrevocably altered. Alone, we'd floundered. But together, we'd risen from the ashes of despair—two people made new, and filled with hope.

Love had done that.

It was love that had guided Sebastian to me, when he hadn't known who I was. Could it have been Liam, reaching through time and space? Had he spoken through the heart he and Sebastian shared, whispered to him when he'd looked at me across the street? Told Sebastian my name? I didn't know. Maybe Liam had led Sebastian to me, knowing he would love me. Or maybe Liam's heart had recognized me, and sought to reconnect with the heart it had once belonged to.

Or maybe it had all been a coincidence, and Sebastian could have just as easily turned and walked the other way.

But I didn't think so.

Because I believed that love worked in ways that defied understanding. It was more powerful than loss. More powerful than grief. Even more powerful than death. And in the end, love would always win.

In us, love had triumphed.

I would always love Liam. I didn't need to forget him, or pretend I hadn't loved him, in order to love again. There was room in my heart for his memory—to acknowledge the ways he had touched my life—and more than enough space to love Sebastian. The deep, abiding, fierce, and passionate love I had for Sebastian didn't need to exist on its own. It was too strong for that. Too sure. It filled me with the strength to choose joy over pain. Hope over grief. Life over death.

Liam had tried to save me from my past. Sebastian had tried to save me for a future he wanted to share. The strength of love had allowed me to choose to save myself. And to give myself to the man I loved. I wasn't perfect. I still had healing to do. But every day, I would choose to live, and to love. For my friends, who were my family. For Liam. For Sebastian. For myself.

People stayed for a while, mingling, browsing, buying books, sipping coffee and tea. The Harpers were in town for a week, so we made plans to show them all our favorite Iowa spots. Charlie and Sebastian were mostly concerned with where we would eat—those two led with their stomachs. Olivia wanted to take me and Mary wedding dress shopping. Sebastian's parents had invited all of us to come out to Waverly for dinner. It was going to be a fun week.

The store emptied and I told Joe I'd lock up. Charlie and Olivia took her parents out for dessert, but we decided to stay behind. Sebastian waited with me while the last of the customers left. I turned things off and made sure everything was closed for the night.

Sebastian held my coat while I slipped my arms into the sleeves. "I rode with Charlie, so we have to walk home."

"That's fine." I pulled my hair out of the back and adjusted my necklace with the corncob charm. "It's a beautiful night."

He held the door and I locked it behind us. The air was cool and the soft sounds of night spoke of a world at rest. A single car drove by while we walked, the hum of its engine fading as it left us behind. Sebastian's hand clasped with mine was warm and comforting. We walked slowly down the sidewalk, beneath tall maple trees, their branches a canopy of green.

Sebastian was quiet. I felt like he was thinking about something. He had a subtle sense of introspection, as if his thoughts were both here with us, and far away.

We got home and he paused on the step in front of the door.

He stood close, and without saying a word, he took my left hand and pressed it against his chest. His heart thumped against my palm, his hand so large it covered mine.

"This heart is yours." He leaned down so our foreheads touched. "It always was, and I'm grateful every day that it led me to you."

With his hand still holding mine against his heart, he reached into his pocket.

"I was going to do this at the bookstore tonight, in front of everyone. It's why I invited the Harpers here. I thought it would be perfect. A nice setting, with the people who care about you. But then I decided to wait. Because this isn't for anyone else—just us."

My heart fluttered as he brought out a velvety gray box. The ring inside was unlike anything I'd ever seen. Three thin bands of gold wound around each other, almost like a vine, with a diamond in the center. The setting looked like a circle of tiny leaves.

He took my hand from his heart and held it while he lowered himself onto one knee. I bit my lip. I wasn't sure if it was to stop me from laughing or crying. I was on the verge of both.

His eyes were intense and focused as he looked up at me. "Brooke, will you marry me?"

"Yes." I touched his face, slid my fingers along his beard. "Yes. I love you so much."

He slid the ring onto my finger and stood. His hands cupped my cheeks and his eyes held onto mine. "I love you, too. We both have a second chance at life, and I'm going to spend the rest of mine loving you."

Our lips came together in a breathtaking kiss. He wrapped his thick arms around me and pressed my body against his. I held him tight, losing myself in the feel of his mouth caressing mine.

The space in my chest that had once felt so hollow was full. Full of love, and the life Sebastian had helped me rediscover.

The life I was going to spend with him—loving him. A priceless gift and a second chance. One for which I would be forever grateful.

EPILOGUE

Two wrongs do not a right make
but two sorrows
come together
to create something more
something beautiful
because love is the ultimate healer
the righter of wrongs
mender of woes
fulfiller of dreams
love makes all things possible
it is breath, heat, and life
creation and truth
the answer to the ultimate question
why are we here
~B

EPILOGUE
BROOKE

*S*ebastian held my hand as we walked down the long path. The sun was warm on my skin and I adjusted my sunglasses against the glare. It had been years since I'd lived in Arizona, and the warm weather in December seemed so foreign. But after the early snowstorm we'd left behind in Iowa, the desert heat was a nice change.

After an intimate wedding in Iowa, we'd moved to Virginia for two years while we finished school. Then we'd done something crazy—even crazier than when I'd decided to move to Iowa with two strangers. We'd sold everything we owned, except what we could carry, bought two plane tickets to Europe, and left.

We spent thirteen months seeing the world. In Europe, we marveled at feats of architecture—everything from ancient Roman aqueducts to Gothic cathedrals to sleek modern skyscrapers. In Asia, we ate octopus and spicy peppers that left our mouths burning for days. Saw museums and temples. We took surfing lessons in South America. Walked through the Amazon jungle with a guide we were pretty sure was just as likely to feed us to a large snake as bring us back to civilization.

We slept in plush hotels, quaint bed and breakfasts, places with bug nets over the bed, and one shack on a beach that had no walls, but was so isolated, it didn't need any. We lived off savings, the last of Sebastian's college fund, and the money I earned as a travel writer for an online magazine.

When we returned to the States, there were still a hundred places we wanted to go. At least. But by then, we were ready for our next adventure. Something a little closer to home.

Sebastian got a job with an architecture firm in Iowa City. He'd applied for jobs in various places. Chicago, Austin, Miami. Seattle. But we both felt Iowa calling us back. We wanted to be near family and friends, and everyone we loved was there. Sebastian's parents still lived in his childhood home in Waverly. Charlie and Olivia had settled in Iowa City. Their daughter, Liliana, was born just two weeks after we got back. Even Brian and Mary Harper were there. They'd relocated to be near Olivia and Charlie.

We bought a pretty house in a neighborhood we both liked, not far from Charlie and Olivia. It wasn't fancy, but it was comfortable. We decorated it with treasures we'd collected in our travels. Art, books, vases, bowls, statues. A big decorative map hung in our living room, with the places we'd visited marked in gold.

Our house represented something so much more than just a roof over our heads. It was a home. A place that was safe and secure. A place where we could put down roots, and build our life together.

A place to raise our son.

I rested my hand on my belly as we walked. I had another eight weeks—give or take—before he'd be born, but it was hard to imagine him getting any bigger. I already felt enormous.

Of course, looking at the man I'd married, if our son took after him, he was bound to be big.

"I think it's over there," Sebastian said, pointing ahead of us.

We walked onto the grass and found what we were looking for. Liam's grave.

I'd only been here once, for his funeral. His family had bought a beautiful headstone, with his name etched in large letters. *Liam Edward Harper*. Below, it read *Beloved Son*, with the dates of his birth and death. He'd been two months away from turning twenty.

I put the bouquet of flowers I'd brought next to the headstone.

Sebastian rubbed slow circles across my back. "Do you need a minute alone?"

I nodded, and he walked a short distance away.

How you doing, Bee?

"I'm really good. Maybe you know that already. I like to think you can see me, but I don't really know." The baby kicked and I rubbed my belly. "I've been to some of the places we put on our map. A lot of them, actually. They were amazing. We came back to the States, and Sebastian and I live in Iowa, now. We have a nice house. And we're having a baby."

I paused, a sudden rush of emotion making my eyes sting and my throat feel thick.

"I'm sorry you couldn't stay." A few tears ran down my cheeks. "But even though you didn't have a lot of time, your life meant so much. So, thank you. Thank you for the time we had. For asking me to that dance. For being my friend—and my family when I didn't have anyone else. And thank you, so much, for the gifts you gave when you left us. Your death meant life and healing for others. If this is the way things had to be, it couldn't have had a happier ending."

I stood for a minute, just breathing. Feeling.

Wiping my eyes, I stepped away. Took a deep breath. Sebastian came back and wrapped his arm around my shoulders, cradling me next to him.

"You okay?" he asked, his voice gentle.

"Yes," I said, and I meant it. "It's still sad, but I'm glad we came. It feels right."

"It does to me, too," he said. "Can I have a minute?"

"Yeah, of course," I said.

I wandered away while Sebastian stood in front of Liam's grave. The baby rolled and poked me with his arms and legs. He was an active little thing. I had a feeling we were going to have our hands full.

After a few minutes, Sebastian turned and nodded. I joined him, slipping my hand into his. He touched my belly and kissed the top of my head.

"Ready?" he asked.

"Yeah," I said. "Let's go."

My heart was full of emotion as we walked back to our rental car, although I wasn't sad. I felt an overwhelming sense of peace. Liam had been a bright spot in the life of a girl who'd known too much darkness. But he hadn't been the love of my life.

That was Sebastian.

He was my best friend. My soulmate. The man I loved with everything I had. His love wasn't a crutch for me to lean on. It was a fire that fed the flame inside of me. We loved each other, believed in each other, and supported each other. We walked side-by-side down the path we had chosen, secure in the bond we had forged.

Sebastian was quiet as we walked. I wondered what he'd said to Liam, but I didn't ask. If he wanted to tell me, he would. But maybe it was something between them—something he didn't need to share.

We drove back into Phoenix and found a restaurant near our hotel. We'd come down for a few days, mostly to visit Liam's grave. I'd felt like I needed to. Like I needed a moment of closure. And with a baby coming soon, it was easier to come now. Two adults traveling was one thing—we were experts at that. But traveling with a baby was going to be a whole new ballgame.

The restaurant was quiet, and the waitress brought our dinners. I was starving—but I was pretty much always hungry lately. When we'd finished about half our meal, Sebastian put his fork down and looked me in the eyes.

"I thanked him for giving me his heart," he said. "For saving my life. And I thanked him for loving you. He was in your life at a time when you needed him, and I'm really glad he was there. I'm glad it was him."

I took a deep breath. "Me too."

He reached across the table and took my hand. Brought it to his lips for a kiss.

"I was thinking about something else while we were there."

"Yeah? What's that?"

"What we should name our baby," he said. "In fact, I'm surprised we didn't come up with this sooner."

I lifted my eyebrows. We'd been going back and forth on names ever since we found out we were having a boy. I was beginning to think we'd never agree. "Seb, we're not naming him Blade. Or Ranger. Or Steel."

"Come on," he said. "Those names are badass. I'm

keeping them on the list for future children. But no, that's not what I'm thinking."

"Okay, what are you thinking?"

He smiled, his green and brown eyes crinkling at the corners. "His name is Liam."

~

AFTERWORD

Organ donation saves lives.

In 2017, 116,000 men, women, and children in the United States alone were on the national transplant waiting list.

Twenty people die every day waiting for a transplant.

Every ten minutes, another person is added to the waiting list.

Ninety-five percent of American adults support organ donation, but only fifty-four percent are organ donors.

One donor can save up to eight lives.

Please consider registering as an organ donor. And make your wishes known to your family and loved ones.

In the U.S. visit www.organdonor.gov.

In the U.K. visit www.organdonation.nhs.uk.

In Australia visit register.donatelife.gov.au.

In New Zealand visit www.donor.co.nz.

In Canada visit www.cantransplant.ca.

ABOUT THE BOOK

Where do I even begin? I've been trying to write this for days.

This book is unlike anything else I've ever written so far. And it's probably my favorite thing I've ever written.

When I set out to write this book, everything about it felt like a risk. I'd just finished releasing my Book Boyfriends series—three sexy, fun romcoms. What were my readers going to think about this book, after those? How many readers were new to me from that series, and would give this one the side-eye? What's up with that dark cover? That description? Where's the lighthearted, romantic, cotton candy book?

Not here, obviously.

I like to challenge myself creatively, and this represented one of the biggest challenges I've ever undertaken (even bigger than redeeming Weston, and that was quite the challenge). There are things about this book that don't fit the typical romance mold. I was worried about that, but as I write this Afterward, I've already had more private messages, emails, and posts in my reader group from ARC readers than I've ever had for any release, ever. And the response is utterly overwhelming. So I think it's safe to say that those risks I was so worried about paid off.

One of the main risks I took was making you wait so many chapters before the hero and heroine meet. Who does that? Everything I've ever read about "how to write a romance novel that readers will love" says you need the hero and heroine to meet early. You want readers to be invested in them getting together from an early point in the story. After all, that's what a romance is about. If there's confusion over who we're supposed to 'ship, we've got issues.

It's one thing to break a rule (or an established genre expectation) because you don't know the rule exists. That's often a mistake, and perceived as such by the reader, even if they're not sure what went wrong. It's another to break a rule on purpose, with a specific intent behind it. And that's exactly what I did.

I knew Sebastian and Brooke weren't going to meet until about a third of the way into the book. At one point, I told my friend Tammi about this and her response was something like, "I trust you, and you can probably take your readers anywhere, but... are you sure?"

Yes, I was sure. I realized very early on—when I was still brainstorming ideas for this book—that Brooke and Liam's story, and the progression of Sebastian's illness, couldn't be treated like regular backstory. It wouldn't be enough to begin the book with Sebastian telling Charlie that he's going to meet the organ donor's family, and then relate the story of his illness through conversations and inner monologue. And it wouldn't be enough to begin Brooke's story with her in the bar listening to Jared's band, and then reveal to the reader her history with Liam through dialogue and memories.

You needed to live it all with them.

Granted, what you're given in Part I are milestones and highlights, not a full storyline detailing those two-plus years of their lives. But you're given the important points that show both what Sebastian lost as a result of his illness, and what Liam meant to Brooke—and what she lost when he died.

If we hadn't lived through that, the impact of this story wouldn't have been the same. We had to suffer with Sebastian while he deteriorated. We had to see him go from a healthy, driven athlete, to a young man ready to give up and die.

We had to experience where Brooke came from—get a taste of what life was like with her mother. And we had to live through her relationship with Liam. Yes, we had to fall in love with Liam, just like she did, in order to understand everything that happened afterward.

My hope was (and is) that readers will hang in there through those early chapters, knowing a connection is being made. Knowing Sebastian is indeed the hero in this romance, and his path is going to cross with Brooke's. That their early stories are compelling enough that you want to keep reading, even if you aren't quite sure where it's all going. Or if you do know, and aren't sure if you want to go there.

I reached a really interesting place while I was writing this. It was a struggle and there were moments when I had so many doubts about whether I could pull this off. As I was delving into Part II, I was holding back. I was trying to keep from going too far with Brooke, especially. Maybe she was just kind of down on her luck. Maybe she'd gone back to school, but she was having a hard time. Maybe she'd sworn off men completely, and she was just lonely.

I was afraid of taking her too far into the darkness, and putting readers off. I didn't want her to be so far gone that no one wanted to read her story. But what that fear produced was a first post-Liam chapter that fell totally flat. It wasn't the Brooke in my mind that I was putting on the page. I was whitewashing it all too much. Afraid to go too far.

Then I said, fuck it. I knew where she'd really gone after Liam died. It didn't happen all at once, but by the time the story picks up again four years later, yes, she's a mess. She's living with some trashy piece of shit. She's drunk half the time. She's lost her job and doesn't have much going for her, because she's hitting rock bottom.

Once I let some of my inhibitions go, the story came to life in a whole new way. I stopped shying away from the darkness inside Brooke. I didn't want her to seem pathetic or weak. I didn't want her to be such a terrible disaster that no one liked her. But I also wanted to be true to the story I was trying to tell. And it had the messy parts in it. So, I wrote them. I left them in.

That's what you have here. A story with the messy parts left in.

There were times when I wasn't sure what the hell I was doing. I told some author friends, "I meant to write a book about a man who gets a heart transplant and falls in love with the woman who'd loved the heart donor, and I wound up writing a book about child abuse, addiction, death, loss, and grief. What have I done?"

But you know what, this was their story. Parts of it weren't pretty. Parts of it were terrible, and tragic, and sad. I'll never be able to read that epilogue without tearing up (at the very least). Death and grief are hard. They're hard to talk about, and hard to live with. But they're also a universal human experience. We've all lost people who are important to us. And sometimes those losses are life-changing and devastating.

I wanted to show that you can come back from that. Even when you've been enshrouded so deep in darkness that you don't think you'll ever feel good again, there is still hope. Love is that hope. Maybe it

won't be the love of your life, like Sebastian was for Brooke. It could be the love of another family member, a spouse, a child, a friend, even a stranger. Love has the power to get us through the worst moments, the worst things we can experience. We can come out on the other side of the most tragic of circumstances and find joy again.

Turns out I had a lot to say about writing this book, I suppose. I'm not sure what to say about the emotional intensity. I'm sorry? I feel like I owe every reader a box of tissues and maybe a glass of wine and some chocolate. But I hope it was worth it. I know it was for me.

Thanks for reading,

CK

ACKNOWLEDGMENTS

I'm always so fortunate to have amazing people in my corner. This book was no exception.

The first kernel of an idea came from none other than my husband. Thank you for challenging me with this story. And for your never-ending belief in me. It means more than I can properly express.

To Nikki, who suffers through my writer-angst and makes sure I'm not screwing up my stories.

To Jodi, who went above and beyond in so many ways. Thank you for your feedback, and for your help hustlin' this launch. You're a wonderful friend and I'm so glad to have you in my life.

Thank you to Elayne for cleaning up my words and asking good questions.

And to all of you reading this book. Each story I write is my gift to you. Thank you for joining me on this journey.

ALSO BY CLAIRE KINGSLEY

For a full and up-to-date listing of Claire Kingsley books visit
www.clairekingsleybooks.com/books/

For comprehensive reading order, visit

www.clairekingsleybooks.com/reading-order/

The Haven Brothers

Small-town romantic suspense with CK's signature endearing
characters and heartwarming happily ever afters. Can be read as
stand-alones.

Obsession Falls (Josiah and Audrey)

Storms and Secrets (Zachary and Marigold)

Temptation Trails (Garrett and Harper)

The rest of the Haven brothers will be getting their own happily
ever afters!

How the Grump Saved Christmas (Elias and Isabelle)

A stand-alone, small-town Christmas romance.

The Bailey Brothers

Steamy, small-town family series with a dash of suspense. Five unruly brothers. Epic pranks. A quirky, feuding town. Big HEAs. Best read in order.

Protecting You (Asher and Grace part 1)

Fighting for Us (Asher and Grace part 2)

Unraveling Him (Evan and Fiona)

Rushing In (Gavin and Skylar)

Chasing Her Fire (Logan and Cara)

Rewriting the Stars (Levi and Annika)

The Miles Family

Sexy, sweet, funny, and heartfelt family series with a dash of suspense. Messy family. Epic bromance. Super romantic. Best read in order.

Broken Miles (Roland and Zoe)

Forbidden Miles (Brynn and Chase)

Reckless Miles (Cooper and Amelia)

Hidden Miles (Leo and Hannah)

Gaining Miles: A Miles Family Novella (Ben and Shannon)

Dirty Martini Running Club

Sexy, fun, feel-good romantic comedies with huge... hearts. Can be read as stand-alones.

Everly Dalton's Dating Disasters (Prequel with Everly, Hazel, and Nora)

Faking Ms. Right (Everly and Shepherd)

Falling for My Enemy (Hazel and Corban)

Marrying Mr. Wrong (Sophie and Cox)

Flirting with Forever (Nora and Dex)

Bluewater Billionaires

Hot romantic comedies. Lady billionaire BFFs and the badass heroes who love them. Can be read as stand-alones.

The Mogul and the Muscle (Cameron and Jude)

The Price of Scandal, Wild Open Hearts, and Crazy for Loving You

More Bluewater Billionaire shared-world romantic comedies by Lucy Score, Kathryn Nolan, and Pippa Grant

Bootleg Springs

by Claire Kingsley and Lucy Score

Hot and hilarious small-town romcom series with a dash of mystery and suspense. Best read in order.

Whiskey Chaser (Scarlett and Devlin)

Sidecar Crush (Jameson and Leah Mae)

Moonshine Kiss (Bowie and Cassidy)

Bourbon Bliss (June and George)

Gin Fling (Jonah and Shelby)

Highball Rush (Gibson and I can't tell you)

Book Boyfriends

Hot romcoms that will make you laugh and make you swoon. Can be read as stand-alones.

Book Boyfriend (Alex and Mia)

Cocky Roommate (Weston and Kendra)

Hot Single Dad (Caleb and Linnea)

Finding Ivy (William and Ivy)

A unique contemporary romance with a hint of mystery. Stand-alone.

His Heart (Sebastian and Brooke)

A poignant and emotionally intense story about grief, loss, and the transcendent power of love. Stand-alone.

The Always Series

Smoking hot, dirty talking bad boys with some angsty intensity. Can be read as stand-alones.

Always Have (Braxton and Kylie)

Always Will (Selene and Ronan)

Always Ever After (Braxton and Kylie)

The Jetty Beach Series

Sexy small-town romance series with swoony heroes, romantic HEAs, and lots of big feels. Can be read as stand-alones.

Behind His Eyes (Ryan and Nicole)

One Crazy Week (Melissa and Jackson)

Messy Perfect Love (Cody and Clover)

Operation Get Her Back (Hunter and Emma)

Weekend Fling (Finn and Juliet)

Good Girl Next Door (Lucas and Becca)

The Path to You (Gabriel and Sadie)

ABOUT THE AUTHOR

Claire Kingsley is a #1 Amazon bestselling author of sexy, heartwarming contemporary romance, romantic comedies, and small-town romantic suspense. She writes sassy, quirky heroines, swoony heroes who love big, romantic happily ever afters, and all the big feels.

She can't imagine life without coffee, great books, and the characters who inhabit her imagination. She lives in the inland Pacific Northwest with her three kids.

www.clairekingsleybooks.com

Made in the USA
Monee, IL
30 January 2025

11228076R00229